The
Treasured
BRIDES
COLLECTION

Three Timeless Romances
from a Beloved Author

The Treasured
BRIDES

COLLECTION

Grace Livingston Hill

BARBOUR
PUBLISHING

Published by Barbour Books, an imprint of Barbour Publishing, Inc., P.O. Box 719, Uhrichsville, Ohio 44683, www.barbourbooks.com

Our mission is to publish and distribute inspirational products offering exceptional value and biblical encouragement to the masses.

ecpa Member of the
Evangelical Christian
Publishers Association

Printed in Canada.

CONTENTS

THE BIG BLUE SOLDIER

Chapter 1

Purling Brook, New York, November 1918

"And you don't think maybe I ought to have had lemon custard to go with the pumpkin instead of the mince?"

Miss Marilla Chadwick turned from her anxious watching at the kitchen window to search Mary Amber's clear, young eyes for the truth, the whole truth, and nothing but the truth.

"Oh no, I think mince is much better. All men like mince pie, it's so—sort of comprehensive, you know."

Miss Marilla turned back to her window, satisfied.

"Well now, if he came on that train, he ought to be in sight around the bend of the road in about three minutes," she said tensely. "I've timed it often when folks were coming out from town, and it always takes just six minutes to get around the bend of the road."

All through the months of the Great War, Miss Marilla had knitted and bandaged and emergencied and canteened with an eager, wistful look in her dreamy, gray eyes. And many a sweater had gone to some needy lad with the little thrilling remark as she handed it over to the committee, "I keep thinking, what if my nephew Dick should be needing one, and this just come along in time?"

But when the war was over, and most people had begun to use pink and blue wool on their needles, or else cast them aside altogether and tried to forget there ever had been such a thing as war, and the price of turkey had gone up so high that people forgot to be thankful the war was over, Miss Marilla still held that wistful look in her eyes and still spoke of her nephew Dick with bated breath and a sigh. For wasn't Dick among those favored few who were to remain and do patrol work for an indefinite time in the land of the enemy, while others were gathered to their waiting homes and eager loved ones? Miss Marilla spoke of Dick as one who still lingered on the borderland of terror and who laid his young life a continuous sacrifice for the good of the great world.

A neat paragraph to that effect appeared in *The Springhaven Chronicle*, a local sheet that offered scant news items and fat platitudes at an ever-increasing rate to a gullible and conceited populace, who supported it because it was really the only way to know what one's neighbors were doing. The paragraph was the reluctant work of Mary Amber, the young girl who lived next door to Miss Marilla and had been her devoted friend since the age of four, when Miss Marilla used to bake sugar cookies for her in the form of stodgy men with currant eyes and outstretched arms.

Mary Amber remembered Nephew Dick as a young imp of nine, who'd made a whole long, beautiful summer ugly with his torments. She also knew that the neighbors all around had memories of that summer when Dick's parents went on a Western trip and left him with his Aunt Marilla. Mary Amber shrank from exposing her dear friend to the criticisms of such readers of *The Springhaven Chronicle* as had memories of their cats tortured, their chickens chased, their flowerbeds trampled, their children bullied, and their windows broken by the youthful Dick.

But time had softened the memories of that fateful summer in Miss Marilla's mind, and besides, she was deeply in need of a hero. Mary Amber had not the heart to refuse to write the paragraph, but she made it as conservative as the circumstances allowed.

But now, at last, among the latest to be sent back, Lieutenant Richard Chadwick's division was coming home!

Miss Marilla read in the paper what day they would sail and that they were expected to arrive not later than the twenty-ninth. And as she read, she conceived a wild and daring plan. Why shouldn't she have a real, live hero herself? A bit belated, of course, but all the more distinguished for that. And why shouldn't Mary Amber have a whole devoted soldier boy of her own for the village to see and admire? Not that she told Mary Amber that, oh no! But in her mind's vision, she saw herself, Mary Amber, and Dick all going together to church on Sunday morning, the bars on his uniform gleaming like the light in Mary Amber's hazel eyes. Miss Marilla had one sudden pang of fear when she thought that perhaps he would not wear his uniform home, now that everybody else was in citizen's clothing; then her sweet faith in the wholesomeness of all things came to her rescue, and she smiled in relief. Of course he would wear it to come home; that would be too outrageous not to, when he had been a hero. Of course, he would wear it the first few days. And that was a good reason why she must invite him at once to visit her, instead of waiting until he had been to his home and been demobilized. She *must* have him in his uniform. She wanted the glory of it for her own brief share in that great time of uplifting and sacrifice that was so fast going into history.

So Miss Marilla had hastened into the city to consult a friend who worked in the Red Cross and went out often to the wharves to meet the incoming boats. This friend promised to find out just when Dick's division was to land, to hunt him up herself, and to see that he had the invitation at once. "*See that he came*," she put it, with a wise reservation in her heart that the dear, loving soul should not be disappointed.

And now, the very night before, this friend had called Miss Marilla on the telephone to say she had information that Dick's ship would dock at eight in the morning. It would probably be afternoon before he could get out to Springhaven, so she had better arrange to have dinner about half past five. So Miss Marilla, with shining eyes and a heart that throbbed like a young girl's, had thrown her shawl over her shoulders and hastened in the twilight through the hedge to tell Mary Amber.

Mary Amber, trying to conceal her inward doubts, had congratulated Miss Marilla and promised to come over the first thing in the morning to help get dinner. Promised also, after much urging, almost with tears on the part of Miss Marilla, to stay and help eat the dinner afterward, in company with Miss Marilla and the young lieutenant. From this part of her promise Mary Amber's soul recoiled, for she had no belief that the young leopard with whom she had played at the age of ten could have changed his spots in the course of a few years, or even covered them with a silver bar. But Mary Amber soon saw that her presence at the dinner was an intrinsic part of Miss Marilla's joy in the anticipation of the dinner; and, as much as she disliked the position of being flung at the young lieutenant in this way, she promised. After all, what did it matter what he thought of her anyway, since she had no use for him? And then she could always quietly freeze him whenever Miss Marilla's back was turned. Mary Amber *could* freeze with her hazel eyes when she tried.

So quite early in the morning, Miss Marilla and Mary Amber began a cheerful stir in Miss Marilla's big sunny kitchen. Steadily, appetizingly, there grew an array of salads and pies and cakes and puddings and cookies and doughnuts and biscuits and pickles and olives and jellies; while a great bird, stuffed to bursting, went through the seven stages of its final career to the oven.

But no, it was five o'clock. The bird, with brown and shining breast, was waiting in the oven, "done to a turn." Mashed potatoes, sweet potatoes, squash, succotash, and onions had received the finishing touches and had only to be served. Cranberries, pickles, celery, and jelly gave the final touches to a perfect table, and the sideboard fairly groaned under its load of pies and cake. One might have thought a whole regiment was to dine with Miss Marilla Chadwick that day, from the sights and smells that filled the house. Up in the spare room, the fire glowed in the Franklin heater, and a geranium glowed in a west window between spotless curtains to welcome the guest. Now there was nothing left for the two women to do but the final anxiety.

Mary Amber had her part in that, perhaps even more than her hostess and friend, for she was jealous for Miss Marilla and was youthfully incredulous. She had no trust in Dick Chadwick, even though he was an officer and had patrolled an enemy country for a few months after the war was over.

Mary Amber had slipped over to her own house when she finished mashing the potatoes and changed her gown. She was putting little pats of butter on the bread-and-butter plates now, and the setting sun cast a halo of burnished light over her gold hair and brightened up the silk of her brown gown with its touches of wood-red. She was beautiful to look upon as she stood with her butter knife, deftly cutting the squares and dropping them in just the right spot on the plates. But there was a troubled look in her eyes as she glanced, from time to time, at the older woman over by window.

Miss Marilla had ceased all thought of work and was intent only on the road toward the station. It seemed as if not until this moment had her great faith failed her, and the thought come to her that perhaps he might not come. "You know, of course, he might not get that train," she said meditatively. "The other leaves only half an hour later. But she said she'd tell him to take this one."

"That's true, too," said Mary Amber cheerily. "And nothing will be hurt by waiting. I've fixed those mashed potatoes so they won't get soggy by being too hot, and I'm sure they'll keep hot enough."

"You're a good, dear girl, Mary Amber," said Miss Marilla, giving her a sudden impulsive kiss. "I only wish I could do something great and beautiful for you."

Miss Marilla caught up her shawl and hurried toward the door.

"I'm going out to the gate to meet him," she said with a smile. "It's time he was coming in a minute now, and I want to be out there without hurrying."

She clambered down the steps, her knees trembling with

excitement. She hoped Mary Amber had not looked out the window. A boy was coming on a bicycle; and if he should be a boy with a telegram or a special-delivery letter, she wanted to read it before Mary Amber saw her. Oh, how awful if anything had happened that he couldn't come today! Of course, he might come later tonight, or tomorrow. And a turkey would keep, though it was never so good as the minute it was taken out of the oven.

The boy was almost to the gate now and—yes, he was going to stop. He was swinging one leg out with that long movement that meant slowing up. She panted forward with a furtive glance back at the house. She hoped Mary Amber was looking at the turkey and not out of the window.

It seemed that her fingers had suddenly gone tired while she was writing her name in that boy's book, and they almost refused to tear open the envelope as the boy swung on his wheel again and vanished down the road. She had presence of mind enough to keep her back to the house and the telegram in front of her as she opened it covertly, trying to keep the attitude of still looking eagerly down the road, while the typewritten, brief message got itself across to her tumultuous mind.

IMPOSSIBLE TO ACCEPT INVITATION. HAVE OTHER
ENGAGEMENTS. THANKS JUST THE SAME.

(SIGNED)

LIEUTENANT RICHARD H. CHADWICK

Miss Marilla tore the yellow paper hastily and crumpled it into a ball in her hands as she stared down the road through brimming tears. She managed an upright position, but her knees were shaking under her, and an empty feeling came in her stomach. Across the sunset skies in letters of accusing size, there seemed to blaze the paragraphs from *The Springhaven Chronicle*, copied afterward in the country *Gazette*, about Miss Marilla Chadwick's nephew, Lieutenant Richard H. Chadwick, who was expected at his aunt's home as soon as he landed in this country after a long and glorious career in other lands, and who would spend the weekend with his aunt, and "doubtless be heard from at the Springhaven Club House before he left." Her throat caught with a strange little sound like a groan. Still, with her hand grasping the front gate convulsively, Miss Marilla stood and stared down the road, trying to think what to do, how to word a paragraph explaining why he did not come, how to explain to Mary Amber so that look of sweet incredulousness should not come into her eyes.

Then suddenly, as she stared through her blur of tears, there appeared a straggling figure, coming around the bend of the road by the Hazard house. And Miss Marilla, with nothing at all in her mind but to escape from the watchful, loving eyes of Mary Amber for a moment longer till she could think what to say to her, staggered out the gate and down the road toward the person, whoever it was, that was coming slowly up the road.

On stumbled Miss Marilla, nearer and nearer to the oncoming man, till suddenly through a blur of tears she noticed that he wore a uniform. Her heart gave a leap, and for a moment she thought it must be Dick; that he had been playing her a joke by the telegram and was coming on immediately to surprise her before she had a chance to be disappointed. It was wonderful how the years had done their halo work for Dick with Miss Marilla.

She stopped short, trembling, one hand to her throat. Then,

as the man drew nearer and she saw his halting gait, saw, too, his downcast eyes and whole dejected attitude, she somehow knew it wasn't Dick. Never would he have walked to her home in that way. There had been a swagger about little Dick that could not be forgotten. The older Dick, crowned now with many honors, would not have forgotten to hold his head high.

Unconscious of her attitude of intense interest, she stood, with hand still fluttering at her throat and eyes brightly on the man as he advanced.

When he was almost opposite her, he looked up. He had fine eyes and good features; but his expression was bitter for one so young, and in the eyes, there was a look of pain.

"Oh! Excuse me," said Miss Marilla, looking around furtively to be sure Mary Amber could not see them so far away. "Are you in a very great hurry?"

The young man looked surprised, amused, and slightly bored, but paused politely.

"Not 'specially," he said, and there was a tone of dry sarcasm in his voice. "Is there anything I can do for you?"

He lifted the limp little trench cap and paused to rest his lame knee.

"Why, I was wondering if you would mind coming in and eating dinner with me," spoke Miss Marilla eagerly, from a dry throat of embarrassment. "You see, my nephew's a returned soldier, and I've just got word he can't come. The dinner's all ready to be dished up, and it needn't take long."

"Dinner sounds good to me," said the young man, with a grim glimmer of a smile. "I guess I can accommodate you, madam. I haven't had anything to eat since I left camp last night."

"Oh! You poor child!" said Miss Marilla, beaming on him with a welcoming smile. "Now isn't it fortunate I should have asked *you*?" As if there had been a throng of passing soldiers from which she might have chosen. "But are you sure I'm not keeping you from someone else who is waiting for you?"

"If there's anyone else waiting anywhere along the road for me, it's all news to me, madam. And anyhow, you got here first, and I guess you have first rights."

He had swung into the easy, familiar vernacular of the soldier now, and for the moment, his bitterness was held in abeyance, and the really nice look in his eyes shone forth.

"Well then, we'll just go along in," said Miss Marilla, casting another quick glance toward the house. "And I think I'm most fortunate to have found you. It's so disappointing to get dinner ready for company and then not have any."

"Must be almost as disappointing as to get all ready for dinner and then not have any," said the soldier affably.

Miss Marilla smiled wistfully.

"I suppose your name doesn't happen to be Richard, does it?" she asked, with that childish appeal in her eyes that had always kept her a young woman and good company for Mary Amber, even though her hair had long been gray.

"Might just as well be that as anything else," he responded affably, willing to step into whatever role was set for him in this most unexpected play.

"And you wouldn't mind if I should call you Dick?" she asked, with a wistful look in her blue eyes.

"Like nothing better," he assented glibly, and found his own heart warming to this confiding, strange lady.

"That's beautiful of you." She put out a shy hand and laid it lightly on the edge of his cuff. "You don't know how much obliged I am. You see, Mary Amber hasn't ever quite believed he was coming—Dick, I mean—and she's been so kind and helped me get the dinner and all. I just couldn't bear to tell her he wasn't coming."

The young soldier stopped short in the middle of the road and whistled.

"Horrors!" he exclaimed in dismay. "Are there other guests? Who is Mary Amber?"

"Why, she's just my neighbor, who played with you—I mean with Dick, when he was here visiting as a child a good many years ago. I'm afraid he wasn't always as polite to her then as a boy ought to be to a little girl. And—well, she's never liked him very well. I was afraid she would say 'I told you so,' if she thought he didn't come. It won't be necessary for me to tell any lies, you know. I'll just say, 'Dick, this is Mary Amber. I suppose you don't remember her,' and that'll be all. You don't mind, do you? It won't take long to eat dinner."

"But I'm a terrible mess to meet a girl!" he exclaimed uneasily, looking down deprecatingly at himself. "I thought it was just you. This uniform's three sizes too large and needs a drink. Besides"—he passed a speculative hand over his smoothly shaven chin—"I—hate girls!" There was a deep frown between his eyes, and the bitter look had come back on his face. Miss Marilla thought he looked as if he might be going to run away.

"Oh, that's all right!" said Miss Marilla anxiously. "Mary Amber hates men. She says they're all a selfish, conceited lot. You needn't have much to do with her. Just eat your dinner and tell anything you want to about the war. We won't bother you to talk much. Come, this is the house, and the turkey must be on the table getting cold by now."

She swung open the gate and laid a persuasive hand on the shabby sleeve, and the young man reluctantly followed her up the path to the front door.

Chapter 2

When Lyman Gage set sail for France three years before, he left behind him a modest interest in a promising business enterprise, a girl who seemed to love him dearly, and a debt of several thousand dollars to her father, who had advised him to go into the enterprise and furnished the funds for his share in the capital.

When he had returned from France three days before, he had been met with news that the business enterprise had gone to smash during the war, the girl had become engaged to a dashing young captain with a well-feathered nest, and the debt had become a galling yoke.

"Father says tell you, you need not worry about the money you owe him," wrote the girl sweetly, concluding her revelations. "You can pay it at your leisure when you get started again."

Lyman Gage lost no time in gathering together every cent he could scrape up. This was more than he had at first hoped, because he owned two houses in the big city in which he had landed and these houses, though old and small, happened to be located near a great industrial plant that'd sprung up since the end of the war, and houses were going at soaring prices. They were snapped up at once at a fabulous sum in comparison with their real value. This, with what he had brought home and the bonus he received on landing, exactly covered his indebtedness to the man who was to have been his father-in-law. When he turned away from the service window, where he had been telegraphing the money to his lawyer in a far state, with instructions to pay the loan at once, he had just forty-six cents left in his pocket.

Suddenly, as he reflected that he had done the last thing left he now cared to do on earth, the noises of the great city got hold upon his nerve and tore and racked it.

He was filled with a great desire to get out and away from it, he cared not where, only so that the piercing sounds and rumbling grind of the city traffic should not press upon the raw nerves and torture them.

With no thought of getting anything to eat or providing for a shelterless night that was fast coming on, he wandered out into the train area of the great station and idly read the names up over the train gates. One caught his fancy, Purling Brook. It seemed as if it might be quiet there and a fellow could think. He followed the impulse and strode through the gates just as they were about to be closed. Dropping into the last seat in the car as the train was about to start, he flung his head back and closed his eyes wearily. He did not care whether he ever got anywhere or not. He was weary in heart and spirit. He wished that he might just sink away into nothingness. He was too tired to think, to bemoan his fate, to touch with torturing finger of memory all the little beautiful hopes he had woven about the girl he thought he loved better than anyone else on earth. Just passingly, he had a wish that he had a living mother to whom he could go with his sick heart for healing. But she had been gone long years, and his father even longer. There was really no one to whom he cared to show his face, now that all he had counted dear on earth had been suddenly taken from him.

The conductor roused him from a profound sleep, demanding a ticket, and he had the good fortune to remember the name he had seen over the gate: "Purling Brook. How much?"

"Fifty-six cents."

Gage reached into his pocket and displayed the coins on his palm with a wry smile.

"Guess you better put me off here, and I'll walk," he said, stumbling wearily to his feet.

"That's all right, son. Sit down," said the conductor half roughly. "You pay me when you come back sometime. I'll make it good." And he glanced at the uniform kindly.

Gage looked down at his shabby self helplessly. Yes, he was still a soldier, and people had not got over the habit of being kind to the uniform. He thanked the conductor and sank into sleep again, to be roused by the same kindly hand a few minutes later at Purling Brook. He stumbled off and stood, looking dazedly about him at the orderly little village. The sleep was not yet gone from his eyes, nor the ache from his nerves, but the clear quiet of the little town seemed to wrap him about soothingly like salve, and the crisp air entered into his lungs and gave him heart. He realized that he was hungry.

It seemed to have been a popular afternoon train that he had travelled upon. He looked beyond the groups of happy homecomers to where it hurried away gustily down the track, even then preparing to stop at the next near suburban station to deposit a few more homecomers. There, on that train, went the only friend he felt he had in the world at present, that grizzly conductor with his kindly eyes looking through great bifocals like a pleasant old grasshopper.

Well, he could not remain here any longer. The air was biting, and the sun was going down. Across the road, the little drugstore even then was twinkling out with lights behind its blue and green glass urns. Two boys and a girl were drinking something at the soda fountain through straws and laughing a great deal. It somehow turned him sick; he could not tell why. He had done things like that many a time himself.

There was a little stone church down the street, with a spire and bells. The sun touched the bells with burnished crimson till they looked like Christmas cards. A youthful, rural football team went noisily across the road, discoursing about how they would come out that night if their mothers would let them; and the station bus came down the street, full of passengers, and waited for a lady at the meat market. He could see the legs of a chicken sticking out of the basket as the driver helped her in.

He began to wonder why he hadn't stayed in the city and spent his forty-six cents for something to eat. It would have bought a great many crackers, say, or even bananas. He passed the bakery, and a whiff of fresh-baked bread greeted his nostrils. He cast a wistful eye at the window. Of course, he might go in and ask for a job in payment for his supper. There were his soldier's clothes. But no, that was equivalent to begging. He could not quite do that.

Here in town they would have all the help they wanted. Perhaps, farther out in the country—perhaps—he didn't know what, only he couldn't bring himself to ask for food, even with the offer to work. He didn't care enough for that. What was hunger, anyway? A thing to be satisfied and come again. What would happen if he didn't satisfy it? Die, of course, but what did it matter? What was there to live for, anyway?

He passed a house, all windows, where children were gathered about a piano, with one clumsily playing an accompaniment. There was an open fire, and the long windows came down to the piazza floor. They were singing at the top of their lungs, the old, time-worn song made familiar to them by community songfests, still good to them because they all knew it so well.

There's a long, long trail a-winding
Until my dreams all come true...

And it gripped his heart like a knife. He had sung that song with *her*, when it was new and tender, just before he had sailed away, and the trail had seemed so long! And now he had reached the end of it, and she had not been there to meet him. It was incredible. She, so fair! And false! After all those months of waiting. That was the hardest part of it—that she could have done it, and then explained so lightly that he had been away so long she was sure he would understand, and they both must have got over their childish attachment, and so on, through the long, nauseating sentences of her repeal. He shuddered as he said them over to his tired heart, and then shuddered again with the keen air, for his uniform was thin and he had no overcoat.

What was that she had said about the money? He needn't worry about it. A sort of bone to toss to the lone dog after he was kicked out. Ah well! It was paid. He was glad of that. He was even grimly glad for his own destitution. It gave a kind of sense of satisfaction to have gone hungry and homeless to pay it all in one grand lump, and to have paid it at once, and through his lawyer, without any word to her or her father either. They should not be even distant witnesses of his humiliation. He would never cross their path again, if he had his way. They should be as completely wiped out of his existence, and he out of theirs, as if the same universe did not hold them.

He passed down the broad, pleasant street in the crisp air, and every home on either hand gave him a thrust of memory that stabbed him to the heart. It was such a home as one of these that he had hoped to have someday, although it would have been in the city, perhaps, for she always liked the city. He had hoped, in the depths of his heart, to persuade her to the country, though. Now he saw as in a revelation how futile such hopes had been. She would never have come to love sweet, quiet ways such as he loved. She couldn't ever have really loved him, or she would have waited, would not have changed.

Over and over again he turned the bitter story, trying to get it settled in his heart so that the sharp edges would not hurt so, trying to accustom himself to the thought that she, whom he had cherished through the blackness of the years that were past, was not what he had thought her. He stopped in the road, beside a tall hedge that hid the Hazard house from view, and snatched out her picture that he had carried in his breast pocket till now, snatched it out, gazed upon it with a look that was not good to see on a young face, and tore it across! He took a step forward, and with every step he tore a tiny fragment from the picture and flung it into the road, bit by bit, till the lovely face was mutilated in the dust, where the feet of passersby would grind upon it and where those great blue eyes that had gazed back at him from the picture so long would be destroyed forever. It was the last thread that bound him to her, that picture. And when the last scrap of picture had fluttered away from him, he put his head down and strode forward like one who has cast away from him his last hope.

The voice of Miss Marilla roused him like a homely, pleasant sound about the house of a morning when one has had an unhappy dream. He lifted his head, and, soldierlike, dropped into the old habit of hiding his emotions.

Her kindly face somehow comforted him, and the thought of dinner was a welcome one. The ugly tragedy of his life seemed to melt away for the moment, as if it could not stand the light of the setting sun and her wholesome presence. There was an appeal in her eyes that reached him, and somehow he didn't feel like turning down her naïve, childlike proposition. Besides, he was used to being cared for because he was a soldier, and why not once more, now when everything else had gone so rotten? It was an adventure, anyway, and what was there left for him but adventure? he asked himself with a little, bitter sneer.

But when she mentioned a *girl*, that was a different thing! Girls were all treacherous. It was a new conviction with him, but it had gone deep, so deep that it had extended not only to a certain girl or class of girls, but to all girls, everywhere. He had become a woman hater. He wanted nothing more to do with any of them. And yet, at that moment, his tired, disappointed, hurt man's soul was really crying out for the woman of the universe to comfort him, to explain to him this awful circumstance that had come to all his bright dreams. A mother. That was what he thought he wanted, and Miss Marilla looked as if she might make a nice mother. So he turned like a tired little hungry boy and followed her, at least until she said "girl." Then he almost turned and fled.

Yet, while Miss Marilla coaxed and explained about Mary Amber, he stood facing again the lovely vision of the girl he had left behind at the beginning of the long, long trail, and whose picture he had just trampled underfoot on this end of the trail, which it now seemed to him would wind on forever alone for him. As he paused on Miss Marilla's immaculate front steps, he was preparing himself to face the enemy of his life, in the form of *woman*. The one thing, really, that made him go into that house and meekly submit to Miss Marilla's guest was that his soul had risen to battle. He would fight Girl in the concrete! She should be his enemy from henceforth. And this strange, unknown girl who hated men and thought them conceited and selfish, this cold, inhuman creature was likely falsehearted, too, like the one he had loved and who had not loved him. He would show her what he thought of such girls, of all girls; what all men who knew anything about it thought of all girls! And, thus reasoning, he followed Miss Marilla into the pleasant oilcloth-covered hall and up the front stairs to the spare room, where she smilingly showed him the towels and brushes prepared for his comfort, and left him, calling cheerily back that dinner would be on the table as soon as he was ready to come down.

All the time he was bathing his tired, dirty face and cold, rough hands in the warm, sweet-scented soapsuds, and wiping them on the fragrant towel, even while he stood in front of the mirror, all polished to reflect the visage of Lieutenant Richard H. Chadwick, and brushed his close-cropped curls till there was not a hint of wave left in them, he was hardening himself to meet Girl in the concrete and get back a return for what she had done to his life.

Then, with a last final polish of the brush and a flick of the whisk-broom over his discouraged-looking uniform, he set his lips grimly and went downstairs, taking the precaution to fold his cap and put it into his pocket, for he might want to escape at any minute and it was best to be prepared.

Chapter 3

Mary Amber was carrying in the great platter of golden-brown turkey when he first saw her, and had not heard him come down. She was entirely off her guard, with a sweet, serious intentness upon her work and a stray wisp of gold hair set afloat across the kitchen-flushed cheek. She looked so sweet and serviceable and true, with her lips parted in the pleasure of completing her task, that the soldier was taken by surprise and thrown entirely off his guard. Was this the false-hearted creature he had come to fight?

Then Mary Amber felt his eyes upon her as he stood staring from the open hall door, and lifting her own clear ones, froze into the opponent at once. A very polite opponent, it's true, with all the grace of a young queen, but nevertheless an opponent, cold as a young icicle.

Miss Marilla, with bright eyes and preternaturally pink cheeks, spoke into the vast pause that suddenly surrounded them all, and her voice sounded strangely unnatural to herself.

"Dick, this is Mary Amber. I suppose you don't remember her."

And the young soldier, not yet quite recovered from that first sweet vision of Mary Amber, went forward with his belligerence to woman somewhat held in abeyance.

"You—have changed a good deal since then, haven't you?" he managed to ask, with his native quickness, the right thing in an emergency.

"A good many years have passed," she said, coolly putting out a reluctant hand to please Miss Marilla. "You don't look at all as you did. I never should have known you."

The girl was looking keenly at him, studying his face closely. If a soldier just home from an ocean trip could get any redder, his face would have grown so under her scrutiny. Also, now that he was face-to-face with her, he felt his objection to Girl in general receding before the fact of his own position. How had that ridiculous old woman expected him to carry off a situation like this without giving it away? How was he supposed to converse with a girl he had never seen before, about things he had never done—with a girl whom he was supposed to have played with in his youth? Why had he been such a fool as to get into this corner, just for the sake of one more dinner? Why, tomorrow he would need another dinner, and all the tomorrows through which he might have to live. What was one dinner, more or less? He felt in his hip pocket for the comforting assurance of his cap and gave a furtive glance toward the hall door. It wouldn't be far to bolt back to the road, and what would be the difference? He would never see either of the two again.

Then the sweet, anxious eyes of his hostess met his with an appealing smile, and he felt himself powerless to move.

The girl's eyes had swept over his ill-fitting uniform, and he seemed to feel every crease and stain.

"I thought they told us you were an officer, but I don't see your bars." She laughed mockingly and searched his face again accusingly.

"This is another fellow's uniform," he answered lamely. "Mine got shrunk so I could hardly get into it, and another fellow who was going home changed with me."

He lifted his eyes frankly, for it was the truth that he told, and he looked into her eyes, but saw that she did not believe him. Her dislike and distrust of the little boy Dick had come to the front. He saw that she believed that Dick had been boasting to his aunt of honors that were not his. A wave of anger swept over his face, yet somehow he could not summon his defiance. Somehow he wanted her to believe him.

They sat down at the beautiful table, and the turkey got in its work on his poor, human sensibilities. The delicate perfume of the hot meat as it fell in large, flaky slices from Miss Marilla's sharp knife, the whiff of the summer savory and sage and sweet marjoram in the stuffing, the smoothness of the mashed potatoes, the brownness of the candied sweet potatoes, all cried out to him and held him prisoner. The odor of the food brought giddiness to his head, and the faintness of hunger attacked him. A pallor grew under the tan of his face, and there were dark shadows under his nice eyes that quite touched Miss Marilla and almost softened the hard look of distrust that had been growing around Mary Amber's gentle lips.

"This certainly is great!" he murmured. "I don't deserve to get in on anything like this, but I'm no end grateful."

Mary Amber's questioning eyes recalled him in confusion to his role of nephew in the house, and he was glad of the chance to bend his head while Miss Marilla softly asked a blessing on the meal. He had been inclined to think he could get away with any situation, but he began to feel now as if his recent troubles had unnerved him, and he might make a mess of this one. Somehow that girl seemed as if she could see into a fellow's heart. Why couldn't he show her how he despised the whole race of false-hearted womankind?

They heaped his plate with good things; poured him amber coffee, rich with cream; gave him cranberry sauce and pickles and olives; and passed little delicate biscuits and butter with the fragrance of roses. With all this before him, he suddenly felt as if he could not swallow a mouthful. He lifted his eyes to the opposite wall, and a neatly framed sentence in quaint, old English lettering met his eye: WHO CROWNETH YOU WITH LOVINGKINDNESS AND TENDER MERCIES, SO THAT THY YOUTH IS RENEWED LIKE THE EAGLE'S.

An intense desire to put his head down on the table and cry came over him. The warmth of the room, the fragrance of the food, had made him conscious of an ache in every part of his body. His head was throbbing, too, and he wondered what was the matter with him. After all the hardness of the world, and the bitterness, to meet a kindness like this seemed to unnerve him. But gradually the food got in its work, and the hot coffee stimulated him. He rose to the occasion greatly. He described France, spoke of the beautiful cathedrals he had seen, the works of art, the little children, the work of reconstruction that was going on. Spoke of Germany, too, when he saw they expected him to have been there, although this was a shoal on which he almost wrecked his role before he realized. He told of the voyage over and the people he had met, and he kept most distinctly away from anything personal, at least as far away as Mary Amber would let him. She, with her keen, questioning eyes, was always bringing up some question that was almost impossible for him to answer directly without treading on dangerous ground, and it required skill indeed to turn her from it. Mary listened and marveled, trying continually to trace in his face the lines of that fat-faced, arrogant child who used to torment her.

Mary rose to take the plates, and the young soldier insisted on helping. Miss Marilla, pleased to see them getting on so nicely, sat smiling in her place, reaching out to brush away a stray crumb on the tablecloth. Mary, lingering in the kitchen for a moment to be sure the fire was not being neglected, lifted the stove lid, and with the draught, a little flame leaped up around a crumpled, smoldering yellow paper with the familiar WESTERN UNION TELEGRAPH heading. Three words stood out distinctly for a second, IMPOSSIBLE TO ACCEPT, and then were enveloped by the flame. Mary stood and stared with the stove lid in her hand, and then as the flame curled the paper over, she saw LIEUTENANT RICHARD—revealed and immediately licked up by the flame.

It lay, a little crisp, black fabric, with its message utterly illegible, but still Mary stood and stared and wondered. She had seen the boy on the bicycle ride up and go away. She had also seen the approaching soldier almost immediately, and the thought of the telegram had been at once erased. Now it came back forcefully. Dick, then, had sent a telegram, and it looked as if he had declined the invitation. Who, then, was this stranger at the table? Some comrade working Miss Marilla for dinner, or Dick himself, having changed his mind or playing a practical joke? In any case, Mary felt she ought to disapprove of him utterly. It was her duty to show him up to Miss Marilla, and yet how could she do it when she did not know anything herself?

"Hurry, Mary, and bring the pie," called Miss Marilla. "We're waiting."

Mary put the stove lid down and went slowly, thoughtfully back to the dining room, carrying a pie. She studied the face of the young soldier intently as she passed him his pie, but he seemed so young and pleasant and happy she hadn't the heart to say anything just yet. She would bide her time. Perhaps somehow it was all explainable. So she set to asking him questions.

"By the way, Dick, whatever became of Barker?" she requested, fixing her clear eyes on his face.

"Barker?" said Lyman Gage, puzzled and polite, then, remembering his role, "Oh yes, *Barker*!" He laughed. "Great, old Barker, wasn't he?" He turned in troubled appeal to Miss Marilla.

"Barker certainly was the cutest little guinea-pig I ever saw," beamed Miss Marilla, "although, at the time, I really wasn't as fond of it as you were. You would have it around in the kitchen so much."

There was covert apology in Miss Marilla's voice for the youthful character of the young man he was supposed to be.

"I should judge I must have been a good deal of a nuisance in those days," hazarded the soldier, feeling that he was treading on dangerous ground.

"Oh no!" sighed Miss Marilla, trying to be truthful and at the same time polite. "Children will be children, you know."

"All children are not alike." It was as near to snapping as sweet

Mary Amber ever came. She had memories which time had not dimmed.

"Was it as bad as that?" The young man laughed. "I'm sorry!"

Mary had to laugh. His frankness certainly was disarming. But there was that telegram! And Mary grew serious again. She did not intend to have her gentle old friend deceived.

Mary insisted on clearing off the table and washing the dishes, and the soldier insisted on helping her. So Miss Marilla, much disturbed that domestic duties should interfere with the evening, put everything away and made the task as brief as possible, looking anxiously at Mary Amber every trip back from the refrigerator and pantry to see how she was getting on with the strange soldier, and how the strange soldier was getting on with her. At first she was a little troubled lest he shouldn't be the kind of man she would want to introduce to Mary Amber. But after she had heard him talk and express such thoroughly wholesome views on politics and national subjects, she almost forgot he was not the real Dick, and her doting heart could not help wanting Mary Amber to like him. He was, in fact, the personification of the Dick she had dreamed out for her own—as different, in fact, from the real Dick as could have been imagined, and a great deal better. His frank eyes, his pleasant manner, his cultured voice, all pleased her; and she couldn't help feeling that he was Dick come back as she would have liked him to be all the time.

"I'd like to have a little music, just a little, before Mary has to go home," Miss Marilla said wistfully, as Mary Amber hung up the dishtowel with an air that said plainly without words that she felt her duty toward the stranger was over and she was going to depart at once.

"Sure!" said the stranger. "You sing, don't you, Miss Mary?"

There was no alternative, and Mary resigned herself to another half hour. They went into the parlor, and Mary sat down at the old square piano and touched its asthmatic keys that sounded the least bit tinny, even under such skilled fingers as hers.

"What shall I play?" questioned Mary. "'The Long, Long Trail'?" There was a bit of sarcasm in her tone. Mary was a classical musician and hated ragtime.

"No! *Never!*" said the soldier quickly. "I mean—not that, *please.*" A look of such bitter pain swept over his face that Mary glanced up surprised and forgot to be disagreeable for several minutes while she pondered his expression.

"Excuse me," he said. "But I loathe it. Give us something else; sing something *real.* I'm sure you can." There was a hidden compliment in his tone, and Mary was surprised. The soldier had almost forgotten that he did not belong there. He was acting as he might have acted in his own social sphere.

Mary struck a few chords tenderly on the piano and then broke into the delicious melody of "The Spirit Flower." And Lyman Gage forgot that he was playing a part in a strange home with a strange girl, forgot that he hadn't a cent in the world and his girl was gone, and sat watching her face as she sang. For Mary had a voice like a thrush in the summer evening, that liquid appeal that always reminds one of a silver spoon dropped into a glass of water; and Mary had a face like the spirit flower itself. As she sang she could not help living, breathing, being the words she spoke.

There was nothing, absolutely nothing about Mary to remind him of the girl he had lost. And there was something in her sweet, serious demeanor as she sang to call to his better nature; a wholesome, serious sweetness that was in itself a kind of antiseptic against bitterness and sweeping denunciation. Lyman Gage, as he listened, was lifted out of himself and set in a new world where men and women thought of something besides money and position and social prestige. He seemed to be standing off, apart from himself, and seeing himself from a new angle, an angle in which he was not the only one that mattered in this world, and in which he got a hint that his plans might be only hindrances to a larger life for himself and everyone else. Not that he exactly thought these things in so many words. It was more as if, while Mary sang, a wind blew freshly from a place where such thoughts were crowding and made him seem smaller in his own conceit than he had thought he was.

"And now sing 'Laddie,'" pleaded Miss Marilla.

A wave of annoyance swept over Mary Amber's face. It was plain she did not wish to sing that song. Nevertheless, she sang it, forgetting herself and throwing all the pathos and tenderness into her voice that belonged to the beautiful words. Then she turned from the piano decidedly and rose. *I must go home at once*—was written in every line of her attitude. Miss Marilla rose nervously and looked from one of her guests to the other.

"Dick, I wonder if you haven't learned to sing."

Her eyes were so pathetic that they stirred the young man to her service. Besides, there was something so contemptuous in the attitude of that human spirit flower standing on the wing, as it were, in that done-with-him-forever attitude, that spurred him into a faint desire to show her what he could do.

"Why, sure," he answered lazily, and with a stride, transferred himself to the piano stool and struck a deep, strong chord or two.

Suddenly there poured out a wondrous baritone, such as was seldom heard in Purling Brook, and indeed is not common anywhere. He had a feeling that he was paying for his wonderful dinner and must do his best. The first song that had come to his mind was a big, blustery French patriotic song, and the very spirit of the march was in its cadence. Out of the corner of his eye, he could see Mary Amber still poised but waiting in her astonishment. He felt that he had already scored a point. When he came to the grand climax, she cried out with pleasure and clapped her hands. Miss Marilla had sunk into the mahogany rocker, but was sitting on the edge, alert to prolong this gala evening, and two bright spots of colorful delight shone on her faded cheeks.

He did not wait for them to ask him for another. He dashed into a minor key and began to sing a wild, sweet, sobbing song of love and loss till Mary, entranced, softly slipped into a chair and sat breathless with clasped hands and shining eyes. It was such an artistic, perfect thing, that song, that she forgot everything else while it was going on.

When the last sob died away, and the little parlor was silent with deep feeling, he whirled about on the piano stool and rose briskly.

"Now I've done my part, am I to be allowed to see the lady home?"

He looked at Miss Marilla instead of Mary for permission, and she smiled, half frightened.

"It isn't necessary at all," spoke Mary crisply, rising and going for a wrap. "It's only a step."

"Oh, I think so, surely," answered Miss Marilla, as if a great point of etiquette had been decided. She gave him a look of perfect trust.

"It's only across the garden and through the hedge, you know," she said in a low tone, "but I think she would appreciate it."

"Certainly," he said, and turned with perfect courtesy as Mary looked in at the door and called, "Good night."

He did not make a fuss about attending her. He simply was there, close beside her, as she sped through the dark without a word to him.

"It's been very pleasant to meet you," he said as she turned with a motion of dismissal at her own steps. "Again," he added lamely. "I–I've enjoyed the evening more than you can understand. I enjoyed your singing."

"Oh! *My* singing!" flung back Mary. "Why, I was like a sparrow beside a nightingale. It wasn't quite fair of you to let me sing first without knowing you had a voice. It's strange. You know, you never used to sing."

It seemed to him her glance went deep as she looked at him through the shadows of the garden. He thought about it as he crept back through the hedge, shivering now, for the night was keen and his uniform thin. Well, what did it matter what she thought? He would soon be far away from her and never likely to see her again. Yet he was glad he had scored a point, one point against Girl in the concrete.

Now he must go in and bid his hostess good-bye, and then away to—where?

Chapter 4

As Lyman Gage went up the steps to Miss Marilla's front porch, a sick thrill of cold and weariness passed over his big frame. Every joint and muscle seemed to cry out in protest, and his very vitals seemed sore and racked. The bit of bright evening was over, and he was facing his own gray life again, with a future that was void and empty.

But the door was not shut. Miss Marilla was hovering anxiously inside, with the air of just having retreated from the porch. She gave a little relieved gasp as he entered.

"Oh, I was afraid you wouldn't come back," she said eagerly. "And I did so want to thank you and tell you how we—how I, yes, I mean *we*, for I know she loved that singing—how very much we enjoyed it. I will always thank God that He sent you along just then."

"Well, I certainly have cause to thank you for that wonderful dinner," he said earnestly, as he might have spoken to a dear relation, "and for all this"—he waved his big hand toward the bright room—"this pleasantness. It was like coming home, and I haven't any home to come to now."

"Oh! Haven't you?" said Miss Marilla caressingly. "Oh, *haven't* you?" she said again wistfully. "I wonder why I can't keep you a little while, then. You seem just like my own nephew—as I had hoped he would be—I haven't seen him in a long time. Where were you going when I stopped you?"

The young man lifted heavy eyes that were bloodshot and sore to the turning, and tried to smile. To save his life he couldn't lie blithely when it seemed so good to be in that warm room.

"Why—I was, I don't know—I guess I just wasn't going anywhere. To tell you the truth, I was all in and down on my luck and as blue as indigo when you met me. I was just tramping anywhere to get away from it."

"You poor boy," said Miss Marilla, putting out her fine, little blue-veined hands and caressing the old khaki sleeve. "Well, then you're just going to stay with me and get rested. There's no reason in the world why you shouldn't."

"No, indeed," said Lyman Gage, drawing himself up bravely. "I couldn't think of it. It wouldn't be right. But I certainly thank you with all my heart for what you have done for me tonight. I really must go at once."

"But where?" she asked pathetically, as if he belonged to her, sliding her hands detainingly down to his big rough ones.

"Oh, anywhere; it doesn't matter," he said, holding her delicate, little old hand in his with a look of sacred respect, as if a nice old angel had offered to hold hands with him. "I'm a soldier, you know, and a few storms, more or less, won't matter. I'm used to it. Good night."

He clasped her hands a moment and was about to turn away, but she held his fingers eagerly.

"You shall not go that way!" she declared. "Out into the cold, without any overcoat and no home to go to! Your hands are hot, too. I believe you have a fever. You're going to stay here tonight and have a good sleep and a warm breakfast; and then, if you must go, all right. My spare bed is all made up, and there's a fire in the Franklin heater. The room's all warm as toast, and Mary put a big bouquet of chrysanthemums up there. If you don't sleep there, it will all be wasted. You *must* stay."

"No, it wouldn't be right." He shook his head again and smiled wistfully. "What would people say?"

"Say! Why, they've got it in the paper that you're to be here—at least, that Dick's to be here. They'll think you're my nephew and think nothing else about it. Besides, I guess I have a right to have company if I like."

"If there was any way I could pay you," said the young man. "But I haven't a cent to my name, and no telling how long before I will have anything. I really couldn't accept any such hospitality."

"Oh, that's all right," said Miss Marilla cheerily. "You can pay me if you like, sometime when you get plenty, or perhaps you'll take me in when I'm having a hard time. Anyhow, you're going to stay. I won't take no for an answer. I've been disappointed and disappointed about Dick's coming, and me having no one to show for all the years of the war, just making sweaters for the world, it seemed like, with no one belonging to me. And now I've got a soldier, and I'm going to keep him at least for one night. Nobody's to know but you're my own nephew, and I haven't got to go around the town, have I, telling that Dick didn't care enough for his old country aunt to come out and take dinner with her? It's nothing to them, is it, if they think he came and stayed overnight, too? Or even a few days. Nobody'll be any the wiser, and I'll take a lot more comfort."

"I'd like to accommodate you," faltered the soldier, "but you know I really ought—" Suddenly the big fellow was seized with a fit of sneezing, and the sick, sore thrills danced all down his back and slapped him in the face and pricked him in the throat and banged against his head. He dropped weakly down in a chair and got out the discouragedest-looking handkerchief that ever a soldier carried. It looked as if it might have washed the decks on the way over or wiped off shoes, as doubtless it had. And it left a dull streak of olive-drab dust on his cheek and chin when he had finished polishing off the last sneeze and lifted his suffering eyes to his hostess.

"You're sick!" declared Miss Marilla, with a kind of satisfaction, as if now she had got something she could really take hold of. "I've thought it all the evening. I first laid it to the wind in your face, for I knew you weren't the drinking kind; and then I thought maybe you'd had to be up all night last night or something—lack of sleep makes eyes look that way. But I believe you've got the grippe, and I'm going to put you to bed and give you some homeopathic medicine. Come, tell me the truth. Aren't you chilly?"

With a half-sheepish smile, the soldier admitted that he was, and a big involuntary shudder ran over his tall frame with the admission.

"Well, it's high time we got to work. There's plenty of hot

water, and you go up to the bathroom and take a hot bath. I'll put a hot-water bag in the bed and get it good and warm; and I've got a long, warm flannel nightgown I guess you can get on. It was made for grandmother, and she was a big woman. Come, we'll go right upstairs. I can come down and shut up the house while you're taking your bath."

The soldier protested, but Miss Marilla swept all before her. She locked the front door resolutely and put the chain on. She turned out the parlor light and shoved the young man before her to the stairs.

"But I oughtn't to," he protested again, with one foot on the first step. "I'm an utter stranger."

"Well, what's that?" said Miss Marilla crisply. "'I was a stranger, and ye took me in.' When it comes to that, we're all strangers. Come, hurry up; you ought to be in bed. You'll feel like a new man when I get you tucked up."

"You're awfully good," he murmured, stumbling up the stairs with a sick realization that he was giving way to the little imps of chills and thrills that were dancing over him, that he was all in, and in a few minutes more, he would be a contemptible coward, letting a lone, old woman fuss over him this way.

Miss Marilla turned up the light and threw back the covers of the spare bed, sending a whiff of lavender through the room. The Franklin heater glowed cheerfully, and the place was warm as toast. There was something sweet and homelike in the old-fashioned room with its strange, ancient framed photographs of people long gone and its plain but fine old mahogany. The soldier raised his bloodshot eyes and looked about with a thankful wish that he felt well enough to appreciate it all.

Miss Marilla had pulled open a drawer and produced a long, fine flannel garment of nondescript fashion; and from a closet, she drew out a long pink bathrobe and a pair of felt slippers.

"There! I guess you can get those on."

She bustled into the bathroom, turned on the hot water, and heaped big white bath towels and sweet-scented soap upon him. In a kind of daze of thankfulness, he stumbled into the bathroom and began his bath. He hadn't had a bath like that in—was it two years? Somehow, the hot water held down the nasty little sick thrills and cut out the chills for the time. It was wonderful to feel clean and warm, and smell the freshness of the towels and soap. He climbed into the big nightgown, which also smelled of lavender, and came out presently with the felt slippers on his feet and the pink bathrobe trailing around his shoulders. There was a meek, conquered expression on his face; and he crept gratefully into the warm bed according to directions, and snuggled down with that sick, sore thrill of thankfulness that everybody who has ever had flu knows.

Miss Marilla bustled up from downstairs with a second hot-water bag in one hand and a thermometer in the other.

"I'm going to take your temperature," she said briskly and stuck the thermometer into his unresisting mouth. Somehow, it was wonderfully sweet to be fussed over this way, almost like having a mother. He hadn't had such care since he was a little fellow in the hospital at prep school.

"I thought so," said Miss Marilla, casting a practiced eye at the thermometer a moment later. "You've got quite a fever. And you've got to lie right still and do as I say, or you'll have a time of it. I hate to think what would have happened to you if I'd been weak enough to let you go off into the cold without any overcoat tonight."

"Oh, I'd have walked it off likely," faintly spoke the old Adam in the sleepy, sick soldier. But he knew, as he spoke, that he was lying, and he knew Miss Marilla knew it also. He would have laughed if it hadn't been too much trouble. It was wonderful to be in a bed like this and be warm, and that ache in his back against the hot-water bag. It almost made his head stop aching.

In almost no time at all, he was asleep. He never realized when Miss Marilla brought a glass and fed him medicine. He opened his mouth obediently when she told him and went right on sleeping.

"Bless his heart," she said. "He must have been all worn out." And she turned the light low and, gathering up his chair full of clothes, slipped away to the bathroom, where presently they were all, except the shoes, soaking in strong, hot soapsuds. Miss Marilla had gone downstairs to stir up the fire and put on irons. But she took the precaution to close all the blinds on the Amber side of the house and pull down the shades. Mary had no need ever to find out what she was doing.

The night wore on, and Miss Marilla wrought with happy heart and willing hands. She was doing something for somebody who really needed it, and who, for the time being, had no one else to do it for him. He was hers, exclusively, to be served this night. It was years since she had had anybody of her own to care for, and she luxuriated in the service.

Every hour she slipped up to feel his forehead, listen to his breathing, and give him his medicine, and then slipped down to the kitchen again to her ironing. Garment by garment the soldier's meager outfit came from the steaming suds, then was conveyed to the kitchen, where it hung on an improvised line over the range and got itself dry enough to be ironed and patched. It was a work of love, and therefore, it was done perfectly. When morning dawned, the soldier's outfit, thoroughly renovated and pressed almost beyond recognition, lay on a chair by the spare room window, and Miss Marilla, in her dark blue serge morning dress, lay tidily down on the outside of her bed to take "forty winks." But even then she could hardly get to sleep, she was so excited thinking about her guest and wondering whether he would feel better when he awoke or whether she ought to send for a doctor.

A hoarse cough roused her an hour later, and she went with speed to her patient and found him tossing and battling in his sleep with some imaginary foe.

"I don't owe you a cent any longer!" he declared fiercely. "I've paid it all, even to the interest while I was in France. And there's no reason why I shouldn't tell you just what I think of you. You can go to thunder with your kind offers. I'm off *you* for life!" And then the big fellow turned with a groan of anguish and buried his face in his pillow.

Miss Marilla paused in horror, thinking she had intruded upon some secret meditation. But as she waited on tiptoe and breathless in the hall, she heard the steady hoarse breathing keep on and knew he was still asleep. He did not rouse more than to open bloodshot, unseeing eyes and close them again when she loudly stirred his medicine in the glass and held the spoon to his lips. As before, he obediently opened his mouth and swallowed, and went on sleeping.

She stood a moment anxiously watching him. She did not know just what she ought to do. Perhaps he was going to have pneumonia. Perhaps she ought to send for the doctor, and yet there were complications about that. She would be obliged to explain a lot—or else lie to the neighborhood. And he might not like it for her to call a doctor while he was asleep. If she only had someone with whom to advise! On ordinary questions she always consulted Mary Amber, but by the very nature of the case, Mary Amber was out of this. Besides, in half an hour Mary Amber very discreetly put herself beyond a question, outside of any touch with Miss Marilla's visitor, by taking herself off in her little car for a short visit to a college friend over in the next county. It was plain that Mary Amber did not care to subject herself to further contact with the young soldier. He might be Dick, or he might not be Dick. It was none of her business while she was visiting Jeannette Clark; so she went away quite hurriedly. Miss Marilla heard the *purr* of the engine as the little brown car started down the hedged driveway, and watched the flight with a sense of satisfaction. She had an intuition that Mary Amber was not in favor of her soldier, and she had a guilty sense of hiding the truth from her dear, young friend that made her breathe more freely as she watched Mary Amber's flight. Moreover, it was with a certain self-reproachful relief that she noted the little brown suitcase that lay at Mary Amber's feet as she slid past Miss Marilla's house without looking up. Mary Amber was going away for the day at least, probably overnight. And by that time, the question of the soldier would be settled one way or the other, without Mary Amber's having to worry about it.

Miss Marilla ordered a piece of beef and brewed a cup of the most delicious broth, which she took upstairs. She managed to get her soldier awake enough to swallow it. But it was plain that he did not in the least realize where he was and seemed well content to close his eyes and drowse away once more. Miss Marilla was deeply troubled. Some pricks from the old, timeworn adage beginning, "O what a tangled web we weave," began to stab her conscience. If only she had not allowed those paragraphs to go into the county paper. No, that was not the real trouble at all. If only she had not dragged in another soldier and made Mary Amber believe he was her nephew! Such an old fool! Just because she couldn't bear the mortification of having people know her nephew hadn't cared enough for her to come and see her when he was close at hand. But she was well punished. Here she had a strange sick man on her hands and no end of responsibility. Oh, if only she hadn't asked him in!

Yet, as she stood watching the quick little throb in his neck above the old flannel nightgown and the long, curly sweep of the dark lashes on his hot cheek as he slept, her heart cried out against that wish. No, a thousand times no. If she had not asked him in, he might have been in some hospital by this time, cared for by strangers. And she would have been alone, with empty hands, getting her own solitary dinner or sewing on the aprons for the orphanage, with nothing in the world to do that really mattered for anybody. Somehow her heart went out to this stranger boy with a great yearning, and he had come to mean what her own—or what her own ought to have been to her. She wouldn't have him elsewhere for anything. She wanted him right where he was for her to care for, something at last that needed her, something she could love and tend, even if it were only for a few days.

And she was sure she could care for him. She knew a lot about sickness. People sent for her to help them out, and her wonderful nursing had often saved a life where the doctor's remedies had failed. She felt sure this was only a severe case of flu that had taken fierce hold on the system. Thorough rest, careful nursing, nourishing broth, and some of her homeopathic remedies would work the charm. She would try it a little longer and see. If his temperature wasn't higher than the last time, it would be perfectly safe to get along without a doctor.

She put the thermometer between his relaxed lips and held them firmly round it until she was sure it had been there long enough. Then she carried it softly over to the front window and studied it. No, it had not risen. In fact, it might be a fifth of a degree lower.

Well, she would venture it a little while longer.

For two days, Miss Marilla cared for her stranger soldier as only a born nurse like herself could care, and on the third morning, he rewarded her by opening his eyes and looking about. Then meeting her own anxious gaze, he gave her a weak smile.

"I've been sick," he said, as if stating an astonishing fact to himself. "I must have given you a lot of trouble."

"Not a bit of it, you dear child," said Miss Marilla, and then stooped and brushed his forehead with her lips in a motherly kiss. "I'm so glad you're better!"

She passed her hand like soft, old fallen roseleaves over his forehead, and it was moist. She felt of his hands, and they were moist, too. She took his temperature, and it had gone down almost to normal. Her eyes were shining with more than professional joy and relief. He had become to her, in these hours of nursing and anxiety, as her own child.

But at the kiss, the boy's eyelashes had swept down upon his cheek; and when she looked up from reading the thermometer, she saw a tear glisten unwillingly beneath the lashes.

The next two days were a time of untold joy to Miss Marilla while she pampered and nursed her soldier boy back to some degree of his normal strength. She treated him just as if he were a little child who had dropped from the skies to her loving ministrations. She bathed his face and puffed up his pillows and took his temperature and fed him and read him to sleep—Miss Marilla could read well, too. She was always asked to read the chapter at the Fortnightly Club whenever the regular reader, whose turn it was, failed. And while he was asleep, she cooked dainty, appetizing little dishes for him. They had a wonderful time together, and he enjoyed it as much as she did. The fact was he was too weak to object, for the little red devils that get into the blood and kick up the fight commonly titled grippe had done a thorough work with him, and he was, as he put it, "all in, and *then* some."

He seemed to have gone back to the days of his childhood since the fever began to abate, and he lay in a sweet daze of comfort and rest. His troubles and perplexities and loneliness had dropped away from him, and he felt no desire to think of them. He was having the time of his life.

Then suddenly, wholly unannounced and not altogether desired at the present stage of the game, Mary Amber arrived on the scene.

Chapter 5

Mary was radiant as the sunny morning in a little red tam, and her cheeks as red as her hat from the drive across country. She appeared at the kitchen door, quite in her accustomed way, just as Miss Marilla was lifting the dainty tray to carry her boy's breakfast upstairs, and she almost dropped it in her dismay.

"I've had the grandest time!" breezed Mary. "You don't know how beautiful the country is, all wonderful bronze and brown with a purple haze and a frost like silver lace this morning when I started. You've simply got to put on your wraps and come with me for a little while. I know a place where the shadows melt slowly, and the frost will not be gone yet. Come quick! I want you to see it before it's too late. You're not just eating your breakfast, Auntie Rill! And on a tray, too! Are you sick?"

Miss Marilla glanced guiltily down at the tray, too transparent even to evade the question.

"No, why—I—he—my neph—" Then she stopped in hopeless confusion, remembering her resolve not to tell a lie about the matter, whatever came.

Mary Amber stood up and looked at her, her keen young eyes searching and finding the truth.

"You don't mean to tell me *that man* is here yet? And you, waiting on him!"

There was both sorrow and scorn in the fine young voice.

In the upper hall, the sick soldier in a bathrobe was hanging over the banisters in a panic, wishing some kind of fairy would arrive and waft him away on a breath. All his perfidy in getting sick on a strange gentlewoman's hands and lying lazily in bed, letting her wait on him, was shown up in Mary Amber's voice. It found its echo in his own strong soul. He had known all along that he had no business there, that he ought to have gone out on the road to die rather than betray the sweet hospitality of Miss Marilla by allowing himself to be a selfish, lazy slob—that was what he called himself as he hung over the banisters.

"Mary! Why, he has been very *sick*!"

"Sick?" There was a covert sneer in Mary Amber's incredulous young voice. And then the conversation was suddenly blanketed by the closing of the hall door, and the sick soldier padded disconsolately back to bed, weak and dizzy, but determined. This was as good a time as any. He ought to have gone before.

He trailed across the room in the big flannel nightgown, which hung out from him with the outlines of a fat, old auntie and dragged down from one bronzed shoulder rakishly. His hair was sticking up wildly; he felt of his chin fiercely and realized that he was wearing a growth of several days.

In a neat pile on a chair, he found his few clean garments and struggled into them. His carefully ironed uniform hung in the closet. He braced himself and struggled into the trousers. It seemed a tremendous effort. He longed to drop back on the pillows, but wouldn't. He sat with his head in his hands, his elbows on his knees, trying to get courage to totter to the bathroom and subdue his hair and beard, when he heard Miss Marilla coming hastily up the stairs, the little coffeepot sending on a delicious odor and the glass of milk tinkling against the silver spoons as she came.

He had managed his leggings by this time and looked up with an attempt at a smile, trying to pass it off in a jocular way.

"I thought it was high time I was getting about," he said, and broke down coughing.

Miss Marilla paused in distress and looked at his hollow eyes. Everything seemed to be going wrong this morning. Oh, why hadn't Mary Amber stayed away just one day longer? But of course, he had not heard her.

"Oh, you're not fit to be up yet!" she exclaimed. "Do lie down and rest till you've had your breakfast."

"I can't be a baby having you wait on me any longer," he said. "I'm ashamed of myself. I ought not to have stayed here at all." His tone was savage, and he reached for his coat and jammed it on with a determined air in spite of his weakness and the sore shivers that crept shakily up his back. "I'm perfectly all right, and you've been wonderful. But it's time I was moving on."

He pushed past her hurriedly to the bathroom, feeling that he must get out of her sight before his head began to swim. The water on his face would steady him. He dashed it on and shivered sickly, longing to plunge back to bed, yet keeping on with his absolutions.

Miss Marilla put down her tray and stood with tears in her eyes, waiting for him to return, trying to think what she could say to persuade him back to bed again.

Her anxious expression softened him when he came back, and he agreed to eat his breakfast before he went anywhere. He sank gratefully into the big chair in front of the Franklin heater, where she had laid out his breakfast on a little table. She had lined the chair with a big comforter, which she drew unobtrusively about his shoulders now, slipping a cushion under his feet, and quietly coddling him into comfort again. He looked at her gratefully, and setting down his coffee cup, reached out and patted her hair as she rose from tucking in his feet.

"You're just like a mother to me," he choked, trying to keep back the emotion from his voice. "It's been great. I can't tell you."

"You've been just like a dear son." She beamed, touching the dark hair over his forehead shyly. "It's like getting my own back again to have you come for this little while and to be able to do for you. You see, it wasn't as if I really had anybody. Dick never cared for me. I used to hope he would when he grew up. I used to think of him over there in danger and pray for him, and love him, and send him sweaters. But now I know it was really you I thought of and prayed for. Dick never cared."

He looked at her tenderly and pressed her hand gratefully.

"You're wonderful," he said. "I shall never forget it."

That little precious time while he was eating his breakfast made it all the harder for what he meant to do. He saw that he could never hope to do it openly, either, for she would fling herself in his path to prevent him from going out until he was well. So he let her tuck him up carefully on the spread-out bed and pull down the shades for him to take a nap after the exertion of getting dressed. And he caught her hand and kissed it fervently as she was leaving him, and cherished her murmured "dear child!" and the pressure of her old roseleaf fingers in parting. Then he closed his eyes and let her slip away to the kitchen where he knew she would be some time preparing something delicious for dinner.

When she was safely out of hearing, rattling away at the kitchen stove, he threw back the covers vigorously, set his grim determination against the swimming head, stalked over to the little desk, and wrote a note on the fine notepaper he found there.

"Dear wonderful little mother," he wrote. *"I can't stay here any longer. It isn't right. But I'll be back someday to thank you if everything goes all right. Sincerely, Your Boy."*

He tiptoed over and laid it on the pillow. Then he took his old trench cap, which had been nicely pressed and was hanging on the corner of the mirror, and stealthily slid out of the pleasant, warm room, down the carpeted stairs, and out the front door into the crisp, cold morning. The chill air met him with a challenge as he closed the front door, and dared him not to cough. But with an effort, he held his breath and crept down the front walk to the road, holding in control as well the long, violent shivers that seized him in their grasp. The sun met him and blinded his sensitive eyes; and the wind, with a tang of winter, jeered at his thin uniform and trickled up his sleeves and down his collar, penetrating every seam. But he stuffed his hands into his pockets and strode grimly ahead on the way he had been going when Miss Marilla met him, passing the tall hedge where Mary Amber lived and trying to hold his head high. He hoped Mary Amber saw him *going away.*

For perhaps half a mile past Mary Amber's house, his courage and his pride held him, for he was a soldier who had slept in a muck pile under the rain, held his nerve under fire, and gone on foot ten miles to the hospital after he was wounded. What was a little flu and a walk in the cold to the neighboring village? He wished he knew how far it was, but he had to go, for it would never do to send the telegram he must send from the town where Miss Marilla lived.

The second half mile, he lagged and shivered, with not energy enough to keep up circulation. The third half mile and the fourth were painful, and the fifth was completed in a sick daze of weakness, for the cold, though stimulating at first, had been getting in its work through his uniform, and he felt chilled to the very soul of him. His teeth were chattering, and he was blue around the lips when he staggered into the telegraph office of Little Silverton. His fingers were almost too stiff to write, and his thoughts seemed to have congealed also, though he had been repeating the message all the way, word for word, with a vague feeling that he might forget it forever if he did not keep it going.

"Will you send that collect?" he asked the operator when he had finished writing.

The girl took the form and read it carefully.

Arthur J. Watkins, Esq.,
LaSalle Street, Chicago, Ill.
 Please negotiate a loan of five hundred dollars for me, using old house as collateral. Wire money immediately Little Silverton. Entirely out of funds. Have been sick.
     Lyman Gage

The girl read it through again and then eyed him cautiously.

"What's your address?" she asked, giving a slow, speculative chew of her gum.

"I'll wait here," said the big blue soldier, sinking into a rush-bottomed chair by the desk.

"It might be some wait," said the girl dryly, giving him another curious once-over.

"I'll wait!" he repeated fiercely, and dropped his aching head into his hands.

The little instrument clicked away vigorously. In his fevered brain, he fancied it writing on a typewriter at the other end of the line and felt a curious impatience for his lawyer to read it and reply. How he wished it would hurry!

The morning droned on, and the telegraph instrument chattered breezily, with the monotony of a sunny child that knows no larger world and is happy. Sometimes, it seemed to Gage as if every click pierced his head and he was going crazy. The shivers were keeping in time, running up and down his back and chilling his very heart. The room was cold, cold, *cold*! How did that fool of a girl stand it in a pink, transparent blouse, showing her fat arms huskily? He shivered. Oh, for one of Miss Marilla's nice, thick blankets and a hot-water bag. Oh for the soft, warm bed, the quiet room, and Miss Marilla keeping guard! But he was a man—and a soldier. And every now and then would come Mary Amber's keen accusing voice, *"Is that man here yet? And you are waiting on him!"* It was that, that kept him up when he might have given way. He *must* show her he was a man, after all. *"That man!"* What had she meant? Did she, then, suspect him of being a fraud and not the real nephew? Well—shiver, shiver—what did he care? Let Mary Amber go to thunder! Or, if she didn't want to go, he would go to thunder himself. He felt himself there already.

Two hours went by. Now and then, someone came in with a message and went out again. The girl behind the desk got out a pink sweater she was knitting and chewed gum in time to her needles. Sometimes she eyed her companion curiously, but he did not stir nor look up. If there hadn't been prohibition, she might have thought him drunk. She began to think about his message and weave a crude little romance around him. She wondered whether he had been wounded. If he had given her half a chance, she would have asked him questions, but he sat there with his head in his hands like a stone image and never seemed to know she was in the room. After a while, it got on her nerves; and she took up her telephone and carried on a gallery conversation with a fellow laborer somewhere up the line, giggling a good deal and telling about a movie she went to the night before. She used rare slang, with a furtive glance at the soldier for developments, but he did not stir. Finally, she remarked loudly that it was getting noontime and "so longed" her friend, clicking the receiver into place.

"I gotta go to lunch now," she remarked in an impersonal tone. "I have an hour off. This office is closed at noontime."

He did not seem to hear her, so she repeated it, and Gage looked up with bloodshot, heavy eyes.

"What becomes of the message if it comes while you're away?" he asked feverishly.

"Oh, it'll be repeated," she replied easily. "You c'n cumb back bime-by 'bout two o'clock er later, 'n' mebbe it'll be here. I gotta lock up now."

Lyman Gage dragged himself to his feet and looked dazedly

about him; then he staggered out on the street.

The sun hit him in the eyes again in a way that made him sick, and the wind caught at his sleeves and ran down his collar gleefully. The girl shut the door with a click and turned the key, eyeing him doubtfully. He seemed to her very stupid for a soldier. If he had given her half a chance, she would have been friendly to him. She watched him drag down the street with an amused contempt, then turned to her belated lunch.

Lyman Gage walked on down the road a little way, and then began to feel as if he couldn't stand the cold a second longer, though he knew he must. His heart was behaving strangely, seeming to be absent from his body for whole seconds at a time and then returning with leaps and bounds that almost suffocated him. He paused and looked around for a place to sit down, and finding none, dropped down on the frozen ground at the roadside. It occurred to him that he ought to go back now, while he was able, for he was fast getting where, from sheer weakness, he couldn't walk.

He rested a moment and then stumbled up and back toward Little Silverton. Automobiles passed him, and he remembered thinking if he weren't so sick and strange in his head, he would try to stand in the road and stop one and get them to carry him somewhere. He had often done that in France or even in this country during the war. But just now it seemed that he couldn't do that, either. He had set out to prove to Mary Amber that he was a man and a soldier, and holding up automobiles wouldn't be compatible with that idea. Then he realized that all this was crazy thinking, that Mary Amber had gone to thunder, and so had he, and it didn't matter, anyway. All that mattered was for him to get that money and go back and pay Miss Marilla for taking care of him. And then for him to take the next train back to the city and get to a hospital. If he could only hold out long enough for that. But things were fast getting away from him. His head was hot and in a whirl, and his feet were so cold he thought they must be dead.

Without realizing it, he walked by the telegraph office and on down the road toward Purling Brook again.

The telegraph girl watched him from the window of the tiny bakery where she ate her lunch.

"There goes that poor boob *now!*" she said, with her mouthful of pie a la mode. "He gets my goat! I hope he doesn't come back. He'll never get no answer to that telegram he sent. People ain't goin' 'round pickin' up five hundred dollarses to send to broke soldiers these days. They got 'um all in Liberty Bonds. Say, Jess, gimme one more o' them chocolate éclairs, won't you? I gotta get back."

About that time, Lyman Gage had found a log by the wayside and sunk down permanently upon it. He had no more breath to carry him on, and no more ambition. If Mary Amber had gone to thunder, why should he care whether he got an answer to his telegram or not? She was only another girl, anyway. *Girl.* His enemy! And he sank into a blue stupor, with his elbows on his cold, cold knees and his face hidden in his hands. He had forgotten the shivers now. They had taken possession of him and made him one with them. It might be, after all, that he was too hot, and not too cold. And there was a strange, burning pain in his chest when he tried to breathe, so he wouldn't breathe. What was the use?

Chapter 6

Miss Marilla tiptoed softly up the hall and listened at the door of the spare bedroom. It was time her soldier-boy woke up and had some dinner. She had a beautiful little treat for him today, chicken broth with rice, and some little bits of tender breast meat on toast, with a quivering spoonful of currant jelly.

It was very still in the spare room, so still that a falling coal from the grate of the Franklin heater made a hollow sound when it fell into the pan below. If the boy was asleep, she could usually tell by his regular breathing. But, though she listened with a keen ear, she could not hear it today. Perhaps he was awake, sitting up. She pushed the door open and looked in. Why! The bed was empty. She glanced around the room, and *it was empty too*.

She passed her hand across her eyes as if they had deceived her and went over to look at the bed. Surely he must be there somewhere. And then she saw the note.

Dear wonderful little mother. . .

Her eyes were too blurred with quick tears and apprehension to read any further. *Mother!* He had called her that. She could never feel quite alone in the world again. But where was he? She took the corner of her white apron and wiped the tears away vigorously to finish the note. Then, without pausing to think, and even in the midst of her great grasp of apprehension, she turned swiftly and went downstairs, out the front door, across the frozen lawn, and through the hedge to Mary Amber's house.

"Mary! Mary Amber!" she called as she panted up the steps, the note grasped tightly in her trembling hand. She hoped, oh, she hoped Mary Amber's mother would not come to the door and ask questions. Mary's mother was so sensible, and Miss Marilla always felt as if Mrs. Amber disapproved of her, just a little, whenever she was doing anything for anybody. Not that Mary Amber's mother was not kind herself to people, but she was always so very sensible in her kindness and did things in the regular way and wasn't impulsive like Miss Marilla.

But Mary Amber herself came to the door, with pleasant forgetfulness of her old friend's recent coolness, and tried to draw her into the hall. This Miss Marilla firmly declined, however. She threw her apron over her head and shoulders as a concession to Mary's fears for her health, and broke out, "Oh, don't talk about me, Mary. Talk about *him*. He's gone! I thought he was asleep, and I went up to see if he was ready for his dinner, and he's *gone*! And he's sick, Mary. He's not able to stand up. Why, he's had a fever. It was a hundred and three for two days and only got down to below normal this morning for the first time. He isn't fit to be out, either, and that little thin uniform with no overcoat!"

The tears were streaming down Miss Marilla's sweet Dresden china face, and Mary Amber's heart was touched in spite of herself.

She came and put her arm around Miss Marilla's shoulder and drew her down the steps and over to her own home, closing the door carefully first, so her mother needn't be troubled about it. Mary Amber always had tact when she wanted to use it.

"Where was he going, dear?" she asked sympathetically, with a view to making out a good case for the soldier without Miss Marilla's bothering further about him.

"I—do–don't know," sobbed Miss Marilla. "He just thought he ought not to stay and bother me. Here! See his note."

"Well, I'm glad he had some sense," said Mary Amber with satisfaction. "He was perfectly right about not staying to bother you." She took the little crumpled note and smoothed it out.

"Oh my dear, you don't understand"—sobbed Miss Marilla. "He's been such a good, dear boy, and so ashamed he had troubled me. And really, Mary, he'll not be able to stand it. Why, you ought to see how little clothes he had. So thin, and cotton underwear. I washed them and mended them, but he ought to have had an overcoat."

"Oh well, he'll go to the city and get something warm, and go to a hospital if he falls sick," said Mary Amber comfortably. "I wouldn't worry about him. He's a soldier. He's stood lots worse things than a little cold. He'll look out for himself."

"Don't!" said Miss Marilla fiercely. "Don't say that, Mary. You don't understand. He is *sick*, and he's all the soldier-boy I've got. And I've *got* to go after him. He can't be gone very far, and he really isn't able to walk. He's weak. I just can't stand it to have him go this way."

Mary Amber looked at her with a curious light in her eyes.

"And yet, Auntie Rill, you know it was fine of him to do it," she said, with a dancing dimple in the corner of her mouth. "Well, I see what you want. And, much as I hate to, I'll take my car and scour the country for him. What time did you say he left?"

"Oh Mary Amber." Miss Marilla smiled through her tears. "You're a good girl. I knew you'd help me. I'm sure you can find him if you try. He can't have been gone over an hour, not much, for I've only fixed the chicken and put my bread in the pans since I left him."

"I suppose he went back to the village, but there hasn't been any train since ten, and you say he was still there at ten. He's likely waiting at the station for the twelve o'clock. I'll speed up and get there before it comes. I have fifteen minutes. I"—glancing at her wristwatch—"I guess I can make it."

"I'm not so sure he went that way," said Miss Marilla, looking up the road past Mary Amber's house. "He was on his way up that way when—" And then Miss Marilla suddenly shut her mouth and did not finish the sentence. Mary Amber gave her another curious, discerning look and nodded brightly.

"You go in and get warm, Auntie Rill. Leave that soldier to me. I'll bring him home." Then she sped back through the hedge to the little garage, and in a few minutes was speeding down the road toward the station. Miss Marilla watched her in troubled silence, and then, putting on her cape that always hung handy by the hall door, walked a little distance up the road, straining her old eyes but seeing nothing. Finally, in despair, she turned back, and presently, just as she reached her own steps again, she saw Mary's car come flying back with only Mary in it. But Mary did not stop nor even look toward the house. She sped on up the road this time, and the purring of the engine was sweet music to Miss Marilla's ears. Dear Mary Amber, how she loved her.

The big blue soldier, cold to the soul of him and full of pain that reminded him of the long horror of the war, was still sitting by the roadside with his head in his hands when Mary Amber's car came flying down the road. She stopped before him with a little triumphant *purr* of the engine, so close to him that it roused him from his lethargy to look up.

"I should think you'd be ashamed of yourself, running away from Miss Marilla like this and making her worry herself sick!" Mary Amber's voice was keen as icicles, and the words went through him like red-hot needles. He straightened up, and the light of battle came back to his eyes. This was *Girl* again, his enemy. His firm upper lip moved sensitively, and came down straight and strong against the lower one, showing the nice line of character that made his mouth beautiful.

"Thank you," he said coldly. "I'm only ashamed that I stayed so long." His tone further added that he did not know what business of hers it was.

"Well, she sent me for you. And you'll please to get in quickly, for she's very much worked up about you."

Mary Amber's tone stated that she herself was not in the least worked up about a great, hulking soldier that would let a woman wait on him for several days hand and foot and then run away when her back was turned.

"Kindly tell her that I am sorry I troubled her but that it is not possible for me to return at present," he answered stiffly. "I came down to send a business telegram, and I am waiting for an answer."

A sudden shiver seized him and rippled involuntarily over his big frame. Mary Amber was eyeing him contemptuously, but a light of pity stole into her eyes as she saw him shiver.

"You are cold!" said Mary Amber, as if she were charging him with an offense.

"Well, that's not strange—is it—on a day like this? I haven't made connections yet with an overcoat and gloves, that's all."

"Look here, if you are cold, you've simply got to get into this car and let me take you back to Miss Marilla. You'll catch your death of cold sitting there like that."

"Well, I may be cold, but I don't *have* to let you take me anywhere. When I get ready to go, I'll walk. As for catching my death of cold, that's strictly my own affair. There's nobody in the world would care if I did."

The soldier had blue lights like steel in his eyes, and his mouth looked very soldierlike indeed. His whole manner showed there wasn't the least use in the world trying to argue with him.

Mary Amber eyed him with increasing interest and thoughtfulness.

"You're mistaken," she said grudgingly. "There's one. There's Miss Marilla. She'd break her heart. She's like that, and she hasn't much to care for in the world, either. Which makes it all the worse what you've done. Oh, I don't see how you *could* deceive her."

"Deceive her?" said the astonished soldier. "I never deceived her."

"Why, you let her think you were Dick Chadwick, her nephew, and you *know* you're not! *I* knew you weren't the minute I saw you, even before I found Dick's telegram in the stove saying he couldn't come. And then I asked you a lot of questions to find out for sure, and you couldn't answer one of them right." Her eyes were sparkling, and there was an eager look in her face, like an appeal, almost as if she wanted him to prove what she was saying was not true.

"No, I'm not Dick Chadwick," said the young man with fine dignity. "But I never deceived Miss Marilla."

"Well, who did then?" There was disappointment and unbelief in Mary Amber's voice.

"Nobody. She isn't deceived. It was she who tried to deceive you."

"What do you mean?"

"I mean she wanted you to think I was her nephew. She was mortified, I guess, because he didn't turn up, and she didn't want you to know. So she asked me to dinner to fill in. I didn't know anybody was there till just as I was going in the door. Then I had to go and get sick in the night and ruin the whole thing. I was a fool to give in to her, of course, and stay that night. But it did sound good to have a real night's sleep in a bed. I didn't think I was such a softie as to get out of my head and be on her hands like that. But you needn't worry. I intend to make it up to her fully, just as soon as I can lay hands on some funds—"

He suddenly broke into a fit of coughing so hoarse and croupy as to alarm even Mary Amber's cool contempt. She reached back in the car, and grasping a big fur coat, sprang out on the hard ground and threw the coat about him, tucking it around his neck and trying to fasten a button under his chin against his violent protest.

"You're very kind," he gasped loftily, as soon as he could recover his breath. "But I can't put that on, and I'm going down to the telegraph office now to see if my wire has come yet."

"Look here," said Mary Amber in quite a different tone, "I'm sorry I was so suspicious. I see I didn't understand. I ask your pardon, and won't you please put on this coat and get into this car and let me take you home quick? I'm really very much troubled about you."

The soldier looked up in surprise at the gentleness, and almost, his heart melted. The snarly look around his mouth and eyes disappeared, and he seemed a bit confused.

"Thank you," he said simply. "I appreciate that. But I can't let you help me, you know."

"Oh, please!" she said, a kind of little-girl alarm springing into her eyes. "I won't know what to say to Miss Marilla. I promised her to bring you back, you know."

His eyes and lips were hardening again. She saw he did not mean to yield, and Mary Amber was not used to being balked in her purposes. She glanced down the road, and a sudden light came into her eyes and brought a dimple of mischief into her cheek.

"You'll have to for my sake," she said hurriedly in a lower tone. "There's a car coming with some people in it I know. And they will think it awfully strange for me to be standing here on a lonely roadside talking to a strange soldier sitting on a log on a day like this. Hurry!"

Lyman Gage glanced up, saw the car coming swiftly, saw, too, the dimple of mischief; but with an answering light of gallantry in his own eyes, he sprang up and helped her into the car. The effort brought on another fit of coughing, but as soon as he could speak, he said, "You can take me down to that little telegraph office, if you please, and drop me there. Then nobody will think anything about it."

"I'll take you to the telegraph office if you'll be good and put that coat on right, and button it," said Mary Amber commandingly. She had him in the car now, and she knew she could go so fast he could not get out. "But I won't stop there until you promise me, on your honor as a soldier, that you won't get out or make any more trouble about my taking you back to Miss Marilla."

The soldier looked very balky indeed, and his firm mouth got itself into fine shape again till he looked into Mary Amber's eyes and saw the saucy, beautiful lights there. And then he broke down laughing.

"Well, you've caught me by guile," he said, "and I guess we're about even. I'll go back and make my adieus myself to Miss Marilla."

A little curve of satisfaction settled about Mary Amber's mouth.

"Put that coat on, please," she said, and the soldier put it on gratefully. He was beginning to feel a reaction from his battle with Mary Amber, and now that he was defeated, the coat seemed most desirable.

"Don't you think it would be a good idea if you would tell me who you really are?" asked Mary Amber. "It might save some embarrassment."

"Why, certainly!" said the soldier in surprise. "It hadn't occurred to me, that's all. I'm Lyman Gage, of Chicago." He named also his rank and regiment in the army. Then, looking at her curiously, he said, hesitating, "I'm—perfectly respectable, you know. I don't really make a practice of going around sponging on unprotected ladies."

Her cheeks flamed a gorgeous scarlet, and her eyes looked rebuked.

"I suppose I ought to apologize," she said. "But really, you know, it looked rather peculiar to me—" She stopped suddenly, for he was seized with another fit of coughing, which had so shrill a sound that she involuntarily turned to look at him with anxious eyes.

"I s'pose it did look strange," he managed to say at last, "but, you know, that day when I came in I didn't care a hang." He dropped his head wearily against the car and closed his eyes for just a second, as if keeping them open was a great effort.

"You're all in now," she said sharply. "And you're shivering. You ought to be in bed this minute." Her voice held deep concern. "Where is that telegraph office? We'll just leave word for them to forward the message if it hasn't come, and then we'll fly back."

"Oh, I must wait for that message," he said, straightening up with a hoarse effort and opening his eyes sharply. "It is really imperative."

She stopped the car in front of the telegraph office. The little operator, sensing a romance, scuttled out the door with an envelope in her hand and a different look on her face from the one she had worn when she went to her lunch. To tell the truth, she had not had much faith in that soldier nor in the message he had sent "collect." She hadn't believed any answer would come, or at least any favorable one.

Now she hurried across the pavement to the car, studying Mary Amber's red tam as she talked and wondering whether she couldn't make one like it out of the red lining of an old army cape she had.

"Yer message's come," she announced affably. "Come just after I got back. An' I got yer check all made out fer yah. You sign here. See? Got anybody to 'dentify yah? 'Tain't necessary, see? I c'n waive identification."

"I can identify him," spoke up Mary Amber with cool dignity, and the soldier looked at her wonderingly. That was a very different tone from the one she had used when she came after him. After all, what did Mary Amber know about him?

He looked at the check half wonderingly, as if it were not real. His head felt very strange. The words of the message seemed all jumbled. He crumpled it in his hand.

"Ain't yah going to send an answer?" Put in the little operator aggrievedly, hugging the thin muslin sleeves of her little soiled shirtwaist to keep from shivering. "He says to wire him immediately. He says it's important. I guess you didn't take notice to the message."

The soldier tried to smooth out the crumpled paper with his numb fingers; and Mary Amber, seeing that he was feeling very miserable, took it from him, and capably put it before him.

Am sending you a thousand. Wire me your post office address immediately. Good news. Important.

(Signed)

Arthur J. Watkins

"I guess I can't answer that now," said the soldier, trying his best to keep his teeth from chattering. "I don't just know—"

"Here, I'll write it for you," said Mary, with sudden understanding. "You better have it sent in Aunt Rill's care, and then you can have it forwarded anywhere, you know. I'll write it for you." And she took a silver pencil from the pocket of her coat and wrote the telegram rapidly on a corner she tore from the first message, handing it out for his inspection and then passing it on to the operator, who gathered it in capably.

"Send this c'lect too, I s'pose," she called after the car as it departed.

"Yes, all right, anything," answered Lyman Gage, wearily sinking back in the seat. "It doesn't matter, anyway."

"You are sick!" said Mary Amber anxiously, "and we are going to get right home. Miss Marilla will be wild."

The soldier sat up, holding his precious check.

"I'll have to ask you to let me out," he said, trying to be dignified under the heavy stupor of weariness that was creeping over him. "I've got to get to a bank."

"Oh, must you today? Couldn't we wait till tomorrow or till you feel better?" asked Mary anxiously.

"No, I must go now," he insisted doggedly.

"Well, there's a bank on the next corner," she said, "and it must be about closing time." She shoved her sleeve back and glanced at her watch. "Just five minutes of three. We'll stop, but you'll promise to hurry, won't you? I want to get you home. I'm worried about you."

Lyman Gage cast her another of those wondering looks, like a child unused to kindness suddenly being spoiled. It made her feel as if she wanted to cry. All the mother in her came to her eyes. She drew up in front of the bank and got out after him.

"I'll go in with you," she said. "They know me over here, and it may save you trouble."

"You're very kind," he said, almost curtly. "I dislike to make you so much trouble—"

Perhaps it was owing to Mary's presence that the transaction went through without question, and in a few minutes more they were back in the car again, Mary tucking in her big patient fussily.

"You're going to put this around your neck," she said, drawing a bright woolly scarf from her capacious coat pocket. "And around your head," she added, drawing a fold comfortingly up around his ears and the back of his head. "And keep it over your nose and mouth. Breathe through it; don't let this cold air get into your lungs," she finished with a businesslike air as if she were a nurse.

She drew the ends of the scarf around, completely hiding everything but his eyes, and tucked the ends into the neck of the fur coat. Then she produced another blanket from some region beneath her feet and tucked that carefully around him. It was wonderful being taken care of in this way. If he only had not been so cold, so tired, and so sore all over, he could have enjoyed it. The scarf had a delicate aroma of spring and violets, something that reminded him of pleasant things in the past, but it all seemed like a dream.

They were skimming along over the road, up which he had come at so laborious a pace, and the icy wind cut his eyeballs. He closed his eyes, and a hot curtain seemed to shut him out from a weary world. Almost he seemed to be spinning away into space. He tried to open his mouth under the woolen fragrance and speak, but his companion ordered him sharply to be still till he got where it was warm, and a sharp cough, like a knife, caught him. So he sank back again into the perfumed silence of the fierce heat and cold that seemed to be raging through his body and continued the struggle to keep from drifting into space. It did not seem quite gallant or gentlemanly to say nothing, nor soldierly to drift away like that when she was being so kind. And then a curious memory of the other girl drifted around in the frost of his breath mockingly, as if she were laughing at his situation, almost as if she had put him there and was glad. He tried to shake this off by opening his eyes and concentrating them on Mary Amber as she sat sternly at her wheel, driving her little machine for all it was worth, her eyes anxious and the flush on her cheek bright and glowing. The fancy came to him that she was in league with him against the other girl. He knew it was foolish, and he tried to drive the idea away, but it stayed till she passed her own hedge and stopped the car at Miss Marilla's gate.

Then it seemed to clear away, and common sense reigned for a few brief moments, while he stumbled out of the car and staggered into Miss Marilla's parlor and into the warmth and cheer of that good woman's almost tearful, affectionate welcome.

"I want you to take that," he said hoarsely, pressing into her hand the roll of bills he had got at the bank. And then he slid down into a big chair, and everything whirled away again.

Miss Marilla stood aghast, looking at the money and then at the sick soldier till Mary Amber took command. He never remembered just what happened, nor knew how he got upstairs and into the great warm, kind bed again, with hot broth being fed him and hot-water bags in places needing them. He did not hear them call the doctor on the telephone, nor know just when Mary Amber slipped away down to her car again and rode away.

But Mary Amber knew this was the afternoon when *The Purling Brooke Chronicle* went to press, and she had an item that must get in. Quite demurely, she handed the envelope to the woman editor, just as she was preparing to mail the last of her copy to the printer in the city. The item read:

Miss Marilla Chadwick, of Shirley Road, is entertaining over the weekend Sergeant Lyman Gage, of Chicago, but just returned from France. Sergeant Gage is a member of the same division and came over in the same ship with Miss Chadwick's nephew, Lieutenant Richard Chadwick, of whom mention has been made in a former number, and has seen long and interesting service abroad.

Mary Amber was back at the house almost before she had been missed and just as the doctor arrived, ready to serve in any capacity whatever.

"Do you think I ought to introduce him to the doctor?" asked Miss Marilla of Mary in an undertone at the head of the stairs, while the doctor was divesting himself of his big fur overcoat. She had a drawn and anxious look, like one about to be found out in a crime.

"He doesn't look to me as if he were able to acknowledge the introduction," said Mary, with a glance in at the spare bed, where the young man lay sleeping heavily and breathing noisily.

"But—ought I to tell him his name?"

"That's all right, Auntie Rill," said Mary easily. "I told him his name was Gage when I phoned and said he was in the same division with your nephew. It isn't necessary for you to say anything about it."

Miss Marilla paused and eyed Mary strangely with a frightened, appealing look, and then with growing relief. So Mary knew! She sighed and turned back to the sickroom with a comforted expression growing round her mouth.

But the comforted expression changed once more to anxiety, and self was forgotten utterly, when Miss Marilla began to watch the doctor's face as the examination progressed.

"What has this young man been doing?" he growled, rising from a position on his knees where he had been listening to the soldier's breathing with an ever-increasing frown. Miss Marilla looked at Mary, quite frightened, and Mary stepped into the breach.

"He had a heavy cold when he came here, and Miss Chadwick nursed him, and he was doing nicely. But he ran away this morning. He had some business to attend to and slipped away before anybody could stop him. He got very much chilled, I think."

"I should say he did," exclaimed the doctor. "Young fool! I suppose he thought he could stand anything because he went through the war. Well, he'll get his now. He's in for pneumonia. I'm sorry, Miss Chadwick, but I'm afraid you've got a bad case on your hands. Would you like to have me phone for an ambulance and get him to the hospital? I think it can be done at once with a minimum of risk."

"Oh, no, no!" said Miss Marilla, clasping one pale hand and then the other nervously. "I couldn't think of that—at least, not unless you think it's necessary—not unless you think it's a risk to stay here. You see he's my—that is, he's almost—like—my own nephew." She lifted appealing eyes.

"Oh, I beg your pardon," he said, with a look of relief. "In that case he's to be congratulated. But, madam, you'll have your hands full before you are through. He's made a very bad start—a very bad start indeed. When these big, husky fellows get sick, they do it thoroughly, you know. Now, if you'll just step over here, Miss Mary, I'll explain to you both about this medicine. Give this every half hour till I get back. I'll run up here again in about two hours. I've got to drive over to Plush Mills now, to an accident case, but I'll be back as quick as I can. I want to watch this fellow pretty closely for the first few hours."

When the doctor was gone, Mary Amber and Miss Marilla stood one on each side of the bed and looked at each other, making silent covenant together over the sick soldier.

"Now," said Mary Amber softly, "I'm going down into the kitchen to look after things. You just sit here and watch him. I'll run over first to put the car away and tell mother I'll stay with you tonight."

"Oh, Mary Amber, you mustn't do that," said Miss Marilla anxiously. "I never meant to get you into all this scrape. Your mother won't like it at all. I'll get along all right. And anyway, if I find I can't, I'll get Molly Poke to come and help me."

"Mother will be perfectly satisfied to have me help you in any way I can," said Mary Amber with a light in her eyes. "And as for Molly Poke, if I can't look after you better than she can, I'll go and hide my head. You can get Molly Poke when I fail, but not till then. Now, Auntie Rill, go sit down in the rocking chair and rest. Didn't I tell you I'd help get that turkey dinner? Well, the dinner isn't over yet, that's all, and I owe the guest an apology for misjudging him. He's all right, and we've got to pull him through, Auntie Rill. So here goes."

Mary Amber gave Miss Marilla a loving squeeze and sped down the stairs. Miss Marilla sat down to listen to the heavy breathing of the sick soldier and watch the long, dark lashes on the sunken, tanned cheeks.

Chapter 7

For three weeks the two women nursed Lyman Gage, with now and then the help of Molly Poke in the kitchen. There were days when they came and went silently, looking at each other with stricken glances and at the sick man with pity. And Mary Amber went and looked at the letter lying on the bureau and wondered whether she ought to telegraph that man who had sent the soldier the money that day. Another letter arrived, and then a telegram, all from Chicago. Then Mary Amber and Miss Marilla talked it over and decided to make some reply.

By that time the doctor had said that Lyman Gage would pull through, and he had opened his eyes once or twice and smiled weakly upon them. Mary Amber went to the telegraph office and sent a message to the person in Chicago whose name was written at the left-hand corner of the envelopes, the same that had been signed to the first telegram.

LYMAN GAGE VERY ILL AT MY HOME, PNEUMONIA, NOT
ABLE TO READ LETTERS OR TELEGRAM. SLIGHT IMPROVE-
MENT TODAY.

(SIGNED)
MARILLA CHADWICK

Within three hours, an answer arrived.

MUCH DISTRESSED AT NEWS OF GAGE'S ILLNESS. CANNOT
COME ON ACCOUNT OF FRACTURED BONE, AUTOMOBILE
ACCIDENT. PLEASE KEEP ME INFORMED, AND LET ME
KNOW IF THERE IS ANYTHING I CAN DO.

(SIGNED)
ARTHUR J. WATKINS

Mary wrote a neat little note that night before she went on duty in the sickroom, stating the invalid had smiled twice that day and asked what day of the week it was. The doctor felt that he was on the high road to recovery now and there was nothing to do but be patient. They would show him his mail as soon as the doctor was willing, which would probably be in a few days now.

The day they gave Lyman Gage his mail to read, the sun was shining on a new fall of snow and the air was crisp and clear. There were geraniums blossoming in the spare-room windows between the sheer white curtains, and the Franklin heater was glowing away and filling the place with the warmth of summer.

The patient had been fed what he called "a real breakfast," milk toast and a soft-boiled egg, and the sun was streaming over the foot of the bed cheerfully, as if to welcome him back to life. He seemed so much stronger now that the doctor had given permission for him to be bolstered up with an extra pillow while he read his mail.

He had not seemed anxious to read the mail, nor at all curious, even when they told him it was postmarked Chicago. Miss Marilla carried it to him as if she were bringing him a bouquet, but Mary eyed him with curious misgiving. Perhaps, after all, there would not be good news. He seemed so very apathetic. She watched him furtively as she tidied the room, putting away the soap and towels and pulling a dry leaf or two from the geraniums. He was so still, and it took him so long to make up his mind to tear open the envelopes after he had them in his thin, pale hand. It almost seemed as if he dreaded them like a blow and was trying to summon courage to meet them. Once, as she looked at him, his eye met hers with a deprecatory smile, and to cover her confusion she spoke impulsively.

"You don't seem deeply concerned about the news," she said brightly.

He smiled again, almost sadly.

"Well, no," he said thoughtfully. "I can't say I am. There really isn't anything much left in which to be interested. You see, about the worst things that could happen have happened, and there's no chance for anything else."

"You can't always tell," said Mary Amber cheerfully as she finished dusting the bureau and took herself downstairs for his morning glass of milk and egg.

Slowly Lyman Gage tore the envelope of the topmost letter and took out the written sheet. In truth he had little curiosity. It was likely an account of how his lawyer friend had paid back the money to Mr. Harrower, or else the details of the loan on the old Chicago house. Houses and loans and such things seemed far from his world just now. He was impatient for Mary Amber to come back with that milk and egg. Not so much for the milk and egg as for the comfort it gave and the cheeriness of her presence. Presently Miss Marilla would come up and tell over some little incident of Mary's childhood exactly as if he were Dick, the real nephew. And he liked it. Not that he liked Dick, the villain. He found himself hopelessly jealous of him sometimes. Yet he knew in a feeble, far-away sense that this was only a foolish foible of an invalid, and he would get over it and laugh at himself when he got well.

He smiled at the pleasantness of it all, this getting-well business, and then turned his indifferent attention to the letter.

Dear Gage, it read, *what in the world did you hide yourself away in that remote corner of the world for? I've scoured the country to get trace of you without a single result till your telegram came. There's good news to tell you. The unexpected has happened and you are a rich man, old fellow. Don't let it turn your head, for there's plenty of business to occupy you as soon as you are able to return.*

To make a long story short, the old tract of land in which you put all you had and a good deal more has come to the front in great shape at last. You will remember that the ore was found to be in such shape when they came to the mining of it that it would cost fabulous sums for the initial operations, and it fell through because your company couldn't afford to get the proper machinery. Well, the government has taken over the whole tract and is working it. I am enclosing the details on another paper, and you will perceive, when you have looked it over, how very much you are needed at home just now to decide numerous questions that have taxed my ingenuity to the limit to know just what you would want done. There is a great deal of timber on those lands also, very valuable timber, it seems, and that is another source of wealth for you. Oh, this war has been a great thing for you, young man. And you certainly ought to give extra thanks that you came out alive to enjoy it all. Properly managed, your property ought to keep you on Easy Street for the rest of your life, and then some.

I took pains to let Mr. Harrower know how the wind blew when I paid him the money you had borrowed from him. He certainly was one surprised man. Of course, I don't speak officially, but from what he said I should judge that this might make a big difference with Miss Elinore. So you better hurry home, old man, and get busy. The sun is shining, and the war is over.

Yours fraternally, as well as officially,

Arthur J. Watkins

Over the first part of the letter, Lyman Gage dallied comfortably, as he might have done with his grapefruit or the chicken on toast they had promised him for lunch. He had lost his sense of world values for the time being, and just now a fortune was not more than a hot-water bag when one's feet were cold. It merely gave him a sense that he needn't be in a hurry getting well, that he could take things easy because he could pay for everything and give his friends a good time after he was on his feet again. In short, he was no longer a beggar on Miss Marilla's bounty, with only a thousand dollars between him and debt or even the poorhouse.

But, when he came to that last paragraph, his face suddenly hardened, and into his eyes there came a glint of steel as of old, while his jaw set sternly and lines came around his mouth—hard, bitter lines.

So it was *that* that had been the matter with Elinore, was it? She had not grown tired of *him* so much, but had wanted more money than she thought he would be able to furnish for a long time? He stared off into the room not seeing its cozy details for the first time since he began to get well. He was looking at the vision of the past, trying to conjure up a face whose loveliness had held for him no imperfections. He was looking at it clearly now as it rose dimly in vision against the gray of Miss Marilla's spare-room wall. And for the first time he saw the spoiled under lip with the selfish droop at its corners, the pout when she could not have her own way, the frown of the delicate brows, the petulant tapping of a dainty foot, the proud lifted shoulder, the haughty stare, the cold tones and crushing contempt that were hers sometimes. These had seldom been for him, and when he had seen them, he had called them beautiful, had gloried in them, fool that he was! Why had he been so blind, when there were girls in the world like—well—say like Mary Amber?

Misjudging Elinore? Well, perhaps, but somehow he did not believe he was. Something had cleared his vision. He began to remember things in Elinore Harrower that he had never called by their true names before. It appeared more than likely that Elinore had deliberately left him for a richer man, and that it was entirely possible, under the changed circumstances, that she might leave the richer man for him, if he could prove he was the richer of the two. Bah! What a thing to get well to! Why did there have to be things like that in the world? Well, it mattered very little to him what Elinore did. It might make a difference with her, but it would make no difference to him. There were things in that letter of hers that had cut too deep. He could never forget them, no, never, not even if she came crawling to his feet and begging him to come back to her. As for going back to Chicago, business be hanged! He was going to stay right here and get well. A smile melted out on his lips, and comfort settled down about him as he heard Mary Amber's step on the stairs and the soothing clink of the spoon in the glass of egg and milk.

"Good news?" asked Mary Amber, as she shoved up the little serving table and prepared to administer the egg and milk.

"Oh, so-so," he answered with a smile, sweeping the letters away from him and looking at the foaming glass with eager eyes.

"Why! You haven't opened them all!" Mary Amber laughed.

"Oh! Haven't I?" he said impatiently, sweeping them up and tearing them open wholesale with only a glance at each, then throwing them back on the coverlet again.

"Nothing but the same old thing. Hounding me back to Chicago." He grinned. "I'm having much too good a time to get well too fast, you may be sure."

Somehow the room seemed cozier after that, and his sleep the sweeter when he took his nap. He ate his chicken on toast slowly to prolong the happy time, and he listened and smiled with deep relish at the little stories Miss Marilla told of Mary Amber's child-hood, the gingerbread men with currant eyes, the naughty Dick who stole them. This world he was in now was such a happy, clean little world, so simple and so good. Oh, if he could have known a world like this earlier in his life. If only he could have been the hapless Dick in reality!

Molly Poke was established in the kitchen downstairs now, and Miss Marilla hovered over her anxiously, leaving the entertaining of the invalid much to Mary Amber, who wrote neat business letters for him, telling his lawyer friend to do just as he pleased with everything till he got back; and who read stories and bits of poems, and played chess with him as soon as the doctor allowed. Oh, they were having a happy time, the three of them. Miss Marilla hovered over the two as if they had been her very own children.

And then, one lovely winter afternoon, when they were discussing how perhaps they might take the invalid out for a ride in the car someday next week, the fly dropped into the ointment.

It was as lovely a fly as ever walked on tiny French heels, and came in a limousine lined with gray duvetyn and electrically heated and graced with hothouse rosebuds in a slender glass behind the chauffeur's right ear. She picked her way daintily up the snowy walk, surveyed the house and grounds critically as far as the Amber hedge, and rang the bell peremptorily.

Miss Marilla went to the front door, for Molly Poke was busy making cream puffs and couldn't stop. When she saw the little fly standing haughtily on the porch, swathed in a gorgeous moleskin cloak with a voluminous collar of tailless ermine, and a little toque made of coral velvet embroidered in silver, she thought right away of a spider. A very beautiful spider, it's true, but all the same, a spider.

And when the beautiful red lips opened and spoke, she thought so all the more.

"I have come to see Lyman Gage," she announced freezingly,

looking at Miss Marilla with the glance one gives to a servant. Miss Marilla cast a frightened glance of discernment over the beautiful little face. For it was beautiful, there was no mistaking that, very perfectly beautiful, though it might've been only superficially so. Miss Marilla was not used to seeing skin that looked like soft roseleaves in baby perfection on a person of that age. Great baby eyes of blue, set wide, with curling dark lashes; eyebrows that seemed drawn by a fairy brush; lips of such ruby-red pout; and nose chiseled in warm marble. Peaches and cream floated through her startled mind, and it never occurred to her that it was not natural. Oh, the vision was beautiful, there was no doubt about that.

Miss Marilla closed the door and stood with her back to the stairs and a look of defiance upon her face. She had a fleeting thought of Mary and whether she ought to be protected. She had a spasm of fierce jealousy and a frenzy as to what she should do.

"You can step into the parlor," she said in a tone that she hoped was calm, although she knew it was not cordial. "I'll go up and see if he's able to see you. He's been very sick. The doctor hasn't let him see any"—she paused, and eyed the girl defiantly—"any *strangers*."

"Oh, that'll be all right." The girl laughed with a disagreeable tinkle. "I'm not a stranger. I'm only his fiancée." But she pronounced "fiancée" in a way that Miss Marilla didn't recognize at all, and she looked at her hard. It wasn't *wife*, anyway, and it hadn't sounded like *sister* or *cousin*. Miss Marilla looked at the snip—that was what she began to call her in her mind—and decided that she didn't want her to see Lyman Gage at all. But, of course, Lyman Gage must be the one to decide that.

"What did you say your name was?" she asked bluntly.

For answer the girl brought out a ridiculous little silk bag with a clattering clasp and chain and took from it a tiny gold card case, from which she handed Miss Marilla a card. Miss Marilla adjusted her spectacles and studied it a moment, with one foot on the lower stairs.

"Well," she said reluctantly, "he hasn't seen anyone yet, but I'll go and find out if you can see him. You can sit in the parlor." She waved her hand again toward the open door and started upstairs.

The blood was beating excitedly through her ears, and her heart pounded in pitiful thuds. If this "snip" belonged to her soldier boy, she was sure she could never mother him again. She wouldn't feel at home. And her thoughts were so excited that she did not know that the fur-clad snip was following her close behind until she was actually within the spare bedroom and holding out the card to her boy with a trembling, little, withered roseleaf hand.

The boy looked up with his wide, pleasant smile like a benediction and reached out for the card interestedly. He caught the look of panic on Miss Marilla's face and the inscrutable one on Mary Amber's. Mary had heard the strange voice below and arisen from her reading aloud to glance out the window. She now beat a precipitate retreat into the little sewing room, just off the spare bedroom. Then Lyman Gage realized another presence in the room and looked beyond to the door where stood Elinore Harrower, her big eyes watching him jealously from her swathing of gorgeous furs, while he slowly took in the situation.

It had been a common saying among his friends that no situation, however unexpected, ever found Lyman Gage off his guard, or ever saw him give away his own emotions. Like lightning, there flitted over his face now a sudden cloud, like a curtain, shutting out all that he had been the moment before, putting under lock and seal any like or dislike he might be feeling, allowing only the most cool courtesy to appear in his expression. Miss Marilla, watching him like a cat, could not tell whether he was glad or sorry, surprised or indignant or pleased. He seemed none of these.

He glanced with cool indifference toward the lovely vision smiling in the doorway now, ready to gush over him, and a stern dignity grew in the set of his jaws. But otherwise, he did not seem to have changed, and most casually, as if he had seen her but the week before, he remarked, "Oh! Is that you, Elinore? Seems to me you have chosen a cold day to go out. Won't you sit down?" He motioned toward a stiff little chair that stood against the wall, though Mary Amber's rocker was still waving back and forth from her hasty retreat.

Miss Marilla simply faded out of the room, although Gage said politely, "Don't leave us, please." But she was gone before the words were out of his mouth, and with a sudden feeling of weakness, he glanced around the room wildly and realized that Mary Amber was gone, too.

Mary Amber stood in the sewing room and wondered what she ought to do. For the other door of the sewing room was closed and barred by a heavy iron bed that had been put up for convenience during the soldier's illness, and the only spot that was long enough to hold it was straight across the hall door. Obviously, Mary Amber could not get out of the sewing room without moving the bed, and she knew by experience of making it every morning that it squeaked most unmercifully when it was moved. Neither could she go out through the spare bedroom, for she felt that her appearance would cause no end of explanations. And equally, of course, she dared not shut the door because it would make a noise and call attention to her presence.

So Mary Amber tiptoed softly to the farthest end of the little room and stood rigidly silent, trying not to listen, yet all the more attuned and sensitive to whatever was going on in the next room. She fairly held her breath lest they should hear her and pressed her fingers upon her hot eyeballs as if that would shut out the sound.

"That's scarcely the way I expected you to meet me, Lyme"—in the sweet lilt of Elinore Harrower's pampered voice.

"I was scarcely expecting you, you know, after what has happened," came chillingly in Lyman Gage's voice, a bit high and hollow for his illness, and all the cooler for that.

"I couldn't stay away when I knew you were ill, Lyme, dear!" The voice was honeyed sweet now.

"What had that to do with it?" The tone was almost vicious. "You wrote that we had grown apart, and it was true. You are engaged to another man."

"Well, can't I change my mind?" The tone was playful, kittenish. It smote Lyman Gage's memory that he had been wont to call it teasing and enjoy it in her once upon a time.

"You've changed your mind once too often!" The sick man's voice was tense in his weakness, and his brow was dark.

"Why Lyman Gage! I think you are *horrid*!" cried the girl, with a hint of indignant tears in her voice. "Here I come a long journey to see you when you're sick, and you meet me that way and *taunt* me. It's not like you. You don't seem a bit glad to see me! Perhaps there's someone else." The voice had a taunt in it now, and an assurance that expected to win out in the end, no matter to what she might have to descend to gain her point.

But she had reckoned without knowledge, for Lyman Gage

remembered the picture he had torn to bits in the dying light of the sunset and trampled in the road. Those same brilliant eyes, that soft-tinted cheek, those painted lips had smiled impudently up at him that way as he had ground them beneath his heel. And this was *Girl*, his natural enemy, who would play with him at her pleasure and toss him away when he was no longer profitable to her, expecting to find him ready at a word again when circumstances changed. He straightened up with sudden strength and caught her words with a kind of joyful triumph.

"Yes, there is *someone else*! Mary! Mary *Amber*!"

Mary Amber, trying not to hear, had caught her name, heard the sound in his voice like to the little chick that calls its mother when the hawk appears, and suddenly her fear vanished. She turned and walked with steady step and bright eyes straight into the spare bedroom, a smile upon her lips and a rose upon her cheek that needed no cosmetics to enhance its beauty.

"Did you call me—Lyman!" she said, looking straight at him with rescue in her eyes.

He put out his hand to her, and she went and stood by the bed, over across from the visitor who had turned and was staring amazedly, insolently at her now.

Lyman Gage put out his big, wasted hand and gathered Mary Amber's hand in his, and *she let him*!

"Mary," said Lyman Gage possessively, and there was both boldness and appeal in his eyes as he looked at her, "I want Miss Harrower to know you. Miss Amber, Miss Harrower."

Elinore Harrower had risen, with one hand on the back of her chair and her crimson lips parted, a startled expression in her eyes. Her rich furs had fallen back and revealed a rich and vampish little frock beneath, but she was not thinking of her frock just then. She was looking from one to the other of the two before her.

"I don't understand!" she said haughtily. "Did you know her before?"

Lyman Gage flashed a look at Mary for indulgence and answered happily.

"Our friendship dates back to when we were children and I spent a summer with my Aunt Marilla teasing Mary and letting the sawdust out of her dolls." He gave a daring glance at Mary and found the twinkles in her eyes playing with the dimples at the corner of her mouth, and his fingers clung more warmly around hers.

The two were so absorbedly interested in this little comedy they were enacting that they had quite failed to notice its effect upon the audience. Elinore Harrower had gathered her fur robes about her and was fastening them proudly at her throat. Her dark eyes were two points of steel, and the little white teeth that bit into the pouting crimson under-lip looked vicious and suggestive.

"I did not understand," said Elinore haughtily. "I thought you were among strangers and needed someone. I will leave you to your friends. You always did like simple country ways, I remember." And she cast a withering glance around.

"Why, where is Aunt Rilla, Mary?" asked Lyman, innocently ignoring the sneer of his guest. "Aunt Marilla!" he raised his voice, looking toward the door. "Aunt Marilla, won't you please come here?"

Miss Marilla, her heart a perfect tumult of joy to hear him call her that way, straightened up from her ambush outside the door and entered precipitately, just as the haughty guest was about to stalk from the room, if one so small and exquisite as Elinore can be said to stalk. The result was a collision that quite spoiled the effect of the exit, and the two ladies looked at each other for a brief instant, much as two cats might have done under similar circumstances.

Mary Amber's eyes were dancing, and Lyman Gage wanted to laugh, but he controlled his voice.

"Aunt Marilla, this is Miss Harrower, a girl who used to be an old friend of mine, and she thinks she can't stay any longer. Would you mind taking her down to the door? Good-bye, Elinore. Congratulations! And I hope you'll be very happy!" He held out his free hand—the other still held Mary Amber's, and the smile upon his lips was full of merriment. But Elinore Harrower ignored the hand and the congratulations, and drawing her fur mantle once more about her small haughty shoulders, she sailed from the room, her coral and silver toque held high and her little red mouth drooping with scorn and defeat. Miss Marilla, all hospitality now that she understood, offered tea and cake but was given no answer whatever. And so in joyous, wondering silence, she attended her soldier's guest to the door.

Lyman Gage lay back on his pillows, his face turned away from Mary Amber, listening, but his hand still held Mary Amber's. And Mary Amber, standing quietly by his side, listening, too, seemed to understand that the curtain had not fallen yet, not quite, upon the little play, for a smile wove in and out among the dimples near her lips and her eyes were dancing little happy lights of mirth. It was not until the front door shut upon the guest and they heard the motor's soft *purr* as the car left the house that they felt the tenseness of the moment relax, and consciousness of their position stole upon them.

"Mary, Mary Amber," whispered Lyman Gage softly, looking up into her face, "can you ever forgive me for all this?"

He held her hand, and his eyes pleaded for him. "But it's all true. There *is* another one. *I love you!* And oh, I'm so tired. Mary Amber, can you forgive me—and—and love me, just a little bit?"

Down upon her knees went Mary Amber beside the bed, and gathered her soldier boy within her strong young arms, drawing his tired head upon her firm, sweet shoulder.

When Miss Marilla trotted back upstairs on her weary, glad feet and put her head in at the door fearfully to see how her boy had stood the strain of the visitor—and to berate herself for having allowed a stranger to come up without warning, she found them so. Mary Amber, soothing her patient to sleep by kisses on his tired eyelids, and the soldier's big pale hand enfolding Mary's little one contentedly, while the man's low voice growled tenderly, "Mary, you are the only girl I ever really loved. I didn't know there was a girl like you when I knew her."

So Miss Marilla drew the door closed softly, lest Molly Poke should come snooping round that way, and trotted off to the kitchen to see about some charlotte russe for supper, a great thankful gladness growing in her heart, for—oh! Suppose it had been that other—*hussy!*

FOUND
TREASURE

A good name is rather to be chosen than great riches,
and loving favour rather than silver and gold.

PROVERBS 22:1

Chapter 1

New York City, Summer 1928

The younger set was meeting in Ethel Garner's summerhouse to make plans for an automobile ride and an all-day picnic that was arranged for the next week.

They fluttered in by ones and twos in their little bright dresses, looking like a lot of dressy dolls on the Garner lawn. They hovered about awaiting a few more arrivals, chattering like a flock of birds just alighted.

"Oh Ethel!" screamed her special chum Janet Chipley, "isn't that a darling new dress! Did your mother make it or did you get it in the city?"

"This?" said Ethel, with a conscious look at the dainty little blue-and-white voile she was wearing. "Oh, it's a little imported frock Mother picked up. It is rather good, isn't it?"

"Imported!" exclaimed Maud Bradley, dashing into the conversation with gusto. "My goodness! They don't import *cotton* dresses do they? Aren't you stylish, wearing imported dresses in the afternoon. Say, Ethel, you look precious in it, though, don't you? That's a pastel shade of blue, isn't it? You ought to save it for the ride. It's awfully attractive. Jessie Heath said she was getting a new dress, too. Her mother ordered it in New York from that great dressmaker she goes to every spring. It's some kind of pink they're wearing in Paris. But I'm sure it won't be any prettier than yours."

"You've got a pretty dress, too, Maud," said Ethel, somewhat patronizingly. "Did you make it yourself?"

"Yes," said Maud with a grimace, "sat up till after midnight last night to finish the hemstitching."

"Aren't you clever. You don't mean to say you did all this hemstitching? Why, it looks just like the imported things. I think you are simply great to be able to do it."

"Oh, that's nothing," said Maud. "I'd much rather do it than study Latin. You know I flunked the exam this year. I get more and more disgusted with it. Say, girls, what do you think? I heard Miss House wasn't going to teach Latin next year. Wouldn't that be great? I'd almost be willing to go back to school another year, just to be rid of her. My, she was a pain! How anybody could get like that puzzles me. But isn't it great that we're done with high school? You couldn't drag me to college. Emily Morehouse says she's going, and Reitha Kent. But they always were grinds."

"Well, I'm going," said Ethel with satisfaction.

"*You're* going!" screamed her friend in dismay. "Why, I thought you said you weren't."

"Well, so I did, but Mother has persuaded me. She says she wants me to get the *atmosphere*! And you really aren't *anywhere* if you haven't been to college these days."

"Mercy," said Janet. "Then I suppose I'll have to go, too. I only begged off by telling Dad and Mother you weren't going."

"Oh, come on, Jan, of course you'll go. I couldn't leave you behind. And besides, we'll have heaps of fun."

"But we aren't signed up anywhere."

"Yes we are; that is, I am. I know Dad can get you in at my college. He's something on the board. Get your father and mother to come over tonight and talk it over with Dad. He'll fix it. There comes Gladys Harper. Come on, girls, let's go back to the summerhouse. The rest will know where to find us, and it's too hot to stay here in the sun. Was that the phone, Flora?" called Ethel as her younger sister came out on the porch. "Who called? I hope nobody is staying away."

"It was Eleanor Martin. She can't come till half past four. They've got the dressmaker there and she has to be fitted."

"I know," said Ethel. "Come on, we're going around to the summerhouse. I wonder what she had to telephone for. She told me that this morning."

Flora, in her bright pink organdy, followed the girls around to the summerhouse.

"Why, it was about Effie," she admitted with a troubled look as they drifted into the big rustic arbor against its background of tall privet hedge and settled down among the cushions with which it was amply furnished. "You know Effie Martin wants to go with us on the picnic. Eleanor is taking their big new car, and Effie wants to drive it part of the time. She asked me to get her an invitation. But Eleanor has found it out, and she doesn't want her to go."

"The very idea!" said Janet Chipley sharply. "Why, that would be ridiculous. Why, *she* doesn't belong to our crowd at all."

"Well, she evidently wants to," said Flora with a troubled sigh, "and I promised her I'd do my best to get her an invitation. She's simply wild to go. And it's really the first time she's ever seemed to care much. What could I do but promise?"

"Well, she's not going to get any invitation if *I'm* on the committee," announced Maud Bradley. "I'll tell you that! Why, she's *unbearable*. Nobody else would want to go if she went, that's certain. Just tell her we had our list all made up and there wasn't room, Flora."

"But she'd say she could ride on the running board," said Flora, still troubled. Flora did not like to be unkind.

"Yes, that's just what she would do," asserted Ethel. "Anything to make a sensation. And she doesn't seem to know how disgusting she is. She has a disagreeable habit for every minute in the day, I believe. She bites her nails continually. It sends shivers down my back. I sat behind her in church last Sunday and I nearly went wild. She just took each finger in turn and chewed right around them, and then she put one knee over the other and swung her foot, jarring her knee against the pew in front where that meek little Mrs. Elder sits. I thought I should shriek she made me so nervous. Mrs. Elder kept turning her head just a little and looking distressed, but she couldn't get the courage to turn clear around and look her in the face and make her stop. I almost disgraced myself sighing with nervousness. I'm sure she heard me, but it didn't make any difference. She didn't even know what it was all about. She turned and stared at me a minute with those great black eyes of hers and kept right on. I don't want any worse punishment than to be obliged to sit beside her in any gathering again."

"Yes, I know just how she is," chimed in Maud Bradley. "She just fidgets and fidgets. She's for all the world as bad as her eight-year-old brother, and he is the most disagreeable little kid in the whole town. *I* sat beside her in church one Sunday when our seat was full, and I was glad when the service was over. She kept turning and twisting and fixing her hat and smoothing her gloves. She had gloves on, so she couldn't bite her nails then. She hummed the tunes while the minister was reading the hymns, and she tore a paper into small bits while the prayer was going on. I didn't have a minute's peace. I'm sure I don't know how anybody could be expected to enjoy her company. She's enough to spoil things wherever she goes. By all means, don't let us invite her. Don't you say so, Cornelia? Wouldn't it simply spoil everything if Effie Martin went along with us?"

Cornelia Gilson, a flashy little girl with copper-colored bobbed hair and a yellow frock, had come in while they were talking and listened with an indignant frown.

"What! That Martin girl? Eleanor's kid sister? Well, I should say so," she answered quickly. "What are you all thinking about? Why should *she* be invited? She never was before!"

Janet Chipley ventured to explain. "Why, Flora Garner says she told her she wanted to go just awfully, and now they have the new car, and Eleanor is to be allowed to take it, and she thinks the girls will ask her."

"Well, we certainly will not!" declared Cornelia indignantly. "She'll find she is mistaken. I should think her own sister would make her understand that. She is not old enough for our crowd.

She's only fourteen."

"Well, I guess she's fifteen," admitted Maud reluctantly, "but she doesn't act like it."

"Girls, you're all mistaken about her age. She's sixteen. Her birthday was last week," spoke up Flora Garner timidly. "She wants to go dreadfully. Her sister doesn't want her to, one bit, and she didn't want to ask her to secure an invitation, so she asked me. I felt awfully embarrassed, for I didn't know what to say."

"Sixteen! Well, I should think she would be ashamed. Why, she acts like a big, tough boy. Last summer at the shore, she came tearing down the boardwalk with her hair flying, chasing Tom Moore and bound to catch him before they reached the bath-houses. I felt awfully humiliated to have her come up to me a few minutes after, when I was talking to Mrs. Earle and her son, and say, 'Hello, Jan!' She was chewing gum, too. And think of it, I had to introduce her. Mrs. Earle is so sweet; she takes in everybody, and she put out her hand and said, 'Is this your cousin, Janet?' Then after I told who she was, Mrs. Earle drew her aside and told her softly, so that her son would not hear, and with a great many 'my dears,' that there was a big tear in her skirt. And what do you think that poor fish did? She just laughed out loud and pulled the tear around and stuck her finger in it and said, 'Oh yes, I know it. That's been there two weeks. Most everybody's told me of it now. It's too much trouble to mend it down here. It's bad enough to have to sew when I'm at home.' Just then Tom Moore came in sight again, and without saying good-bye or anything, she started and ran, calling, 'Ho, Tom, you can't catch me again! I dare you to!' I was so mortified I could have sunk down into the sand with a good will and never come up again. Lawrence Earle looked after her with the most curious expression. If she had seen him she would never have held up her head again."

"Oh yes, she would, Janet," said Maud, laughing. "You don't suppose a little thing like that would bother her. Why, she's got brass enough to make a pair of candlesticks. The thing I don't understand is how she happened to be so utterly ill-mannered, with so lovely a mother."

"Well, surely, girls," said Ethel Garner, "if her own sister doesn't want her, we can't ask her to go along. What is the use of discussing her any further? I, for one, am tired of the subject. She is full of disagreeableness and apparently has not a single virtue."

"You're forgetting, Ethel," put in Janet Chipley sarcastically, "she can ride a bicycle!"

"Oh yes, she can ride a wheel"—laughed Ethel with a sneer and a curl of her lip—"but she does even that like a clown. She would rather stand on the saddle with one toe and go flying down Main Street than anything else in the world. She just wants to show off her acrobatic feats! I can't understand why her mother lets her. She's too old to ride a bicycle. None of the other girls do."

"You were just saying she wasn't old enough to go with us," urged Flora mischievously.

"Well, you know perfectly what I mean, Flo. Don't try to be clever! She acts just like a great big, overgrown small boy. And the way she plays baseball and tries to get in with the boys! She thinks she's so smart because they praise the way she pitches. She thinks it's so wonderful to be able to pitch like a boy! I think it's unlady-like. And she goes whistling through the streets, and she never looks even *neat*! Her clothes are simply a mess! And her hair is a fright! If she went along, she'd be sure to disgrace us all in some way. Decidedly, no! She's a flat tire if there ever was one. Don't you all say so, girls?"

"Yes I do," said Maud Bradley. "Come, let's drop her and get to work. There's the route and the time and the lunch to plan for, and the afternoon is going fast."

The little company of brightly dressed girls settled themselves in the hammocks and chairs that were plentiful in the summerhouse and went to work in earnest.

Meantime, on the other side of the carefully trimmed hedge, stretched full length on the soft, springy, sweet-smelling earth, her elbows on a mossy bank, her face in her hands, her cheeks very red, her eyes on an open book, lay Effie Martin, the subject of all this conversation. She had taken her book after dinner and slipped off to this group of trees between her father's lawn and that of Mr. Garner's. It was a favorite retreat for her, away from the noise of her teasing brother, and the possible calls of conscience when she heard the work of the house going on and knew that she ought to be helping. She did not like to work, and she did love to read. She often came here when she wanted to be alone. She had found this particular bit of mossy turf, covered by clean, spicy pine needles. She did not know that in the summer arbor, opposite, Ethel and Flora Garner would receive their friends that day.

She would not have hesitated on that account if she had known. It did not occur to her that she would be liable to hear conversations not meant for her ears. When she had first heard voices approaching the hedge on the other side, she had paid little heed to them, but had read on until she suddenly heard her own name and became aware that she was the subject of much unpleasant remark. Her cheeks flamed with anger, and her big black eyes sparkled dangerously. It did not occur to her that she was an eaves-dropper or that she ought to get up and go away. She would probably not have gone if it had occurred to her. It had never been fully impressed upon her that there was anything wrong in listening to what is not intended for one's ears, especially when the theme is one's self.

The girls on the other side of the hedge went on discussing her personal habits. It had never occurred to her that she had personal habits before or that those habits could be agreeable or disagreeable to others. There was something startling in hearing them portrayed in such unpleasant tones. Her heart beat fast with indignation. So this was what they thought of her. Her first impulse was to start to her feet and rush into their midst, but what could she do? They were but stating their opinions.

She had half started to get up, but now she sank back again. Alas! she could not deny the statements they had made about her, either. She glanced down at her stubby fingers, whose nails, worn to the quick, gave sad evidence of being daily bitten. Now that she recalled it, she supposed she did bite her nails in church. She was tired and longed to get out of doors, and that seemed to give her relief from what seemed to her a dull meeting. She glanced down at her dress. It was even now torn and spotted in many places. She had never paid much attention to her clothes before. She had not minded a few spots or rents, more or less. Now she suddenly saw what others thought of her. How they went on scorning her— those girls of whose circle she had so earnestly aspired to be one. How she hated them for it! What a hateful world she was in! How could they talk that way? Those pretty, simpering girls who could not ride as she could—not one of them—nor pitch a ball so that the boys would as soon have her in the game as one of themselves! They had nothing but nonsense in their heads and were very silly. Why should she care what they said? But all the time, as the talk went on, her cheeks burned redder and redder and her heart throbbed with its painful mingling of emotions.

Meanwhile the girls, unaware of the angry little listener on the other side of the hedge, arranged their program. They were to rest and refresh themselves at a farmhouse, a pleasant distance from home, and return in the evening by moonlight, if the night was clear. Then came the question of the chosen guests. All the usual girls were named, Eleanor Martin, Effie's older sister, among the rest. A spasm of almost hatred again passed over Effie as she thought of the selfishness of her sister, who was unwilling that she should take part in the coming pleasure. Eleanor could have managed it for her if she had chosen, but Eleanor was nineteen and did not care to be troubled by "kids," as she chose to designate her sister, albeit she never breathed this in the presence of their mother. Mrs. Martin disliked slang, and endeavored, as much as in her power, to bring up her daughters properly. But it was a hard task with so many feet to guide, so many mouths to feed, so little in the family treasury. This was, perhaps, the reason that poor Effie had been so often obliged to shift for herself.

The letters in the book before her were blurred into one long word. Effie felt no further interest in the hero of the historical novel that she had been reading. History was empty and void. Her own life had loomed up and eclipsed the ages, so that there was nothing of interest outside it. She felt that no one had ever been so miserable, so helpless, so disliked, so ill-treated, so utterly unhappy as herself. How could she go on living after today? She had suddenly seen herself as others saw her. Her feelings must have had a little touch of what Eve felt when she had eaten of that forbidden fruit and no longer saw the world about her fair. How could she ever endure it? Her thoughts surged through her brain without beginning or end. And through it all she longed to jump through that hedge, with vengeance in her eyes, and pounce upon those hateful girls and make them take it all back, make them suffer for what they had said, or do something that should assuage this dreadful feeling that oppressed her.

The planning on the other side of the hedge went on. The anticipated pleasure was discussed in animation. This was heightened somewhat by the arrival of a little sister of Janet Chipley, who brought a book her sister had sent her after and contributed this information as she was running away again to play: "Say, Janet, did you know Lawrence Earle had come home? I saw him just now coming from the station in the car with his mother, and he's going to be home all summer, for he said so, and he's going to play tennis with me a lot, for he's promised. Isn't that lovely? And he isn't a bit different from a year ago, if he *has* been to college. I thought perhaps you'd like to ask him to your ride." And Bessie Chipley flew away to her game, leaving the girls in high glee over the arrival of the young man who had won a most brilliant record in a noted college, and for whose society the girls were all eager.

"Oh, isn't that lovely!" "Of course we'll ask him!" were some of the exclamations from the delighted girls.

But the listener, on the other side of the hedge, only felt the blood burn hotter in her cheeks as she remembered what the girls had said she had done the year before at the seashore, and that this young man had been a witness. She really felt humiliation on her own account now, as she realized how she must have appeared in his eyes, tearing along like a boy and careless about the great rent in her gown. A year ago she would scarcely have understood why this should have been embarrassing, so much of a child had she been. But now young womanhood was stirring in her heart, with a sense of pride, self-consciousness, and the fitness of things. Self-consciousness had been very slight indeed, until now, but her eyes had been opened and she was ashamed—and Lawrence Earle, of all people! The boy who had taught her to pitch a ball when she was a mere infant. Of course, he was a great deal older than she was—five or six years at least, and had probably forgotten all about her. But she had always remembered him as an ideal hero!

"We must have another girl to make even couples," they were saying, and Effie's humiliation was so complete that she scarcely felt the pang of disappointment that she could not be chosen for the vacant place. No, rather stay at home forever than that she should be of the same company with that immaculate youth who had witnessed her degradation. This was what she felt. Suddenly her feelings rose to such a pitch she could no longer keep still, and scrambling to her feet, she fairly fled from the place where she had so suffered. The tears had gathered in her eyes, and once she fell with a stinging thud to the ground, having tripped over a hidden root. This only brought the tears the faster. And when she reached the house she threw her book upon the floor, ran through the house, slamming all the doors after her, tore up the stairs to her own room where she locked herself in, and threw herself upon the bed in an agony of weeping such as she had very seldom experienced.

Her patient mother, who had been trying to take a nap with the fretful, teething baby, was awakened by her rushing through the house and sighed. "Oh, there goes Effie! What shall we do with that child?"

Chapter 2

Effie had cried perhaps half an hour. Hers was too vehement a nature to do things by halves, and her weeping was so violent that she was thoroughly exhausted. Then she lay still and began to think things over. Why was it that those girls disliked her and she seemed to be so unwelcome everywhere? For now that she thought of it, she saw there were quite a number of people in the world who did not care to have her around. Her mother loved her, she felt sure, but somehow her mother always sighed when she came into the room. Why was that? Was she not wanted in the world? She could not help it, she supposed, or could she? What the girls had said about some things was quite true, though she had never felt before they were things that mattered to others. If she wanted to bite her fingernails, what business was it of theirs? She never troubled their fingernails. She had a right to do with her own as she pleased, so long as she let other people's alone. But here, it seemed, these personal habits of hers did trouble other people, and she must not expect to be wanted if she could not make herself pleasant. She looked at her stumpy fingers through her tear-dimmed eyes. They certainly did not look pretty. But it had never occurred to her that biting them had anything to do with that.

The girls had said she made them nervous. She hardly understood why, but if it was so, why, of course, it was. The question was, could she stop doing it? And if she could, and should, would that make any difference in the feelings of those girls for her? But then, she did not intend to try to please those girls! No, indeed! They were not worth pleasing. But there were people in the world to whom she would like to seem lovely—her mother, for instance, and perhaps Flora Garner, for she had been nice and sweet about asking to have her invited to the ride. Everybody said Flora Garner was sweet. She had that reputation wherever she was known. It was a great thing to have people feel that way about you and say nice things. And then her poor, swollen cheeks burned again at the thought of the hateful things that had been said about her. But would it be worthwhile to try to make things better, so that people might think well of her? A fierce desire to get on her bicycle and fly away into the gathering shades of the dusky night that was drawing on seized her. It was suppertime, but she wanted no supper. She would go, and she jerked herself up from the bed, caught her hat, and without waiting to wash the tearstains from her face, dashed downstairs. It was like her. Effie always did everything without thinking. As she went out the door, she heard her mother sigh and say to her baby brother, "Oh baby, baby, if you would only just sit still on the floor for ten minutes longer till I finish this seam. My back aches so that I cannot hold you and sew any longer."

Effie went straight on out the door, feeling sorry for her mother, having a dim sense that the baby was unreasonable, and life hard, anyway. But it never occurred to her that she had anything to do with it until she was flying along the south road fully a mile from home, and the fresh breeze fanning her face had somewhat cooled the tempest in her heart. She was beginning to feel more like herself and trying to decide if there was any way in which she might change that would affect the feelings of others toward her. There was Mother, for instance, again—yes, Mother, sitting in the gathering shadows at this moment, stealing the last rays of light to sew the dark garment that she expected to wear on the morrow to pay her last tribute to a dear old school friend who was done with this life. Mother's little excursions and holidays, somehow, were almost always set apart for last sad rites and duties of neighborly kindness. It was strange about Mother, how she never seemed to have any good times for her own. Effie never thought of it before. How nice it would be if Mother was on a bicycle, flying along by her side! But Mother on a bicycle! How funny it would be! She couldn't learn to ride in the first place, she was so timid. And then how could she get time? She was at this minute doing two things at once, and that baby was very hard to take care of. It was hard that Mother couldn't even get her dress done without being hindered. Well! There was something. Why had she not thought of that before?

She turned her bicycle so suddenly that a little dog that was trotting along in the road, thinking he knew just where Effie was going, almost got his tail cut off.

Back she flew faster than she had come, and bursting in the door, threw her hat on a chair and grabbed the baby from the floor at his mother's feet, where he was vainly endeavoring to pull himself up to a standing posture by her skirt. Mrs. Martin gave a nervous jump as Effie entered, and another anxious "Oh, take care, Effie!" as the baby was tossed into the air. But Effie, intent on doing good for once in her life, was doing it as she did everything else: with a vengeance, and she went on tossing the baby higher and higher, regardless of her mother's protests. Each crow of the baby made Effie more eager to amuse him. She whirled around the room with him in her arms, tumbling over a chair occasionally, but not minding that in the least. She danced along to the middle of the room under the gas fixture, and just as her mother rose hastily and dropped her sewing, saying, "Effie, I insist—" she tossed the excited baby high into the air and brought the curly head sharp against the chandelier. Then the fun ceased. The baby screamed, and the mother rushed and caught him to her breast, and with reproachful looks at the penitent Effie, sent for hot water and Pond's Extract. The others coming in gathered around the darling of the house and hesitated not to reproach Effie for her part in the mischief until her anger flamed forth. Seeing that the baby had recovered and was apparently not seriously injured, she rushed from the room to her own in another torrent of weeping. This time she knelt before the open window and watched the lights through her tears, as they peeped out here and there over the village, and felt bitter toward them and toward everything. Why should she be the one always to blame for everything that happened? Here she had given up her ride when she was having a good time, and had come home to help Mother and was greeted only with an exclamation of fear, and then this had happened—a thing that might have happened if he had been with any of the others, she thought. She was scolded for what she had intended should be a relief and a help to Mother, and that was all the good she had done. Much progress she had made in her own reformation! She would not be likely to go on in it very far if this was the result of her first trial, and her heart grew hard and bitter again.

By and by, the dinner bell rang and she went sulkily down, took her place, and ate in silence until Eleanor, full of her afternoon, put another sting in the already very sad heart of her sister. It appeared that she had gone to the committee meeting at the Garner's, probably after her sister had left the hedge.

"Mamma," she said, with the haughtiness of her lately acquired young ladyhood, "I do wish you would reprove Effie. She is forever making herself obnoxious. I found out that she had been poking around trying to get in with our crowd. She's nothing but a child!"

"It's an awful pity you and Eff have to live in the same town with each other, Nell, she gives you so much trouble," put in Johnnie, the outspoken younger brother.

"Johnnie, you're very saucy, and that isn't smart at all," responded Eleanor, flattening her eyelids down in a way she had that she fancied was very reproving to her brother.

"Mamma, I wish you would tell Effie that you won't allow her, under any circumstances, to go with us next week on our ride. She is getting very troublesome. I—"

But Eleanor was interrupted by Effie, whose black eyes flashed fire and tears as she rose from the table, her dinner only half finished.

"It isn't in the least necessary for you to ask Mamma to do any such thing. I wouldn't go if you dragged me! I know exactly every word those precious girls of yours have said about me this afternoon, and they are a mean, selfish lot, who care nothing about anything but clothes! I only hope you'll enjoy the company of those who speak that way about your sister. I should not, not even if they had been talking about *you*. But you may rest easy about me; I won't trouble you anymore. I've been made to understand most thoroughly that nobody in this world wants me. I'm sure I can't tell what I was made for, anyway." And with a voice that trembled with her utter humiliation and defeat, she stalked from the room, her lifted chin and haughty manner barely lasting till the dining-room door shut her from the family gaze, when she burst into uncontrolled tears and rushed upstairs for the third time that day to her own little room.

"Why, what does she mean, Eleanor?" asked the pained voice of the father, laying down the evening paper, behind which he had been somewhat shielded from the avalanche of talk around him. "What have you done to the child? Why hasn't she as much right to go riding as the rest of you? I thought that was why we bought the seven-passenger car, so there would be plenty of room for anybody that wanted to go?"

"You don't understand," said Eleanor with reddening cheeks, and she attempted to explain to her father the fine distinctions of age and class in the society in which she moved. But somehow her father could not be made to understand, and the end of it was that Eleanor was told that if her sister was not welcomed on the ride, then she could not go. Rebellious and angrier than ever at Effie, she declared she would stay at home then. So it came about that the Martin household was not in a happy frame of mind that evening at the close of their evening meal. And the two sisters lay down to rest with hard thoughts of each other.

Effie, as she turned her light out, knelt a moment beside her window to look at the stars and murmur the form of prayer that had been so much a part of her bringing up that she scarcely realized what it all meant. "Help me to be good," was one of the oft-repeated sentences, and Effie no longer felt it necessary for her thoughts to stay by to see that these words were spoken to the One above who was supposed to be her guard and guide. She fancied herself, on the whole, rather good as goodness in girls went. Now, tonight, as she finished her petition, which was rather a repetition, she looked up to the stars she loved and thought of a scrap of poetry she had picked up in her reading, which she was not well-enough taught to know was wonderful. It ran thus:

> *All that I know*
> *Of a certain star*
> *Is, it can throw*
> *(Like the angled spar)*
> *Now a dart of red,*
> *Now a dart of blue;*
> *Till my friends have said*
> *They would fain see too,*
> *My star that dartles the red and the blue!*
> *Then it stops like a bird; like a flower hangs furled:*
> *They must solace themselves with the Saturn above it.*
> *What matter to me if their star is a world?*
> *Mine has opened its soul to me; therefore I love it.*

Poor little, lonely, disagreeable Effie wished as she looked out into the night that she could be like that star and be able to dartle red and blue for someone, so that others might hear of it and want to see her and know her. How nice that would be! That star language evidently meant people, and it meant there was someone, somewhere who could see beauties in some star that everybody could not see. She wondered if ever anybody would think they saw anything good like dartles of red and blue in her, and would feel that they didn't care after that whether other people's worlds were great or not, so long as they had her red and blue dartles.

But how silly such thoughts were. If those hateful girls who had talked about her that afternoon had known she had thoughts like this, how they would have screeched with laughter! Her cheeks burned hotly in the darkness at the very thought, and she arose and slammed the window down, warm night though it was, and went to bed feeling utterly miserable. How was it possible for her ever to be different? She could not. She had tried that afternoon and failed most miserably, and she was not one who was likely to try again in the same direction.

Was there anywhere else to turn? Oh, if she but had some wise and good helper who would tell what was the matter, and if she must go on being hated all her life as she had begun.

Then the thought of what the girls had said about her clothes came and drowned all other thoughts, and she drifted off to sleep, planning how she would fix up an old dress that should be the envy of all the town.

Poor child, she was only a little girl yet at heart and was just waking up to the fact that she was growing up and a great deal more would be expected of her.

Perhaps her guardian angel standing by, remembering that she was dear to her heavenly Father, and knowing for a surety there was light coming to her darkened pathway, brushed the tears in pity from her young face, for she dreamed that a soft hand touched her forehead and cooled and comforted her.

But downstairs, Effie's father and mother were having a serious conference about her.

"I'm sure I don't know what to do with her," her anxious mother was saying. "She grows more heartless and careless every day. Today she nearly killed the baby with her impetuosity, and when I tried to stop her before she hit his head against the chandelier, she simply ignored my commands. I wonder if it would do any good to send her away to school. I never believed much in finishing schools, but Effie really needs something to tone her down. She goes rushing through life, without any idea of manners or any thought of others. I'm sure I don't see how we came to have a child like that!"

"I am afraid nobody understands her," said her father, with troubled brows. "She seems to me so much like my own little sister Euphemia for whom she is named, and she was a wild little loving thing like Effie, but she would fly up into flinders if people were unjust to her—"

"Nobody has been unjust to Effie," said her mother coldly. "Everybody would love her if she would be less selfish and rude. I have tried to tell her but she doesn't even seem to hear me. And Sam, she isn't in the least like your sister Euphemia. She was mild and gentle and lovely, as I remember her. We should have named Effie Joan of Arc or some outlandish masculine name, for she never will be anything but a disgrace to your sister's name, I'm afraid."

"Oh, don't say that Hester," said the father in a pained voice. "I'm sure our little Euphemia will grow up some day and understand. If you would just try to talk with her a little about—"

"Talk to her!" said her mother wearily. "I've talked and talked and it rolls right off from her. She goes tearing in one door and out the other on her own affairs, and never minds whether I have a headache or whether the baby is asleep or whether there are dishes to be washed on the maid's day out! She seems a hopeless cause!"

"Now, now, Mother. You mustn't talk that way about our little girl. I sometimes think perhaps the other children put upon her. Eleanor, now, is a bit overbearing since she has grown up, and she wants to have the whole right to the car. That really isn't just to Euphemia. The child has as good a right to go on that ride as she."

"Not if the other girls don't want her," said the mother. "They feel themselves older, you know—"

"But they're not much older, are they? Eleanor is only two years older than Euphemia. That ought not to be such a great difference. And those Garner girls, why the youngest one was born two days later than Euphemia, for I remember congratulating her father on her birth. There is something wrong somewhere. Why don't they want Euphemia? Aren't her clothes right?"

"Why, yes—" said her mother hesitantly, a new trouble gathering in her eyes. "She is as well dressed for her age as need be. She has never complained. She doesn't care much for dress. She always preferred getting out and away to play ball or hockey or skate, no matter what she had on."

"Well, perhaps that's it," said the pitying father. "Perhaps she needs something a little more fancy, Mother. We haven't realized that she was growing up, too, and needed things. She ought to be dressed right, of course. I know you've been trying to economize so we could get the car, but things are beginning to look up at the office a little, and I think pretty soon we'll have things a little easier. You get Euphemia what she wants, Mother. I can't bear to have her look the way she did tonight. It isn't right for a child."

"But she really has never expressed a desire for new clothes," said her mother thoughtfully. "All she wants is to get off on that bicycle of hers. I'm afraid she'll never grow up."

"There are worse faults than that, Mother, worse faults. I believe it might be worse to grow up too soon."

"Yes," sighed the mother. "I'm afraid Eleanor has done that. She seems really hard on her sister sometimes, although I think it's just because she's so sensitive about what the other girls think. Eleanor is a good girl."

"Well she is all wrong in this matter. She really has no right to cut her sister out of going on a ride."

"Now Father, I'm not so sure," said the mother. "You know Eleanor didn't get it up. The girls invited her, and they didn't ask Effie."

"Well they should have! They asked for the car, didn't they?"

"Well, but that didn't make it necessary for them to ask all of the children, and Effie has never been in that crowd."

"Well, if she wants to go now I think she has a right!" declared the father.

"No, not unless she has made herself welcome. I'm afraid it is Effie's own fault that she is not invited."

"Well, Mother, you look into the matter and see if there can't be something done for Euphemia. I can't have my sister's namesake turning out a failure in life, and that's what she'll be if something isn't done for her. I'm afraid I will never forget her face when she said she didn't know what she was born for anyway, and that she had found out there wasn't any place in the world where she was wanted. That's a pretty serious thing for a girl to get into her head, I think."

"It isn't likely that she really meant all that," said her mother. "She was just angry. She'll likely have forgotten it all by tomorrow. I never heard her say anything like that before. She usually doesn't care in the least what people think about her. She is utterly independent and goes her own way, no matter what anybody says. She is more like a boy than a girl."

"I can't think that, Mother," said Effie's father, shaking his head. "There was a real depth to her tones. You look into it and see if you can't get at the inwardness of this thing. Somebody must have done something pretty ugly to her to make her look as she did at the dinner table tonight."

But the next morning Effie came swinging downstairs, whistling in loud piercing tones and waking the baby, who had had a bad night with two teeth he was cutting and had just dropped off to sleep. Both Father and Mother looked at her with stern eyes and sharp reproofs. Indeed, to the newly awakened Effie their words were so unjust and cutting that she slammed out of the back door without her breakfast and, jumping on her bicycle, rode off into the country and spent a furious two hours pedaling away and thinking hard thoughts of her parents, her sisters, all the girls in town, and her world in general, finally working off the surplus fury and coasting back down the hills toward home another way around, whistling to keep up her courage. No one should know how hard she was hit and how much she cared that no one loved her. Let them all be hateful to her if they would. She could stand it, and she would see if she could not beat them all in spite of everything. Maybe if she got her dress fixed up they would think more of her. Now that she thought about it, everybody was always loving and nice to Nell when she had a new dress on. Nell could get anything out of her father when she was dressed up. Dress must make a great difference in this world. She had always scorned it as among the necessary bothers of living. Now she began to see that it might be a desirable accessory. At least she would try it.

She rode into the yard with grim determination upon her face, skirted the driveway, and entered by way of the kitchen. She secured a few crackers, an orange, and some cake and stole up the back stairs to her room, where she set herself to examine her wardrobe and see what could be done with it.

Chapter 3

It was like Effie not to take anyone into her confidence, but to embark on her new enterprise alone. She even took some of her own hoarded money that she had been saving to buy a new tennis racket and went and bought some fashion magazines instead of going down and asking Mother for hers. She had a feeling that if she worked this thing out, it had to be done wholly on her own initiative. Nobody else must know. In fact, she felt if anybody did find out that she was trying to be different, she would certainly have to stop trying.

All the spare time that Effie had outside of the duties actually required of her, she spent in her room, with an occasional intermission when she would mount her bicycle and ride afar furiously, returning to a new attack upon her self-imposed task. She meant to get that new dress done by the day of the ride! Not for any special hope or reason that she entertained, not for the possibility of being seen by any of the party, for she scorned such praise, but just for her own satisfaction, she wanted to get that dress done before the day of the ride.

If anyone had been in the habit of noticing Effie's movements, she certainly would have excited the family curiosity now, for it was unheard of that she should remain in the house while the great out-of-doors called her. If they thought anything about it or noticed that she did not go out so much, or was absent from the public tennis courts or the baseball field where she had been wont to hover, they merely thought she was off in the hammock somewhere reading. Nobody paid much heed to Effie, from morning to night, except to blame or complain of her. Only the mother, with her reawakened anxiety, watched her, listened at the hall door for her step, hovered near her locked door, anxious lest some new phase of this ugly duckling's development was in the process of being evolved, relieved that no apparent catastrophe seemed to result from her long sessions in her room.

For Effie had decided, in the course of her meditations, that the very first thing needed in the building of a noteworthy character was a neat, stylish sport suit she could wear on her bicycle or for tennis or golf, if she ever got a chance to play. And while that is perhaps not the usual way for a young person to set about living a different life, nevertheless, her mother and her guardian angel were pleased.

Effie was not fond of sewing, neither was she adept in the art, for she loved her books and her outdoor life too dearly. But she was ever one who, if her will and desire were great enough, could do almost anything she tried to. So it was not surprising, as the days went by, that she really was accomplishing marvels in the way of making quite a pretty sport dress out of her sister's old school dress, having actually thought so far as carefully to rip, clean, and press it before beginning to make it up.

Effie had also surprised her father and sister when she found out what commands her father had laid upon Eleanor concerning the ride. She had gone to him and asked him to allow Eleanor to go, telling him she honestly did not wish to go and would not feel at all happy to have Eleanor kept at home. This she did, not because she had attained any great degree of self-sacrifice in her spirit, but being of a practical turn of mind, she saw no sort of use in keeping her sister away from a pleasure, which she knew by personal yearnings, she would enjoy so much, just because she, Effie, was debarred from it. Furthermore, she knew Eleanor would be sure to tell the girls why she could not go, and they would probably feel obliged to ask her for Eleanor's sake, and she wanted to have nothing more to do with that ride. Her cheeks burned with the thought of it. Ugly ride! And ugly day when she had lain and listened to a description of herself as others saw her. She felt as if she had grown years older since then. Now and then when pride and pleasure in her new dress would lift her up beyond her gloomy thoughts, there would come to her with a sudden pang the thought, *What is the use of making it when I'm not wanted anywhere to wear it?* But she kept steadily on, and through her mother's help, given unsuspected here and there, for the mother had more sympathy with her untamed little girl than the child knew, she actually had it in a wearable condition a few days before the day of the picnic.

And now there was a revelation for the mother, for she found that Effie, her third daughter, the girl who was always a tomboy and tore her clothes as soon as they were on, or soiled them, or put them on awry, and who had come into the family after so many others that she had been obliged by the force of circumstances and the state of the family purse to wear other people's cast-offs so much, now stood arrayed in a dress that fitted her lithe, strong young form, and was neat, trim, and stylish. She was actually pretty. Never had anyone called Effie pretty since she was a little baby and the aunt for whom she was named had come to see her and said she was a pretty baby, but it wouldn't last, she could see that with half an eye. Pretty babies always made ugly grown folks, and everybody had repeated that until it came to be a settled fact that Effie was not pretty. She had long ago understood it so herself and accepted the fact firmly, if a little bitterly. Eleanor, everybody agreed, had beautiful eyes, and with rich complexion and ready wit was not only handsome but very bright. But now the mother saw in this other daughter a pretty vision where she had not expected it, and suddenly put her arms around her child's neck, folded her close, and called her "My little Euphemia," as she had called her when she was a wee baby and her mother had had time to sit for three whole weeks and just love her and cuddle her and see all her baby charms.

Effie felt a sudden joy in those words of her mother's. She was glad she had tried to do something, even if it was only to make a dress. She went back to her room, surveying herself a long time in the mirror. What a difference it made to have a pretty dress instead of the torn skirt and soiled blouse she had been wearing. Some hint of a Bible verse floated through her head—she was not sure at all that there was such a verse—righteousness probably. She wondered if any robe of righteousness could feel better upon anyone than this little gown she had made with her own hands.

And then a new idea came to her. Why not make more dresses?

With Effie, to get an idea was to carry it out, and forthwith she hurried up to the attic to an old trunk, where all the cast-offs of the family were stowed away.

Fifteen minutes later she came down with her arms full of faded, soiled georgette crepe.

To anyone with less determination than Effie, the bundle would have looked utterly hopeless. The color had originally been pink but had faded to a sickly, yellowish saffron. But Effie, while she ripped off yards of crystal beading, was planning how she would buy a ten-cent package of rose dye and make that discouraged-looking material seem like a summer sunset cloud.

Patiently, she ripped and snipped away until at last it was all apart, a seemingly worthless pile of dirty pink. There was one consolation; there was enough of it. For the dress had been made long ago, when dresses were long and wide and full of ruffles and shirring and pleats, and there was material enough to make three dresses of the modern kind, if it had all been in good condition.

When it was all apart, Effie made a suds of soap flakes and put it soaking while she jumped on her bicycle and rode down to the drugstore for a package of pink dyeing soap.

An hour later, she stood surveying her finished work with satisfaction. The georgette was washed clean, and dyed a lovely shell pink, and lay in soft billows of cloud like a sunset sky on the chair in her room, smooth and apparently as good as new. The last length was stretched smoothly on her bed and pinned firmly, inch by inch, along the edges. She had discovered that it took each strip from five to ten minutes to become perfectly dry and smooth, and she was overjoyed with the result. Now she would have a real evening dress. She had always wanted one when Eleanor and the other girls came trooping in with their pretty, bright, fluffy frocks. Of course, she had no place to wear one, but then it would be a joy just to have such a dress hanging in her closet, to know it was there if any occasion ever should come to wear it. She had openly scorned "dolling up" as she called it, but in her secret heart had wished often that she, too, might look pretty and be admired like the other girls. Well, probably nobody would ever see her in this dress, but she meant to have it ready. Perhaps sometime she would put it on and surprise them all and let them see that tomboy Effie could look nice, too. Anyhow, it would be lots of fun to make it and not let a soul, even Mother, know until it was done. Perhaps if it looked nice, Mother would call her little Euphemia. "My little Euphemia." How that warmed her wild young heart! And Mother's tone had been so dear when she had said it. Perhaps she could make her say it again.

She studied the fashion books for a long time to select the right style for this dress, for Effie had ideas even if she had never paid much attention to dress. She wanted it to be prettier than any pink dress she had ever seen before.

She hesitated for a long time as to whether she would finish the edge with picot or with binding, but finally decided on binding. In the first place, there was so much of the material there would be plenty for binding. And while picot would be much easier for her, saving more than half the labor, still it would cost something, and she had already spent more than half her little hoard. She experimented with a few small pieces of the georgette and found that, after some awkwardness, she was going to be able to manage the binding, and it somehow appealed to her because it was so exceedingly neat. Picot edges were apt to grow taggy. Eleanor's did. And she wanted nothing about her to suggest untidiness. Those girls should see she could be as neat and trim as any of them when she tried. She even planned to make a flower for her shoulder out of the pieces of georgette, like the picture in the fashion magazine, and she grew so interested in trying to cut the long slim petals and make them curl up at the edges by drawing them under a pencil-end quickly, that she forgot to go downstairs and set the table for her mother, a duty that was supposed to be hers on the maid's day out. "Heedless Effie!" the family called, and her cheeks grew red with the truth of the adjective as she hurriedly put aside her materials and rushed downstairs when the dinner bell rang.

She was quite silent at the table, glowering with drawn brows when Eleanor said sarcastic things about how she slipped out of all her duties.

"I suppose you were off with the boys, playing ball or something," said Eleanor with a sneer. "I declare, Mamma, I should think you'd be ashamed of having her act like a tough boy! She's getting so big and bony, and she doesn't care how she looks. The other day I was passing the boys' ball field late in the afternoon, and here was Effie in that old gray skirt with John's red sweater on, and her hair all over her eyes, and she had a baseball bat in her hand and was hitting and running with great strides, kicking up her heels like a wild child. I was mortified to death to think I had a sister like that. I thought when vacation came she would stop playing baseball, but it seems she plays every day—"

"That's a lie!" said Effie, rising with fury in her face. "I haven't been out this week! Mother knows I haven't!" And with a glance of reproach at her mother, she dashed from the room and rushed to her refuge upstairs. She was so blinded with her tears that she forgot all about that last breadth of georgette pinned out on her bed and flung herself despairingly right into it, and never knew she had done it until a pin caught her cheek and tore an ugly scratch across its flushed surface.

Downstairs, she had left an uncomfortable scene again. Effie's father had risen from the table, pale with distress, his lips actually trembling. "Now, now, children, this must stop!" he said. "I can't have Euphemia treated this way. Eleanor, you are very much to blame. You have no right to talk that way about your sister before everybody. She is getting almost to hate everybody. You are grow-ing hard and sharp as you grow up. I am distressed beyond measure at your attitude toward your sister."

"Well, do you want me to shut my mouth and let her be made a laughingstock in the town?" retorted Eleanor. "That's what she is. None of the girls will have anything to do with her. She isn't like a girl; she's like a big, tough boy. I thought it was my duty to tell you."

"You should come then, privately, and tell your mother or me. You should not bring Effie out in a disgraceful way before the family. I insist that this must stop. Your sister was generous enough to come and ask that I allow you to take the car and go on your excursion even though your friends were unwilling to invite her, a daughter of the house as much as you are. It seems to me that you reward your sister in a very hateful way."

"Well, you're not around her much, Dad. You don't know how mortifying she is. Why, nobody wants her around. Nobody!"

Eleanor's voice floated up through the open window and came straight to poor Effie's ears, and her tears started afresh. How ter-rible was life when her own sister could say things like that! Oh, if she could only die! If she could only get out of it. Nobody would care, only perhaps her father, a little, and well—yes—her mother—remembering her voice when she had said, "My little Euphemia!" But after all, if she were gone, it would be a relief to everybody. She was only a duty, never a delight. Now see how it had turned out today, of all days, when she had meant to be so good and help her mother! She hadn't done a thing to help. Just stayed in her room and worked for herself. And it would probably always be so. She couldn't be like other girls and think of things. She couldn't! Oh why should she try! If there was only someone to help her! Some kind friend who would understand and to whom she was not afraid to go for advice. Perhaps there was a way.

But there wasn't. There was no one in the whole wide world who cared or would help. They expected her to be just what they wanted her to be, and they had no patience with her that she was not, and that was the whole of it! There was no use trying. And why should she bother to make herself pretty clothes? No one would like her any better if she had them. Eleanor would likely laugh and ask her if she was going to play ball in the pink georgette, if she did succeed in making it up so it looked like other girls' things.

So she viciously pulled the pins out of the pretty pink stuff and rolled the whole thing unceremoniously into a box and put it on the top shelf of her closet, resolving never to touch it again. Then she crept into bed and cried herself to sleep.

For what was the use of trying to overcome her name? She had a bad reputation. Everybody expected her to be boisterous and forgetful and rough and uncivil, and they thought she was even when she wasn't. They would say in that superior tone of theirs, "Oh, you can't expect anything else of Euphemia!"

Euphemia! Why did she have to have a hateful name like that? It was a piece of all the rest. She was an odd number with an ugly name. Her hair wouldn't curl, and her face was fat, and her bones were large, and she liked to play ball with the boys better than anything else in life, and that was the truth, so what was the use of trying to please anybody, anyway?

And at last she fell asleep.

She did not know that a few minutes later her mother, coming up with a glass of milk and a plate of nice things, found her asleep with the tears on her cheeks and a sob still in her throat. And she knelt beside her a long time, praying for her dear, wild little girl, that she might be led into the paths of peace and righteousness, and find out the true secret of right living.

Chapter 4

The morning of the picnic dawned bright and clear. It seemed as if it had been made especially for the occasion, and Eleanor came down in a pretty new dress that the dressmaker had finished especially for the occasion.

Effie, too, donned her new sport dress, but not until after breakfast, and until she had watched her sister leave the house, driving the new car cheerfully, for the rendezvous at Maud Bradley's.

Then she turned, with a long, quivering breath of envy and hopelessness, and went to get her little new frock from the closet.

She had not taken it out since the night she hung it there, when her new resolves had suffered such a rebuff. The georgette still reposed in an unceremonious roll in the box on the closet shelf, and she wondered why she had tried, anyway, to make a sport dress. She couldn't wear it to play ball with the boys very well. She would feel hampered lest she would soil it. She couldn't slide to a base with a pleated silk skirt on, and she couldn't pitch her ball right for fear she would split the shoulders. But anyhow, she had decided she didn't want to play ball with the boys anymore. Eleanor had taken all the pleasure out of that. Eleanor would presently take the joy out of everything she had ever cared to do.

Nevertheless, she got herself into the little brown frock with its simple, stylish lines and its bright touch of burnt orange. It was only Eleanor's old cast-off crepe de Chine, but it did somehow have an air. It really was quite attractive. It made a soft rose color bloom out in her healthy cheeks and matched the brown of her eyes and hair. She stared at herself almost in wonder, and somehow her lonely, wounded heart felt a little comforted. For it was nice to look pretty and pleasing, almost like the other girls.

So she put on her little brown hat, taking unusual care with her thick, unruly hair to put it into smooth and attractive order, and was amazed again to see what a difference a little care made in her appearance. Well, perhaps it was worthwhile to look nice anyway, just for her own self, even if no one else noticed it.

She slipped downstairs, taking care that no one saw her as she stole out to the back kitchen where she kept her bicycle, and in a moment more was riding off down the street.

It was no part of her plan to come into contact with the excursion party that day. Hateful things! She wouldn't have them see her for the world. It never entered her head that they would not have known her if they had seen her now, riding along in this neat and attractive rig, trim tan shoes and stockings, sitting like a lady on her bicycle, her jaws not working rhythmically chewing gum, her whole lithe figure poised gracefully. She did not in the least resemble the girl whom they all despised, who usually tore along on her bicycle with her head down, shoulders humped, jaws working hard, hair hanging over her eyes untidily, a tear in her skirt, a hole in the elbow of her brother's cast-off sweater, and her old canvas sneakers covered with mud. No, they would not have known her.

Her object was to go as far from the planned route of the party that day as pleasant roads and her own will could take her. And her mother, watching the trim figure out of sight, so entirely one with the bicycle she rode, sighed and wished she might give her a little of the happiness she knew Effie had longed for so much. Then the mother prayed to her heavenly Father to guide this loved one's footsteps into His ways and turned back to her baby and her crowding household cares. If she had not been a mother who confided in her heavenly Father, she could not have tolerated the burdens of her daily life.

Effie's main object was to ride fast and cross the old township road before the party, which had planned its route along that highway, should reach there. Then she would be far beyond any sight of them, and could forget them, and speed away into the sweet country, and try to enjoy herself. For the very act of riding, even though she was all alone, brought intense pleasure to this girl. She rode fast and daringly. She sat up straight and dropped the boyish lean that she had pretended of late, and which she instinctively felt was a part of what Ethel Garner had meant when she had depreciated her riding. She put her chin on a self-respecting level, her eyes flashing a little defiance as she remembered those girls. She would show them sometime that she also could ride like a lady.

That cut about her riding had gone deeper than she was willing to acknowledge even to herself, for she was proud of her ability to ride well. She would chew no more gum as she rode, and she would maintain an irreproachable position. Thinking these thoughts, she sped along faster than she realized and soon had crossed the township road and was fairly out into the open country. The thought of the party was hateful to her. She tried to live in a world of fancied friends of her own, where she was admired and her company sought after, and where no one spoke of her but to praise. She turned her head slightly and smiled in an imagined talk with a pleasant friend of her own conjuring. Her brown suit became the finest of imported garments. The modest home behind towered into a stately mansion; her mother sat in it at leisure, arrayed in rich silks and costly jewels. The fretful little brother was a lovely child with a French nurse, and there were no more cares or troubles or disagreeable things in her joyful life. Naturally, surrounded by such an atmosphere, she was sweet and lovely herself. Not that Effie had ever sat down and charged her own faults to her surroundings, but her inference was that one who had everything lovely about one could but be lovely one's self. At least, she would for one afternoon be that ideal person and have things just as she pleased. She even met the other riding party in fancy and had them look at her with envy and call to her to join them, while she pursued the even tenor of her way, sorry for them that they had to be disappointed, but altogether so engaged with these other and worthier friends of hers, she scarcely remembered that they had passed, five minutes after.

Even the young man, Lawrence Earle, came into the story, as she in imagination gave him a distant nod in response to his eager greeting of open admiration.

Thus drenching her bruised spirit in the healing uplift of her own imaginings, she sailed out into a day that was perfect as any June day could be. The sky was blue without a sign of cloud. The blossoms here and there, all the way from dandelion to wild grape, were filling the air with sweetness, and the birds were fairly crazy with song, pouring it out into the air like living, visible gold. As she rode along her spirit rose to meet the day, and more and more the sorrows of her life dropped away and left her free. She was like a butterfly, skimming the golden sunshine, a bird on the wing, as lithe and happy, so happy she could almost burst into song herself.

She tried it a little in a clear, throaty contralto, humming a song the boys sang at school. She forgot she was ugly and unwanted, forgot there were excursions from which she was excluded, forgot there were obnoxious young snobs from college who laughed at little tomboys with holes in their skirts and sweaters, forgot there was anything in this world but free air and sunshine and happiness. In short, she was just the little careless Effie again, as she had been before she heard those hateful girls down behind the privet hedge in her own side yard.

She whizzed past a farmhouse with three old ladies sitting knitting on the porch and was gone before they discovered she was a girl and not a boy. She shied around a red rooster that was strutting in the road; she flashed by a great dog who was lying in wait to bark at her and chase her, as she pedaled up a long, slow hill with the ease of a bird on wing, coasting down again with a broad sweep of meadow and the crossroads ahead of her.

Then suddenly her golden visions vanished and she was hurled back into her hateful world of self-consciousness again. For there, ahead of her, she saw a shining new car, halting at the crossroads, as if its driver were uncertain which road to take, and another glance at him showed something familiar about the set of his shoulders. Was it, could it be that that was Lawrence Earle? And he had missed the way, of course. He had probably meant to join the party on the pike and missed them, or perhaps they had not carefully outlined their route to him.

She knew perfectly which way they intended to take. She had heard it talked about when she was behind the Garner's hedge and by Eleanor at the dinner table. If this had been anyone else in the world, or any other party of excursionists that he was intending to join, Effie would not have hesitated an instant. She would have ridden with all her might and reached him and told him where he ought to go, that he should turn back at once and take the cross-road to the pike three miles back.

But this was not the usual Effie. This was an awakening girl with a fierce grievance and a heart full of bitterness. What? Warn this young man that he was going away from the rendezvous? Never! She would sooner do anything than that. Help those hateful girls and that supercilious young man who had made fun of her once to come together and have a good time? Not if it were to pour the largest, hottest coals of fire on their heads! She would glory in their separation. It served them right. And there settled down over her a sense of satisfaction that there was an occasional balancing of punishments in this world, and those girls were getting one now. Nevertheless, it made her a little uncomfortable when she looked back to see Mr. Earle riding along on the road she had taken, getting farther and farther away from where he was supposed to want to go, when a word from her might have set him right. He would probably pass her in a moment, so she concluded to put him out of mind by putting him out of sight; and setting spurs to her steed, she wheeled sharply into a road at the right, level as a table, and tried to rejoice in her sense of freedom. Let him go on and lose his way. It was nothing to her!

Suddenly she became aware that for some minutes there had been a sound of rapid hoofs behind her, but she had been enjoying herself too much to pay heed to them. Now as the sounds drew nearer, and she turned her head to see who was driving so madly, she saw it was a grocery wagon, driverless, coming at full speed, the horse apparently almost beside himself with fear, the lines flying in the wind, and its only occupant a little fair-haired child, a tiny boy with golden curls blowing in the breeze, too young to understand, and just old enough to cling to the seat and be frightened. It was a miracle that he had not been thrown out on the hard pavement some distance back. In a moment more that horse would pass her. Instinctively, she swerved aside to be out of his way. And now he had passed her, and the blue-eyed baby looked at her and gave a cry and a beseeching look, and it made her think of her own baby brother's face when he was frightened or hurt. Just ahead, a quarter of a mile, was a sharp turn and a steep hill with a great yawning quarry hole at one side. The baby would be almost certain to be thrown out there, and there was scarcely a chance of any rescue, unless—oh, could she? With a thought of whether she had a right to risk so much when she had so little power to help, she put all her strength to her bicycle and shot down the road after the horse. She could easily outdistance him in a moment or two if she tried and then—but there was no time for thought—she *must* ride alongside and catch the bridle or the reins, or something, and stop that horse. She must, or the baby would be killed, and if she did not try, she would all her life feel responsible for his life. Not that she really thought this out. It might be said to have flashed through her brain. She acted. Quick as light flashes so her bicycle obeyed her motion. She leaned forward now with all her might to get the greatest power and make the quickest time, with no more thought of trying to ride in a ladylike position. She wished a man were here to act instead of herself, and so increase the chance of saving the baby. She saw no man ahead now and thought of the one she had just passed, and wished he were there, for maybe he could help. She forgot that she had just been hating him. She forgot everything but just what she was doing, and then as quick as thought she was beside the foaming horse, wheeling steadily step-by-step abreast of him, and making ready for her next move. Now her boyish practice of riding this way and that, standing on one pedal or on the saddle, riding on the front and the back and the side, and every other part of her bicycle, stood her in good stead. Just how she did it she could not tell afterward, but she caught that horse by the bit and held him for one long, awful, rushing minute, when everything in the world she had ever done passed over her head in clear sequence, and she felt that the end had come. She heard a car coming. Would it be too late? The horse was rearing and plunging again. Could she possibly hold out till someone came? Then a strong hand was placed firmly over hers, and a steady voice said, "Whoa, now, whoa! Steady, boy, steady!" And the horse gradually slackened his pace, and she caught a glimpse of the golden-haired baby still clinging to the seat. She dropped in a little heap somewhere in the road not far from her bicycle, and everything grew black and still about her.

Chapter 5

Lawrence Earle was one of the most admired and envied young men in town. Since he had been a little child, playing in the yard of his father's beautiful home, people had watched him and pointed him out and said, "See, that is Lawrence Earle. His father is the wealthiest man in this part of the country, and his mother is one of the very finest women you will find. She is beautiful and dresses like a flower and has everything her heart could wish, that money can buy. And yet she is just as sweet and gracious and good as if she had nothing to make her proud."

Lawrence did not grow up behind stone walls and high hedges, too good to have anything to do with the other boys. He went to the public school and took his place with the rest. He played baseball better than anyone else in his class, they used to say, even when he was in the primary grades. He could swim and climb anything, and he could fight if it became necessary to set something right.

But Lawrence Earle had always stood for fine things. He was always on the level, honest, even if it went against him to be, and the boys said he was so decent that he couldn't be any more decent.

He stood high in his classes, in spite of the fact that he went out for athletics and was always ready for fun. While he was in grammar school and high school, his house was always the center of all the school social doings, and his mother always ready to help in any sudden party or picnic proposed. She was one of them, "a good sport," they used to call her. The boys adored her, and girls admired her and tried to imitate her.

One of the nicest features of these social affairs was that there were no class distinctions; all, whether rich or poor, were welcomed alike.

But when Lawrence went away to college, these social affairs at the Earle home largely ceased. Nearly all of Lawrence's close friends were also away at college or gone to work somewhere. Therefore, it was that the younger set, of whom the Garner girls and Eleanor Martin were members, knew Lawrence and his famous good times only afar. They had been the little children when Lawrence was growing up.

When, therefore, it began to be noised abroad that Lawrence had graduated and would be coming home in a few days, all the younger set, who now considered themselves "the" set, began to scheme how they might get hold of him, for they longed to experience for themselves some of those wonderful good times they had heard their older brothers and sisters talk about.

Lawrence had gained distinction in college, of course, and the news of his successes had drifted home in one way or another. Several of the town boys were in the same college with him, and there was no lack of knowledge concerning his attainments and successes.

Football, basketball, baseball, and scholarship alike seemed to claim him as a hero. The scores he made as captain of this team and that were watched in the papers. When he made Phi Beta Kappa, there was a long article about it in the town paper. And everybody who had any acquaintance whatsoever with him or his family spoke of it to everybody else and said how nice it was, and that it was, of course, to have been expected of a boy like Lawrence. In fact, there were no other boys just like Lawrence, they all agreed.

In short, Lawrence was in a fair way to have his head turned, and a stranger hearing all his praises sounded would have been likely to feel that Lawrence Earle was a most spoiled, conceited, impossible youth. He was rich and good-looking and smart. What more could a young man have?

But Lawrence Earle had a sensible mother who had early taught him that nothing he had was really his own, only a gift from God, to be most carefully and generously used, else it might be taken from him. And as he grew up, he showed that he had not a grain of selfishness or conceit in him.

Yet in spite of what he had been, the friends and neighbors who had watched him grow up and learned to love and admire him, watched for his homecoming with fear and trembling. For how could it be that a boy with as many things to make him proud as this one, could possibly go through college with such honors as he had won and not grow proud, at least to some extent?

Speculation was rife among the elders. What would the young man do when he came back with his education completed? Would he study law and accept a partnership with his uncle, who was somewhat famous as a lawyer in that region? Would he take up a business career as his wealthy father had done? Or would he have a line of his own, journalism perhaps, or philosophy, or art? Everyone was interested and wondering.

But the young girls were all a flutter to get him to their parties, and Eleanor Martin secretly took a few lessons in dancing, though her father and mother did not approve of that amusement, in order that she might not appear awkward before this elegant stranger when he should return and invite them all to his parties, perhaps.

But Lawrence Earle rode into town late in the evening in his own car and drove quietly up to his mother's door, and made no fuss at all about his homecoming. And when he found on the desk in his old room a pile of invitations, he swept them all aside, and said, "Mother, I don't have to go to any of these things just yet, do I? I'm bored to death with functions. I just want to spend a little quiet time with you for a few days before I see anyone, can't I?"

And his mother, with a light in her eyes, smiled and assented.

"Dear, it's to be just as you want it. If you have any friends you want, they'll be welcome as always. But it will be my greatest joy to have you all to myself for a while, if that will please you best."

"Suits me to a T, Mother dear! I want to take you off on one or two long drives, and we'll have a smashing old-time picnic all by ourselves, like we used to when I was a little kid. I need that to get back to living again. And besides, I've a lot of things to tell you that have developed this year and I hadn't time to write. We've got to have a little leisure for this. About the middle of next week, Jimmy and Bryan will come on for a few days on their way to India. I must tell you all about them. They're great! You'll like 'em. And Ted will run down for a few days, and we'll have to get some of the boys together to meet him, but aside from that I've no plans. If you have, I'm perfectly willing, only wait a few days, won't you, so I can get my bearings?"

His mother smiled, the glad light growing in her eyes. Her boy was unchanged, unspoiled. She held her head proudly.

"There aren't many of the old crowd left, are there? Sam Jones and the Mills boys are down at the foundry, you said, and Fetler is married. Poor little fish! Why didn't he wait till he had enough money to support a wife? And Cappellar is in California, and Jarvis is gone to New York to study medicine, and Butler and Williams went to South America, and Judson is dead. That leaves Brown and Tommy Moore and the Ellsworths of my class, doesn't it? I was counting them up on my way home. Not many for a reunion."

"You don't say anything about the girls," suggested his mother.

"Oh, the girls. Well there weren't so many of them that mattered. Margaret Martin is married, you wrote. I hope she got a good man. She certainly was a peach of a girl! And Wilda Hadley eloped. She always was a fool. Lilly Garner married, too, didn't she? Lives in New York, you said. What became of Evelyn Bradley? She was the prettiest girl in the class, and knew it, too, didn't she? Remember the time I caught her posing before that mirror at our senior class party?"

"Evelyn is out in Hollywood in the movies," said Mrs. Earle, a little sadly. "It was a great disappointment to her mother. She tried to keep her at home. Evelyn has a younger sister now who is even prettier than she was. Don't you remember Maud, a little bit of a black-eyed girl with soft black curls?"

"Can't say I do," answered Lawrence. "I suppose all those babies have grown up, haven't they?"

"Yes"—smiled the mother—"it's the babies that were then who are inviting you now. I think Maud is one of those girls in that picnic tomorrow. They came here to ask me if I thought you would come, and I promised to tell you all about it. The Garner girls and Eleanor Martin and Janet Chipley, and a new girl, Cornelia Gilson, very modern with glorious red hair. I'm not sure that I admire her type. Oh, you wouldn't know the parties nowadays, Lawrence! They're nothing like the good times you used to have here at home. Why, they wouldn't be satisfied three minutes with the games you used to play and have such grand times with. They've got to dance, dance, dance, and flirt. 'Petting' they call it now. My dear! But you haven't lived out of the world, Son. You know what life is now."

"Yes, I've lived out of it a good deal, Mother, though I know what you mean. I had sort of hoped it wouldn't have penetrated to our town yet, but I suppose that wasn't to be expected. But if it's like that here, too, we'll just cut it out. I haven't any use at all for it. Will you make my excuses to those girls, Mother, or shall I have to write?"

"I suppose you had better write a note, Son. But even then they may come down upon you and carry you off. They are perfectly crazy to have you go on this excursion. They have been planning it for days and arranged the time with a special view to your being here."

"Well, I can't help it; I'm not going," said Lawrence, with a firm set of his jaw. "I hate that sort of thing anyway. Why shouldn't you and I run off for a day, take a drive to Aunt Lila's or something, and don't return till the blamed thing is over?"

"I'd love to," said the mother, "but unfortunately I've got a meeting for that day, the Mite Society, and it's away, out in the country at old Mrs. Petrie's. You remember her? She is lame and blind and the ladies are going out there to give her a little pleasure, as she can't come in to the meetings anymore. I'd get out of it if I hadn't promised to take Mrs. Mason's place leading the devotional, and then I'm also chairman of the refreshment committee and have to look after the luncheon, and in the afternoon we're going to present Mrs. Petrie with a little purse, and they've asked me to make the speech."

"Well, of course, you've got to go. I'll drive you over. How'll that be? And then I'll take a run around to all my old haunts and come back for you in the afternoon? What time do you go?"

"The meeting starts at half past ten, and it isn't over till three. I'm afraid you'll get tired traveling around all that time. Why not come back to lunch with us? Mrs. Petrie would be delighted, and so would all the old ladies. And your mother would certainly be proud to show you off to her old friends."

"Well, I might if I get around. I'll see. So that's settled. But how about our getting off early in the morning before anybody can possibly come around or call up or anything. Wouldn't you enjoy a ride out to the Rocks, say, before you go to Petrie's?"

"I certainly would. How ideal. I feel like a girl again with my best boy going to take me out." And Mrs. Earle stooped and kissed the handsome brow of her son tenderly. "Dear son. It's so good to have you home again."

So Lawrence wrote his note and posted it by special delivery, and when Maud Bradley called up in the morning to present a few added attractions and beseech him to reconsider, Lawrence Earle and his mother were driving along the highway at a joyous speed, bound for old Mother Petrie's, via "the Rocks," with an ice-cream freezer, two cake boxes, and a big basket of sandwiches stowed in the trunk of the car.

"It's just too provoking for anything!" said Maud, explaining it to the Garner girls over the telephone. "There I went and made an extra angel cake just for him, and I sat up almost all night to finish the embroidery on my new dress! They say he is just the same as he used to be but I don't believe it. He's a snob. He thinks we're too young for his Royal Highness! But I mean to drag him into our set yet. Mamma's going to invite him over to dinner Saturday night. She says he used to be real close with Evelyn when they were in school together. We'll get him yet, and then we'll have another of these picnics, won't we?"

"I suppose he thinks we're too small potatoes," said Ethel. "But when he learns how speedy we can be, he'll sit up and take notice. Never mind, Bradley, he'll come next time. Wait till he hears all we do on this trip. I'll take measures to have his mother hear all about it. Aunt Beth runs in there often to see her, and Aunt Beth will tell her all about it. By the way, you knew Eleanor was going to be allowed to take her new car, didn't you? Well, I planned you and the Hall boys and Joe Whiting and Aline would go with her; Minturn, too, can squeeze in if he doesn't get his own car from the repair shop in time. Reitha and Betty Anne are going with Sam and Fred, and the Loring boys and Jessie Heath will go with us. But it does seem as if half the day was spoiled without Lawrence Earle, doesn't it? When we've counted so on his going, too! Isn't it hateful?"

"Yes, it is," gloomed Maud. "If I had known he wasn't going, I wouldn't have tried to finish that dress, and I'd have had some sleep. As it is I'll just have a miserable headache all day long, and all for nothing."

"Well, you got your dress finished, didn't you? You can be glad of that much."

"Yes, but what's the use? The other boys never notice what you have on. All they want is something to eat at a picnic."

"Well, give them your angel cake and forget it." Ethel laughed. "We'll have a good time anyway, and just remember to be thankful that we didn't have to cart that disagreeable Effie Martin along. If Lawrence Earle had gone with us and she had been along, I'd have died of mortification to have him think she was one of us."

"Yes, so should I. You'd better keep Flora away from her vicinity next time. Flora is too soft hearted."

"Well, I've fixed her. She knows what to say the next time Effie Martin asks her for an invitation. I made her understand that we don't want to be mixed up at any time with a girl who has a reputation like Effie's! Well, good-bye, I've got to finish putting the salt and pepper and olives and things in. Don't forget the paper plates and napkins." Maud hung up the receiver with a sigh.

Chapter 6

The fresh, bracing air and the relaxed position soon brought Effie back to consciousness. At first she was just a little bewildered at her surroundings, for in that brief interval of unconsciousness she had thought herself lying in her mother's armchair at home and listening to her mother's sweet voice saying, "My little Euphemia."

She had never liked her name. It was so strange and old-fashioned, just like the aunt for whom she had been named. But now in her mother's tones, with that note of pleased surprise in her appearance, she was conscious as she returned to life again that the name sounded pleasant.

Then the scene was suddenly changed, and she lay in the road with a group of curious strangers about her, and heard a strong voice—that same voice that had spoken to the horse in such commanding tones—say, "Raise her head a little. There! She's opening her eyes. Now, where is that cup of water?" She looked up and saw

Lawrence Earle bending anxiously over her.

With her constitutional impulsiveness, she sat up, told them she was all right, and then jumped to her feet, but found she was more unstrung than she knew by her faint, for she tottered and would have fallen again had not Earle reached out a strong arm and supported her. He made her sit down on the bank a few minutes, and someone brought her a tin cup of water from a wayside spring. Effie felt very much astonished, for she could not remember to have been of so much importance since she had scarlet fever many years ago and her mother had given up everything else and ministered to her.

At first she sat on the grass, dazed, not really understanding what had happened, but by degrees her memory returned and she began to realize what she had been through. Then she started up and asked anxiously, "Where is the kid? Is he all right?"

"All right," said the young man soothingly, as if she were a sick baby. "The woman in the farmhouse took him in to give him a drink of milk. He was only badly frightened. But if he had gone on a few yards farther, nothing could have prevented a catastrophe. You saved the child's life. The quarry hole is just ahead—"

"I know," murmured Effie, as if she were remembering a story she had read. "That's why I jumped at him just then."

"Well, you certainly did just the right thing," said Earle heartily. "I never saw a rescue more neatly made. You hurled yourself at that horse as if you had been doing it every day of your life. You certainly had your courage with you all right! Some girl, I should say."

Effie's cheeks suddenly flushed red with self-consciousness. "Oh, that wasn't anything!" she said almost sullenly, her eyes clouding over with bitterness as she remembered the day and why she was off riding alone when she would much rather have been on an excursion with the other girls.

"Well, I guess you'll find that kid's parents will think it is something when they get here," said Earle earnestly. "Why that baby would be lying down in the quarry hole now, if it hadn't been for you. They say a big rock has fallen from the bank this side of the road, and there wouldn't have been room for the wagon to pass if the horse had tried to go through. It would have been certain death for the child, if you hadn't saved him."

"Well, there wasn't anybody else to do it," said Effie. "I had to do my best." Her voice was still bitterly gloomy.

"Well, you did it all right, and you're a heroine, though you don't seem to know it yet." The young man smiled.

"Humph!" said Effie scornfully, "People don't make heroines out of my kind of stuff. You'll find out. They'll simply say I'm an awful tomboy and I ought to have stood back and waited for some man to take care of the kid. I know; I've heard 'em before!"

A rush of sudden tears came surprisingly into Effie's eyes. She wasn't a girl inclined to crying in public, but the shock of her recent experience had shaken her up. She brushed the tears away angrily and jerked herself up from the bank.

"Where's my bicycle?" she asked roughly, as a small boy might have done. "I've gotta get out of here before anybody comes around. I'll never hear the last of this. And I've torn my new dress, too!" she ended helplessly, looking ruefully down at a jagged tear under one of the pleats.

"You shouldn't worry," said the young man lightly. "You saved the kid's life. There are more dresses in the world, but you can't get a new child to take the place of one you love. You sit down again.

You aren't fit to start out yet. You've had a shock and must rest."

"Aw rats!" said Effie inelegantly, relapsing into her boy vernacular. "I'm not a baby doll. Where's my wheel?"

"Your wheel is pretty badly damaged," he told her gently. "The wagon ran over it when you dropped it, and the horse kicked it and stepped on it once or twice, but I think it can be put in shape. However, don't you realize that doesn't matter? There are also other bicycles in the world."

"Not for me!" snapped Effie. "This was my new bicycle. I bought it myself with money I had saved up. Where is it? I've got to get away from here."

"Look here, sister, I'm here to take care of you just now, and you've got to sit still and rest till the doctor gets here and I'm sure you're all right. You don't seem to know it, but you had a narrow escape yourself. That horse came within an inch of kicking you in the temple when you fell after I took hold of him, and I'm going to make sure you were not injured before you start home, if I have to bind you hand and foot to do it. Now will you be a good child? Look here, what's your name? I think we ought to notify your folks that you're all right, don't you? Bad news travels fast. They might be worrying about you."

"Nobody ever worries about me," said Effie petulantly. "They expect me to do crazy things. They're ashamed of me for doing them. They say I'm too big to ride a bicycle."

"Well, this morning's work is nothing to be ashamed of, I'll testify, and I'm not so sure you're correct about their not worrying. People sometimes worry a lot and never say anything about it. As soon as the doctor gets here and the kid's parents come to take him home, I'm going to bundle you into my car, wheel and all, and take you home, too. We'll leave your bicycle at the best repair shop in town, and I'll promise you, it will come back to you in a day or two as good as new."

Effie looked at him half belligerently a moment, and then said, somewhat ungraciously, "Thanks, but you needn't bother with me. I can walk home and wheel my bicycle myself. You ought to be on your way, Mr. Earle, they've gone over the township road. You must have passed it three miles back and missed your way. I might have told you before, I suppose. I saw you back at the crossroads. But if you hurry, you can catch them. They'll probably wait for you till the last minute, and they'll be awfully disappointed if you don't get there. They're counting on you, and I'm sure I don't want to spoil their pleasure. It won't make things any better for me to have them have a horrid time."

The young man stared at her in astonishment.

"I beg your pardon," he said in a puzzled tone. "You seem to have the advantage of me. I've been away so much that you girls have grown out of all recognition, although I've thought there was something familiar about you from the first. Who are you, please?"

"You won't know any better when I tell you," she snapped, "and you better get on as fast as you can, for the girls will be frightfully angry at me if they find out I was what kept you and made you late."

"Made me late? What can you mean? Won't you explain, please? I'm not aware I'm late for anything. I was just riding around looking over my old haunts, with half the day before me and nothing to do."

"But weren't you going on the picnic with the girls and boys?"

asked Effie perplexed. "Perhaps you've got the dates mixed. I know you were going, for I heard the girls talking about it. They fixed the date so you would be home. The Garner girls and Maud Bradley, you know."

Effie was talking earnestly now, like a girl who was trying to do her duty at last and meant to do it thoroughly, even though it cost her everything.

Lawrence Earle smiled.

"No," he said, showing all his white teeth gleefully. "No, you're all wrong. I wasn't going on that excursion. I declined. I wanted the day to do as I pleased. I wasn't ready to go out into society yet. But you're awfully kind to try to set me right. I appreciate that part of it."

"I'm not kind at all," said Effie crossly, feeling an odd lump in her throat. "I didn't want to tell you at all. I wanted you to get lost and them to be disappointed. But, of course, that wasn't right."

The young man regarded her amusedly.

"And may I ask why you wanted them to be disappointed?" he inquired. "There seems to be something interesting behind all this. Perhaps we're comrades in guilt, who knows? Because I'm not conscious of caring much myself whether they are disappointed or not. They're all strangers to me. Come, tell me why you wanted them to be disappointed."

Nobody had ever coaxed Effie in this pleasant, merry way before. She scarcely understood such treatment. She swept him a searching glance to see if he was kidding her.

"Tell me," he urged in a kindly tone.

"Because they didn't want me to go along," she blurted out at last.

"Oh!" said the young man, with twinkling eyes. "So that's what's the matter. Well, I think they showed very poor taste indeed, myself. Tell me about it."

He dropped down on the grass by her side and began to pull long dandelions and split up their pale green luscious stems into two neat ringlets.

But Effie felt a sudden rush of dumbness come over her. There was something in his kindly comradeship that choked her and made words impossible. She did not remember ever to have had anyone talk to her in this friendly, confidential manner. It fairly overwhelmed her.

He watched her quietly for a moment, saw that for some reason she could not talk about it, and then went on in the same even, pleasant tone.

"First, tell me who you are. I'm sure I ought to know you. You still seem somehow strangely familiar."

Then words rushed to Effie's lips. "No, you don't know me. At least you wouldn't remember me. The last time you saw me you laughed at me."

The quick color sprang to the young man's cheeks.

"Oh, surely not!" he exclaimed. "Aren't you mistaken? Perhaps you misunderstood. I'm sure I never meant to."

"No, I didn't misunderstand," said Effie bitterly. "All the girls said you did, and I remembered it, too, when I heard them talk about it. But you did have a reason, of course. I had torn my dress and your mother told me about it, and I said I knew it, that it was too much trouble to mend it when I was off at the seashore."

Light broke on the young man's face.

"Oh, you're the kid that was having such a good time with

Tommy Moore, aren't you? I remember. Why, kid, I wasn't laughing *at* you, I was laughing *with* you. Didn't you know that? I thought it was refreshing to see a real girl once more, after the specimens of painted dolls I had been talking with. For a fact, I came near throwing down my hat and joining in your game of tag. If it hadn't been that I was taking Mother to call on an old friend who was leaving that night, I believe I would, if for nothing else than to shock that Bradley girl. I detest her! I've watched her and her sister grow up, and they're the most artificial girls I ever saw. I enjoyed you because you were so happy and spontaneous."

"But I wasn't a bit polite," said Effie reluctantly. "I was rude and unmannerly. The girls said so. They said I was a flat tire, and all sorts of things and, of course, I knew it was true, only it made me mad for them to say so and not to want me on the ride. I didn't want to go for their sake. I can't bear them, they're so stuck-up and silly about boys. And I didn't want to go to be on their old picnic either, but I did want to drive the car partway. Father said I might, and I wanted to, and it would have been fun."

"Of course it would, but there are lots of other chances to drive cars, and if I were you, I wouldn't have a regret about that picnic. For my part I'm having a better time right here and now than if I had gone. I wouldn't have missed seeing that rescue this morning for worlds."

Effie flashed him a look of wonder and sudden joy. Could anybody say a thing like that to her and really mean it? He must be only meaning to be polite.

"But you know you haven't told me your name yet. Aren't you going to? I suppose I should remember which one you were from the last time I saw you, but I hadn't paid the slightest attention to any of their names. The only girl I was sure of was that Bradley girl, and I didn't know which one she was, for sure."

Effie's flash of joy vanished into her habitual gloom.

"Well, you wouldn't have remembered it if you had heard it, and I don't think anybody mentioned it that day. It wasn't thought necessary. I'm only Effie Martin, the girl that nobody likes."

"Well, that's not true," said Earle heartily, "for I like you. Even seeing you just this morning I can't help liking you, and why shouldn't everybody else? But say—why—you can't be the little Euphemia—Margaret Martin's little sister, that I taught to pitch a ball, can you? Say, now, I believe you are!"

Effie's face lit up with a glow that made it almost beautiful, and she nodded, shyly, wistfully.

"Sure!" she admitted, almost embarrassedly. Her mother wouldn't have known her by her manner at all, it was so sweet and shy and pleased.

"Well, now that is great!" said Earle. "I can see that you and I are going to be great friends. I always liked your sister Margaret better than any of the other girls. They tell me she has got married. You must miss her, don't you? But say, this is going to be fine. Can you pitch a ball yet?"

Effie dropped her eyelashes, ashamed.

"Yes," she admitted. "But they make a lot of fun of me. They call me a tomboy and say I'm too old for things like that!"

"Nonsense!" said Earle. "Bologna! We'll teach them better. Let's make it the fashion to pitch ball, and then we'll see all those girls out in their backyards practicing. When can I come over and have a game of ball with you? I want to see how you have progressed. You were wonderful as a child, and I'll bet you have become a beaut at it. Say, do you know I never forgot you. I remember finding the meaning of your name one day when I was studying. Do you know what it means? Euphemia?"

"No," said Effie shortly. "I only know I hate it. I wish I had a decent name. Everybody makes fun of it."

"Oh, but they oughtn't. Euphemia means 'of good report.' It bears a recommendation on the surface, you see. Your very name is a good reference."

Euphemia was still for a moment, and then she said, "Well, it doesn't fit me." She said it so bitterly that the young man yearned to help her.

"Make it fit then," he said earnestly.

"How?" she asked, with an eagerness that showed she had asked that question in her thoughts before.

He was silent for an instant.

"Whatsoever things are true, whatsoever things are honest, whatsoever things are just," he quoted, "whatsoever things are pure, whatsoever things are lovely, whatsoever things are of good report; if there be any virtue, and if there be any praise, think on these things."

He was still for a minute, and then he added, "There is One who will help you in that, Euphemia. I wonder if you have Him for your friend and Savior. He is mine, and He is able to help in everything like that. I know, for I've tried it."

"Oh, but you've never been disagreeable as they say I am!"

He flashed her a look of sympathy.

"Euphemia, you don't know what I've been. But anyhow, that doesn't make any difference. He's able to keep us from any kind of falling, if we let Him. We'll talk about this sometime again, if you will. There's a lot I would like to tell you. I see a car coming now. I think the doctor is here. Would you like to go up to the house, or shall we stay right here?"

Chapter 7

Eventually they got into the big car that drew up in front of them and rode with the doctor into the driveway and up to the big old farmhouse, where the little runaway boy was having the time of his life chasing a lot of downy yellow chickens.

The grocer boy was there, much disturbed, shouting an account of the affair over the telephone to his employers. It appeared that he had arrived on a motorcycle while Effie was still unconscious, having requisitioned the motorcycle to chase his horse. The owner of the motorcycle was there, too, enjoying the general excitement and eating gingerbread and milk. The farmer's sons were there outside the door, rubbing down the excited horse after the most approved method, talking wisely about horseflesh in general and this thin, old, cranky grocer's horse in particular. The farmer's wife was there, comforting the beautiful little boy and telling him his mamma was coming right away. And the horse was there, still snuffing and snorting occasionally, giving furtive side glances and side-stepping himself with nervous jumps at each little sound or movement, rolling the whites of his eyes wickedly and lifting his velvety lips with a snarl to show his great yellow teeth.

The grocer's boy at the telephone was telling his story in loud tones, "You see how 'tis. I was up ta Harrisses' waitin' fer the check as you tol' me, an' the kid clumb in the wagon. He often does. He's allus crazy ta ride when I got up there, an' I kid him a lot. Wha's that? No sir. I didn't let him get in. No sir, I don't never 'low him ta get in. I ain't got tha time. No sir, he jus' clumb in of hisself after I was gone in the house, see? Yessir, I was standin' right where I could see the wagon, an' I called to the kid ta get out, see? But he jus' laughed and kep a-jerkin' the reins, an' jus' then the missus she sent down the check, an' I heard a car come up. It was a d'livery truck, ice er somethin', an' it blew it right in that hoss's ear, an' she ups and clips it. I knowed what would happen when I see that car a-comin' an' I flew down them steps, yessir, but I couldn't get a holt of the lines, they was on the other side of her, an' she was makin' fer round the house and down through the other gateway. So I turns around to head her off at the front, but they was diggin' some kind of a ditch fer a drain pipe or a water pipe or a gas pipe or somethin', an' I fell plumb in an almos' broke my ankle, and stunned myself, so when I got up that there hoss was dashing outta the front gate, an' up the road, an' I hadn't got no chancet, see? Yessir, I know. Yessir, I did. I saw a feller comin' on a motorbike, an' I hailed him an' he brung me along. An' I got here almos' as soon ez she did, but some plucky girl on a bike had stopped the hoss. Yessir. No sir, the kid ain't hurt none, jus' scared. Yessir, he's playin' about big as life. Yessir. The doctor's come an' says he's all right. No sir, the mother ain't come yet but she'll be here in a minute. Yessir, I will. I'll come along back as soon as she gets here. Yessir, the meat's all delivered 'cept Mrs. Buckingham's over on the pike, an' she won't kick; she's a lady, she is. Yessir! All right, sir. Good-bye!"

Effie took the doctor's examination of her with something of resentment. Of course there was nothing the matter with her, but she submitted to having her pulse taken and her heart listened to with something of her old belligerent air. It was only when Earle smiled at her that she lost her strained attitude and relaxed into a normal creature. Her face lit up once more with that sweet wonder that anybody should care to be so nice and pleasant to her, and she remembered the wonderful words her new friend had just repeated, with something like a thrill in her heart. Was this going to be a way out of her difficulty, she wondered? It sounded unpractical, but it also sounded beautiful—"think on these things"—it was something to hide in her heart and study out, anyway. Where did he get those words? They were somewhere in the Bible, she felt sure. It seemed as if she could remember her Sunday school class droning the verse out in concert sometime back through the years, but she couldn't be sure. They were strangely familiar, yet she never remembered to have thought they meant anything in particular before.

But another surprise was in store for Effie. Another great car presently drew up before the farmhouse steps, driven by a uniformed chauffeur. A slim, stylish lady in beautiful black satin, with a long string of pearls around her neck, got out and rushed at the little boy.

She held the child in a long embrace, and when she finally put him down and turned back to speak to them all, there were tears on her face and she was pale around her mouth.

"Where is the girl who saved my son's life?" she asked, searching the group with the bluest eyes Effie thought she had ever seen.

And then she rushed at Effie and kissed her, and Effie felt as if an angel had touched her. Such soft lips, like Mother's, only softer and younger. Such delicate perfume, like violets. Such a sweet voice. Effie was thrilled again. What wonderful things were happening to her all at once.

"Why, I didn't do anything at all," stammered Effie, honest and frank as ever. "I only held on till Mr. Earle came. He really did it, you know."

But the lady only said, "Oh, you dear child! But suppose you hadn't held on!" And then she kissed Effie and cried again. And after that she turned around and tried to thank Lawrence Earle, and cried some more. Effie stood in awe and wondered what all those girls who had criticized her would think if they knew where she was now. They would likely blame her, somehow, for being there. And then and there, she resolved that they should never know, if she could help it.

Then the whirl and excitement of it all began to make her feel sick and giddy. And all at once, she found Lawrence Earle's eyes upon her, and he said very pleasantly that he really must take Miss Martin home now, and unless there was something else he could do, they would go at once.

All at once the bottom seemed to have dropped out of things for Effie. She began to look around for Miss Martin. Was she then to have no further opportunity to ask her new friend where to find that Bible verse? Most likely she would never see him again, either. Somehow, the chair by which she was standing seemed to rise up and shake off her unsteady hand, and all the people in the room got dim and misty and whirled into one mass. Then she heard the doctor's voice saying something about more air, and the next thing she knew, she was out on the driveway, being helped into Lawrence Earle's beautiful car. His arm was around her, and a voice was saying—it was the sweet voice of the baby's mother—"Oh, I do hope she isn't going to suffer any ill effects from this. Are you sure, doctor, that's she's all right?"

When they brought the child to say good-bye and thank her, she realized they had been talking about her, and she managed to smile in her old swaggering manner and declared there was nothing at all the matter with her.

Out on the road at last, she found her companion was looking at her anxiously.

"You are perfectly sure you are all right?" he asked.

And then she found herself smiling at him.

"Why yes," she said. "I just felt a little strange in there. I'm all right, now I'm out in the air. Isn't this car grand?"

"Do you like it? So do I," he said. "Now will your mother worry if we don't go right home? It's after twelve o'clock, and you ought to have something to eat at once. Then you'll feel better. There's a tea room over here, a mile or so. Shall we go and get a bite? I'm hungry as a bear myself. I would have urged you to eat something in there when the woman offered it, but I thought it would be better for you to get off where it was quiet to eat. You have been through a lot of excitement, you know."

Effie laughed.

"Why nobody minds how much excitement I go through. That never made any difference with me," she said brightly.

"But you don't make a practice of making flying leaps from bicycles at runaway horses every day, you know. And you did faint clear away, you know, and almost did it again just now."

"Well, I guess that was because I forgot to eat any breakfast," said Effie apologetically. "I was busy, and then I was in a hurry to get away."

"Ah!" said Earle. "I thought you were hungry. Now we'll have some good, hot soup and perhaps a cup of tea or coffee, and whatever else we can find. We're out for a good time, you know. Shall I telephone your mother that you won't be home for lunch?"

"Oh no," said Effie in surprise, "they never expect me till I get there. They never worry about me."

"I wouldn't be so sure of that," said Earle, looking at her thoughtfully. "People don't always tell all they are feeling, you know. Here's our tea room. Now, do you feel like getting out?"

Effie sprang out, quite like her old self, only wondering a little at the weak feeling in her muscles and the wan feeling around her lips.

She sat at the dainty table in the wayside tea room, wondering at herself. To think that she was here, being taken to lunch by a young man! What would those hateful girls say if they knew! A pang, almost of pity for their disappointment, shot through her. They would never forgive her for having the young man they coveted, when they could not get him! But, of course, they need never know. She would tell her mother sometime, perhaps. But it was enough that she should enjoy it all to herself. They would somehow manage to spoil it all for her by some catty remark if they found out. Why have it desecrated?

So Effie ate her delicious lunch, ordered with a view to giving her strength, and enjoyed every mouthful of it, feeling every bit herself when it was finished. Soup and salad and ice cream, delicious tea and delicate crackers, creamed chicken on toast! Somehow such feasts had seldom come her way, lacking in modest luxuries on occasion. But this was wonderful. And the feeling of comradeship. It was so new and sweet to the girl that it made her throat sting and her eyes smart to think about it.

After the lunch was over, they drove around by a new road that even Effie, with her habit of scouring the country on her bicycle, had not known. It was a crossroad through a lovely wood, with ferns and maidenhair and wildflowers in profusion as if this was their special secret hiding place from the world, where they only blossomed for God and those who came to seek His special treasures.

They stopped and picked some of them. Effie was laughing and cheerful and at ease, all the bitterness gone out of her voice, a lilt in it like other girls.

"You don't know how much you are like your sister Margaret," said the young man impulsively, as he helped her back into the car again, and his eyes lingered on her face pleasantly, bringing the happy color into her cheeks. "Your sister Margaret was one fine girl, I thought," he added earnestly.

Effie looked thoughtful.

"I wish she hadn't got married," she said impulsively. "We always had good times when she was at home. She was the only one who never got impatient with me. She—seemed to understand how I felt."

"She had straight, fine brows like yours," mused the young man, looking at her again with a pleasant smile. "I think you must be like her."

"Oh no! I'm not," disclaimed Effie frankly. "I'm not a bit sweet-tempered like her. I get angry and impatient at everything, and I'm untidy, and homely, and lazy, and selfish. I know, for everybody tells me, and I can see it's true."

"Oh, now look here," said Earle, laughing. "That's not the way to give yourself a good report. Don't go to work and blacken your character like that. I don't believe it. See? I know you are not any of those things. I know you are not going to be, either. I can read your character better than that. Besides, you know you can have a Helper anytime when you see those tendencies cropping out. He is always ready to help."

"I think you are wonderful!" burst out Effie. "I didn't know young men ever talked like that. What made it? Was it your mother bringing you up that way? I know she is sweet and dear. My mother likes her a lot. But I never heard the other girls tell about your being this way, almost like a minister. They told how you were a great athlete, and had wonderful parties and all sorts of doings at your house and were a wonderful tennis player and awfully kind and all that, but they never said you were—well—this way. I wanted someone to help me awfully, but never would have thought of coming to you. I didn't know young men and boys ever thought much about God."

It was Earle's turn to look thoughtful now.

"You see, there is something the matter with my report, too, sister," he said at last.

"Oh no," began Effie, deeply chagrined at what she had said. "I didn't mean that. I meant—"

"I know you didn't, little Euphemia," he said gently. "You

didn't mean it at all, but it was there all the same. Well, I'll tell you. I guess you never got the report that I was much of a Christian because when these people here knew me, I wasn't. That's the truth. I hadn't found God yet. I didn't know that He wanted me to live as close to Him and realize Him as I would an earthly friend. I didn't realize Jesus Christ at all as a factor in my daily life. Oh, I believed what I had been taught—that Christ was my Savior from sin in a general way. But I didn't feel much of a sinner, and I didn't spend much of my time thinking about what it meant to have a Savior. Why should I when I didn't realize I needed Him? I didn't read the Bible, either, very much. Of course I knew a lot of it. Mother saw to that, but it was only in my head, not in my heart. But all that is changed now. Everything is different. Last winter I met Jesus Christ!"

"What do you mean?" asked Effie with bated breath. "How could you meet Him?"

"Do you remember the story of Saul on his way to persecute Christians in Damascus? Well, it was something like that. Oh, no light or anything. And I wasn't trying to put over anything like a persecution, but I guess I'd been pretty much against a little crowd of fellows in the college whom I used to call fanatics. And then, one night, one of them got run down by a truck as he was crossing the road to our car to find out the score on a game we had played. And it fell to my lot to take him back to the dormitory and stay with him all that night while he was dying, and the next day when his folks came, too late. And I tell you I never experienced anything like it. That fellow just lay there in all that terrible suffering and talked to us with his failing strength, told us how great it was to serve his God, and looked death in the face with a smile. I'll never forget it. I saw God with my heart that night, and I resolved I'd try to take his place after he was gone and let my life witness for God the way his had done. It was a great life! It was just Christ living in him!"

Earle was talking now, more as if Effie were an older person and he had to justify himself in her eyes, prove his case, and bring her to see as he saw. And she listened with wonder as to a story in a book that had suddenly walked out and become true.

He drew up then, in front of a pretty country home, and looked at her.

"I'm due here to get my mother. Do you mind?" he asked with a smile. "I meant to ask if you would rather I took you home first, but we've talked so hard I forgot it."

They had stopped once on their way and left the bicycle at the repair shop and had driven on, talking so intently that Effie had not noticed which way they were going. Now she started and became instantly self-conscious and uncomfortable.

"Oh, of course not," she stammered, but she did mind, exceedingly. To have Earle's beautiful, well-bred mother see her here in her son's car, as if she had tried to get his attention! She remembered also the tear in her dress and tried to smooth it down and cover it up. What would Mrs. Earle think when she found little, disreputable Effie Martin riding around with her son? The minute or two that they waited for Mrs. Earle to come out to the car were most painful to the girl as she sat silent and distraught, wishing she dared climb out and run away. But that was like the old Effie, and she was done with that Effie forever, she hoped. The new Euphemia must sit still and face whatever came, and try to be a woman.

She came to herself sufficiently to offer to get into the backseat and let Mrs. Earle occupy the front seat with her son, but the lady declined with the loveliest smile.

"Indeed, no, dear! I always sit in the backseat and love it. I would rather you sat right still where you are. Besides, I have a lot of baskets and things to pile in beside me and must have plenty of room. Lawrence, all those things on the step are to go in. Can you manage to stow them away?"

Then Mrs. Earle leaned forward and asked Effie about her mother and the baby, whom she had heard was not well, and Effie found she could open her mouth and speak quite naturally in answer. In a moment more, Lawrence had jumped in beside her, slammed the car door shut, and they were off again into the sunny afternoon. What a day she had had! She sat still and let the wonder of it roll over her while Mrs. Earle asked her son how he had occupied his time.

"Why, Mother, I ran right into an adventure as soon as I left you."

"You don't mean it," said his mother in a voice that entered into her son's adventure with the zest of his own age.

"Yes," he said cheerfully. "I was hesitating which way to turn when I saw this young lady whirl by on a bicycle, and I was tempted to follow down the road she had taken, for it looked a pleasant way. And the first thing she did was to chase after a runaway horse and save a baby's life, and get herself almost killed in the bargain, and so that was where I came in. We picked ourselves up and got some lunch after a while, and took the bicycle to the repair shop, and here we are. What do you think of Euphemia, Mother? Doesn't she look like her sister Margaret?"

"Why, I believe she does," said Mrs. Earle, looking at Effie with the friendliest smile. "I never thought of it before, but she really does."

"Well, you ought to have seen her catch that horse! It was great!"

Effie's cheeks burned with shyness and joy over the kindly words of Mrs. Earle, and she was so pleased and dazed with all their praise that she was quite subdued and sweet when they put her down at her own door. Mrs. Earle said she hoped she would suffer no ill effects from the adventure, and they whirled away.

Effie turned and walked into the house, as if she had suddenly stepped out of a dream into reality.

There was no one in sight. Well, then no one had seen her return. That was good. She need not tell anyone. She might keep this precious experience to herself and not have the life of it ridiculed out of her by the teasing of her family.

She went upstairs to her room, shut and locked the door, and went and stood in front of her mirror, looking into her own eyes with steady glance.

"Euphemia," she said slowly, softly, to herself in the mirror. "You've got to be different after this. You've got to be of good report." Then she turned and dropped upon her knees beside her bed and prayed, whispering the words in a voice of awe, "Dear Christ, please do that for me, too. Please show me how to be a witness. I want to have You help me."

Chapter 8

The famous picnic, which had been so carefully planned and eagerly anticipated, was not such a great success as had been expected.

In the first part, the guest of honor was not present, the guest for whom Maud Bradley had secretly planned it, though she had not let the girls know she knew he was coming at that time.

Maud had done her best at the last minute to get hold of him, in spite of his polite note of refusal. She even went herself to the Earle house, as early in the morning as she thought it discreet to appear there, but found to her dismay that both Lawrence and his mother were gone for the day. That, alone, was enough to spoil the party for Maud, for she had laid her plans so that she might hope to retain the young man for her own special escort. In fact there was not one girl in the bunch, with the possible exception of Flora Garner, who was not in some form or other cherishing some quiet plan to take possession of the guest of the day as her own private property. Even Eleanor Martin had decided to make much of Lawrence Earle's former friendship for her older sister, Margaret, in order to claim his attention. It was a great thing for the whole crowd to have the young man back at home after his long absence, and the halo that surrounded his reputation made him the more desirable.

When, therefore, the company gathered, car by car, and the news was broken to each one that Lawrence Earle would not be with them that day, there was dire dismay. Several girls, against the advice of their mothers, had worn their best dresses, with the young stranger especially in mind. And these looked down at their crisp, new frocks in dismay, for there was no denying the wisdom of their mothers' sage advice. The dresses would never be so fresh and pretty again after a day of frolicking, part of the time in the woods and part of the time crowed into automobiles. And now there would be no fresh frock for the next occasion, when the young man might be more gracious.

Janet Chipley even went so far as to try and get her carload to turn back to her home, on the pretext of having forgotten a box of mints, thinking to slip upstairs and make a change in her garments while they waited. But the driver of her car persuaded her otherwise, and the day began with a number of girls being much upset in temper.

This attitude on the part of the girls gradually had its effect on the boys of the party.

"Oh, Jan, give us a rest on Earle. We're sick of his name. What's he, anyway? He doesn't belong to our crowd. Forget it. I'm glad he didn't come. You girls wouldn't have had eyes for anybody else. He's nothing so great, anyway! Other men have made Phi Beta Kappa. Other men have been captains of teams and nines, and won honors. For Pete's sake, forget him and pass the sandwiches!"

Then they had taken the wrong road, and turning back, failed to find the charming picnic spot they had started for, or the spring where they expected to drink.

There was salt in the ice cream, and someone had forgotten to bring sugar for the Thermos bottles of hot coffee. Jessie Heath tore her new dress on the fallen limb of a tree and blamed it all on Jimmy Woods, who happened to step on the other end of the limb when it caught her dress, and they had such a quarrel that they went on the rest of the way in separate cars.

Eleanor Martin was especially unhappy, for in spite of her best-laid plans, her car was loaded up with two of the girls whom she detested and the stupidest boys in the bunch. She would have protested, but by the time she reached the rendezvous, having had trouble with her makeup and been delayed longer than she realized, the others were all seated, ready to start, and there was nothing to do but take those left standing on the sidewalk waiting for her.

One of the boys who had fallen to her lot was determined to drive the car for her, and after resisting as long as she thought she could, she let him drive for a few miles. And during that episode they had two narrow escapes from a smash-up and one pretty nasty puncture in the new tire, which set them back several miles behind the rest of the party who went happily on their way, shouting out that they would unpack and have the lunch ready when they got there.

Moreover, Eleanor's conscience troubled her, for she knew her father would be cross about that puncture, and she knew she had broken her word in letting Fred Romayne drive.

Redmond Riley had brought a strange boy from New York with him, and this young man had a dashing way with him and carried in his hip pocket a flask that he kept passing around. Eleanor was too well brought up to partake of its contents, but she had not courage to prevent its being passed among the others in her car. And presently the whole carload became most uproarious, finally demanding to stop at a place on the way, where Red said they could get the flask filled up.

Eleanor knew that her father would not approve of such doings, and she had a few ideas herself of what was the correct thing to do. Still, she lacked moral courage to insist, and the consequence was that she suffered tortures all day both from her conscience, which continued to annoy her, and also from the actions of the hilarious boys who were carrying things with a high hand. After the lunch eight of them jumped wildly into her car, which she had unfortunately left unlocked, and drove madly off through the woods, singing and shouting at the top of their lungs, their feet scoring the new leather of the seat, their driver dashing along the wood's road without apparently noticing where he was steering, the brakes grinding in a loud scream just in time to save a collision with a large tree.

Eleanor ran after them, shouting, pleading, wringing her hands, but too late. They dashed on and were gone for an hour and a half, returning with the beautiful new car splashed with mud and one fender bent. The stranger from New York had been driving. He had filled his flask again somewhere and apparently had distributed it generously among the others, for they were all wilder than ever.

Eleanor had to lock the car and hide the key to prevent their going off again later. And in despair she climbed into the driver's seat and refused to leave it, saying she must drive the car herself or they could not ride with her.

She tried to get rid of Red and his friend from New York, but none of the girls wanted them, and the remainder of the day became a nightmare to her.

Moreover, the moon, which they had counted upon for their return drive, withdrew behind a cloud, and rain began to fall to add to their discomforts.

They arrived home, long after midnight, in the midst of one of the most terrific thunderstorms the season had known. And those of the new dresses, which had escaped thorn and briar and crushing and wet moss and spilled cocoa, got a thorough drenching before their miserable young owners got safely into their respective homes.

Altogether Eleanor was not very happy when she met her father's stern eye and tried to explain why they hadn't come home at the time they had promised, and why the fender was bent, and the tire flat, and a long jagged scratch in the leather of the backseat. Tried also to explain the stain on the new carpet in the back and the strong smell of liquor that pervaded the whole dejected, mud-splashed outfit.

Altogether, Eleanor was anything but happy as she went to her room that night, and she was not in a much better mood when she came downstairs the next morning, so late that the breakfast table was cleared off and everything edible put away.

The Garner girls were not much happier, either. They telephoned Eleanor that their father was very angry about the behavior of the crowd. For it appeared that someone had passed them earlier in the evening and recognized them, and had brought back a report of their doings, which had spread through the town with various additions, and the Garner girls were in trouble. Their father considered them responsible to a certain extent. They intimated that he also considered that Eleanor had been responsible for the young men who were in her car. The whole thing was making a most unsavory stir, and the Garner girls were very unhappy.

Later there came word from Janet Chipley. Her mother was taking her away immediately. She did not wish her daughter's name to be mixed up in the affair. It appeared that Red and his New York friend had called upon Janet that morning to return a silver spoon, which they had somehow carried away in one of their pockets, and had much offended Mrs. Chipley. Later advices from other members of the select junior crowd showed even more horrified parents, as the day wore on and the stories grew. For be it known that the crowd the Garner girls and Eleanor Martin belonged to had been considered beyond reproach, and now the young ladies sat in dust and ashes and indignity.

Euphemia Martin, as she resolved to try to have herself called hereafter, had spent a quiet evening in her room after her day's experiences, searching her Bible for the verse that Lawrence Earle had quoted. With the help of an old concordance from the library, she found it at last and made sure that its words were thoroughly graven in her memory.

She went to sleep, saying them over to herself: "Whatsoever things are true, whatsoever things are honest, whatsoever things are of good report; if there be any virtue, and if there be any praise, think on those things!"

And she had never in her life thought on any of those things. It had never made the slightest difference to her whether anyone thought her true or honest or of good report or lovely or anything else. She had gone on her own selfish way, doing what she pleased and boasting to herself that she did not care what people thought of her, feeling proud of the fact that she was going against public opinion. And here it was in the Bible all the time that that was one of the things God wanted her to do—think about being lovely and true and having a good reputation.

Now that she thought about it, there was another verse she had learned when she was a child, something about avoiding even the appearance of evil.

Well, it was strange that she should have run across this young man in this way. The very person she would have avoided if she had known he was there. And to think he should have been the one to show her the way in the darkness. Just that morning she had been wishing she had someone she dared ask what to do about making herself right, and then he had been sent. He must have been sent, for it was all so strange and out of the ordinary, everything that had happened the whole day. It must be God had sent him to help her!

What a wonderful young man he was.

She went over the story he had told her of his own awakening. That must be what old-fashioned people used to call "conversion." People didn't talk about such things nowadays, at least Euphemia had not heard them, unless it might have been a minister now and then mentioning it in a sermon. But Euphemia had never been in the habit of listening much to sermons.

But Lawrence Earle was sincere. She could see that. He believed everything he said, and he carried conviction when he told about it. She felt sure he was right. She was comforted by the fact that God cared to guide her and that He had promised to help her. She longed to know more about this mysterious life of the Spirit that Lawrence Earle seemed to live in and understand. Could it be that a young, unloved, unlovely girl like herself could ever get that great hold on God that Lawrence Earle seemed to have?

And what a witness he was going to make for Christ. Why, he even cared to stop and witness to her, just a young, wild, awkward girl with nothing about her to catch his interest.

Oh, what a great thing it would be to go about a living witness of Christ! For that, one would not mind giving up anything else. But, of course, she never could. A girl who wasn't considered good enough for the other girls of the neighborhood to associate with could never be fit for the indwelling of the great Christ, the divine Savior of the world.

But perhaps He could make her fit. Lawrence Earle had said He was able to keep anybody from all kinds of falling, and to present them faultless—wasn't that the rest of that verse? They used it in benedictions. She knew it by heart because she had usually been so glad that the service was over that she followed the benediction to its end, ready to bounce out into the aisle the minute the amen had come. "Now unto Him that is able to keep you from falling, and to present you faultless before the presence of His glory with exceeding joy—" Did that mean that He was able to make one so faultless that it gave Him joy? He was not ashamed to present one whom He had made faultless, even before the presence of God's glory? How wonderful!

Euphemia had never thought about holy things like this before. But she lay for a long time in her bed, in her dark room, going over these thoughts. And at last she slipped from her bed to her knees and spoke aloud in a very low tone, as if she felt the Presence to whom she was speaking standing close beside her.

"Oh, Jesus Christ, if You are able to make anything out of me with all my faults, won't You please take me and do it? I don't see how You can, but I believe You can do it if You say so, and I do want to be faultless. I would like to be a witness for You, if You think You ever could make me fit."

When the terrible thunder began to roll over the town, and the lightning flashes lit up the darkest corners of rooms, and the rain dashed in sheets against the windows, Euphemia lay sweetly sleeping on her pillow with a smile of trust on her young lips.

She came downstairs the next morning with a light of anticipation in her eyes. She was actually looking for God to answer her prayer.

Chapter 9

There were two surprises in the Martin home that morning. The first occurred when Lawrence Earle drove up to the door in his car and inquired of Johnnie whether his sister had recovered from yesterday and if he might see her a moment. It's true that he spoke a name, one that sounded strangely to Johnnie—Euphemia—but he supposed Eleanor was meant, of course. Who but Eleanor was ever inquired for by a young man? Margaret, the eldest sister, was married and in a faraway Western home. Eleanor was the one to be called upon now. And naturally, Eleanor would be supposed to be recovering from her ride of the day before. Indeed, she had just arisen and was taking a belated breakfast at that moment by herself in the pantry. Johnnie, like the usual small boy, knew all his sister's comings and goings, and he was aware that this young man had been asked to join the ride the day before, also that Eleanor was much interested in him.

The living room was in charming order. This was owing to the careful thought that Effie had bestowed upon that clause, "whatsoever things are lovely," the night before. Effie began to see that there were a great many things which might be lovely and that it was this clause in which she seemed to be most lacking.

Johnnie, having seated the guest, hastened to the kitchen in search of Eleanor.

"Say, Nell, where are you?" he called. "Come out o' there. There's a man in the sitting room to see you—that Earle fellow. He wants to know if you've recovered yet from your pleasure excursion, and I expect he wants you to go and ride. He's got his car, so you'd better get your clothes on. You look like last week's milkshake in that rig."

Then Johnnie put his hands in his pockets and, having done his duty, whistled himself out of the kitchen door before his sister had recovered from her astonishment enough to ask him any questions. She quickly laid down the piece of apple pie she was eating and slipped up the back stairs to follow Johnnie's advice, pondering all the while why Lawrence Earle had come to see *her*. And planning what a delightful time she would have riding with him, the envy of all the other girls. She decided that he had probably come to make his excuses for not going with them yesterday. But why had he come to her, instead of to those other girls who had sent out the invitations? She was in a flutter of excitement and tossed over her boxes and drawers for a certain string of beads she wanted to wear. Euphemia, in the next room, was getting the baby to sleep and singing softly. The words floated through the half-open door occasionally and down through the hall to the waiting visitor.

I ask You for a thoughtful love,
Through constant watching wise,
To meet the glad with joyful smiles
And wipe the weeping eyes;
A heart at leisure from itself,
To soothe and sympathize.
I ask Thee for the daily strength,
To none that ask denied,
A mind to blend with outward life,
While keeping at Thy side;
Content to fill a little space,
If Thou be glorified.

He smiled to himself as he listened, and thought, *If that is Euphemia, and I think I know her voice, she did not need that I should guide her to Him, for she evidently knows Him already. Perhaps she has caught the secret.*

Then Eleanor came down the stairs, smiling and fresh. Eleanor was very pretty, and she was graciousness itself now. She was pleased to have him call. It was kind of him, and they had been so disappointed yesterday. Earle seemed a little surprised, but he was courteous. He asked about the ride and said it had been a perfect day, but other plans had prevented his going. He did not, as Eleanor expected, ask her to ride, though she was arranged in the prettiest of garments. Instead, after a few words about the weather, the roads, and the town in general, he told her she had changed a lot, that he shouldn't have known her, and then he asked if he might see her sister, Euphemia. For a moment Eleanor was puzzled. She was just about to say she had not a sister, Euphemia, when it dawned upon her whom he meant. And she said, "Oh, Effie? Why, yes, I think the child is around somewhere. You never can tell where to find Effie. I'll go and see if she's been heard from lately." And she left the room bewildered. What in the world did he want with Effie? Had she been getting into some sort of a scrape and had he come to find out what she knew of it? Her face burned with shame over the thought.

Effie's low-voiced singing over the baby, as she laid him carefully on Mother's bed in the darkened room, caught her sister's ear, and she hastened to summon her.

Effie had discovered that virtue brings its own reward to a certain degree, and was feeling real pleasure in the work she had accomplished, as she softly covered the baby with Mother's white shawl and tiptoed out of the room. She was startled to find her sister, Eleanor, standing in the hall, frowning at her. "For pity's sake, Effie!" was her greeting. "What a fright you are! Go and brush your hair and put on something decent. Lawrence Earle is downstairs and wants to see you. He wants to know 'if you have recovered from yesterday.' What in the world does he mean? Have you been getting into some scrape, and has he come here to let us know it, asking after you in a very polite way not to hurt our feelings? I just know you have."

But she found herself talking to the empty hall, for Effie, her face lighted up with pleasure that her new friend had come, flew down the stairs without waiting for brush or collar or any adornment, and never paused till she stood in the doorway and realized her untidy working dress.

Eleanor, too vexed to know what to do, followed her sister downstairs, thinking to apologize for her carelessness, and find out, if possible, what was the matter. The busy mother passed through the hall at that moment, and they all met at the door, just as Lawrence Earle was saying cheerfully, "Good morning, Euphemia. How are you? Not all in after yesterday? Well you are some sport!"

Eleanor wondered with disgust if Lawrence Earle supposed Effie was one of the crowd and had perhaps been the one to invite him yesterday. Likely he had gotten them confused, and she must set him straight at once before Effie got her head turned.

But the young man went on speaking.

"How about it? Do you feel like having a few minutes' exercise? I brought a baseball over. I'd like to see how my old pupil has progressed. Can you spare her, Mrs. Martin? Or is this a busy time, and should I wait till afternoon?"

"Why no, of course not, go ahead, dear," responded her mother, heartily glad that some real fun had come to her usually unwelcome daughter.

Effie flew upstairs to make a few changes in her apparel.

"You have a wonderful daughter," said Lawrence Earle earnestly, looking from Mrs. Martin to Eleanor. "You certainly would have been proud of her yesterday. Not a girl in a thousand could have done what she did!" And then he turned as Euphemia, her eyes bright with pleasure, came flying back downstairs in a clean blouse, which she had hastily donned on the fly, as it were, and they went laughing off together into the yard.

"What does he mean, Mother?" asked Eleanor in an offended tone. "What on earth has Effie been doing now?"

"I'm sure I don't know," said her mother, watching them with half-perplexed pleasure. "He isn't spoiled a bit, is he? I was afraid he might have changed, with all the adulation he has had."

"I'm sure I don't see how you can tell he isn't spoiled," said Eleanor discontentedly. "I don't think he's very polite, to say the least. He might have asked me to play, too. I'm the oldest daughter."

"Great cats!" said Johnnie, who had come into the dining room door and was listening. "Nell, you never could throw a ball, nor catch it neither. Wouldn't you make a great figure out there pitching ball!"

"Why, I thought you scorned ball-playing, Eleanor," said her mother, innocently surprised. "I don't suppose it occurred to him that you would care to play."

"Well, I wouldn't!" snapped Eleanor shortly. "I was only saying how impolite he was. The idea of his coming over here and making Effie a laughingstock in her own yard. I shouldn't think you'd allow it, Mother! I should think you'd put a stop to it before anybody sees her! I'm ashamed to have the girls know my sister acts that way."

"I don't see what you mean, Eleanor. Your sister is not behaving in any unseemly way, and as far as I can see, she is very graceful in her movements. That little blouse she made out of your old white dress fits her very nicely."

"No, you never can see any harm in anything Effie does," said Eleanor. "You don't care how much humiliation I have to bear on her account. That's nothing to you."

"Aw, shucks!" said Johnnie, watching out the window. "If you could sling a mean ball like that, you'd be out there, too; you know you would. You're just jealous, that's what you are, Nell!"

"Johnnie! You mustn't speak that way to your sister!"

"Well! She is!" said Johnnie, vanishing out the back door to slump down in the grass by the edge of the ball space and watch the game, ready to run after the ball if it should elude the skillful catcher's hand.

Eleanor went discontentedly upstairs to watch the performance from her curtained window, but she managed to be sitting down on the porch when the two finally finished their play and came sauntering toward the house.

Mrs. Martin came through the hall with her arms full of clean laundry, which she was about to carry upstairs as they came up the steps.

"I'll carry that for you, Mother," said Euphemia, with new thoughtfulness, springing up the steps. "You don't mind if I go for a ride, do you?"

Eleanor made eager talk while the visitor waited for her sister to come down, hoping that she would be asked to go along, and resolving to put Effie in her place if she did. The very idea of Effie's usurping the best new young man in town!

But Lawrence Earle did not ask Eleanor to accompany them, though he was as pleasant as possible while he waited. And as he left, he said to Mrs. Martin, "You won't worry if I keep her out late this afternoon, will you? I've promised to show her a new road that she's never seen, and Mother told me to bring her back with me to lunch. I think I demonstrated my ability to take care of her yesterday, didn't I?" And he touched his hat and went away laughing, as if they understood.

Euphemia's cheeks glowed as she looked back at her mother and sister, but she said nothing, and Mrs. Martin stood looking after them, wondering.

"Something very nice must have happened yesterday, or something rather"—she paused for a word—"dangerous, perhaps." Her eyes took on an anxious look.

"Nonsense!" said Eleanor sharply. "Something disgraceful, I'll bet. That girl can stir up more trouble in a given time than anybody I know. I bet she just did this for spite, whatever it was, because she wasn't allowed to go on that picnic. I might have known, when she came around so softly sweet and asked Papa not to forbid my going, that she had something up her sleeve. I declare, Mamma, I think it's terrible the way you let Effie disgrace us all!"

There were tears of vexation in Eleanor's eyes. She stood gloomily beside the window, looking after them and drumming on the sill. "Mamma," she said, as her mother passed again through the room. "Do you think it's quite safe to allow such a child as Effie to go off with strange young men? You know Lawrence Earle has been at college, and you never can tell how boys change when they go away from home."

The mother gave her a look of astonishment. "Why, Eleanor, daughter, what can you be thinking of! Lawrence Earle is one of the finest young men I know. It seems to me, you were very anxious just yesterday to go off with him yourself. I'm afraid if you would examine your heart, you would really find something like jealousy there."

The mother passed on, and Eleanor went glumly upstairs to settle down to a novel.

She was presently roused, however, to answer the bell. And this time a handsome car driven by a liveried chauffeur was drawn up in front of the house, and a gentleman, holding by the hand a lovely little child, entered and asked for Miss Euphemia Martin. He seemed much disappointed that she was not at home and asked after her health most solicitously. Could he see her father or mother? When Mrs. Martin was summoned from the kitchen, accompanied by the ever-wakeful baby, he overwhelmed her with words of gratitude for her daughter's prompt and brave action, which had saved the life of his child. He was anxious to know if he had Euphemia's full name written correctly. He said the little boy had a small gift, a slight token of the gratitude they felt. He had telephoned into the city for it late the night before and had it marked with the name the people who were standing about on the road had given him, so he hoped it was correct. The gift had come by special delivery that morning. And at a sign from his father, the beautiful baby presented to the mother a small white box, carefully wrapped and tied with white ribbon.

Mrs. Martin took the little white package and looked at it curiously, bewildered.

"But I don't understand," she said. "I don't know of anything that my daughter, Euphemia, has done to merit any thanks. There must be some mistake. Perhaps it is another Miss Martin you mean."

"Oh no," the gentleman said, "the grocer's boy directed me here. He said he knew the young lady quite well, and that she was very brave and fearless."

"But what did she do?" asked the mother, fearful now lest this was another of poor Effie's escapades that would turn out to be not half so praiseworthy as the stranger seemed to think.

The caller proceeded to tell the story then to the wondering mother and sister, with all the details which he had gathered from the onlookers. And Mrs. Martin's eyes grew bright with pleasure over the praise her little girl was getting.

"She was always quite fearless," said her mother. "I am glad it has served to some good purpose. I have sometimes despaired of her ever growing up and settling down. But I rejoice that my daughter was able to save this dear child's life." And she laid her hand tenderly on the little golden head of the boy, who looked up at her with a confiding smile, and said, "Hoss wunned an' wunned! I awful scared! Dirl 'top him. Nice dirl 'top horsey!"

When the callers finally left, promising to come again and thank the young lady personally, Eleanor stood watching them ride away with stormy eyes.

"Weren't there any men around to catch that horse without Effie having to rush forward and make a display of her riding? Effie is always putting herself forward. Here, let's see what she's got. Some worthless trinket, I suppose. Such people think they can discharge a debt like that with a few words and a plaything." And with a most disagreeable expression on her face, she reached out her hand to take the package her mother held.

"Eleanor!" said her mother sternly. "What can have come over you? I am thoroughly ashamed of your actions. You will most certainly not open your sister's package! It is hers to open when she comes." And her mother left Eleanor feeling very uncomfortable.

Chapter 10

Out on the sunny road, under a clear blue sky, with a pleasant morning before her, rode Effie. At another time, she might have stopped to think what the girls would say when they saw her companion, and she would have had a feeling of triumph. But her humiliation had been so recent, and this young man's coming had been so like an angel to her in her utter self-abasement, that she looked upon him with a sort of awe and desired only that she might be worthy of this morning's great honor. So it was that she rode calmly by the Garner's place and never saw the two girls sitting on the wide front porch, nor noticed Janet Chipley and Maud Bradley coming down the street, until her companion lifted his hat. She raised her eyes then, and when she saw who they were, the color flamed into her face. Lawrence Earle noticed it, but gave no sign. He had had a purpose in directing their course around this way. A young cousin of his, quite close to the little Chipley sister and the little Garner sister, had unfolded some of her beliefs regarding Effie Martin to him at dinner the night before, when he had told his mother of his afternoon's experience and the young girl's part in it.

"Cousin Lawrence," she had said earnestly, "I think those girls treat Effie Martin real mean. They wouldn't let her go with them yesterday. I heard them talking. They say she climbs trees and bites her nails and isn't old enough. But I know she wanted to go real bad. Don't you think they were mean? They wanted you though, real much. I heard them say you would be the lion of the 'casion."

He laughed at the little maid's earnestness, but some inkling of Effie's feelings and what she had been through began to dawn on him, and his indignation grew toward those other girls, who he felt needed a lesson. Therefore, he rode with Effie through the main part of town. But out upon the smooth country road, two good miles between themselves and all disagreeable circumstances or memories, he made her forget herself and think only of the beauties about her. He even quoted one or two rare bits of poetry, in order to watch her face and see if their beauty touched her soul and awakened an answering chord. And he enjoyed her wonder and evident delight in all he said. He also discovered that she had been no mean reader herself, for a girl who made no pretension to things literary.

They had a most delightful morning. Euphemia felt that she never had enjoyed herself so much before. It was on her way back that she summoned courage to ask a question. "Would you mind telling me just what you meant yesterday by repeating that verse? How could I make my name fit? I hunted out the verse last night, but I'm not sure I understand."

"Certainly," said he, his face lighting up at her question. "Suppose we stop under this tree and you read the verse for yourself in the original. I always carry my little Greek Testament with me in my pocket."

"Oh, but I can't read Greek, you know."

"Perhaps not, but I think you can read your own name. It is in that verse. Do you know that it's there in the form you wear it in your name? 'Whatsoever things are lovely, whatsoever things are Ευφημία.' Those are the exact words."

They stopped under a chestnut tree, and the young man took out of his pocket a copy of the New Testament in Greek that looked as if it had seen much use. He opened to chapter and verse, as if he knew the way to it well, and pointed out the words to her, reading slowly until she recognized her own name in the strange Greek characters.

"You see," he said, looking at her eagerly, "all the things which go to make up a good report are summed up here: to be true, to be honest, to be just, to be pure, to be lovely. If we are all these, we are sure to have a pretty good report given of us. But the trouble is most of us are not all, nor even many, of these things all the time. And we find it quite impossible of ourselves to be either, so what are we to do? The Book says, 'think on these things.' You know, one's character generally takes color from what one thinks about most. If I think about and love the world, I am worldly. If I think about evil, I make it easy for evil to develop in me. Now, if you think much on these things that are Christly, they are likely to grow in you so that you literally become Ευφημία, of good report. But that is not all. Did you notice the last clause in the next verse? 'And the God of peace shall be with you.' So, you see, you don't have to do it alone. It would be utterly impossible to grow Christly by our own efforts. It is really Christ who works it in us, Christ dwelling in us. And when you begin to 'think on these things,' you open your heart for the Christ to come in and dwell there. And He has promised to keep your heart in all peace."

It was all new to Euphemia. She listened with her soul in her eyes, and afterward she could shut her eyes and seem to remember every inflection, every flash of his eyes, and every curve of his lips as he spoke the words that seemed to mean so much to him. He seemed so eager to impart his own knowledge to her.

All too soon the morning was gone, and they drove back to the Earle house for lunch, and now indeed Euphemia had a taste of unsought triumph. For the Garner girls and Maud Bradley and Janet Chipley came driving past, just as Lawrence Earle turned into his own driveway. And they all saw that the despised Effie Martin was with him, and that they were laughing and talking as if they had been having a good time together. And he was taking her home to lunch! That was plain to be seen, for Mrs. Earle was even then on the porch, waiting to receive her guest. The traffic lights held the girls until they had seen Mrs. Earle come forward and greet Effie affectionately, as if she quite expected her and was pleased at her coming.

"Did you ever!" said Janet Chipley crossly. "Well, he always was odd! So that's that! Effie Martin, of all girls! But, of course, he doesn't know what she is!"

"Oh, he'll find out soon enough," prophesied Ethel Garner. "Effie Martin can't keep herself in the background long."

But what they did not know was that Effie Martin was gone, and there was to be in her place Euphemia Martin, a different girl, as different as if she had indeed been born again.

The beautiful day was over at last, and Lawrence drove her home, leaving her at her father's door with the promise of coming for her soon again.

Effie came slowly into the house, thinking of all the happy, helpful day, and wondering how she should begin to live her new lesson when she was met by Johnnie, bursting at every pore with information and curiosity.

"I say, Eff, hustle along, there, won't you? There's a package here for you, and Ma wouldn't let us open it till you came. A fellow in a big swell car and a pretty little boy that looked like a girl was here and left it for you. Say, I think you were real mean not to say a word about that runaway. You must have had a regular picnic of a time."

She opened the little white box wonderingly, and found inside another white box of velvet lined with blue, and in this lovely case, a tiny platinum wristwatch, set about with jewels, tiny diamonds, and sapphires. And on the back it was inscribed: To EUPHEMIA MARTIN, IN GRATEFUL ACKNOWLEDGMENT OF HER BRAVE ACTION IN SAVING THE LIFE OF CLINTON CARROL.

She looked long at the dainty, jeweled timepiece and the inscription. Here was a testimony to at least one good action she had done. This "Euphemia" inscribed on the precious metal surely meant "of good report." She looked at it so long and so thoughtfully that the others, who were impatient to see it, pressed closer and took it from her, and as they handed it from one to another, exclaimed over its beauty and the bounty of the giver and what the younger ones termed "Eff's luck." She slipped out from among them, leaving it still in their hands, and stood looking out the window, deeply stirred. What a lovely thing had come to her as a sort of seal and memorial of the new life she was going to try to live.

She was roused from her thoughts by her sister Eleanor's words, "The idea of giving a child like you such a magnificent jeweled watch! It will never be of the least use in the world to you. It's too fine for you to wear. Where would you ever go, to dress up enough for that? And when would you ever get the silks and velvets fine enough to wear with it? You'll just have to consider it a medal of good behavior. Perhaps by and by, when he moves away and forgets about it, you might sell it and get something worthwhile."

"Humph!" said Johnnie, looking at her curiously. "I bet you'd wear it quick enough wherever you went if you got it. You'd never think anything too fine for you. Gee whiz! A thing like that's fine enough without any silks and velvets. I think I see you swelling round with it on! You better put it away carefully, Eff, or you'll find it 'out for the evening' some of these fine times when Nell goes to a party."

He was interrupted in this speech by a stinging slap on his cheek, followed by a box on his ears, and Eleanor blazed angrily at him for being an impudent little boy. In the midst of this, Effie took her beautiful watch and fled to her own room. She had been very happy but a moment before, but now her happiness was clouded. She had seen like a flash, since she turned from the window at her sister's words, two distinct ways in which she might work out that "whatsoever things are lovely," and she did not want to work them out. She sat down in her little rocker by the window to think and to look at the beautiful watch. That seemed to embody to her the first thing. She had seen that Eleanor liked the watch and would enjoy it very much if it were hers. Of course, she could not give it away when the gentleman had given it to her. That would not seem right, but she might lend it to her sister sometimes. That seemed a hard thing indeed to her. Her pride and her love of possession and carefulness for her watch all clamored together in her against such a proceeding. Why was it necessary? Eleanor had a watch of her own for which she had saved the money from the small handfuls that fell to her share. She never would allow Effie to wear it. In fact, Eleanor had never shown any great amount of love for Effie. Why should she put herself out for her? Ah, "whatsoever things are lovely"! If she would win love, she must be lovely. It would be lovely to give Eleanor this pleasure sometime.

She put her watch away with a sigh at last, wondering if she ever could come to that sacrifice and resolving to think it out and try to do what was right. There was yet another subject to hold her thoughts—her brother Johnnie. Could she help him in any way? He and she had always been more nearly like companions than she and Eleanor, in spite of the difference in their ages. She knew she had some influence over Johnnie. Perhaps she could win him to be a better boy. Then she thought of the words Lawrence Earle had spoken that morning about God being with you, "that God of peace," and she remembered how many times she had heard people talk about having "the peace which passeth understanding." How she wished she had it! How glad she would be to know and feel that the God of peace was beside her, and that she might look up to Him as she had done to the young man and ask Him to show her where to go and what to do! He would love her. She felt sure He would. Perhaps it was true that He was beside her now and this throb of something strange like a new joy was His smile as He told her He was glad she wanted His love.

In a sort of shamefaced way, she went and locked her door, drew down the window shades, knelt beside her bed, and prayed. She was not used to praying, except at night when she went to bed, and then only as a sort of form that she had kept up since babyhood. She was not quite sure that she had really prayed when she rose from her knees, uncertain whether she really ought to add an amen to such an intangible prayer as that, but in her heart she felt that in that act of kneeling and praying, she had taken the decisive step toward beginning a new life. She had meant by it to let God know she was intending to "think on these things" and wanted Him to come and be with her and show her how, and most of all, to love her. She drew up her shade and looked out the window through the green branches of the trees to the exquisite blue of the sky, and said softly to herself, "I almost believe that I love God a little, and I wonder why, because I know I did not feel so yesterday nor last night. I wonder what has made the difference. It seems as though He has sent me some kind of a message that made me know He was here." She closed her eyes a moment, just to be glad in the thought. It was so new to her to stop and think at all, or to have anyone's love around her in that way. Then with her characteristic quickness, she began to look around for something to do. "I must go down at once and begin," she told herself, smiling. And a careful observer would have seen in that smile a touch of the peace that was to settle down upon her brow, more and more, as the days went by, and she went on "thinking on these things."

She opened her bureau drawer for one more peep at the lovely jeweled thing that seemed to be so much alive, with its musical little tick going, going on all the time—her very own. And yet even in the few minutes since she laid it there, and although she prized it just as highly, it did not seem to her a selfish image of her own pleasure, but rather a token that she was beginning a different life with more joy in it. The watch might be used in God's service now, without causing so severe a pang as a few minutes before.

Chapter 11

W hen Euphemia opened her door, she heard a sudden, piercing scream from the baby downstairs somewhere, and her feet fairly flew to see what was the matter. Was this an opportunity to carry out her new resolves?

As she opened the dining room door, a strange scene met her eyes. The baby was seated on the floor with something in his hands that he seemed to be fighting, while he screamed at the top of his lungs and appeared to be in mortal terror.

The cat was rolled in paper from which she was unable to free herself and was rattling frantically about the room, now landing on the top of the sewing machine and entangling herself further in a spool of silk, now arriving on the dining table that was already set for the evening meal.

Johnnie, from the porch doorway, was howling with joy, and Eleanor was laughing with all her might. Neither of them had made the slightest attempt to rescue either baby or cat. The kitchen door opened and Mrs. Martin appeared, a kettle of hot potatoes in one hand, the colander in the other, saying in an anxious voice, "What is the matter? Why don't you do something, one of you?"

A quick investigation showed that both cat and baby had become entangled in the sheets of flypaper that the careless servant had left on a chair when she started to set the table for dinner. In such catastrophes, it was the custom in the Martin family for the children to stand by and enjoy the discomfiture of the victim until their mother came to set things right. They were running true to form this time, and so great was the power of habit that Euphemia on first sight had almost joined them in their merriment. But a glance at her mother's face reminded her of her vision of better things, which she had just had upstairs during her few moments of communion with her unseen Guide. Instantly, she knew that here was her chance to begin her new life.

"Johnnie, catch that cat!" she cried, springing to rescue the frightened baby, who had just started to apply his face to the flypaper. "Never mind, Mother, we'll have it all right in a minute," she called, and then she rapidly pulled the paper from baby while she held his fat, flying fists firmly, and directed Johnnie, who had proceeded to have a regular game of catch with poor pussy to the great danger of everything breakable in the room.

The cat was frightened almost out of her nine lives. She flew from one article of furniture to another and came within a hair's breadth of knocking over the milk pitcher and carrying the butter plate to the floor with her.

"Open the door, Johnnie," called Effie, "and get me some

water and a rag, quick. Maybe this stuff is poisonous and the baby has some of it in his mouth."

Eleanor was aroused to help then, and they finally managed, after trying water and soap and kerosene, to get the sticky paper from the poor, pink fingers of the frightened baby. Then Effie took him, and they went to look for the cat and Johnnie. And by and by, kitty and baby were comfortably clean, and baby was hushed to sleep. Effie felt very hot and tired, for the baby was heavy, and his struggles had made him hard to hold. She looked dubiously down at her new brown suit and found several daubs of flypaper varnish on it, and knew that it would take a vigorous cleaning to make it as good as new again. The new life wasn't going to be all rose color after all, she perceived.

Then it was dinnertime, and she went in to be greeted by her father, with an unusual smile. "Well! So it seems our girl was very brave yesterday," he said. "They tell me, Mother, that she hung on to that horse after it had reared and lifted her from the ground three times. There were plenty of men about, but none of them moved to help. Our little girl did it all. It's terrible that you went through all that, Daughter, but it was a very brave thing to do. I'm proud of you! It was a great thing to be able to save a life!"

Euphemia's cheeks grew red with the unwonted praise, and she caught her breath. So much virtue and so much praise coming to her all at once! Even more than she deserved.

"If there be any virtue, and if there be any praise," chanted a little line in her soul, and then added, "whatsoever things are honest."

A sudden chill came over her gladness. Ought she to tell her father that the account he had heard had been overdrawn? It was so sweet to hear his praise! And, of course, the details did not really matter. Still, "whatsoever things are honest." Suddenly she looked up.

"I didn't stop the horse quite alone, Father," she said, with a clear-eyed look. "Lawrence Earle came almost immediately and put his hands over mine and held him, or he would have got away from me. He was a very strong horse. But all I did was catch him first when there was no one else near enough to reach him. I was on my bicycle, you know."

"Oh, indeed!" said Eleanor sarcastically. "I thought they were making a terrible fuss over a little thing. I think Lawrence Earle ought to have that watch, then, instead of you."

"Nevertheless, it was a very brave thing to do, Daughter, and you deserve all the praise anyone can give you," said Mr. Martin. Then turning to his elder daughter, he said severely, "Eleanor, it seems to me that it ill becomes you to make remarks like that. It was Lawrence Earle himself who told me the story of the rescue. He was driving his car and was practically helpless at the critical moment. He had to stop his car and spring out, but he said that before he reached your sister's side, the horse had reared three times, lifting her from her feet, and that it's a miracle that she was not killed! Your criticisms are in very bad taste. You ought to be rejoicing that your sister is still alive."

Euphemia was deeply grateful to her father, and her heart throbbed with a new love for him, but her sister's scorn stung deep in the midst of her joy. It was a little thing, perhaps, but it hurt. Johnnie had been watching her thoughtfully, and after dinner, he said to Euphemia, "Aw, gee! Eff, whaddya go an tell that ya didn't do it all, for? Nell has to get her old face in everywhere. I wouldn't a given her the chance."

"But Johnnie, it wouldn't have been honest," said his sister.

Johnnie gave her a quick look. "What's the difference?" said he.

"It makes a difference, Johnnie," she said with a sigh, thinking of all the differences she wished it would make in her.

"How long since?" he asked curiously.

"Johnnie, I'm going to try to be honest always after this. Why don't you, too?" She said it earnestly, almost wistfully. And the boy, quick to follow a leader, and interested always to do something in partnership with someone older than himself, assented.

"All right, I will." He evidently had no question of what would and would not be honest. He surveyed his whole life in one comprehensive glance and knew in a general way where he would have to make a change. "And say," he added, "do you mean we'll size up together, say every Sunday night, how we've done it?"

Effie foresaw trials in this proposed plan, but she also saw possibilities, and she agreed. Then she went in to see what her new Guide had for her, of work or trials or thought.

The next day looked bright ahead of her as she went to bed that night, after a last look at the dear little jeweled watch lying in its satin bed.

But she certainly would have been astonished if she could have heard what her sister, Eleanor, was saying at that very minute when she laid her head upon her pillow.

Eleanor was spending the evening with the Garner girls, and they were out on the porch talking over their unfortunate picnic.

"What do you think," Eleanor was saying, "My sister Euphemia—"

"Your sister *who?*" screamed Janet Chipley. "I never heard you call her that."

"Well, we do, a great deal," said Eleanor. "Mother feels she is getting too old for Effie now. But what do you think? She had the velvet after all, yesterday. She didn't get to go with us, but she had the guest of honor all to herself, and an adventure besides. I suppose you'll hear about it tomorrow for it will likely be out in the paper, so I may as well tell you. Euphemia is very shy about mentioning it. She never said a word herself till Lawrence Earle came over and spoke about it. He and Euphemia are awfully old friends, you know. He really is responsible for my sister's boyishness. He taught her to pitch ball, you know, when she was quite little."

The girls were all agog, listening with bated breath and jealousy in their eyes. Had they not seen the hated Effie riding with the much coveted prize of the town? What did it all mean? And Eleanor talking in that half proud, pleased way about her sister! Oh, if Euphemia, on the way to dreamland, could just have heard and seen! But perhaps her guardian angel knew it was best not, and so drew a kindly veil for the present and sheltered her from too much uplifting praise.

But it is a pity that Johnnie, too, should have been asleep and not have been there, for Eleanor's good, at least.

For Eleanor was enjoying not a little reflected glory from her sister's brave deed. She sat back in the big porch rocker and swayed back and forth with satisfaction.

"Yes, indeed!" she went on, "they've always been quite chummy. I suppose if we had asked my sister, there wouldn't have been any doubt but that she could have coaxed Lawrence to come with us. Strange, I had forgotten how fond he was of her.

"But you know Effie—I mean Euphemia—hasn't the slightest idea of being set up about it all—"

"But what did she do?" interrupted Maud Bradley jealously. "You're not telling us."

"Do?" said Eleanor, smiling, "oh, nothing, only chased a runaway horse that was about to dash over the quarry ledge out by Brocton's Corner and saved the life of Charles Clinton Carroll's only son and heir! Wasn't that some trifle? And she nearly got killed herself, incidentally. Dad and Mother are terribly upset about it. They can hardly speak about it. And Effie—I mean Euphemia—comes in as casually as possible and never tells a word."

She waited a second for the impression to deepen, and then she went on. "It seems Lawrence had seen the runaway himself and had been chasing them, only of course he was hampered by his car, but he got there as quickly as he could—the horse was terribly frightened by the sound of the car coming after him, and all the people standing round were simply petrified with fright. And Effie—Euphemia—would certainly have been killed if Lawrence hadn't arrived in the nick of time and just barely saved her. She was a couple of hours coming to, and Lawrence brought her home, of course. Oh, yes, she's all right this morning, went out and played ball with Lawrence for a while, and then went off to lunch with him and his mother. Of course they begged me to go but I simply couldn't think of leaving Mother with all there was to do this morning, and anyhow it wasn't fair to Ef—Euphemia!"

Eleanor was making quite a case of reflected virtue and rather enjoying it. She studied the faces of her friends and saw a wave of incredulous perplexity passing over their faces. It was time to change the interest.

"But you ought to have seen that darling baby, little Clinton, when he came with his father to thank Eh–phemia! His mother couldn't come, she was so overcome with the shock, so Mr. Carroll himself came; and he couldn't say enough about E–phemia, how wonderful and brave she had been. It seems the horse lifted her clear off the ground three times, trying to shake her when he reared. It must have been frightful! It seems as if I couldn't get it out of my mind. I couldn't sleep a wink last night for thinking about it!"

Amazement held the tongues of her companions silent. This was an entirely new Eleanor! Was she real?

"Mrs. Carroll is coming tomorrow to thank Ef–phemia! But they sent the darlingest gift! I simply had to go out of the house not to open it when it came, Ef—she wasn't at home you know—but of course I wouldn't have opened it for the world till she came. That is half the fun in getting a present, to open it. Don't you think so? Well, when she got home we all stood around and watched her, and what do you think it was? Why the darlingest platinum watch, all jeweled! It's perfectly precious! Wait till you see it. Ef— she would have let me wear it over tonight to show you if I had asked her, but I couldn't bring myself to—not the first night. But you'll see it. It's the sweetest thing I've ever seen. I'm so happy for her, I don't know how to stand it. Isn't it great? And it has a perfectly stunning tribute to Ef—her bravery engraved on the back. It will be something she can keep forever and hand down to her children. We're all so pleased for her. It's better than getting something yourself to have a thing like that happen to your sister, you know."

And all the girls sat in wonder, and oh–ed and ah–ed, and decided that, after all, they ought to have asked Effie Martin to their picnic. How perfectly humiliating to have been left out of all that!

Chapter 12

Euphemia arose the next morning with a heart full of joyful anticipation. She seemed to be standing on the top of the world, looking over into the morning land. What was it that made life so well-worth living? Ah, she was a new creature with a new name and a new friend to help her. Two new friends, in fact. One, the God of peace who was able to keep her from falling and to present her faultless before God's glory—His pure, righteous, searching glory! The other, the friend who had led her to that God of peace and made her understand that He was her Savior, able to save her at every turn of the way.

She wondered shyly whether she was to see her friend Lawrence Earle again soon. Of course, she couldn't expect that his interest in her would keep up. He was four or five years older than she was, belonged in a different social set from any she would enter. If she ever did belong to any social set. . .she doubted it. Also, he had many vital interests. Among other things that they had talked about, he had told her of his hopes to go and witness for God in some corner of the earth where witnessing was most needed. He had told her he was studying, preparing for his life's work, and she knew he expected to be very busy that summer attending conferences here and there where notable Bible teachers were to be present. She sighed wistfully and wished that she might be able to hear some of the good things that he was to have. But perhaps he would come over now and then and tell her about them. And her heart thrilled at the thought of how she would get books and study by herself, so that she would be better able to understand what he told her when he did come.

Then she went downstairs to eat her breakfast and help wash the dishes, for it was the maid's day off. And almost as soon as they were done, he appeared in an old sweater, with his baseball in his hand.

"I thought we might have a little practice this morning," he said, smiling. And she went joyously out to play, feeling that life had never, never held so much joy for her as it did just now.

They played for an hour—and the Garner girls had collected quite a little group of the girls behind the hedge and were watching, though of this Euphemia was scarcely aware, she was having such a good time. And then they sat down under the cherry tree, with the sunshine glinting between the branches on their heads, while Lawrence read to her a chapter in his New Testament in Greek and translated as he went, demonstrating a new thought that he had found.

It seemed like heaven opening to the girl whose inner life had been starved so long. And the thought of the summer stretched wide and sweet and helpful as she sat with dreamy eyes and listened to words that opened up a new life to her.

It's strange how lives touch for a moment in this world and then move apart for years. How interesting it will be hereafter, if we are allowed to study the wise working of Providence and understand all the whys and wherefores.

It would seem to a casual observer that Euphemia Martin needed that sweet new influence that had come into her strong young life and turned it into a new channel, needed it for some time to come, in order that she might be strengthened and taught, and not fall back. But perhaps the Father saw otherwise, saw that this was a soul that could be put to the testing almost at once.

However that was, right there in the middle of a sentence of Gospel truth, Johnnie came rushing into the picture with a message from Mrs. Earle. A telegram had come that her sister in California was very ill, dying perhaps, and wanted her to come. Would Lawrence come home at once?

Of course, Lawrence would come at once. He sprang up, startled, and turned for an instant to the dismayed girl who stood up beside him, her eyes full of disappointment.

"I'm sorry, little pal," he said, using the old name he used to call her in her baby days when he taught her to throw a ball. "I've got to go—probably will have to go with Mother. If I don't get back, you'll know. It's been awfully good to have these nice times with you. And I won't forget—! You won't forget, Euphemia! You'll go on thinking of these things, won't you?"

Euphemia, with a sudden choke in her throat and a sudden stinging of tears in her eyes, put her hand in his and promised. She would go on. She would not forget!

"And we will both pray—" he added, "for each other!" Then with a quick pressure of her hand, and a sudden lighting of his eyes that she never forgot, he was gone.

And that was the last time that Euphemia Martin saw him for five years.

They left on the noon train for California. Of course Lawrence went with his mother.

He wrote Euphemia a beautiful letter en route, explaining and saying how sorry he was that they could have no more games or rides or reads together, but promised to send her a book he thought she would enjoy, which would help along the lines they had been interested in.

And so Euphemia Martin entered into her testing time.

It would seem that the devil might have been laughing in his sleeve at how quickly the props were knocked out from under this girl's new resolves. Now, how would she be able to live her saintly life of virtue without anyone to show her the way? The old life, the old temptations, the old hindrances, the old jealousies, all were left, and it would be easy to drop back into the old ways again.

And for a little while, it seemed to the girl that this must be inevitable as her dream of the summer joys faded, and she knew she must struggle on her new way alone.

Yet she was not alone. She remembered that she had "the God of peace" with her, and He was "able and willing to keep her from falling," any kind of falling her new friend had said. If she would only let Him!

Well, she would let Him as far as she knew how.

It cannot be denied that she felt disheartened when she found that her new friend had gone away. It could scarcely be called a disappointment because his friendship had been so unexpected. But his help had been so great that for a few days she was utterly discouraged and made so many failures and relaxed into her old ways so frequently that she seemed, even to herself, to merit most of the sharp criticisms she had heard of herself. But her soul had grown sensitive by the little praise she had received, and she dreaded again to deserve cold looks and the kind of despairing reproach her mother had in her eyes sometimes. She wanted her mother's approval, and she wanted most of all to be true to her name. Why was it that she failed so miserably? "The God of peace shall be with you," the promise read. Why did He not help, then? Perhaps it was because she did not ask Him aright. Perhaps if He was with her, she ought to talk with Him more. In a general way she knew that people who were trying to be Christians read the Bible and prayed every day. She had never stopped to ask herself if she were a Christian before, but now that she thought of it, she supposed she was. But she realized in her heart that she was a very poor specimen.

She was standing by the window one night looking out into the dark. There were no stars shining. Her lamp was still unlighted. All of her life looked dark to her. She felt herself very wicked. The tears chased one another rapidly down her face. Her thoughts grew bitterer until sobs came, and sometimes grew audible as she sank down upon her knees beside the window and abandoned herself to thinking how utterly hateful everything was, including herself.

Mrs. Martin, passing through the hall on the way from tucking in the baby, heard a strange little wail coming from this daughter's room and went to investigate. And Effie, crying too hard now to notice the opening door, felt her mother's work-hardened hand in gentle touch upon her head, and then her mother's arms around her tenderly; and her mother's voice said, "My poor Euphemia, what is the matter? Will you not tell Mother all about it?"

For a few minutes, the girl cried all the harder, just because of the sympathy and love that had come to meet the ache for it in her heart. But by and by the sobs ceased, and she sat up and told all, beginning with that afternoon under the trees when she had heard herself talked about, every little word she could remember, even down to the biting of her poor fingernails.

It was very hard for her mother to feel that her girl had been so talked about, and thought of, by others. And perhaps it was a hundredfold harder because the mother could see at once that it was because of habits formed in her as a child, which should have been broken; because of the lack of gentleness and politeness and sweet womanliness that she should have tried to train daily in the growing soul. Mrs. Martin blamed herself for not seeing this before and guarding her daughter. She blamed herself none the less that her life was already so overcrowded, and she so overburdened, that there seemed not one minute of time left for anything more. She sighed heavily and was indignant with those girls, and yet could not altogether blame them. But oh, she did so want all her children to be good and beloved and admired. Effie went on to tell of her ride and runaway, and then her meeting with Lawrence Earle, and her talk with him and his helpfulness. And the mother blessed him in her heart.

Mrs. Martin had never talked her religion to her children. She had not known how to open the subject with them. But she did trust in her Lord, and she lived her life with gentleness and patience, even through days that were hard and wearing to her soul. And now that Effie brought her story to her mother, that mother knew how to point her on the right way she had chosen and to give her much-needed encouragement. Well for her that she had a parent who was acquainted with the Lord Jesus Christ. Before Mrs. Martin left her daughter that night, she came back from the door hesitating, and gently, quickly, drew her down beside her on her knees. Then in a low, almost inaudible voice that trembled with the fright of hearing itself in prayer before another, she asked her heavenly Father to guide her little girl. She kissed her and was gone. It had been very hard for the mother to pray aloud because she had never been accustomed to such a thing. She had been embarrassed even in the dark. But she had done it.

After that night her mother never called her anything but her full name, Euphemia, and then she began to teach the baby to call her so, and by and by Johnnie and her father and the others took it up, and within a year she was known to them always as Euphemia. The mother hoped by this constantly to remind her daughter of the meaning of her name, and she did not hope in vain. Euphemia was glad to lose her old and rather despised name and gain a new one with her new life.

There began days in which the mother said gently, "Euphemia, I would like you to help in this," or "Euphemia, if you want to be helpful this morning, there is that," or "Daughter, dear, that disorderly room is a burden to me this morning. Could you set it to rights?"

This helped Euphemia. She always remembered what she was trying to do when her mother spoke like that. There followed, too, many evening talks with Mother, brief necessarily, because of the many cares, but helpful. It was Mother who suggested ways of helping Johnnie and who seconded her efforts to please her elder sister, and Mother who bade her not despair when she had failed and forgotten all her good resolves. And it was Mother who arranged it so that she should have a certain little quiet time to herself in her room undisturbed, to "think on these things" and to pray. This, after all, was the source and center of her life. She learned to commune with Jesus in those daily thinking times.

And the wonderful peace of God "which passeth all understanding" began to settle down upon her brow in unmistakably sweet and gentle lines. The others could not help but feel it. She was careful for others; careful of their feelings, and of her own actions, to make them pleasant to others. She curbed her desires more often now and tried to do as others wished and not as she would please.

Not that she accomplished this all at once. She had days when everything seemed to settle back to something worse than it had been at first and when she seemed to lie again upon that green moss and hear those voices on the other side of that hedge criticizing her. At such times she would sometimes be brought back from almost despair of heart by glancing down at her hands. The nails upon her fingers were now well shaped and carefully cared for, with dainty white rims and the pink flush of health. There was no need for her to hide those hands now. She never bit her nails anymore; neither did she fidget in church. Certainly, in those things she had been helped by hearing what others thought of her, though it had been very bitter at the time and nearly destroyed her faith in life and humanity.

Lawrence Earle did not return to his hometown within a few weeks as he had told Euphemia he would, and as he had confidently expected to do when he left. His aunt lingered at the point of death all through the summer, and finally crept slowly, but surely back to life. She seemed to need her sister, and Mrs. Earle did not feel that she could possibly leave her, and as there was nothing especially urgent to call Lawrence back alone, he remained.

He wrote Euphemia that he had found a wonderful Bible school out there, where he was taking a course that was most helpful, and from time to time there came to her pamphlets and books and a little magazine, which both cheered and helped her on the way in which she had set her course. It put her into touch with a new world, a world of the spirit, where she found that they were a great fellowship who believed this way and were waiting upon the Lord and "thinking on these things." When she first realized this she felt greatly strengthened, and it seemed easier to know there was a host of people scattered everywhere doing what she was trying to do.

Then there came a letter one day from Lawrence Earle telling her that he had received a call to go out to India to do some "witnessing" for a year or two and had decided to accept it. He was sorry not to get back for another game of ball and another chance to read Greek with her, but it could not be helped, and he felt sure this call was from God. He sent by the same mail some more literature and a precious copy of a remarkable translation of the New Testament directly from the original, which he said would help her greatly. In the package was also a small but beautifully bound copy of the Scofield Bible, which he said was a gift from his mother to her. His mother and aunt were planning to take a trip abroad and would accompany him partway, as his aunt was able to travel.

So that was that, and Euphemia looked up from her letter with a sad but patient face. Well, she had known in her heart that she would probably never see him again when he went away, but it was somehow a wrench to be sure that he would not be back for a long time, if indeed he ever came back. India! It seemed like going out of the universe. A kind of blankness filled her soul. But then she realized that she must not feel that way. She must be thankful all her life that his way had touched hers for a few days, for oh, what a difference he had made in everything to her! She could never lose the help he had given her, even if she never saw or heard from him again.

So the days and the weeks went by, and an occasional postcard with strange pictures and stranger postmark reached her. Once or twice, a brief letter came telling of the wonders of the new land, but they were hurried letters from a busy man. Already he seemed like a prophet who had larger interests than just to help her little life.

Euphemia put the letters all away in a little old writing desk with inlaid top and a lock and key, which had been the property of her Aunt Euphemia long years ago and had fallen to her lot. Nobody would ever open this, and here she hoarded all her little treasures. Sometimes she took them out and read them over, for they seemed somehow related to her Bible closely, and always there were quotations and suggestions which made her Bible study more interesting.

But the days grew into months, and the months into two and then three years, and Lawrence Earle was still in strange lands, connected with some island mission, preaching, teaching, traveling and establishing new stations, and training new teachers. He did not write much about himself when he wrote at all. She gleaned most of her information concerning his movements from the little magazine that came to her regularly from its far home and gave her a vivid picture of life as he was living it.

Still, it all seemed quite far away and unreal, and more and more she came to depend on her Bible and prayer for her daily strength.

Euphemia had finished school, had graduated from high school with honors not a few, in a gown that was faultless as to fit and appointments, and amid open admiration from her classmates. For the years had brought her a measure of good looks all her own, and her new ways had taught her to be always well groomed, and she looked as pretty as any of them. Flora Garner, who had been ill and had to stay back a year, graduated in the same class with her and seemed quite willing to be friendly with her, always making a point of walking to and from school in her company, and Euphemia was not anymore the lonely, wild thing she used to be.

But Euphemia had worked hard and had not taken much time for social life aside from keeping up her tennis, swimming, and skating, and these latter she managed to do very often in company with her brother John, who with a group of his "gang," as he called them, was devoted to her and always ready to have her join them in their sports. So, in a measure, she was the same independent girl, walking much apart from the girls of her age.

Her mother worried over it sometimes, but she had her hands so full with Eleanor's affairs that she had little time to do anything about her next daughter's social life. The father said, "Well, Mother, don't worry, perhaps it's a good thing for the child. She hasn't half as many temptations as Eleanor, and she has twice as much character as all those silly girls put together."

"But she'll grow old all alone," mourned the mother, "and perhaps she'll blame us."

"Not she," said her father. "She's too sweet a nature for that. And she'll not grow old alone; don't you be afraid. Somebody'll snap her up someday, somebody that knows a good thing, and then what'll we do without her? Besides, if she should happen to grow old all alone as you say, she'll be such a blessing as she goes that her life will be a happy one anyway. So don't you worry about Euphemia! I have always told you she would turn out all right. You do your worrying for Eleanor. She needs it! Euphemia doesn't."

And Euphemia, who happened to be in the library at the time consulting the dictionary, heard them talking and smiled tenderly. At least she had won the good report with her father and her mother.

And Euphemia had developed a beauty of a kind, also.

Perhaps it was the peace that sat like a light upon her sweet face that made people turn when she went by and say, "Look! Did you see what a distinguished-looking girl that was?"

Her soft olive complexion, untouched by cosmetics, still had the healthy wild-rose glow, and her dark eyes had lost their unhappy restlessness and wore a constant light of settled joy and peace in them. Her heavy hair she had not kept bobbed, but had let it grow, and it set off her vivid face softly, in rich dark waves that would not brush entirely smooth, and needed no curling iron or any such thing, for it had a permanent wave of its own. Neither did she need lipstick on her lips, for they were red with nature's own touch.

Neither was her body big and awkward anymore, for her outdoor life, and her suppleness, had made the muscles firm and given a fine slender line to her erect carriage. Altogether she was good to look upon, and Eleanor often watched her half jealously because of her free, graceful movements so utterly without self-consciousness.

For Eleanor was having a time of her own, and while she was a little more tolerant toward her sister now, because Euphemia often did a great deal for her in the way of mending and making over her dresses, and relieving her of her natural share of the household labors, still she had very little time or thought or love for anybody in the world but Eleanor Martin.

Chapter 13

Eleanor was going to be married.

Sometimes it seemed to Euphemia as if Eleanor felt that no one worthwhile had ever been married before. Eleanor was determined to have the very best of everything, and plenty of it.

Euphemia overheard her father telling her mother that things at the office were in a very bad mix-up and money was going to be scarce for the next six months, and he wished she would go as easy as possible in spending for a while. But Eleanor wept bitterly when Mrs. Martin suggested buying more inexpensive clothes than she had picked out, and the household resolved itself into a gloomy place. Then up rose Euphemia.

"Eleanor, why can't I make your lingerie? I'm sure I could save a lot of money on it. It's ridiculous for you to pay five and six dollars apiece for those little wisps of crepe de Chine and lace, when we could make them for a dollar or two apiece."

"The idea!" sneered Eleanor, and dissolved into tears once more. "If—I ca–can't have a decent outfit, I w–won't get m–married at all."

"But you don't want Father to go into debt for it, do you? He can't buy things without money, can he?"

"He can borrow some money!" said Eleanor sharply from behind her sopping handkerchief.

"Well, Mother says he can't. Mother says he has already borrowed up to his limit to save the business from going to the wall. Now it seems as if it is up to us to do a little something to help. Father went without a new suit when he bought the car to please you. He went without heavy underwear and got pneumonia the winter he bought your new piano. He does without things all the time to get us the necessities of life. I know, for I heard him talking to Mother. And there are going to be enough new things you'll have to have for very decency without spending a fortune on imported underwear. I'm going to make some for you."

"But you couldn't *possibly* make them the way I want them. Those imported things have lines, and nobody but a French dressmaker can get those lines. Besides, they are perfectly darling, with lace insets and rosettes and satin rosebuds. It would be perfectly dreadful to have just plain things in my trousseau. I would be ashamed to show them to the girls!"

"Well, I don't see that it would be an absolute necessity to show them to the girls, but even if it was, I don't see that that has any point. You can't buy what you can't afford, and if you spend all that money on under things you can't even have a wedding dress, let alone hat and shoes and going-away things. I heard Father say the check he gave you was positively all he could spare and we must make it do."

"Well, if this is your wedding, go ahead and do what you like. Make your old patched-up lingerie. I won't wear it."

"You'll have to, if there isn't any other. And Eleanor, you can take me down to the stores and show me just what it is you would like to buy, and if I can't make exactly as good and pretty and everything for less than half the price, I'll say no more. I can copy anything I ever saw in that line."

It ended in a compromise. Eleanor and Euphemia went shopping, saw all the prettiest lingerie, and Eleanor purchased a single garment of each style she desired for a copy. So Euphemia laid aside the precious books and her own preparations for her coming winter at college and plunged into the intricacies of glove silk and filet lace, and lingerie ribbons, and pink and blue and apricot and orchid, until the whole upper story of the house looked like a rainbow.

There were endless discussions in which Eleanor was constantly either weeping angry tears or blaming her parents for the things they had not done for her, until life became almost intolerable.

Mrs. Martin went about with a constant sigh on her lips, and her brows lifted in the middle anxiously. Sometimes Euphemia noticed that her lips were trembling and her hand trembled as she raised it to her aching head. And Euphemia was the buffer between the two. Euphemia gave up her own ways and her own plans and took as much of the burden as possible from her mother's shoulders.

In those days also Father Martin was grave and abstracted, coming late to his meals and hurrying away, having eaten scarcely a bite sometimes. He lived on strong coffee. Euphemia, as she went about trying to help, trying to lift the burdens her parents were carrying, trying to hide Eleanor's selfishness, and to lessen the household expenses, and to fling herself generally into the breach, wondered what the end was to be.

Then it developed that the wedding dress must have some real lace on it, and Eleanor demanded the best. Thirty dollars a yard was the lowest price she would hear to and said with a toss of her head that even that was not nearly as good as Margaret had had on her dress.

Now Euphemia had in her precious inlaid box, wrapped in soft old tissue paper, several yards of wonderful lace, yellow with age. Her heritage that came with her name, Euphemia, handed down from Aunt Euphemia, who had come into possession of it through her husband's family. It was lace such as Eleanor never could hope to own, and Euphemia knew that she had often envied her for having it. And of course, the sacrifice that presented itself to this patient, thoughtful younger sister was that she ought to lend her lace to her sister. It was much the same breathtaking sacrifice that she had once contemplated about her watch, only that sacrifice had never been permitted by her parents. When she had hesitantly proffered the watch once to Eleanor to wear until her own was mended, her father had most summarily given his command, "That is Euphemia's watch, and it's a valuable thing that she will want to keep always. She alone is responsible for it, and it is not right for anyone else to have it. Eleanor, you get along without a watch until your own is mended. You are too careless to have charge of Euphemia's, and we can't run any risks of losing a thing like that. It couldn't be replaced, you know."

Euphemia stood at her bedroom window in the starlight when the idea first came to her that she must lend Eleanor her lace for the wedding, and had it out with her soul. She felt a little dismayed that she found so much selfishness still lingered in herself, but resolved that it should be conquered. So after kneeling down to ask for strength to make this sacrifice as if it were a joy, she sought her sister's room at once, not wishing to leave the matter until the morning lest she might weaken.

She found her mother sitting in the moonlight beside Eleanor's bed, trying to reason with the weeping Eleanor.

"Listen, dear," Euphemia broke in, with a throb of almost joy in her voice. "Don't worry another minute about that lace. You're going to wear mine, of course. You know every bride has to wear something borrowed. 'Something old and something new, something borrowed and something blue,'" she chanted happily. Switching on the electric light, she took out the lace in all its filmy yellowed richness. It settled down upon the pillow in a most amazing heap, a treasure that a princess might have been proud to wear.

"Oh, my dear!" said her mother, with a mingling of relief and protest in her voice. "Your lace! Your wonderful wedding lace! The lace that Aunt Euphemia left you!"

Eleanor sat up and mopped her red eyes and stared.

"You're not going to let me wear your lace, are you, Pheem?" she asked in astonishment. "You certainly are a peach! Say, Pheem, you won't mind if I don't tell it's yours, will you? You don't mind if I say it's an heirloom?"

"But it was to have been *your* wedding lace, my dear," protested her mother fearfully, seeing in Eleanor's request a hidden danger.

"I'm not being married myself yet. The lace won't wear out in one wedding by any means," said Euphemia lightly, trying to put down the rising lump of apprehension in her throat.

"Oh, Mother, Pheem's not the marrying kind, and anyhow she doesn't care for dresses. She's too good!" declared Eleanor cheerfully, slipping out of the bed and going to the mirror to drape the rich flounce of lace around her shoulders and tip her head to one side to get the effect. "It suits me, doesn't it? It's just perfect, Pheem; you're a peach! Would you mind if I cut it, darling? There's enough to make a flounce on the skirt, too. Isn't it gorgeous?"

"No!" said Euphemia sharply, wheeling toward her lace. "No, I *cannot* have it cut! I'll arrange it so it will be pretty without that, but it must not be cut. It's an heirloom!"

She turned appealing eyes to her mother, and Mrs. Martin seconded her.

"Certainly not, Eleanor, you mustn't think of cutting the lace. Isn't it enough that your sister has loaned it to you without your suggesting such a thing? It would be a defamation."

Eleanor pouted.

"Oh, dear! It wouldn't hurt it in the least. It could be pieced together again without any trouble. Well, I don't know as it will do then! I'll have to buy some after all! I couldn't think of putting it on if it doesn't look right."

"It isn't in the least necessary to cut it, Eleanor," said Euphemia patiently, and she took pins and tried to show her sister what effect could be got without cutting the lace.

Eleanor haughty, offended, and only half convinced, finally yielded to the inevitable, knowing in her heart that no money she could ever get together could buy half such priceless lace as this.

It was like this all the way through. Eleanor wanted a caterer, and Mrs. Martin insisted that they could not afford it. She and Euphemia baked and planned and worked with everything they had in them as the day drew near. And then it appeared that there was a bridesmaids' dinner to be planned for and that she must furnish the bridesmaids' dresses; or at least Eleanor had told the girls she was going to do so in order that they might be just what she wanted. She had planned for eight bridesmaids, and she insisted that Euphemia should have a new outfit of most expensive materials. And there were gifts to the bridesmaids, little gold vanity cases. Eleanor went to the city herself and got them, and had them charged to her father at a most expensive place where he had never had a charge account before. He was vexed almost beyond endurance.

All these things were accomplished finally as Eleanor desired, in very self-protection for the family, for Eleanor wept and wailed her way through till she got what she wanted, silk and satin and lace, flowers and ribbon and frills.

"Vanity of vanities, all is vanity," quoted Euphemia as she surveyed the house two nights before the wedding. "And what is going to happen after it's all over?"

Eleanor was marrying a man from another state, and a number of his relatives came to the wedding. Eleanor demanded that a good many of them be entertained at the house. There seemed to be no end to the things that Eleanor wanted. Wouldn't it ever be over? Euphemia wearily wondered, as she toiled down to the laundry and ironed a couple more old curtains for a window that had been forgotten in a room that had been hastily requisitioned for an extra guest room. Wearily she dragged herself up the steps again and found a rod and a hammer and screws and put up the curtains. She looked in on the array of handsome presents set out on their white-draped tables in the upstairs sitting room.

"Whatsoever things are lovely!" she quoted to herself, and

wondered if things like these counted in the scheme of life. Of course they did count, somehow, else God would not have made so many lovely things, but hadn't they somehow got out of proportion, sort of overrated their value? Weren't there other things that were lovelier and more lasting? Euphemia was too tired to philosophize about it.

She saw her mother dragging up the stairs just then, looking old and tired to death. And forgetting her own weariness she flew down, and gathering her little mother in her strong arms, she carried her up and put her down on her bed.

"Now Mother dear!" she said, stooping to kiss the tired brow, "you're not to get up until early morning. No"—as her mother tried to rise—"I don't care how many things you have left undone; you are not to stir until morning. Wedding or no wedding, guests or no guests, you have got to rest."

She helped her mother undress, in spite of protests, and put her inside the sheets, turned down the light, and closed the door. Fifteen minutes later the bride burst into the house and stirred them all up again. She woke her mother from the exhausted sleep into which she had sunk at once, with the startling announcement that Everett's great uncle (Everett was the name of the bridegroom) was stopping off on his way to California and wanted to meet her parents and see the presents. No, he couldn't stay overnight. He had to catch the midnight express to meet an appointment, but he was bringing a set of solid silver salt and pepper shakers, and her mother simply must get up and meet him.

Euphemia protested, and even tried to frighten her sister by saying that their mother would not be able to go to the wedding if she did not get some rest. But Eleanor swept her aside and dashed into her mother's room, switching on both lights and deluging her startled mother with the whole story in a breath.

"You must put on your violet silk, Mother. He won't be here to the wedding and he won't know it is *the* dress. I want you to appear at your best. I'll get my curling iron and fix your hair. You'll have to hurry like the dickens. Everett only got the telegram ten minutes ago. He's driven right down to meet him, and the train is due in about five minutes. Everett is *very* particular about him. He wanted me to make you understand that. He is *very* rich, you know."

Half bewildered and sodden with weariness, Mrs. Martin dragged herself up and let them dress her.

Euphemia, with set lips, went about getting her things and putting up her hair, while Eleanor sat down and hurried them like a bumblebee.

When the car drove up, their mother lay back in the big chair in the living room, looking pale and spent in her pretty new dress. Euphemia was so worried about her and so angry at her sister for being so inconsiderate, that she very nearly said some sharp things to Eleanor. Eleanor acted almost as if it didn't matter at all whether or not there was any mother left after the wedding was over.

But Eleanor would not have heard even if she had said the words that sprang to her lips. She was fluttering to the door to meet the guest.

And after all, the great uncle was deaf and indifferent and nearsighted, and didn't even seem to see their mother, merely acknowledging the introduction haughtily and passing on to the room where the presents were spread out.

Euphemia hurried her mother back to bed as soon as they were gone, thankful that Eleanor had gone down to the midnight train with them to see the disagreeable uncle off again.

Euphemia, the next night, in her golden draperies, her arms full of yellow expensive roses, walking slowly, steadily, up the church aisle as maid of honor, studied the solid flabby face of the bridegroom and wondered what Eleanor saw in him to make her willing to sacrifice her whole family to please his dictatorial fancy. If Everett wanted to do expensive things for Eleanor after she was married, that was all right, but he had no right to insist on Eleanor's family mortgaging their very souls to make his wedding appear great before his friends and family.

Coolly she walked up the aisle, her regal head lifted, her face full of something that seemed to lift her above the rest of the procession and make people look at her rather than watch for the bride. "Just look at Euphemia," they whispered. "Isn't she beautiful! She's prettier than her sister."

But Euphemia was looking her future brother-in-law over and weighing him in the balance as it were, in the light of his actions during the past weeks, and she was sorry for her sister. That selfish little puckered mouth, those expressionless eyes set too close together, the characterless chin. What had been his power over Eleanor? Was it his reputed wealth? She almost shivered at the thought as she drew nearer to the waiting bridegroom, and dropped her eyes to her flowers, taking her place at one side to await the bride. A wave of thankfulness went over her that it was not herself who was being married to Everett Wilcox. Would Eleanor be happy? Oh, would she? She had never been happy at home, although she had always got almost everything she cried for. But if one might judge from that stubborn, selfish mouth, Everett would never be one to give in to weeping. Poor Eleanor. For all that, disagreeable as she had been, Eleanor was her sister and she loved her.

As the awesome words of the marriage ceremony went forward, Euphemia's thoughts followed them tremulously. Such terrible things to promise, if one were not *sure*. How could Eleanor promise all those things for Everett? Her very soul revolted at the thought. She felt sure that she herself would never be married. There would never be anyone who would care for her, who would be wise enough and great enough and dear enough to give one's self to in such solemn pledges.

She came out from the ceremony with a saddened heart. It seemed as if they had just handed Eleanor over to suffer somehow. She could not get away from the thought. Strange that this feeling should have come down upon her so suddenly. Perhaps it was because she had been too busy before to realize that her sister was going out from the household forever.

It was over at last, the showers of rose leaves and rice, the white ribbons on the car, and the shouts and shrieks as the couple made their way to escape. The last guest was gone at last, the last hired servant paid, and the door locked. Euphemia turned to see her little frail mother sink suddenly down in her silken garments, a small, pathetic heap of orchid silk with a pale, white face above it.

She cried out as she sprang to kneel by her side, and her father rushed to them and knelt on the other side, his face ashen-gray in the garish light of the rooms still decorated for the wedding with flowers he could ill afford.

They got her to bed and telephoned for the doctor, but it was almost morning before they settled down to get any rest themselves. Even then they hardly dared to sleep, for their hearts were so anxious.

The next morning Mrs. Martin tried to get up, but found she could not. She said she was only tired and would get up in a little while, but when the doctor came in a little later, he wore an anxious look and asked a great many questions and commanded that she lie still for several days.

The several days stretched into a week, and then two, and three, and still she was unable to get up and go about.

At first the doctor talked cheerfully enough, saying she needed a good long rest, but as the weeks went by, it became evident that the trouble was more deep-seated than they expected. The poor nerves which had stretched and stretched until they almost snapped did not react, and Euphemia and her father gradually began to realize that the mother who had carried all their burdens and smoothed all their ways was down and out. And it was a serious question whether she would recover at all.

The knowledge of it came upon Euphemia like a crushing blow after the long hard going, for there was the house to be kept, and the poor servant utterly unable to cope with the situation, to say nothing of the mending and cleaning and baking, and the four-year-old baby to look after every hour in the day. There was her mother to be cared for like a baby herself; and there must be the most tender care, or she might slip away from them in a breath.

Mrs. Martin seemed satisfied only when Euphemia was with her. Of course a trained nurse might have relieved the situation greatly, but there was Mr. Martin harassed with a business crisis, submerged in debt, and struggling to pay some of the enormous bills that Eleanor had contracted for the wedding. The plain fact was they could not afford a nurse. And there was John, older, of course, a little, but still full of noise and mischief, and seemingly eager to coast down every wrong pathway of life that presented itself to his willing feet. More than half of their mother's burden had been this same John, whose companions and habits had been for two years past wholly unsatisfactory and the last few months a plain daily anxiety. Something must be done for John. There was no end. And nobody but herself to fill the breach and bear all the burden. And there were her beloved books and her dreams of college by and by, and a wider sphere, although there was no need to complain of the narrowness of her sphere just now. It seemed to embrace almost every class and variety of work.

She sat in her room and thought about it awhile after the doctor had gone, when her mother and the restless four-year-old were asleep. "Whatsoever things are true, whatsoever things are lovely, if there be any virtue, and if there be any praise," kept going over and over in her mind. She was accustomed by this time to putting all her actions to that Philippian test. She knelt to pray and rose to shut her hopes and her books away in her closet and turn the key. Then she went down to her daily duties. This time she did not find the cat and the baby in the flypaper, but she found dismay and dreariness, for mother was upstairs sick, shut away from the household troubles. Mother could not bind up a cut finger, nor kiss a bumped head, nor get a boy bread and jelly when he was hungry, and the worst of it all was that there was uncertainty how long this terrible state of things might last. The young hearts whose heaven was Mother's face could not see any light.

Then Euphemia found that she could comfort; she could think to do this thing and plan for that thing and give up her own ways and plans; teach a spelling lesson to one, tell a story to another, and yet with the help of God keep patient and sweet through it all.

She still kept her little time by herself alone to commune with Jesus, or she could not have done it. Here she brought all her troubles and worries to think about. Sometimes it seemed so strange to her to think her life, that had always somehow been under a sort of cloud, was cut off from things that other girls had. She would go back in her memory often to that lovely day and that ride when she met Lawrence Earle and recall the only really grown-up pleasure she had ever had in all her young womanhood, and wonder if it would always be the only one. Very likely it would, because she was growing old so fast. Poor child! She felt almost gray-haired.

But she did not sigh after those things long. Perhaps it would have been harder for her if she had been accustomed to going out a great deal. She was so continually busy and so really interested in her daily round that she had not time to be sad-hearted now. She sometimes got out her books, too, for after the first few months of self-abnegation, she saw that it was not necessary for her to sacrifice all her reading and study, and so she was not growing stupid. Sometimes when all was quiet and dark, she would wonder to herself if the only person besides her mother who had ever promised to pray for her had forgotten. Probably he had long ago forgotten her existence. It was a year since she had received even a postcard from him. She was not even sure in what land he was at present exiled. If he thought of her at all, he probably remembered her only as a disagreeable little girl whom he had tried to help to peace and happiness. And how wonderfully he had done it! If his witnessing in foreign lands for the rest of his life brought no results, he yet might count a humble star in his crown for the light he had brought into her discontented young heart. She would bless him always for it.

And what would she have done under this crisis if she had not found a refuge and stronghold in Christ? Surely the prayers of Lawrence Earle had been what had kept her from slipping away from God during those first months when she had been so discouraged, and perhaps they were helping even now. It gave her comfort to think that this was so and to feel that somewhere, somehow, she had an earthly friend, as well as a heavenly, who would at least care and pray for her, if he knew her need. Then she would drop softly asleep and waken to another day full of labor and sunshine, for she was the sunshine of her mother's room.

Chapter 14

Mrs. Martin went down to the verge of the grave and lingered for weeks, merging into months, but at last, slowly, gradually, so gradually that they could hardly be sure from day to day whether it was true or not, she began to creep back to them again. To take a little interest in their coming back and forth to her room, tiptoeing in with bated breath to watch her quiet face upon the pillow; to open her eyes and smile; to lift her head one morning for a flower that Euphemia brought in, and then to ask after the baby and want to see him.

Eleanor had not come home. They had not told her how ill her mother was. The doctor said it would not do for her to have the excitement of Eleanor's coming.

Eleanor was "doing" the West in a wildly exciting wedding trip with all the accessories that money could provide. She wrote brief, breezy occasional postals home, saying very little and conveying less. Euphemia seemed to feel an undertone of discontent even yet, and wondered, but there was little time to think of Eleanor.

Her mother was coming back to them, from the grave, and Euphemia's heart was full of deep, sweet joy. God had heard her prayer. Almost with awe she gave thanks. It seemed that she had come very close to Christ during her time of trial and was coming to trust Him more and more restfully.

The day that her mother was first able to sit up for a little while was like a grand holiday. Father came home and sat with her and brought roses! The kind he used to bring Mother when he was courting her. And Euphemia noticed with another thrill of joy that the worn look was passing from his face, and his tired eyes were lit with new hope.

"Well," he said, after he had sat for a while holding his wife's hand and looking at her hungrily. "Mother, I guess it won't do you any harm to know we're going to pull through in the business now."

"Really?" said Euphemia, springing softly up and coming to lay her hand on her father's shoulder.

"Yes, we signed the big contract today. We get it all, and it means that by this time next year, we'll be entirely out of the hole. We are practically now, only the money won't all come in at once. But we're standing on firm ground at last, thank God. And Euphemia, little daughter," he added, turning to the girl, "it's partly due to you. There was a time just after Mother took sick when I thought I couldn't weather it. And then you took hold and lifted burden after burden from my shoulders. And you stayed at home from college, and saved all that expense, and cut down the expenses here at home, and saved Mother for me. Little girl, I never can tell you what you have been to me, to your mother, to John, and to the baby and all of us! You are a daughter such as no father and mother ever had before. Isn't she, Mother?"

And the mother's eyes lighted with the old sweet light as she said tenderly, "She's all of that and more."

Euphemia thought that her cup of joy was filled, but her father went on.

"There's another thing, Daughter, too, that I must mention while I'm singing your praises. I want Mother to know what you have done for John. Mother knows how anxious we were about him. He had got going with a bad crowd and it seemed as if nothing could stop him, but somehow you have woven an influence about him that has pulled him away from it all. He came down to the office today and told me he wanted me to take him in and train him for a partnership. He wanted to begin at the bottom and go up as fast as he was able. And I told him I'd be glad to. It will be better for him than fooling his time away at college the way he did last year. And I think he really means business. I'd have been glad to have him have the rest of his college course, but he says, and I agree with him, that he can go and take the rest of his course later if he finds he needs it. It's never too late to study. And he knows I cannot afford to send him just now. He says when he goes he's going on his own money. And I feel that is the right spirit. But I think his change of attitude is all due to his sister!"

It was sweet living those days, with Mother coming back fast to daily life now, and the spring coming on, and all the good things her father had said to think about. And Euphemia went about with a continual smile upon her lips.

And then, one day when Euphemia was walking home from an errand with her hands full of lilacs that a neighbor had sent to her mother, she noticed that the windows of the Earle house were open at last, and a few minutes later met another neighbor who told her that Mrs. Earle was returning that afternoon.

Euphemia came home with her eyes bright with the news. She wondered to herself many things. Would Lawrence Earle come, too? Probably not. She knew that his mother had been during the past year in California again with her invalid sister, and that the sister was not expected to live long. That was the news that had drifted back to the hometown. In a general way, Lawrence Earle was supposed still to be in foreign lands pursuing an occupation which the town was beginning to call by the name of "missionary." Some new kind of missionary, they said he was, doing something about Bible teaching.

Mrs. Earle had indeed returned and began at once to set her house in order, and it began to be rumored that her son was coming later and would perhaps spend the whole summer with her. The story drifted out and around, without Mrs. Earle's having even dropped a hint of any such thing. But some of her neighbors gathered, perhaps from things she had not said, that her son was going to bring someone home with him, presumably his bride. The suppositions grew to the proportions of confident statement and were spread abroad as such. They came to Euphemia Martin's ears. Now Euphemia Martin was too happy over her mother's recovery to be other than glad over anything, and when she thought about this report at all, she wondered if Lawrence Earle's wife would be one in whom she could confide. Of course she would, she told herself, for he would choose no other than a good and true and lovely woman. And so in her heart she liked to think the coming Mrs. Earle would be a friend of hers. She held Lawrence Earle in a kind of awe, as someone higher than the ordinary mortal, who had condescended for a little time to help her. He had forgotten her long ago, but she would always revere him. Euphemia would always be of humble mind after that severe experience she had had of seeing herself as others saw her.

One bright spring morning, when Mrs. Martin was feeling quite well and was able to be about the house once more, doing what little her efficient daughter had left for her to do of household tasks, Euphemia picked a great bunch of fragrant violets from the bank in their backyard, and with heart throbbing over her temerity and cheeks flushed slightly from the excitement of what she was about to do, went timidly to call on Mrs. Earle and leave her gift of violets.

She had a pleasant call. It seemed delightful to her. Mrs. Earle put her arms about her, drew her gently in, and called her "my dear." It all seemed very, very charming. Euphemia wished she had ventured before, and was even moved to ask some questions that in times past had troubled her so much, and which on account of her mother's illness she had been obliged to solve without a counselor. Before she went home, Mrs. Earle showed her some photographs of her son and several pictures taken during their trips abroad. In two or three of them there were other friends, whom Mrs. Earle said had been traveling with them. One sweet-faced girl was among those. Euphemia wondered if that was the coming Mrs. Earle, Jr., but lacked the courage to ask. She carried the vision of that face home with her and began to make a friend of it at once. Mrs. Earle asked her to come again, and there was begun a friendship, which to both became very pleasant. Thus the springtime passed and summer was already at hand, and scarcely a day went by but Mrs. Earle ran over to bring some delicacy to her old friend, Mrs. Martin, or Euphemia ran in to take some message from her mother. The old friendship was renewed and knit the closer between the two older women because the young girl was so dear to them both.

And nearer and nearer drew the day for the homecoming of the son, but Euphemia somehow was strangely silent when the mother spoke of him. It seemed a subject in which she now had no part, save as an onlooker. A glad one, of course, but still a mere outsider.

Chapter 15

Lawrence Earle boarded the New York Express, and after settling himself comfortably, took an unopened letter from his pocket.
It was from his mother and had arrived just as he was leaving for
the station. Being attended by a friend with whom he had spent
the night in New York, he had put the letter by until he was at leisure
on the train. He leaned back to enjoy it. His mother's letters were
always a luxury. He read on through page after page of the closely
written letter, smiling here and there at some sentence or expression
that sounded so like his mother. He was greatly amused at the story
she had to tell him of his supposed marriage, and stopped in his
reading several times to look out of the window and laugh heartily.
His mother had much talent in describing the words and tones of
some of her many curious neighbors, and her son enjoyed her bits of
quaint humor.

"They've settled it all, my son, even down to the bride, and whether she is to have charge of the house or not. I don't know what they will say when you come home without her. And I must say, my boy, though I know I should lose much of your precious society and be no longer first in your thoughts as I have been, that I could wish it were true. For you know, I cannot always stay with you, and you are getting to be 'quite a man.'"

At that sentence the young man smiled, while yet the moisture gathered in his eyes, and a tender expression about his mouth.

The quotation was from the oft-spoken comment of an old neighbor who used to annoy him when he was a child by always telling him that he was getting to be "quite a man." When his mother wanted to be playful she often used the phrase. There followed some words about a certain young woman they had met abroad, and he stopped his reading once more to look thoughtfully out of the window. But at last he seemed to shake his head slightly and went back seriously to his letter. There was a description of the changes she had made in certain rooms and of repairs and additions she thought it would be pleasant to make. There were little items of pleasantry about the town and the people. She told of the changes in certain families during their absence. "But there is no one who has changed more and for the better than your little friend. You will remember her, Euphemia Martin. She called to see me soon after my return in the spring. She seems to be a very lovable girl. I hear good things of her on every side. She has not only beauty, but character in her face, and not only that, but chastened, sweetened character. She is one of Christ's own children. I liked her sweet and gentle manners and her neat and graceful dress. She certainly has grown into a lovely girl and is going to be another such as her mother was before her. Her mother was a beautiful woman before she took upon her heavier cares than she was able to bear. She, by the way, has been very ill for the past two years, and Euphemia has become the mainstay of the home and the very life of her mother. I am really growing extravagantly fond of her. I had no idea she would ever develop into such a lovely character. Some people used not to like her, and now everyone in town has a good word for her. The pretty sister, Eleanor, whom I always thought looked selfish, you remember, has married and gone to California to live. And to tell you the truth, I am thankful for I was always afraid you would become fond of her. You thought so much of the older sister Margaret when you were a mere boy. But Eleanor was no more like Margaret than night is like day. Euphemia seems to be more like Margaret, yet with an added charm which I cannot quite describe. You will have to see her to understand."

The letter went on to mention other friends or neighbors.

"Maud Bradley married a movie actor, and there are rumors that she is very unhappy and thinking of applying for a divorce. Ethel Garner and her sister, Flora, are both married and gone— Ethel to New England, Flora to live in the south, Virginia, I think. Janet Chipley was killed in an automobile accident. Her little sister, Bessie, you remember, with whom you used to play tennis, has grown into a pert little upstart of the modern times, with her hair cut close like a boy and an impudent, loaferish way of intruding herself into the public eye. She is very pretty, but exceedingly unpleasant to watch. She seems to have lost all sense of all the graces of womanhood.

"Do you remember a flashy little girl with copper-colored hair who used to wear bright yellow and burnt orange so much? Her name is Cornelia Gibson. She married your friend John Babcock.

I think they ran away and got married, and John's father was so upset by the affair that he had a stroke of paralysis and has never been able to get around since. I understand that Cornelia is making John very unhappy. John looks twenty years older than when you saw him last. His hair is beginning to turn gray. He will be glad to see you again. He looks so wistful I feel sorry for him. I thought you ought to understand the situation before you see him. What a pity he could not have married someone like Euphemia Martin instead of that heartless little flirt!"

There was more in the same strain about other friends and neighbors, and a page telling how happy she was to have her son coming home at last to stay in his own country, and how delighted she was that he was to be employed in the Lord's service in a great work that was opening up.

When Lawrence Earle had finished reading, he folded the letter thoughtfully and put it into his pocket.

All the time he had been reading he had been conscious of a pair of scrutinizing eyes turned upon him by a grizzled old man who sat across the aisle. He had been so occupied that he did not look at the man until the letter was folded and put back in his pocket. And then he became aware of that steady gaze once more and instantly recognized an old farmer from near his native town. Lawrence Earle, as a little boy, had many a time hitched his sled to this man's load of wood. He rose and went to him at once, and the man seemed pleased beyond measure.

"Wal, yas," he said, "I am a good piece out o' my way. Been up to Bawson to my brother's funeral. I calc'lated to git back yesterday, but couldn't settle up things in time. I be'n a-settin' here spec'latin' on whether this was you or not. You seem to have growed some, and yit you ain't changed so much, after all."

The old man eyed the clean-shaven, tanned face before him with keen satisfaction. There was something about Lawrence Earle that was most winning. The old man was tremendously flattered that he had come over to speak to him, and that he had remembered who he was. There were not so many young men in these days who bothered to talk to plain old men. But Lawrence Earle always was somehow different from the other boys. The old man grew talkative, giving bits of information about the changes in the hometown; how the courthouse had been torn down at last and a new one built: how the Presbyterian church had a new tower for the chimes that Mr. Blakesley had given in memory of his wife; how they were building two new public schools to accommodate the children; how the old political boss was dead and the new one had no use for farmers and was doing all he could against the farm bills they were trying to get through.

Then he relapsed into gossip about the townspeople.

"And there is that youngest Martin gal; they used to call her Effie. There ain't anybody more changed than she. She's growed up strong and straight as a young saplin', and she ain't lost none of her sooppleness either; she can pitch a baseball as good as ever. I seen her do it last week at the church picnic. She's just as fine, an' purty and healthy-lookin' as ever, spite of having nursed her mother through a long sickness for nigh about three years, and took care of the house and her father and all. She'd be affine wife for some young feller. Why, sir, that gal was jes' the mainstay o' that family. Her pa, he couldn't akep' up nohow, with his wife down with nervous prostration for two year goin' on three, if that gal hedn't a done fer him and cheered him up. They do say she's done ez well ez her mother could by them boys, too, and her a little slip of a thing that hed never done a thing but play, when her mother was took sick."

The young man went back to his seat after a time and mused on what he had heard. So the little girl had been thinking on those things of good report all these years, and had found the virtue and the praise.

At New York he changed for his homeward-bound train, and here again he met a friend, a clerk in the home bank, on his way back from business in New York. They talked together a few moments while they waited for the train to be called. "Speaking of changes," said young Brownleigh, "do you remember a little Martin girl, a regular tomboy? Effie, they called her. Well, sir, you wouldn't know that girl now. She dresses plain, but awfully neat and well fitting, and they say she makes all her own clothes, too. Oh, yes, she's good, too, altogether too good for comfort! But a fellow would almost be willing to be good to get a girl like that to smile on him."

Lawrence Earle listened in wonder and a growing delight. How strange it was that he should begin to hear Euphemia's praises sounded the moment he came near the hometown!

And then, at the station, he was met by an eager group of very young girls, headed by his own little cousin, among them the Bessie Chipley of whom his mother had written. There was a small Garner girl and a small Bradley sister and a number of other children who were mere tots when he went away. They surrounded him noisily and demanded that he make a "date" with them at once before any of the older girls had a chance to invite him. They considered that he was their own property, their friend of the years. One would have thought to hear them talk that he was to have nothing else to do but attend parties and rides. They talked eagerly and all at once. He felt that same note of hardness in their speech that his mother had deplored. Yet they were still children. Perhaps they could be helped back to things clean and fine. He thought of Euphemia, and just then his cousin spoke of her, eagerly, almost out of breath in her excitement.

"If we can only get Euphemia to go with us tomorrow. She always makes things move so smoothly, and looks out for everything, and you don't have to do a thing but have a good time. Everybody likes her, too, and you'll be crazy about her. Do you remember her? She's the youngest Martin girl. The only thing is, everybody is after her. I don't know whether she can spare the time."

Lawrence Earle paused in the framing of an excuse for not going on the ride, and with sudden interest in the affair and a new light in his eyes, said, "Yes, by all means, Louise, get Euphemia to go!"

THE PATCH
OF BLUE

Chapter 1

New York City, Fall 1932

Christopher Walton closed the hymn book, put it in the rack, carefully adjusted his mother's wrap on her shoulders as she sat down, arranged the footstool at her feet comfortably, and then sat back and prepared to get himself through the boredom of the sermon time.

Chris had no idea of trying to listen to the sermon. He never even pretended to himself that he was listening. He carried his tall, good-looking self to church regularly because it was the thing required by both Father and Mother that the household should attend church; but his soul was far away as possible from the dim religious light of the sanctuary. Nobody suspected, of course, that behind his handsome, polite exterior, the world was rushing cheerfully on in his thoughts. It would have been a most astonishing thing if the world in which his thoughts were reveling could have suddenly appeared in church. It would have created quite an uproar.

Sometimes it was a football game with the grandstand rooting wildly, and he himself making a glorious touchdown. Sometimes it was a party he had attended the night before, with jazzy music stealing all through his thoughts. Sometimes it was a medley of his own plans for life, when he saw himself alternately writing a book that should set the world on fire; or becoming a central figure on the floor of the stock exchange; or again, a wealthy stockbroker who would finally get to the place where he could give great sums to charity and education.

But none of these things figured in his thoughts this morning. His mind was full of college. Three weeks more and he expected to be gone from this pew, gone back to college life. He drew a breath of secret satisfaction as he remembered that a college student could do as he pleased about attending divine service. If he had important lessons to study, or wasn't feeling up to the mark, he could just stay away. There would be no compulsion. Oh, of course, there was no real compulsion at home. Nobody would have forced him to go if he had taken a grand stand against it perhaps; yet his father's expectation and the grieved look in his mother's eyes were as good as a law to him, and he would have felt most uncomfortable and out of harmony with his family if he had attempted to cut church here. And Chris loved his family. He enjoyed pleasing his father and mother, even though it was sometimes a bore.

His father was getting old, he reflected with a pang. His hair was deeply silvered. There were heavier lines coming into his kindly face. Chris was still a little anxious over the look that had come into his face at the breakfast table, as he finally yielded to their pleas that he stay at home this morning and nurse up the binding headache that had made it impossible for him to eat his breakfast.

Chris settled back comfortably in his father's place at the head of the cushioned pew and reflected briefly on what a pleasant family he had. Nothing must ever be allowed to happen to his family! He paid them each brief tribute. Such a sweet mother, natural pink in her cheeks and a delicate look of refinement and peace about her. His sister, Elise, pretty and stylish and smart. She was off at a weekend house party today, and he missed her from her corner of the pew. They had always been good comrades. He was going to miss her when he went back to college.

College! Ah, now he was off! College! It would be his senior year. It was going to be great! Dad had been just wonderful about it. He had arranged to have him take one of the very best rooms in the whole dorm. And it was practically settled that Walt Gillespie was to be his roommate in place of that dub, Chad Harmon. They were to have a suite—two bedrooms and a spacious sitting room between. Of course, there were many students who couldn't afford an outfit like that. And Mother had given up one of her finest oriental rugs, the one he had always admired the most, for his floor. Of course, she would have to buy a new one in its place, but he knew she loved this blue one, yet wanted him to have it. She said they wanted his last year to be the best of all. Then Dad was making a generous donation to their new fraternity building, and there had been a hint dropped that he would be suggested for president of their chapter next semester. Dad had been awfully generous in the way of money, too. Said he wanted him to have everything during his college life because one went to college only once. Dad had been pleased that he had been popular in his father's fraternity. Of course, it was Dad's influence that had gotten him in here at all, right at the first. They were a terribly exclusive bunch. It was wonderful having a father who was well off and able to put one into the front ranks of things.

And then, the crowning joy of all, Dad was going to let him have a car, one of the very best to take him. He had picked it out and it was coming tomorrow morning. He was to take it out on a trial trip alone and try it out thoroughly before the final deal was made. But it was practically bought already, for he was sure he would find nothing wrong with it. It was a great car.

The shining new car, in all its glory of flashing chrome and deep blue body, rolled slowly down the aisle, past his pew, and let him study it as the minister rose in the pulpit to announce and introduce a visiting preacher that morning. Chris was so interested in his car that he hardly heard what was going on, scarcely noticed the stranger on the platform.

Chris was thinking how he would take Gilda Carson out for a ride tomorrow after he had had a good long tour by himself. Gilda was rather snobbish and always boasting about Bob Tyson's car and how he had taken her here and there. But Bob Tyson's car wasn't worth mentioning in the same breath with his new one. Gilda would boast about his now, he was sure.

Not that he cared so much what Gilda thought or did. She wasn't especially his girl, but it had been a bit irksome having her always talking about Bob's wonderful car. Well there wasn't going to be anything wrong with his new car. It was a wonder. Such a purring engine, free-wheeling, adjustable seats, marvelous shock absorbers, and above all, speed! The car was doing eighty and even ninety now, up and down the stately aisles of the church, and Chris sat with a saint-like expression on his face and watched it. He almost wondered that the people about him did not turn and look after it in admiration.

Suddenly a new voice broke into his meditations. The minister had introduced the stranger.

He was announcing his text now—two texts. "Oh give thanks unto the Lord for He is good!" and "How can we sing the Lord's song in a strange land?"

Chris recognized the first text as a part of the responsive reading they had just had, but the second seemed a little bit out of the ordinary, and he wondered idly what it could possibly have to do with the first. The opening words of the preacher's sermon arrested his attention for an instant.

"It is easy enough to thank God when everything is going well and we have all that we want in our lives. The true test of a thankful heart is to be able to sing praise when things are going all wrong. When we have lost our money or our friends or are disappointed in our dearest ambitions, or when we are in a strange, unhappy environment, then we cry out, 'How can we sing the Lord's song in a strange land?'"

That was about all Chris heard of that sermon, and he only wondered idly a moment about it before he drifted back into his own thoughts. He averred to himself that, of course, it was ridiculous to expect anybody to be thankful for sorrow and disaster, for poverty and sickness and loss. The minister seemed to be giving an instance of someone who had said he was grateful for every trouble that had ever come to him, and through his disappointments had learned to praise the Lord for every one. Well, that was absurd. No one could thank the Lord for unhappiness. He was thankful that his life was laid in pleasant surroundings, and he paused long enough in his reflections to give a quick thanksgiving for his home, his parents, his pleasant environment, the happy college days that still lay before him, his new car. And then he was off again into the anticipations of his senior year at college and what he had to do before he went back. He tabulated different items mentally on his fingers, things he must not forget. Not the least among them was the trial of the new car tomorrow, and presently the car was rolling up and down the aisle again before his happy vision, and the minister with his absurd message about being glad for unhappiness was utterly forgotten.

He had arranged a full schedule for the next few days when, at last, the closing hymn was announced, and he found the place for his mother and arose with relief to join in the hymn of praise. He noticed, with a vague annoyance, there was a line in the hymn that conveyed that same illogical suggestion about giving thanks for trouble that the minister had suggested in the beginning of his sermon. But he raised his voice a little louder when it came to the refrain of praise and steadily thought of all the thrilling joys of his own life with true thanksgiving. He certainly was grateful that the lines had fallen to him in such pleasant places, and just now he was, more than all, grateful the service was over and he would soon be free to go back to the delightful details of everyday living.

Out in the lovely summer day at last, he drew a breath of relief and began to talk eagerly to his mother about the new curtains she was going to select the next day for his college room. He had decided ideas of just what he wanted, built upon a college room of a famous athlete he had seen last spring.

Chris was glad his father's headache seemed to be better and that the dinner table was a cheerful place, with all the things he liked best to eat. His father seemed a bit grave and silent, but he attributed that to the headache, for he responded smiling to anything that was said. Chris tried to persuade himself that he had only imagined those lines of care on his father's face. He talked eagerly of his new car, and his father seemed pleased and promised to take a drive with him if he would come down to the bank between eleven and twelve o'clock the next day.

Monday morning, Chris came whistling down the stairs with a light in his eyes. His mother stood in the hall just below him, and he paused at the foot of the stairs to stoop and touch a light kiss on her forehead. Such a pretty little mother! But he knew just what she was going to say, and he wished to forestall it. She was a little peach of a mother, of course, but she always had been afraid of things, and he was so full of his own joy this morning that he felt a little impatient toward her fears.

"Oh, Chris, you will be careful, won't you?" she implored, just as he had known she would do.

"Sure, Muzzie. I'm always careful. Why, what's the idea? You act as though I had never driven before."

"But, a new car, Chris, that's different. You don't know how it will act. And a new kind that you have never driven before. That free-wheeling. I'm afraid of it. You don't know how to work it. They tell me it's quite different from other driving. I wish you'd take a serviceman along with you the first day or two."

Chris laughed cheerfully.

"Well, I like that! A serviceman! I think I see myself. Why, Mud, you know Uncle Eben's car was just like this one, and I drove it for him all the time he was here, every day for two weeks. But, Mother, seriously, you must stop worrying about me. I'm not a kid anymore. I'm a man. This is my last year at college, remember.

And besides, there isn't a car made that I can't drive. Why do you suppose I've hung around Ross Barton's garage all these years, if not for that? I'm considered a good driver. Why don't you go along with me and prove it? I'll give you a good ride and leave you wherever you say, then you will have more confidence in me."

"Oh, I can't, Chris, I have a committee meeting here at the house this morning. But you won't be late for lunch, will you? You know I'll be worried."

The boy stooped and silenced her with a real kiss on her soft, anxious lips, now.

"Now, look here, Mother," he said earnestly, "you've just got to stop worrying. You're just making trouble for yourself. Besides, I'm stopping at the bank at eleven for Father, and you know he'll come back on time. You've got him well trained. Sure you don't want to go along, just for a little spin? Well, come on out and look at the car, anyway. Did you see it yet from the window? Look!"

He flung the front door open.

"There! Isn't that a winner! Isn't it the niftiest car you ever saw? Long, clean, sporty lines. Dad was great to do all this for me. It's going to make all the difference in the world in my college life, having this car."

His mother smiled indulgently with a wistful look in her eyes and patted his arm.

"Your father feels that you deserve it, Chris," she said lovingly. "We want you to get the greatest enjoyment possible out of your last year in college."

She stood in the open doorway and watched him drive away, thinking what a happy lot was hers with such a son. Then she turned with a bit of a sigh of anxiety, and yet a smile, and went back to her pleasant, sheltered life, thinking how good God had been to her.

Chris drove out into the clear September morning, his face alight with satisfaction. Down through the pleasant village street of the pretty suburb where he had been born. He wanted, first of all, to ride around the old familiar streets and get used to the idea that this wonderful car was his.

As he thrilled to the touch of the new wheel, he remembered that first old Ford he had bought for ten dollars. He had to tinker with it for three weeks before it would run. He had never been so happy with it then, till the kindly policeman who had known him all his young life stopped him because he was too young to drive and had no license. But he never dreamed that day that only a few years more and he would be driving one of the best cars that was made, and thrilling to the thought that it was all his own.

It was practically his own now. Dad would see to the red tape of the purchase tomorrow morning. He had promised. And then he would drive it back to the home garage, and it would be his. It made him feel like a man to think of it. He had a sudden memory of his express wagon, and how serious life had looked to him as he had taken it out on that first morning after Christmas, on the street, and showed it to his playmates. And his first bicycle! Dad had always been so good to him, getting him everything he wanted. How he loved that wheel!

But boy! It had been nothing like this first car! This was great!

Skimming along with the top down and the wind in his hair! There was nothing like it!

He was skirting the edge of the little grove just outside of town now, where they used to have the high school picnics. The trees were golden, with here and there a vivid coral one. They were early in turning. The yellow leaves against the blue of the autumn sky filled him with an ecstasy. He wished he had someone to talk to who would understand, yet he felt that it would be impossible to put into words what he was feeling. College and car and the glory of the day all mixed up in his soul. Boy! It was great!

He whirled back into town again and traversed the streets, going slowly by his own house and waving to his mother, whose face he could see at the window, just to give her confidence in his driving. His mother waved back to him. She was a great little mother. She was a pretty good sport after all, fearful as she was. Some mothers would have made a terrible kick at having their sons go off to college with a high-powered car. Mothers were always so afraid of accidents.

There was Natalie Halsey. He would pick her up and take her for a spin. She had her arms full of bundles and would perhaps be glad of the lift. He had never had much to do with Natalie, although they had been in the same class in high school. She was a quiet, shy girl, always hurrying off home right after school and never going to any parties or high school affairs, a bit shabby, too, with very few friends among the high school clique. Had he heard that her father died this summer? He wasn't quite sure. It would be better not to mention it. He hadn't seen Natalie for a year or two. He couldn't remember when it was.

He drew up alongside the girl and called out, "Hello, Natalie, want a ride? I'm going your way."

Natalie turned with a delighted smile and surrendered heavy bundles as he sprang and took them from her.

"That will be wonderful!" she said, turning a tired smile upon him, and he wondered that he had never noticed before what blue eyes she had. "I was just wondering whether I could get these things home. I twisted my arm yesterday, and it aches so I could hardly hold on to everything."

"You oughtn't to try to carry such loads," reproved Chris in a grown-up tone. "Why didn't you have them sent?"

"Well, you see, the grocery stores don't deliver," said Natalie frankly, "and we can't afford to go to any other." She laughed cheerfully as if it were a joke, and he looked at her with a wondering pity. He had never realized before that people who were decent at all had to consider such trivial matters. It embarrassed him. He hastened to change the subject and took naturally the one uppermost in his mind, which was college.

"You're going back to college this fall, I suppose? I forget where you went."

Natalie laughed again, this time wistfully.

"No such luck for me," she said. "I went for two years to the university, but last year Mother was too sick to leave, and this year—well—I oughtn't to complain," she added brightly, "I've just got a job, and I'm very fortunate in these hard times."

"A job!" said Chris in dismay, and looked at her wonderingly. Why, she seemed just a kid out of high school. So slender and frail looking.

"You know my father died last spring," added Natalie sadly. "I needed a job badly."

"Oh, I'm sorry," said Chris. He felt he was making a bungle of things. He recalled suddenly that Natalie had not been at the high school commencement exercises three years ago. Someone had been sick. Her essay, which had received honorable mention, had been read by someone else. Poor kid! She must have been having a rotten time.

"I just got the job," confided Natalie, almost eagerly. "I'm to be cashier at the grocery store on the corner of Park Avenue. I'm so pleased."

There was a ringing to her voice that told of anxiety and need, and Chris looked at her wonderingly, pityingly.

"Oh, I say," said Chris, as they neared her home, "wouldn't you like to take a little spin? You don't have to go in yet, do you? I've just got this new car and I'm trying her out. Want to go?"

"Oh, I'd love to," said Natalie breathlessly, "but I've got to get home. You see, my mother's been very sick again, and I've left her all alone this morning. It was only a bad case of the flu, but she's very weak, and I don't like to leave her long. My sister had to go on an errand. But the car is wonderful, and I thank you for this much of a ride. I shall remember it a long time."

He helped her out and carried her bundles to the door of the plain little house for her, and suddenly thought of the contrast between this home and his own. There was something touching and lovely in the way Natalie thanked him. Her voice was sweet and womanly. He felt a deep discomfort at the thought that this pretty, frail girl had to work in a grocery store and make change for all kinds of people.

The discomfort lasted as he spun away from the door into the bright September day again. He half wished he had not picked Natalie up and got to know the unhappiness in her life. He couldn't do anything about it, of course.

He whirled into another street, and there was Betty Zane coming around the corner.

"Hello, Betts!" called Chris. "Wantta ride in my new buggy?"

"Oh boy! Do I?" replied Betty eagerly, clambering in without waiting for him to get out and help her, and they whirled away into the sunshine.

Betty was pretty and stylish and a great chatterbox. Betty admired the car and in the same breath told of one as wonderful that Bruce Carson had just bought. Betty had much gossip to tell of the different members of the old high school class, and she threw out hints as to parties that she might be induced to go to with the boy that got the earliest request. Betty talked of college and what she expected to do there, decried the fact that Chris was not attending a coeducational college where they might continue their acquaintance, openly said she would like more rides in his wonderful new roadster, and left him reluctantly when it was time for him to go for his father.

Chris had forgotten Natalie and her difficulties when he rode downtown toward his father's bank. His mind was full of the things that Betty Zane had told him. When he closed his eyes, he could see the bright red speck that had been Betty's little sharp painted lips and the dancing sarcastic eyes. He still heard ringing in his ears some of the flattery she had handed him. He knew that some of the things Betty had said had been bold, things his mother would not have liked. But, of course, Betty was a modern girl. Mother would have to learn that girls were not as they were when she was young. Then why should he suddenly think of Natalie? She was a girl more like the girls of his mother's day. But then that was probably because she had had no chance in life, no good times. She was old-fashioned, poor thing! But she was nice. Too bad she couldn't have had a better chance!

Then he turned downtown and made his way through increasing traffic toward his father's bank.

Within a half block of the bank he came to a traffic light. As he waited for it to change, he noticed an unusual jam in traffic and stretched his neck to discover the cause.

Then he saw a double line of people were blocking the sidewalk in front of the bank and surging out into the street, right in the way of traffic. What would it mean?

The light flashed green, and Chris moved on a few paces nearer to the scene of confusion. There must have been an accident. There were so many people and cars he could not see what was the matter.

Then as he drew nearer, he saw ugly, menacing faces in the crowd, and he heard a rough voice call out, "There he is, the son of the president, ridin' round in a five-thousand-dollar car, while we have to sweat fer our money!"

Then a kind of growl passed over the crowd like a roll of muffled thunder, and suddenly a little thickset man in the crowd picked up a brick from a pile along the curb where the road was being mended and hurled it straight at Chris. It crashed through the beautiful glass of the windshield, barely escaped hitting him in the temple, and glanced off through the open window at his left. Chris was too much astonished to even be frightened at first.

But the shattering glass had fallen among the crowd and cut hands and faces here and there, a bit got into someone's eye, and all was confusion. Fists were shaken in his face, angry threats were hurled at him, and Chris was hard put to know what to do, for the car was tight in traffic and he could not move it.

Then suddenly, he heard the voice of his friend the policeman at his left.

"Better get out of here quick, Chris," he said in a guarded voice. "Start yer engine. I'll make a way fer ya." And the mounted officer of the law rode fearlessly into the crowd, hitting this way and that with his club, till the mob separated enough for Chris to go through, escorted by two or three burly policemen who appeared out of the throng. They battled an opening through to the side street that led to the alley of the bank, but as they turned the corner Chris heard the report of a shot, and a bullet whistled by his ear, straight through what was left of the windshield. Then Chris knew he had had a close call.

As he reached the alley back of the bank where he had meant to turn in, the mob surged from the other end of the block coming toward him.

"Get into that back doorway there quick, and lock it after ya," said the friendly policeman, riding close. "I'll look after yer car. Be spry there."

Chris slid from the car and another officer slipped in behind him. Chris sprang to the doorway, but the door was locked. He began to beat upon the door, and the mob, with yells of delight, surged toward him. He put his shoulder to the heavy door, but he could not even shake it. The crowd were all but upon him, when suddenly without warning the door gave way and he fell across the threshold!

Chapter 2

Chris never knew exactly what happened for the next minute or two. Someone kicked him as he lay there across the threshold, and a cruel blow from a heavy club hit his arm. Someone shouted "Kill him!" and then he heard a policeman's whistle and wild confusion. Someone had caught him from within the door and was pulling him inside the building. Someone else caught his feet from without and pulled. His shoe came off in the struggle. Something hit him on the head with a dull thud. There were wild yells and a sudden blank.

The door was shut when he came to, and he was inside. Anxious faces were about him. He couldn't quite distinguish them, but he tried to straighten up from the hard couch he was lying on in a storeroom for old records and files.

"I'm all right!" he said unsteadily, as he tried to stand up, thinking of his father somewhere in the building. Then a memory of his mother came and quite brought him back to his senses. His mother must not hear about this. All her worst fears would be justified. She would never feel safe about him again.

Then came, with a pang, the thought of his beautiful car. Where was it? Was it ruined? Oh, what had happened anyway? Why was all that mob out there, and what was going on? Had there been an accident? And had they mistaken him for someone else? He was still dazed from the blow on his head.

Someone brought him a glass of water and he drank it slowly, trying to remember just what happened. His blood was beginning to boil with indignation over the indignity done to himself and his car. He was beginning to be furious with himself for not having jumped into that crowd and seized that fellow who had thrown that brick. What was the matter with him, anyway, that he had weakly submitted to being led away by the police? He should have done some heavy tackling to show that crowd where to get off. What was the use of being a star football player if one couldn't act in a time of emergency? Of course, it had taken him by surprise, but he should have done something even so. He turned toward the door with a thought of going out yet and getting somebody, but even as he turned things went black before his eyes, and he caught himself from falling by the headrest.

"Better lie down again," advised an anxious voice that he vaguely identified as one of the cashiers in the bank. Then another put out a kindly hand and tried to lead him to the couch, but the motion brought him back from the confusion of his mind again.

"No, I'm quite all right now, thank you," he said, blinking at them. "Where's Dad? I'd like to see Dad."

They looked at one another, whispered, and one of them

stepped to the door and tapped. Another whispered conversation, and he came back.

"Your father's in consultation, but he'll see you in about ten minutes," he said gravely.

Chris sank down on the hard couch again and began to take account of what had happened. It was then he missed his shoe.

"Say, did that hyena get my shoe?" he asked, with a shade of his old grin coming back to his face.

"He sure did!" responded one of the cashiers gravely, looking out of the grating above the door. "What's left of it is out there in the alley, I guess, but you wouldn't want to wear it. I have an extra pair in the closet. I'll get them. Maybe they will serve you for the time till you can do better."

He brought the shoes, and Chris had recovered sufficiently to laugh at the fit of them. He arose, trying to get back some of his old assurance and poise. Then someone opened the door to his father's office and beckoned him, and he had to throw his whole energy into the effort to walk steadily through that door. He must not frighten his father. He felt a good deal shaken up, but he was all right.

"You're lucky you came off as well as you did," murmured the cashier as he closed the door behind him.

Then Chris walked into his father's presence and stood in dismay. For the bank president was sitting at his beautiful mahogany desk, with his head down upon his arms on the desktop and a look of utter despair about his whole drooping figure.

"Dad! What's the matter?" Chris cried in alarm, quickened out of his daze by the sight of the stricken look of his beloved father.

Slowly the father lifted his head, struggled upright in his chair, and looked at him with such a ghastly haggard face that his son was more alarmed than ever. Why, his hair seemed to have silvered more in the few hours since breakfast, and those deep lines in his face were terrible to see.

"What's the meaning of all this, Dad? Are you sick? Oh, *Dad*!"

His father passed a trembling hand over his forehead and eyes and struggled to make his voice steady.

"No, Son, I'm not sick. I'll be all right. It's—just—been a shock, of course."

"But—what is it, Dad?" And then with dawning comprehension—"What's the meaning of all that crowd outside in the street? Has something happened? There hasn't been a run on the bank? Dad—*has there*?"

He saw the look in his father's face that it was true, and sought to find the right word of encouragement.

"But it can't be anything serious, can it, Dad? Our bank? *Your* bank?"

"It's serious, Son," answered his father huskily. "It couldn't be more so. There has been a traitor at work inside our ranks."

"Oh, Dad! But don't look that way. It'll be righted somehow."

"Yes, it'll be righted," agreed the utterly sad voice, humiliated to the depths. "It'll be righted for the depositors, I trust. At least they won't lose much, we hope, perhaps nothing in the end. But it means utter ruin for us! For your mother and you and me! For your uncle Ben, Mr. Chalmers, and the Tryons."

Chris looked perplexed.

"But," he said, looking at his father bewildered, "I don't understand why you—"

"No, you don't understand, Son. It is too astounding. You couldn't understand. But Son, it means that we as officers and directors will have to give up everything in order to satisfy our depositors. It means that even our house and furniture must go, everything that will bring in anything. It means that your mother and I will have no home and no income, and I am too old to begin again, Chris. It couldn't be done!" He ended with a groan, and Chris staggered across the room and laid his hand upon his father's silver head that was down upon his arms again.

"Never mind, Dad," he found himself saying bravely over the terrible lump that had come in his throat. "You've got *me*. I can carry on."

The father's answer was another groan, and then he lifted his head and the boy saw there were tears in his father's eyes.

"You don't understand yet, Chris. It means that I can't send you, my only son, back to college! It means I can't buy you the car I promised, nor do any of the other things for you and your sister that I've always meant to do. And how are you going to carry on without a college diploma in these days? I can't do a thing for you. I, too, have failed!"

"There, Dad! Don't feel that way!" said the boy, patting his father's arm awkwardly. "What's the difference? I don't mind! I oughtn't to have had a car yet anyway. I–It—" and then suddenly he knew that he must not tell his father what had happened to him and the car as he was coming in. If he was going to be a man and help his father now, that was one thing he would have to take care of himself without his father's help. Whatever he was liable for that had been damaged, he would pay himself. Perhaps it would be covered by insurance, he didn't know. But he closed his lips tight and resolved that he would tell nothing about it. His father had enough to bear.

"Look here, Dad," he began again, "can't you get out of this place and go home? Does Mother know anything about what's happened?"

"I trust not," said the man hoarsely, his whole frame shaken by a convulsive sob. "Not yet."

"Well, there, what's the use in taking it so hard? There'll be some way out. Doesn't Mother own our house? Can't you keep that?"

The gray head was shaken solemnly.

"She owns it," he said wearily. "I put it in her name long ago. But only for her need in case of my death. We talked it over then, about men who did that to protect themselves when they knew they were about to fail. Mother said then, and I know she'll stick by it now, that she wouldn't think of keeping a house when others felt we were in debt to them. It wouldn't be honorable, Son. We've got to do the right thing even though we are penniless."

Chris was silent a moment, taking it all in. Then he answered bravely, "Sure thing, Dad. Of course we have!"

And somehow the father felt a little thrill of comfort from the way the boy said that "we," including himself in the wholesale sacrifice. The father put out his hand and grasped the hand of his boy. "Thank you for that, Son. You're going to stand by, and that'll help a lot. I feel that I'm awfully to blame not to have discovered sooner what was going on, but we'll work it out, somehow, *together*. You've helped me a lot already, boy. Now, I'm going out there and speak to the crowd."

"Oh no, Dad!" cried Chris in quick alarm. "Listen! You mustn't.

I've been out there. I know what it's like. The people are seeing red just now. It wouldn't be safe. Wait till tomorrow, Dad. Wait till you've made some kind of statement in the papers. Wait till the people have cooled off a little."

"No, Son! I'm going now. I've got to face the thing or I couldn't live with myself overnight. There are people out there in distress. Widows, and orphans, who trusted me with their all. They've been telephoning all day till I'm nearly crazy. Mrs. Manders, the widow of my old friend. Mrs. Byers, that poor little old paralytic, and those two Johnson sisters, sewing their fingers to the bone making clothes for people and putting it all in here for a rainy day. Oh! It's a burden too great to be tolerated! But I must tell them I'll do my best."

"Oh, but not yet, Dad! Not today!"

"Yes, today! Now! I couldn't go home and face my wife with it undone. She would expect it of me. She would want it. Don't worry, Son, I've sent for a band of police to stand about in the crowd lest there might be some lawless ones. There are always those when there is any excitement."

"You don't understand, Dad. You mustn't go out now. It would be suicidal."

"Yes, I understand. And I must go. You stay here, lad."

"No, Dad, if you're going out, I belong with you!" protested Chris.

"Listen, Son, there isn't any danger, of course, but if there should be, I'd rather you were safe in here to take care of Mother."

"No, Dad, she'd want me to stand by you!" declared Chris, linking an arm in his father's.

So they stood when Mr. Chalmers, one of the directors,

tapped at the door and entered.

"They've come, Mr. Walton," he said respectfully, almost deprecating, "but I wish you'd be persuaded! The chief says he'll do his best but he wishes you wouldn't go today."

"Thank you," said the bank president, lifting his distinguished-looking head a trifle in a way that meant he could not be persuaded. "I'm ready." Then he looked down at Chris, whose young head was thrown back with that same look of determination, and smiled gravely, adding, "We are ready."

Mr. Chalmers opened his lips with a glance at Chris to protest, and another director, Mr. Tryon, in the doorway said, half under his breath, "Oh, do you think that's wise?" Then they closed their lips and stood back with respect in their eyes for the father and son. There was that in the eye of each other that made it necessary for them to go and to stand together.

The wild-eyed crowd, milling together, battling for the first place next to the great bronze grafting doors, turning feverish glances toward the entrance, calling out threats now and then, pushing, selfish, almost crushing the new, frightened, determined women who had joined themselves to the mob, were suddenly brought to amazement by the unexpected opening of the doors.

Those immediately in front were precipitated into the marble entranceway, falling at the feet of the advancing two, the father and the son.

Two cashiers had opened the doors, swinging them back noiselessly behind the noisy, unnoticing crowd who had stood there for five hours beating upon the door and screaming out threats, and who were now so busy with their own madness they did not even see the opening doors.

Just for an instant the crowd blinked and wavered, as the four bullies who had occupied first place in the doorway rolled backward upon the floor, then four others were quick to mount over them and clamber on, wild for their rights and their money.

But two officers with clubs quickly beat back the throng and brought them to their senses, and the crowd drew closer and cried out with many voices for a helping and their money. The women were pleading now, with clasped hands and tears rolling down their cheeks. It was a wild scene of confusion, and Chris's heart stood still with the horror and the sadness of it, as he stood for that first instant in the doorway until the fallen men could be removed from their way. The pitifulness of life! For the first time in his few short years, he realized a little sense of the sorrow and the helplessness of a great part of the world. He had never thought before for his fellowmen who were not as fortunate as himself. Now he began to see and understand, and his heart swelled painfully with the greatness of misery, and the thought that, indirectly perhaps, his beloved father, and therefore himself also, had been the cause of it. For the first time he realized the reason for that stone that'd been flung through his beautiful new windshield a few short minutes before, and for that cry he had not recalled until now: *"There he is, the son of the president, riding around in a five-thousand-dollar car!"* He could see how they had felt, and he was filled with a new kind of shame.

Then out they stepped, the president of the bank with his only son, and a wild cry burst from the mob in the street. One moment they stood there, side-by-side, then the president of the bank raised his hand and the mob hushed for an instant, just one breathless moment. And while the silence hung in space, before it should break into chaos, Christopher Walton Sr. spoke.

"Friends," he said, and his voice was steady and clear so that it was heard to the utmost edge of the crowd.

Then from across the street there came a missile, swift and hard and sure, aimed straight for the brave man's face. It was Chris who saw what was coming and drew his father aside, just a hair's breadth. The ball of slime and mud hit harmlessly the grill of the door before which he stood, and glanced off, only spattering his face. But even then he did not waver. He merely took out his white handkerchief and wiped away the mud from his cheek and eyes, and then lifted his hand again for silence.

The sheer bravery of the act silenced the crowd again for an instant, and while it lasted he spoke.

"Friends, I am here to tell you that you will get back every penny of your savings just as soon as it is possible. I personally pledge to give up all I have, my home and personal property, and I know the directors will do the same. This thing has come about through a circumstance which is just as surprising and heart-breaking to us as to you, and to the last cent we have, we'll make good. We ask you to go quietly to your homes, and within a few days, just as soon as it is physically possible to find out the extent of our trouble and our resources, we'll communicate with every one of our depositors and let them know what is coming to them. We ask your cooperation, and it is to our mutual benefit to work together."

He paused an instant and glanced down at his son, standing so straight and tall beside him, almost reaching his father's height; then he added, with the first smile that had lightened his sorrowful features all that day, "My son is here beside me to say that if anything happens to his father before his promise is made good, he stands ready to see that it is fulfilled. Isn't that so, Chris?"

"It sure is, Dad," answered the son, with a clear ring in his voice.

Then the crowd, always ready to be swayed either way, broke into a cheer, and some of the women openly wept.

Only on the outer edge of the crowd, where the policemen were quietly handcuffing a youth with slime on his hands, was there a low menacing undertone, like a growl of distant thunder.

Then a hand drew the father and son within the sheltering doors again, and most of the crowd turned and drifted slowly, hesitatingly, away.

Sometime later, a closed car drove up around the corner of the alley, back of the bank, and took the Waltons and two of the bank directors to their homes. And the region about the bank, and the streets where they had to pass, were well patrolled.

Mrs. Walton was in a high state of excitement when they finally arrived at home.

"Where have you both been?" she cried tearfully. "I've been so worried. I thought there had been a terrible accident and you were both killed. I even tried to telephone the bank, but got no answer except that the wire was busy. I thought I should go crazy."

"Oh," said the older Walton sympathetically, "that was because so many people were calling up constantly. I'm so sorry. I never dreamed that you would be worried yet, and I did not want to tell you until it was necessary, not until I could come home and explain it myself. My dear, we have been passing through terrible times this morning." He passed a frail hand over his furrowed forehead and looked at her with weary eyes. Chris, watching him, seemed to see him suddenly grow old before his eyes. He saw his mother put her hand hastily over her heart in quick premonition, and while his father explained about the run on the bank, it all swept over him what it was going to mean to his mother to lose her home and be poor. Gosh, that was tough on Mother! His little pretty mother! It suddenly came to him that he must somehow stand between her and this so great calamity.

Then, amazingly, he saw her face relax, her fears drop away, her face grow calm, and almost a smile come out upon her lips.

"Oh, is that all?" she said with great relief. "I thought you must have some awful sickness or a stroke, or you were going to have to have a terrible operation."

Suddenly Chris began to laugh.

"Oh, Mother," he cried, "excuse me, but—why!—you're only afraid of the things you imagine, things you get up yourself out of nothing! When it comes to real things, Muz, you've got nerve. I'll say you're a real little old hero!"

"But Mary," said the father anxiously, "you don't understand. It will mean that we will have to give up our house and all the beautiful things you have gathered through the years, rugs and jewels and pictures—"

"Of course," said Mother, nonchalantly. "Why speak about such trifles. We've been poor before. Besides, don't you remember what the minister said on Sunday, that we must thank God for the hard things that come into our lives as well as for the nice things? There's probably some wise reason in all this, and maybe by and by we'll see it. Come on, now, let's go to dinner. It's waited long enough. And it's a good dinner, beefsteak and mushrooms. If we're not going to be able to afford such things anymore, we can at least enjoy this one—unless, Christopher, you think we ought to give this dinner to some creditor?" she asked with a twinkle.

Christopher Senior took his wife in a tender embrace and smiled, his whole anxious face relaxing, and Chris Junior murmured as he turned away to brush aside a strange blurring that came into his eyes. "Gosh, Mother, you're a whiz! Who'd ever think you'd take it like that?"

"But I'm getting old, Mother," said the banker wistfully. "It's not as if I could begin all over again."

"So am I," said Mother cheerfully. "But Chris is young, and an old head and a young head together are more than twice as good as a young head making young mistakes. Come, hurry and carve that steak!"

And, surprisingly, they sat down at that belated dinner, laughing.

If the prowler in the shrubbery outside the dining room window heard that laughter, it perhaps only added fuel to the fire in his heart, his angry heart that wanted his money, wanted it tonight, and meant to get it, somehow, soon.

It was not until Chris got up to his own room a couple of hours later, for they had lingered, talking it out and clinging together for reassurance, that he suddenly realized what this change of circumstances was going to mean to him. On the bed lay a pennant in flaming colors bearing the name of his college. He had bought it today to give to Gilda to put on her wall, and now he was not going back to college.

He was filled with the consternation of this fact as he finally put out his light and opened his window, and he failed to see the lurking figure with the menacing pale face in the hedge beyond the rhododendrons. He got into his bed and began to look his misfortunes in the face, and it was not till those still deep, dark hours toward morning that he fell into a light sleep.

And suddenly a shot rang out, almost in the room, and he sprang out of bed in alarm.

Chapter 3

W hen Natalie Halsey entered the house after watching Chris drive off, she tiptoed softly down the little dark hall and cautiously opened the door into the kitchen to lay down her bundles on the kitchen table. Then she peered through the half-open door into the front room, which had been temporarily converted into a bedroom during her mother's sickness. The house boasted of but four rooms, two upstairs and two down, with a little lean-to shed for a laundry.

"Yes?" said a quick, alert voice from the shadows of the sick room, and Natalie threw the door open wide and gave a cheerful little laugh.

"I can't move without your hearing me, can I, Mother dear!" she said, coming to let the brightness of the day in. "I hoped you would have a good long sleep while I was gone. You scarcely slept a wink all night, and you simply have to make it up, you know, or you'll have a relapse. Didn't you even get a nap at all this morning?"

"Oh yes," said the invalid indifferently. "I think I did, but I kept one ear open for your coming." She gave a funny, brave little laugh as if it were not a matter of importance. "I'm really not tired, you know. I'm quite rested. And I've decided to get up today and go to work. I've got to finish that hemstitching for Mrs. Baker."

"Now, Mother, look here. You've got to behave," cried Natalie firmly. "You're not getting up until the doctor says so, and even then unless you are good. As for that hemstitching, I may as well tell you that Janice finished it weeks ago and took it to Mrs. Baker, and she was wonderfully pleased with it and paid for it right away. So you don't need to think of work yet awhile."

The mother gave her a startled look.

"The dear child," she said tenderly. "Was that what she was doing so quietly when I was supposed to be asleep? And I thought she was studying."

"Oh, she studied, too," said Natalie cheerfully.

"But"—the mother's eyes had a worried look—"the money must be all gone. I can't see how you have kept things up—and gotten luxuries, too. I know you two have just starved yourselves."

"Do we look starved?" chirped Natalie cheerily. "Mother, you just quit worrying and I'll tell you some good news. Listen. I've got a job! Not just a little snatch of work, but a real job with a regular salary and hours. I start on Monday morning at eight o'clock sharp! Now, will you be good?"

"Oh, Natalie! Child! Where is it?"

"Well, maybe you won't like it so well, but it's really a good job, and easy hours, and quite respectable and nice. Just think how wonderful it will be not to have to worry from one six months to another. And then not know whether the dividend we ought to get from our one-and-only is really coming or not."

"Tell me, dear! Where is it?"

"Well, it's cashier in the grocery store. Now, Mother, don't look that way. It's a really lovely store, clean and light and airy, and the nicest, courteous manager. He treats me like a queen. He's having my little glass den all painted up new for me and getting me a stool that will be comfortable. He's married, and kind, and he says his wife told him that it made all the difference in the world what kind of stool the cashier had, whether she got tired and cross or not."

Mrs. Halsey made a little sound of a moan.

"Oh, Natalie, my baby! To think of your having to work in a store with a lot of rough men! Oh, how badly your father would feel if he knew we had come to that! He was so particular about his dear girls."

"Nonsense, Mother!" said Natalie, a trifle sharply because of the sudden lump that came in her throat and threatened tears. "Father would be glad I had the chance of such a nice place. They are not rough men, any of them. They are just nice boys that work so hard they haven't time to look at anybody. It's mostly ladies that I'll have to do with. People who come shopping. I'll be sort of shut away in a little glass room, you know, and people come to the window with their checks and money. I think it'll be fun, Mother. You know I always could make change accurately, and anyway, there's a machine to do it. It will be just nothing but fun."

"You're a brave little girl," said her mother, wiping away a few tears with a feeble hand.

"There, now, Mother dear, just stop those sob-tears this minute. This is nothing to be sad about. Just be glad. Why, Mother,

I thought you taught me that God takes care of us and nothing that He does not allow can come to people who are His own. Don't you think He can take care of me as well in a grocery store as in a fine parlor?"

"Oh yes," sighed the sick woman. "Of course, but—"

"But it's not the way you would like it done? Is that it, Mother? Well, say! Don't you think He loves me as much as you do? Come, Mother dear. Cheer up. We're on the road to wealth. Can't you rejoice with me?"

"Oh yes," said the mother, fetching a watery little smile. "You're a good girl."

"No, I'm not particularly good. Don't make the mistake of over-estimating my worth," said Natalie comically. "I'm quite natural and normal as a human girl. I envied Gilda Carson this morning. She was out with a great lovely hound on a chain. I'd teach him to run alongside and never stray away or bark at other dogs. Say, Mother, you don't know how I came home just now, do you? Did you happen to hear me arrive? I just came home in a wonderful new car, with a perfectly good, handsome young man. I wish you had been at the window just to see how fine I was. He asked me to take a ride, too, only I knew I had to get the soup on for dinner, so I declined."

"A young man?" said the mother fearfully. "Oh, Natalie, *who?*"

"Oh, you needn't sigh like that, Mother. He was perfectly all right. He has the reputation of being as good as he is good-looking. It wasn't a tramp nor a drummer, not anybody wild from down on the Flats. It was the son of the president of our bank, if you please. Christopher Walton, with a brand-new car that his father has given him to take back to college."

"Natalie! How did he happen to ask you?"

"Oh, he just rode alongside the sidewalk and asked me if he could give me a lift. You know I had some groceries, and I suppose I may have looked overburdened," said Natalie, taking half the joy out of her unexpected ride by this flat facing of facts. "He's always been noted for his kindliness."

"That was—*nice* of him," said the mother thoughtfully. "That's the kind of young man you might naturally have had for a friend, if all things had gone well with us and your father had lived. Of course, he wouldn't think so now, though. He wouldn't know from present appearances that your father was just as good as his."

"Oh, Mother, don't talk that way!" said Natalie, with a sudden, brief impatience. "We all had Adam for a remote grandfather, anyway. What's the difference about family?"

"Because—dear child, you don't understand. But class really means a lot to most people. It probably does to him. Most young men in his station in life would only look upon one in your position as someone to condescend to."

Natalie was silent for a moment.

"Well, suppose he did?" she said, with matter-of-factness in her tone. "I had a nice ride anyway, and he talked to me just as if I was any nice girl. He used to be in my class in high school, you know. It really wasn't anything so very notable, just a few blocks in a pretty car, but it was fun and I'm glad I had it."

"Yes, of course," the mother hastened with belated pleasure to state. "So am I. How I wish you had a car of your own."

"Oh now, Mother, what would we do with a car of our own, here in this street? Where would we keep it? On the front porch or out in the little old, forsaken chicken coop?"

At last Natalie got her mother to laughing a little. Then she suddenly sobered.

"Dear child!" she said, with a quiver in her voice. "There's something else about this that makes me troubled. I wouldn't want you to get interested in a handsome young man who might offer you a ride now and then, and mean nothing by it, and then break your heart."

Natalie sat down in the rocking chair and broke out laughing, perhaps to help her hold back the tears, which were very near the surface this morning, for in spite of her brave words and cheery manner, things were looking pretty serious for her. She didn't mean to tell her mother that there were only thirty-seven cents of the hemstitching money left after she purchased the supply of necessities she had just brought home. And that they had asked the landlord to let the rent run along until her first week's pay came in before he might expect an installment on it. Poor child! She had been up and down, several times a night, trying to soothe her mother to sleep; rubbing her back with steady, patient hand; bathing her aching forehead with witch hazel; getting her a glass of milk, and the strain was beginning to tell on her. To tell the truth, it had been hard to contrast the difference between her own life and that of some of the members of her class whom she had seen in brief glimpses as she passed them on the street that morning, and her brave spirit had faltered several times.

So now, she had to hide her tears and put on a cheerful little comical manner.

"Oh, Mother dear! What a silly fraidycat you are! Do you take me for an absolute fool? Don't you know I have no intention of falling for any boy, no matter how fine or how plain he might be.

I'm going to hold Mother's hand and stay at home and make life happy for you. Perhaps Janice will marry, and when I get old, I'll make bibs and dress dolls for her children; but I'm just cut out for a grand old maid. I'm not going to break my heart for anybody. Now! Will you be good? It's time for your broth, and if you find any more causes to worry, I'm going to send for the doctor. So there!"

So with coaxing and wiles she cheered her mother to a real smile and fed her broth, and chattered on about how she was going to make over her old green serge for a school dress for Janice, till the day settled into a quiet, peaceable groove of homely duties.

Then Janice breezed in with an announcement that she had an order to sew for a dozen handkerchiefs, and three pairs of pillowcases to hemstitch, and the sun shone in the tiny parlor bedroom.

Later when the mother was taking an afternoon nap and the sisters were doing up the brief kitchen work, and having a cheery conversation together about how they were both going to make ends meet, Natalie confided to her sister the story of her ride and her mother's fears.

"Mums is afraid I'm going to lose my heart at once, of course." She laughed.

"Well," said Janice thoughtfully, "I shouldn't think it would be a hard thing to do, Natty. I think he's perfectly grand. There isn't a single one of your class in high school that's as good-looking as he is, nor as polite and really courteous. And he's smart, too."

"Oh, sure!" agreed Natalie, out of a heart that had held those same opinions through four long, lonely years in high school and three hard-working empty ones since. "That goes without saying. Why look lower than the best? That's why I'm getting ready to be a cheerful spinster. I couldn't possibly aim for the highest, so why aim at all? Oh, Jan! For pity's sake, let's talk about something practical. Do you realize that I've got a job, and that if we can get through till next Saturday, I'll have a pay envelope? But how to get through till then is the problem. Suppose you take account of stock. Can we do it? There's still thirty-seven cents in the treasury, but Mother's wee dividend doesn't come in for another six weeks yet. How about it? Could we live on beans for a day or two and leave the thirty-seven cents for mother's extras? We can charge beef for broth for a week, if it comes to a pinch."

"Sure we can," said Janice gallantly. "I've got two pounds of rice, a box of gelatin, half a pound of sugar, and some junket tablets hidden away in case of emergency, and there's still a quarter in my once fat pocketbook. We'll manage to rub along. With all this you brought in today, we'll live like kings. That meat will make a wonderful soup, and we'll eat the meat, too, and then sandwiches and hash. Oh sure! And you got a stalk of celery. You extravagant thing! That'll just put pep into any meal."

"He threw that in," said Natalie, laughing.

"Oh, *he* did!" said Janice, looking at her sister sharply. "Well, I guess Mother'll have something else to worry about. Which is it to be, Natty, a bank president or a grocery man that I'm going to have for my best brother-in-law?"

"Oh, stop your nonsense," said Natalie good-naturedly. "Come on and let's clean this cupboard shelf, and find out, just to a grain, how much of everything we really have left. I shouldn't wonder if by next week Mother will be able to be up a little each day, and perhaps the next week you could go back to school. Then we'll have to work out a regular schedule of home work, so you won't have too much on your hands while I'm in the store."

So they scrubbed the cupboard shelves and set their meager array of eatables out grandly, apportioning them for each day of the week, jubilant that it was going to be possible to get through to the first paycheck.

"A shredded-wheat biscuit apiece, six days," counted Natalie, "not counting tomorrow. We have oatmeal enough left for tomorrow."

"His sister is very nice, too," mused Janice, measuring out the rice carefully and putting it in a clean glass jar.

"What?" said Natalie, whirling around upon her sister. "Whose sister?"

"Chris Walton's sister," said Janice, her eyes on a tiny bag of raisins that suggested possible rice pudding, if an egg and a little milk could be spared. "We could have rice pudding for Mother's birthday," went on Janice thoughtfully. "She could eat that, surely. You know Friday is her birthday. We really ought to have some chicken broth. How about my going out and making a raid on our neighbor's hencoop?"

"Is she indeed?" said Natalie. "What's her name? How do you happen to know that she's nice?"

"Who? The hen I'm going to raid? Now how could I possibly tell what her name is till I've met her?" said Janice, in an aggrieved tone.

"I was speaking of the bank president's daughter," said Natalie in a dignified tone, "but if you wish to be trivial, it doesn't matter. What's a stolen hen among friends?"

"Why," said Janice, giggling, "she's in my class in school. Her name is Elise. I think she's nice because she never has any runs in her stockings, and she doesn't use lipstick. We don't have much to do with each other, of course, how could we? She has her own friends. But she smiled at me the other day when we passed in class. I like her. I think you can usually tell, don't you? Even if you don't know people very well. She never makes me feel the darkened-up runs in *my* stockings the way Gilda Carson does, nor how much too short my old blue dress is getting, and—anyhow, I like her."

"Well, that's nice," said Natalie, irrelevantly. "So do I, if she smiled at you." And she suddenly bestowed a resounding smack on the curve of her sister's cheek.

"How about stewing these eight prunes?" said Janice, rubbing off her sister's kiss with a grin. "Maybe Mother would like a taste, and they really have been here a long time. Not that I like them," she finished with a grimace. "When you get to be a bank presidentess, or a lady grocer, whichever it is, please don't let's have prunes anymore. I'm ashamed to look a prune in the face, I've hated so many of them."

"No, my dear, we'll never have another prune when I attain either of those great estates. We'll have grapefruit served in cracked ice or honeydew melon with lemon juice or black grapes from South Africa, just on one provision however, and that is if you cut out that nonsense and never speak of it again. Even in fun I don't like it, Jan," she added seriously. "If I should ever meet Chris Walton again, I should be ashamed to think we had ever talked such utter nonsense. Promise me, dear, you won't!"

"You dear old funny, serious darling!" said the younger sister in a burst of admiration, "Of course not, if you don't want me to. I was only kidding anyway. But seriously, Nat, I do wish you had some nice friends like that, and some good times like other girls."

"I have all the good times I want," said Natalie with a firm shutting of her lips. "Haven't I the chance to go to Bible study? You don't know how glad I am of that. I've wanted it ever since that first time I went. I'm so glad it doesn't cost anything. I just love every minute of the hour. You are sure you don't mind giving up Monday evenings?"

"Why should I mind, dearest dear? Where would I go? To the opera, or to Gilda Carson's dance at the country club, or did you suppose a host of boyfriends were waiting outside the door to convince me to go to the movies or some other place of entertainment? No, rest your conscience, serious sister, I'll only be falling asleep over my hemstitching or stealing an hour at a hoarded magazine story."

"Oh, Jan, I wish you had some good times! I mean you will, too, when I get on a little further."

"Oh, certainly, we'll all have good times," said Janice, waving the dish towel. "Now, if you don't mind, I'll retire to my hemstitching and earn a few honest pennies for a rainy day without prunes."

Softly laughing, the two girls scurried upstairs to get their sewing, walking quietly lest they awaken their mother. They had good times together, these two girls, who were almost isolated from their own kind. They were perhaps closer to one another than most sisters, just because hard work and poverty had separated them from the girls who would have been their natural mates, if their father's fortune had not been swept away when they were very young, and sickness and death had not changed their environment. They chattered quietly as they worked, talking over all the people they had met, all the little trifles that went to make up their days. Natalie asking questions about Janice's school friends, recalling incidents of their older brothers and sisters, and Janice curious about the grocery store and her sister's new environment.

At last Janice folded away her hemstitching.

"It's getting too dark for you to work on that green serge any longer, Natalie," she said, "and I can't see to pull the threads. We can't afford to get glasses, so we better stop. What's for supper? I'm hungry as a bear."

"Toast and tea and a cup of junket for Mother," said Natalie, folding the breadths of the skirt she had just succeeded in cleverly piecing so it wouldn't show.

"There's codfish enough left for you and me," she added firmly, "creamed codfish on toast with a dish of dried applesauce apiece, and warmed-over cocoa. We simply have got to hoard every crumb till next Saturday. Can you stand it, Jan?" She looked at her sister anxiously.

"Sure thing," said Janice bravely, almost blithely. "Aren't I husky enough to survive a week of codfish and applesauce? I might even give up the applesauce if you'd ask me, especially the dried part. I'm not particularly partial to dried apples. But, of course, they're not nearly as scratchy to the tongue as dried peaches. I abominate *them*!"

"We're having codfish tonight so we can have a meatball apiece tomorrow," appeased the sister.

"Noble sacrifice!" Janice giggled. " 'On to the codfish! Let joy be unconfined! No sleep till morn while youth and beauty meet—' Is that the way it goes?"

"Stop your nonsense," said Natalie, smiling. "You'll wake Mother."

"Mother is awake. I heard her stirring as I came by the door. I'm going to light her lamp now. Is her toast ready?"

So they presently gathered about the mother with a tempting tray, tempting as to the delicacy of its preparation if not filled with rare food. And the three of them settled down to cheer one another, a cheerful, brave little trio, trusting God and upholding one another in all the bright, tender ways at their command.

Chapter 4

The sound of a body falling below stairs brought Chris swiftly to his senses. He sprang into action, but even so, his mother was there before him. He found her kneeling at the foot of the stairs, stooping over his father, who lay huddled here with blood upon the floor beside him, and blood on the breast of his bathrobe.

"Call Dr. Mercer!" she said in a low strained voice, and Chris hurried to the telephone, his heart beating wildly. What had happened? Was his father shot through the heart? Oh God, what had happened? He thought he should always see that picture of his mother in her delicate blue robe kneeling beside his stricken father, her soft gray curls falling over her slender shoulders, and that look of bravery in her eyes. How pretty his mother must have been when she was a girl! That was a strange thought to come at such an awful time, yet it flung itself at him as he lifted down the receiver.

He was back to the hall in an instant.

"He's on the way," he said soothingly. "Can't I lift him up?"

"No, we'll wait till the doctor comes. Get a glass of water!"

He sprang for the water, noting as he passed the dining room window that it was pushed halfway up from the bottom.

"What was Dad doing down here?" he whispered as he brought the water.

"He heard a noise and came down to investigate," murmured the mother. "I tried to make him wait and telephone the police but he wouldn't."

There was a sound at the door. The doctor had arrived, with a policeman just behind him wanting to know what had happened. The next half hour was a confusion of horror to Chris. Policemen coming and going silently, low murmured directions, fingerprints on the windowsill, footprints outside the window. A quick, low gasp of pain from the stricken man as he came back to conscious-ness under the doctor's ministrations. Anxious waiting during the search for the bullet that had entered somewhere around the lungs. Bandages, subtle pungent odors filling the house, the swift arrival of a trained nurse from the hospital, a bed brought downstairs and his father moved to it. It all seemed like one awful nightmare that could not be true. His father! And yesterday everything had been so wonderful, and he had been so thankful that there was nothing dreadful in his life.

Strange that that peculiar, unnatural sermon of Sunday should come back to him now. That one sentence, rather, from the sermon, that he had heard above the joyful reverberation of his thoughts. That suggestion that men ought to be thankful for the hard things that came to them. Bosh! How could they? That was ridiculous! What possible good could come from an experience like this one?

How could one believe that terrible experiences were sent in love to anyone?

Things settled down into quiet at last. That fearful probing for the bullet was over. It had been found in a gravely serious spot, close to the lung. His father lay sleeping under opiates, with the white-capped nurse in charge and silence reigning. The mother was going about with white face and bright eyes, getting ready in the kitchen something that the doctor had ordered.

"It's a very serious situation," the doctor told Chris plainly, "but if all goes well, he has an even chance of pulling through. You'll have to be a man and take the burden from your mother, Son."

Chris, with heavy heart, straightened his strong, young shoulders and bowed gravely. He felt as if the burdens of the universe had suddenly settled down upon him. He felt as if the ground under him was sinking away and everything that he had known and trusted in was swimming, toppling about him. But he bowed the doctor out, took all the directions, went and helped the nurse arrange a curtain to keep the light out from her patient's eyes, helped his mother in the kitchen, and then persuaded her to lie down and save her strength for later, when she might be needed. And at last he was free to go to his own room and change his bath-robe and slippers for more suitable clothing.

He stood in the middle of the room and looked about him, dazed. Looked at his watch and stared about again. Was it only three short hours since he had heard that shot? Why, ordinarily at this hour, he would still be in his bed, sleeping. It was only six o'clock in the morning, yet that house had seemingly passed through a whole day's work!

Was it only yesterday morning he had been so happy, getting

his things in shape for packing? There on his desk lay a pile of papers he had sorted out to burn. And there were the piles of undergarments his mother had marked yesterday and laid on the window seat for him to put in his trunk. College! He couldn't go now, of course. And that car? Where was it? He ought to hunt up the police and find out what they did with it. He hadn't thought of it since.

Softly, he tiptoed to the telephone in the back hall and finally got in touch with the police station. They assured him the car was safe, what was left of it, and his heart sank. His next duty would be to communicate with the owner. Would he be liable for the damage or would the insurance cover it? He knew very little about insurance rules. A five-thousand-dollar car—its beautiful glitter defaced! Another five thousand dollars to add to the hundreds of thousands, perhaps, that his father owed. Well, he would look after that, anyway. Somehow, he must find a job. He must! He must be a man now and take cares upon himself. Maybe his father would never recover. Even if he lived, he might be always an invalid after this. There was that possibility to face.

Yesterday, he was facing another happy year of college life: football, basketball, baseball, fraternities, honors—all that college life meant. Today he might as well be an old man and be done with it. He had debts and a family dependent on him. He dropped his head down wearily on the telephone stand and sighed. If he had not been ashamed he would have cried. He could feel the tears in his eyes and down his throat. He swallowed hard and fought them back. He was a man. He had to be! And Dad, his perfectly wonderful dad, was lying in the living room between life and death. Dad might not get well. What did it matter whether he went to college or not? If Dad ever got well, he wouldn't care whether he owned a sport car or not.

Presently, he roused himself enough to telephone the agency of the car, ask anxious questions about insurance, and disclose the whereabouts of the car. He was gratefully relieved when they said they would take care if it and let him know later about the insurance. He left the telephone with a sigh, tiptoed to the door of the living room, and looked wistfully in. The nurse came and spoke to him in a noiseless voice, telling him to go to bed and snatch some sleep. Chris dragged himself upstairs and threw himself across his bed. The sun was high and bright, flinging its rays half across the room, but he did not notice it. He was utterly weary in soul and body, and dropped asleep as his head touched the pillow.

There followed long days and anxious nights, when the affairs of the world were practically forgotten in the more vital question of whether the husband and father was going to live or die, and Chris felt that he was aging a year an hour. College was a thing of the past, and he stuffed away all the pennants and athletic articles in a dark closet and tried to forget there was such a thing as being a boy with a carefree life. Yet there wasn't much to actually do. Hang around the halls, listen for the slightest sound from the sick room, go on the trivial errands for the nurse or doctor, sometimes in a wild hurry, with the helpless feeling that the beloved father's life was slipping away no matter what they did. Once, he had to go to the train to meet a famous specialist who was coming in consultation. That was a terrible day that seemed ages ago.

As Chris looked back to the afternoon when he and his father had stepped out of the bank door and stood together before that angry mob, it seemed years past. Yet he was sometimes curious of a thrill of pride in his father. If Dad had to go out of life, he was glad he had this last brave act to remember. Sometimes, when he closed his eyes to try and sleep, he could set the noble, unafraid look on his father's face as he opened his lips to speak and stood there so controlled and quiet when the mud was thrown in his face. At such times, his blood would boil over the indignity till it seemed he just must get up and out and hunt for the criminal who did it and throttle him. Then he would get up and begin to pace back and forth in his room, like a caged lion, till remembering his father was downstairs, who might hear. He would force himself to lie down again.

Affairs at the bank seemed a distant and vague interest. Every day someone would call up and ask after the president and give some hint of how matters were going. Chris knew that a bulletin had been sent out to depositors giving them hope of an installment in the near future. He knew that his mother had signed over all properties in her name or in a joint account. He knew vaguely that other directors had done the same and that there was hope of putting the bank back someday, on some kind of a working foundation. But he seemed to have drifted so far away from it all that it did not interest him. His heart seemed frozen, deadened. His universe had turned to stone. He wondered, sometimes idly, why God could let a catastrophe like this come to his father and mother, such wonderful Christians. And himself! He had never done anything so very bad that he should have to be treated like this. It almost looked as if his father and mother had put their trust vainly in God.

One day on the street, Chris was hurrying along with medicine for which the nurse had sent him, and a man, passing, looked keenly into his eyes with a pleasant glance. The lean, kindly face was vaguely familiar. Somehow battling in his mind against that kindly glance was a former impression of startled antagonism. He glanced back after the man, and suddenly it came to him that this was the man who had preached that sermon about being thankful for the hard things as well as the pleasant things that came into one's life. Chris stabbed him in the back with a black scowl and passed on.

Good guy, that is! Knows a lot about it, he does! he meditated. *Like ta lose all he's got, wouldn't he? Like to have his father dishonored and shot and lying between life and death for weeks. Like ta give up his chance of getting anywhere in the world because he couldn't finish his college education. You bet he'd be thankful for all that handed out ta him in one day, wouldn't he?*

There remained with him an impression of deeply graven lines of sorrow, though the man did not look old.

Gradually, as the days passed, the tension in the sickroom let up a little. The burden on their hearts was not quite so heavy. The father seemed to be improving just a little, and hope sprang up fearsomely.

Then, one morning, there came a telephone call from Walter Gillespie's sister. Walter was coming home for a few hours and wanted to see him very much. Could he take lunch with him? He wanted to consult with him about something.

Chris was whistling softly under his breath as he got ready. It was good to have the cloud lifted, even briefly, to feel that things were not quite so hopeless in the sickroom as they had been and that he might go out for a few hours without that dread feeling clutching at his heart that death might have entered during his absence. It was good to see Walt again, even though he had been gone from home but a short time. It gave him a warm, pleasant feeling to know that Walt wanted to see him, a thrill to think of hearing how things were going at college. It was a salve for his hurt pride that even though he was not coming back to college, they valued his opinion enough to consult him about something.

As he walked down the street, he began to wonder what it could be that Walt wanted. Probably to discuss some questionable men who were up for consideration by the fraternity. It might be Dick Bradford. If so, he was absolutely against him. He was yellow. You couldn't depend on him.

As he approached the Gillespie home, he suddenly realized that he was on foot instead of driving the handsome new car that he had talked with Walt so much about when he was thinking of getting it. It may have been this thought that obsessed him as he went up the steps, or was it possible that Walt, as he came down the stairs and met him in the hall, had just the slightest shade of condescension about him as he greeted him? He must be mistaken, of course. Walt was never that way with him. With anybody. Walt and he had been buddies since they were little kids. No, of course, he was just sensitive.

Yet he felt it again up in Walt's room, when they were going over the history of the last few weeks in college—Walt telling about the new boys, the prospects of the fraternity, the changes in the faculty. Especially what was being done in the fraternity. Walt had been made president! A sudden pang shot through Chris. There had been strong hints that he himself was to be made president this semester. Then he generously arose to the occasion and put out a cordial hand for the old-time grasp!

"Congratulations, Pard!" he said eagerly, his ready smile beaming out. "That's great!"

Walt accepted his eagerness a bit languidly, as befitted one in a higher position, and went on to tell of the men that had been pledged.

With studied casualness, Walt announced, "And oh, yes, we're taking in Dick Bradford. That'll be a help."

Chris froze at once. Dick Bradford! Walt knew what he thought of Dick Bradford. Then Walt hadn't come to consult him about that. It was all settled. Chris felt strongly the condescension in his former comrade's manner, and he closed his lips quickly in a firm line and then opened them to say with decision, "You'll be making a great mistake, Walt. He's yellow. I thought I told you what happened last spring—"

But Walt waved him aside.

"He's got personality, Chris. There isn't a man in the new bunch that can match him for that. And we need men with personality, outstanding men, that can represent us anywhere and make a good impression. We feel that we have done a good thing in securing him. In fact we lost him to the Deltas. They had him all but pledged."

"He's a typical Delta," said Chris, with his old haughty manner that used to bring Walt to terms in the old days. But Walt simply lifted his chin a shade higher and smiled superciliously.

"You always did have it in for Dick," he said condescendingly, "but your advice is a bit late. Dick was pledged last night, and we feel that he's the right man. He has charm, you know. And now, kid—"

Chris frowned with a sudden chill at his heart. This wasn't the old kindly "kid" of his childhood; it was a condescending tone, a term of diminution. It was as if they had suddenly changed places, and the admiring deference that Walt had always paid him had suddenly been demanded of him. Did it do this to Walt to become president of the fraternity for a semester?

Would it have done that to *him*?

But Walt was talking fluently now.

"We had a get-together last night, some of us who are in the heart of things, and decided it wasn't fair to your college to have a man like you drop out just at the end this way."

He spoke as if Chris had dropped out through sheer wantonness. Chris looked up at him in astonishment.

"We feel that it's due the college and our class that you should finish. You had a fine record all the way through, both athletics and studies, and neither the class nor the teams can afford to lose you at this stage of things. We feel you should come back and finish."

Chris lifted his chin and looked at his old comrade coldly. This was not even the old tone of sympathy and love that he felt he had a right to expect from Walt. He was talking as if he were an officer who had a right to rebuke him.

"In short," went on Walt, putting on a grown-up official manner, "we felt that something should be done for you. So we have looked around and found several ways of helping out. With an athletic scholarship, we can fix things so that you will have practically nothing to pay. Of course, you wouldn't be able to occupy the suite that we had expected to take together." Walt's eyes were on the floor now, fitting the toe of his well-polished shoe into the oriental rug. "You wouldn't expect that. And anyway, Dick has taken over your share in the apartment, so that would be impossible even if you could afford it. But there is a room vacant on the fourth floor, and I think you could be fairly comfortable there. Of course, it's among the freshies, but that would be a part of the concession I believe from the college. Some duties up there—"

He paused suddenly and looked up, worried by the stony silence with which Chris was receiving his offer.

Chris was sitting there with his haughtiest manner, his head thrown up, his eyes angry, looking at his friend as if he had suddenly become an alien enemy.

Walt began to fidget around uneasily. He knew that look on Chris's face but had never happened to have it turned on him before. He hastened to speak in quite a different tone.

"Why, what's the matter, old man? You don't understand. I'm offering you a chance to finish your college course. I've come down on purpose. The frat sent me. They're back of me, and they'll be back of you. And the college wants you."

"Sorry!" said Chris stiffly. "It's quite impossible."

"But look here, Chris," said Walt, getting nervous. He had thought this thing was going to be put through so easily. "You don't understand. It won't cost you a cent. It's a free gift. The college feels you're worth it to them! They haven't a man who can come up to you in athletics, and they really need you."

"That's gratifying, I'm sure," said Chris, assuming his most grown-up manner and shutting his lips with that kind of finality that made his former playmate remember other occasions and understand that this was going to be a real hand-to-hand battle.

He settled down to argue. He still had several good reasons why Chris should come back with him today to college.

"Why, I've had this ready to propose for a week, but I wouldn't do it until your father was out of danger," he said, in a conciliatory tone that helped a lot toward soothing Chris's wounded pride.

"My father isn't entirely out of danger yet," said Chris, in a serious tone. "He's better, but we have to take very great care of him."

"Oh, certainly! Of course!" said the other young man, a trifle impatiently. "But a nurse can do that! He would get well twice as quick if he knew you were back in college getting all that's coming to you. Why, I've had my sister on the quiet watching the bulletins from the doctor, and she wired me the minute he said your father was better."

"That wouldn't make any difference," said Chris, and suddenly knew he was right. "It will be a long time before my father is well, and I'm needed right here. I have responsibilities. And you're mistaken about Dad. I'm just sure now, under the existing circumstances, that Dad would expect me to stand by."

But Walter Gillespie did not give up. He argued it this way and that. It presently appeared that another member of the fraternity had come down with him. An alumnus was to be there to lunch, and Chris had it all to go over again.

But Chris did not weaken. As the argument went on, he only grew stronger in the knowledge of what he had to do. A vision of that angry mob in front of the bank the day he stood by his father and promised to see that his covenant with the people was made good came vividly to his mind, and convinced him that unquestionably his place was here at home, helping his father to make good, cheering and helping his mother.

Later, when he was by himself, all the tempting things they offered would come back to him and stab him to the heart with longing to go. For before they were done with him, the jobs they had secured for him, the fourth-story dormitory, and the condescension were scrapped, and the beautiful suite of rooms with Walt for roommate was even offered free, with the promise to put Dick Bradford elsewhere. There was satisfaction, of course, in the thought that they wanted him so badly. It healed his wounded pride when the dignified alumnus even descended his patronage and humbled himself to tell Chris he was the only man who could come in at this time and tide the fraternity over a certain crisis through which it was passing.

But when it was all over, Chris could only say it was impossible, that he had other obligations that came first.

Of course, on the way home that afternoon, having seen Walt and the alumnus on the two-fifty train, he suffered a reaction and began to think perhaps he had been a fool to refuse such an offer. Perhaps his father would blame him for taking things in his own hands this way. Yet there remained, like a wall of adamant, back in his mind, the knowledge that he should stay and work and help to pay back his father's debt, if possible. At least help him in his present need.

A deep gloom settled down upon him as he turned his steps toward home. Here was he, with the way open to go back and get his last college year, which any fool would tell him he needed before he would be worth much in the business world, and yet the way so effectually blocked by honor that the offer might as well never have come, save for the satisfaction of knowing how the college people felt toward him.

But when he entered the house and found that his father's condition had not been quite so good that day, he forgot all about college again as the mantle of anxiety returned upon his weary, young shoulders.

Chapter 5

There came a morning when the doctor came out of the sick-room with a look of bright triumph on his face.

"Well, sir," he said to Chris, as he got himself into his fall overcoat and took up his hat, "your father's going to get well. I didn't tell you before because I wasn't sure but there might be a setback. He's come through his worst danger now. The lung is all cleared up, and he's on the way to health again. From now on you won't need to keep quite so still when you walk through the hall, and in a few days he'll be up and around. But don't worry him about business, hear? Not till he's strong. Positively not a word. I've told him I won't have it."

But the sick man seemed strangely apathetic about the affairs of the world. Somehow, in the dimness of that darkened chamber, he had caught a vision of something bigger than earthly things, and he lay back and rested.

One night, shortly before Thanksgiving, when Chris, just in from the crisp outside air, came as usual to the invalid chair to which the Father had been promoted, he looked up and smiled wistfully at his son.

"Sorry, boy, about college, but—maybe there'll be a way yet," he said sorrowfully.

"Oh, Dad!" cried the boy, summoning a simulated brightness which he did not feel. "Don't you worry about college! I'm all right. Just so you get well, that's all we care."

"Well, you're a good boy!" said the father tenderly, "and please, God, I'm going to get well. The doctor promises me that by the fifteenth of December, if I'm good, I may go down to the bank. So, you see, I'm really progressing. And Son, Mother and I have been talking about this house. We think the sale ought to be through as soon as possible for the sake of our creditors."

"The doctor said you mustn't talk about business yet," said the boy, feeling as if his father had struck him.

"No, I'm not going to, Chris, only I didn't want you to be utterly unprepared if somebody comes here to look at the house. The doctor said it wouldn't do me any harm. In fact, it is a great relief to me to feel that I am doing all in my power to make up to my creditors. You won't mind, Chris."

"Of course not!" said Chris shortly, swallowing the lump that had begun to rise in his throat and the utter rebellion in his heart. He thought bitterly of the deputation that had come from college to say they'd arranged a way in which his last college year could be financed, but he had not even told his mother about it. He knew he was needed at home for a long time yet, and that even if his father regained his usual health and was not actually physically dependent upon him, that he should stay at home and get a job, stick by and make it as easy for the family as he could. He knew this was right. But he was feeling just a little proud of himself, and set up, too, that he had taken the stand, refusing the offer courteously but definitely, and had kept his mouth entirely shut about it. He felt quite a little bitter at the world, and unconfessedly at God, too, for "handing him out such a raw deal," as he phrased it.

But the next day Chris began to look for a job in good earnest. Up to that time he had not felt that he should be away from the house more than a few minutes at a time, lest he should be needed.

It is true that Chris had, from the beginning, felt easy in his mind about job hunting. Of course, he knew all about the unemployed situation, and that older men than himself, with families dependent upon them, were looking vainly for jobs. He knew this in a general way, but still it never entered his head that he would have a hard time hunting something to do, a real paying job. He felt that his father's son would be welcomed as an employee in any one of a dozen big concerns in town. He wasn't expecting to be a bank president right at the first, of course, but he did expect that several places would be open to him at a good salary just because he was Christopher Walton Jr.

He had carefully looked the situation over, weighing the wisdom of undertaking a position as a bond salesman, as a cashier in a bank, as an assistant in a real estate office looking toward a partnership, or something in insurance. They all appealed to him in various ways. A managership in one of those big oil corporations might be good, too. Of course, he expected six month's training in anything before he would be put in a responsible position with a worthwhile salary.

No, Chris was not conceited, as we usually count the meaning of that word. He was simply judging probabilities by his old standards, as his father's son, the son of the leading bank president in town. He had, as yet, no conception of what it meant to be a bank president whose bank had closed its doors and put hundreds of poor people in destitute situations. A bank president, it's true, who had promised to give up everything and stand by his creditors, but after all, a failure. And Chris was yet to find out that even nobility sometimes begets contempt. He even came to the place once where he wondered if some people would not have respected his father more if he had kept his own millions and lived on in his big house, with servants and cars galore. He came to the place where he found that some men respected money more than even honesty—bowed to it, deferred to it, honored those who had it. His young, furious, indignant soul had many things to learn and many experiences to pass through before he found peace.

So Chris started out early the next morning to find his "position," as he called it, expecting to be able to announce his success to his father on his return.

Chris went first to three best-known bond houses in the city, the heads of which were supposedly personal friends of his father. The head of the first was in conference and declined to see him that day. The head of the second was in a hurry and told him so at once, but informed him coolly that there was no opening with their house at present. They were thinking of dismissing a couple of men, rather than taking on any. Perhaps in the spring. How was his father? He glanced at his watch, and Chris knew the interview was over.

The third one told him frankly that there was no business at present to warrant taking on new men, and that even if there were, he, Chris, should finish college before he thought of applying for such a job. He suggested that money could be borrowed for his last college year. And when Chris indignantly told him he was needed at home and informed him of his invitation to go to college under scholarships, the man shook his head and told him it was simply crazy to decline that offer, that his father would never allow him to be so foolish when he was well and 'round again.

There might, of course, be truth in some of the things the man said, but Chris closed his lips and left. He could not tell this friend of his father's how utterly destitute they were going to be and how he must work to help his father and mother. He simply closed his lips and left.

All that day he went from place to place, marking each one off his list as he left, his heart growing heavier and heavier, and more bewildered, as he plodded on. The bright prospects, which he had held as many and to be had for the asking, were receding fast.

His sad heart was not made lighter by meeting Gilda Carson, just getting into Bob Tyson's car. She was home from college for the Thanksgiving holiday, and she tossed him the most casual smile, hardly as if she knew him at all. Never an eager lighting of the face, nor a joyous calling out to him to be sure and come over that evening. Just a cool bow, and she was off, smiling up at Bob as they drove away together.

He frowned and walked half a block beyond his destination, telling his bitter heart that he didn't care in the least what Gilda did, nor what Bob Tyson thought, nor anything. He didn't care! He didn't care! He didn't care! But yet he knew in his sad heart that he did care. He cared that his pride had been hurt. Gilda herself wasn't worth caring about, of course. In a sense he had always known that, but he had enjoyed taking the prettiest girl in school about and getting away from others whenever he chose. And to have her freeze him out this way, just because his father had lost money! Well, he was off her for life anyway, and he'd show her, he said fiercely to himself.

He thought, with a pang, of the fellows off in college, the boys he had played baseball with, and football. If the fellows were only back home, about town, it would be different. He wouldn't feel so alone. Boys never snubbed like girls. If Walt Gillespie were only home now, he would show them all a thing or two. Walt was his best friend. Of course, Walt had been a bit lofty when he first began to tell about his being president of the fraternity, and about Dick Bradford; and come to think about it, Walt hadn't written since he went back. Of course, college took a lot of time and fellows weren't keen on writing letters. But—well—if it had been Walt who had to stay home, he wouldn't have left him cold, without word that way. He might have found time for a postcard. Just some word about the winning of a game or how the frat was going or something.

A new pang shot through him, and his bitterness continued to grow.

He came home at night dog weary, his young face almost haggard, with gray lines about his eyes and mouth. His mother watched him anxiously across the table but asked no questions. She knew, as mothers know without asking, that he had been out to hunt a job and had not succeeded.

Then, next morning, when he started on his rounds among a less aristocratic group of firms, he had his jaw set firmly. Before night he would find something. He would force himself in somewhere. It was ridiculous that nobody wanted him. There was a place for him somewhere. He hadn't tried but one day, yet. Of course, he would find something before night.

About ten o'clock, as he was passing the station, he spied Betty Zane descending from the train with her suitcase, home for Thanksgiving from her coeducational college.

"Hello, Chris!" She waved to him. "Can't you take me home in your lovely new car?"

There seemed to Chris's sensitive ear a mocking tone in Betty's voice. Betty Zane knew, of course, that he had no new car now. She must have been thoroughly informed of all that happened since she went away. If no one else would tell her, her sharp-eyed kid sister Gwendolen would have done so. Betty was just trying to make him confess that he had no car. Betty was like that. She used to pin a butterfly to her desktop in school and enjoy watching the poor fluttering wings. Chris hardened his heart, remembering Gilda's freezing bow of yesterday, and he gave Betty a very good male imitation of it, and answered quite rudely for a boy who had been brought up to be courteous, "Nothing doing. I'm out of business. There's the taxi."

Betty stared at him and tossed her head, then turned her back upon him, and Chris moved on out of her sight, all the more out of sorts with the world because he knew that he ought to be ashamed of himself.

So he tramped on, bitter and pessimistic. Grand day this, he ought to be ashamed of himself.

Oh, of course, he was glad and thankful that Dad was getting better and Mother wasn't breaking under the strain. But even that had a sting in it, for what prospect had Dad but bitterness and disappointment? It would be better, perhaps, if they all died together rather than to live on and see such a difference between their former life and now. How could they ever be happy again? Dad would probably find that men in the business world could be just as offish as the young folks. Dad wouldn't keep that cheery, exalted look long, after he got back into business life again. He would find he was up against it. It was all well enough to be so relieved that his good name was to be cleared and no one have to suffer for the bank's troubles, but just wait till the excitement blew over. Dad would suffer. Just suffer! And so would Mother, and it was up to him to do something about it. He'd simply *got* to get a real paying job.

Then he let himself into the house to find that his father and mother were rejoicing, yes, actually rejoicing that the beautiful family car they had had for only about four months, and which had been the delight of their hearts, had been sold at a good price. What did they care how much the old thing brought since they had to give it up?

Father had family prayers as usual, reading a chapter about the goodness of the Lord and actually thanking God that the car had been so well sold! Well, it was just inexplicable, that was all. For his own part, he felt so rebellious at the going of their car that he could hardly make his knees bend to kneel down with them. Thank God for that? There wasn't a chance!

As they rose from their knees after prayer, Mr. Walton said, with a ring to his voice that his son could not understand, "I heard today of a possible buyer for the house. If that be so, we may soon be on an honest basis."

"Honest?" burst out Chris.

"Yes, Son," said the father, turning wise, kind eyes toward him. "I shrink every day from coming out of a house like this when many depositors in the bank that was under my care, people who trusted in me to take care of their all, are almost without food or shelter."

And Chris perceived that his father and mother were bent on one thing, the paying of their debts, and that possessions meant nothing to them so long as a single creditor had anything against them.

He opened his lips to ask, "But where shall we go, Dad, if the house is sold?" And then was ashamed in the face of such nobility as both parents were displaying, and closed them again.

So, the house was going, too! That was another thing to dread! It was like standing on a tiny speck of land in the midst of a wild, whirling ocean and seeing the land crumble away under one's feet bit by bit. The car had gone today, college yesterday; the house where he was born would perhaps go tomorrow. And where were all the friends of the years? Would any of them stick, or would they melt away, one by one, till they stood alone in an alien world?

Chapter 6

It was not until the week after Thanksgiving that the buyer came to look at the house. Chris had almost begun to hope that he was a myth and no one would come.

He was a big pompous man who murdered the King's English and wore an enormous diamond on his fat little finger, as if it were a headlight.

He had a large family of untamed children who swarmed cheerfully, boldly through the house, fingering Mrs. Walton's embroideries, staring into her private room rudely, yelling at one another from one story to another, and even attempting to be what Chris called "fresh" with him, the son of the house.

They freely discussed the furnishings; laughed at some things as funny and old fashioned; were frankly curious about some of the rich tapestries, which the Walton's had counted among their finer treasures; asked questions without stint, gaining new viewpoints, one could see, with every icy answer that Chris made as he showed them over the rooms at his mother's request. As he progressed from cellar to attic, his rage and indignation increased. Why did they have to stand this sort of thing from these low-down, common people? It was bad enough to have them buy the house without this torture. If they wanted it, let them take it and keep still. If they didn't, let them go away! He had no patience with his mother's smiling sweetness, her gentle courtesy. He knew it was hard for her as for him. Yet she kept her strength and sweetness. How could she? These insufferable people! They were fairly insulting and acted as if the house already belonged to them. One daughter with too much lipstick said she hoped he would call on her often. It would be nice and cozy having someone come who knew the house well, and he'd likely be homesick and would enjoy coming back. He looked at her coldly and said nothing. He waded deep into the waters of humiliation that day.

It was rumored that the father was a bootlegger and had made an enormous sum of money, which he didn't know how to spend. He was voluble in his delight in the house, offered to buy the pictures and hangings and furniture, even the precious works of art Dad and Mother had picked up abroad. They wanted the house just as quick as the Waltons could possibly get out. They made no question about the price that was asked. They even offered to pay a bonus if they could have possession in two weeks.

Chris, with a furl of disgust on his lip, looked to his father for a quick refusal, but when he saw the relief on that pale, beloved face, and realized that what his father wanted more than anything in life was a speedy release from indebtedness, a quick relief from his depositors, he closed his lips hard on the protest he was about to make. After all, of course it was a good price the man was paying, and a bonus would help, too. He must remember they were paupers and had no right to pick and choose.

Oh, those were bitter days for Chris, tramping the streets all day, sometimes far into the evening, sometimes walking miles into the country to reach a man who had no influence.

Then came the question of where they would go. Chris faced it bitterly, thinking of lodging houses or a boardinghouse or a hotel apartment. But the next night, when he came home and heard the plan his mother and father had agreed upon, he thought his cup of humiliation was full.

There was a little run-down house on a back street whose kitchen windows looked out upon the railroad, a street where the washerwoman lived. It had recently come into Mr. Walton's hands through the death of a man without a family, who owed him a debt of long standing and had given him a judgment note against the house. Chris's family was actually planning to move into it next week and vacate their noble family mansion for the bootlegger's family. Chris sat down in the nearest chair, aghast.

Elise was there, having been summoned home from her aunt's, where she had been while her father was ill. Elise, in her pretty blue dress, with her fair curling hair and her lovely, big blue eyes. Somehow, she had never looked so lovely before to her brother's eyes as when he thought of her in Sullivan Street living next to their washerwoman!

Before he could shut his lips, so carefully guarded during all the weeks when his father lay ill, one awful sentence about Elise and Mother living next to the washerwoman slipped out, and Chris saw the dart of pain in his father's eyes at once.

"But," said Elise cheerfully, "she won't have to be our washer-woman anymore, you know, Chrissy, because, as I understand it, we can't afford any washerwoman. We have to do the wash ourselves. I think it'll be fun." She ended with a grin of good sportsmanship.

"I know!" sighed the father, with a piteous look around upon them all.

"Nothing of the kind!" said Elise. "Mother and I are going to enjoy it, aren't we, Mother? It'll be the chance of a lifetime for me to learn to be a good cook and housekeeper. Forget it, Daddy! This is only a game. Get into position and smile!"

And her father, in spite of his heavy heart, smiled at the pretty girl.

"Maybe it'll be for a little while," he murmured, trying to make his voice sound hopeful.

That night Chris bought a paper and spent two hours studying the want ads and marking them. As he finally got into his bed, he thought of the fellow who had preached that fool sermon the last time he went to church, and wished he could wring his neck. A lot he could be thankful for the things that were handed out to him now, couldn't he? Mother and Elise in a place like Sullivan Street! Good night! He'd *got to* get a *job*!

He didn't call it a position anymore; it was just a plain job. He felt he might even be a little thankful if he could just have a few dollars coming in to help out. No creditor was going to get his money, not till he was making enough to put Mother in a comfortable position anyway.

The next morning he started out early and answered three advertisements, but found a long line of discouraged-looking applicants waiting for each. While he was waiting for a fourth place, which had named a time for applicants to arrive, he stepped around to Sullivan Street and found it even worse than he feared.

The house was whitewashed, or had been once, but there was scarcely enough of the original to identify it. It looked, through dirty windows, to have but five rooms and a lean-to kitchen. There were four dirty, limp cords fastened from stakes in the hard ground to the top of the window sash, and twined about them were four dead, dried ghosts of morning glory vines, waving disconsolately about in the chill November breeze. They typified to Chris their family of four Waltons, come down to Sullivan Street from the glory of the ancestral home that had been theirs.

The dead leaves waved and rasped emptily, back and forth against the broken windowpane, making a sad little minor refrain of weird music that sent a lump into the boy's throat. He dashed around the narrow path to the backyard, a mere patch, mostly paved with ashes, and saw a tattered clothesline stretched from the corner of the house to the fence and back, and fancied his beautiful young sister hanging up the family wash thereon in a chilly wind like this. The tears stung into his eyes. He hurried off and tried to forget it all, wishing for a genie and a magic lamp with which to bring an immediate fortune for the family. He went on to the next place on his list, was told they wanted only college graduates, and turned with more bitterness in his heart.

Thankful for a thing like that? Not he. Where was his father's God, anyway? Had there really been any God at all, he wondered as he buttoned his coat closer and pulled his hat over his smarting eyes. He had a feeling at the pit of his stomach, like his memory of the day he first discovered there wasn't any real Santa Claus.

What was going to happen next, he wondered desperately, and pulled his hat further down over his eyes.

The next few days were soul-trying ones for Chris, beyond anything he had ever experienced before. He was appalled to find his mother and father were both determined to move to the Sullivan Street house. Even the first desolate glimpse of the house had not discouraged them.

He had watched them as they came in sight, walking, the first time they had been out since the car was sold, walking down the plebian street like common folks. Chris raged inwardly and followed behind them, dropping his eyes, hoping they would not meet anyone who knew them.

"I'm afraid it looks pretty hopeless," sighed the father. "If I just didn't remember what wonders you can work with very simple things, I would give up in despair. But we could be happy there for a little while, couldn't we, Mary? Perhaps something will change, and we can get into a better neighborhood soon."

"We can be very happy!" said Mary with a toss of her head and that bright smile she had worn ever since her elderly lover had begun to get well.

"A little paint will work wonders," she said. "We can save on butter and things, and buy paint, and Chris and I can put it on. I'll do the inside and Chris will do the outside. There's a pair of nice new overalls I bought for the chauffeur and never gave him. They will do for Chris, and we have a ladder, haven't we?"

Whether it was the vision of himself in overalls on a ladder painting that Sullivan Street house, or the rainbow cheerfulness of his mother's voice, one or the other, or both, brought sudden tears to Chris's eyes. And he had to duck his head down quickly and pretend to be trying to pick up a round bit of tin that looked like a dime from the sidewalk, lest his father should see him crying. Tears! In a fellow old enough to be in college! Why, he hadn't felt like crying since he was a baby and licked all the boys in the street, and then found his nose was bleeding and one eye wouldn't open.

Mother hadn't been discouraged with the inside of the house, either. She had said how it was good they had never sold that coal range in the cellar at home. Nobody would want to buy that. They were out of date now. But it would practically heat the house in mild weather, and a coal range was wonderful to cook with. You could broil a beefsteak to perfection over hot coals that would make a gas-broiled steak blush with shame. Cheerily like that she talked along, suggesting the old red sofa from the attic—the one that had been her mother's and she had never been willing to part with, even though it was shabby and old-fashioned—would fit in between the side windows that looked out on the alley. She recalled, also, a little stand and a strange old pine desk that had been her father's and a few over-stuffed chairs. It had been mere tender memories that had kept them in the attic instead of sending them to the dump. But now, why! She looked almost glad with that tender touch in her eyes, as if she were actually pleased that they were to come into their own again. Her son stood by the dusty window and looked out, marveling.

And the very next morning, he came home and found his mother washing that dirty window, out of which he had looked! He had come home for lunch, and the one maid who was staying with them till they were moved said lunch was ready but his mother had gone down to "the other house." The words gave his heart a wrench. As if that dump down there could be called a house! "The *other* house!" He had followed hotfoot after her and found her washing the windows, her sleeves rolled up, an old sweater pinned around her closely, and a stray lock of wavy gray hair fallen into her eyes, her face as eager as a child's. The wife of the president of the Fidelity Bank washing windows in late November in a cold house!

He took her home summarily, walking so fast she was almost out of breath and scolding her all the way, but she only smiled. After that, he went back after lunch and finished the rest of the windows himself. He didn't do them very well. They had streaks all over them, but at least the dust was off. Then he looked around in dismay at the work still to be done. Walls and floors had to be swept and washed. Dirty paper, dirty paint! Ugh! How could his mother bear it? It was harder to wash a window than to play an afternoon's game of football. He was trembling from head to foot. After serious consideration he went home and collected some of his treasures—his camera, several tennis rackets, and a set of golf clubs—and took them to a second-hand place and sold them. Then he hunted up a man who did whitewashing and got him to promise to scrub the whole house early the next morning.

After that Chris abandoned his vain search for a job until the moving should be over. Chris and Elise went to work, Chris with a frown on his handsome face, and Elise with laughter and cheerful songs, jokes, and an indefatigable ability to sit down on the stairs anywhere and giggle at his efforts. Often he got furiously angry at her. He found it impossible to treat this whole catastrophe of the family like a joke. It was serious business, the wreck of their whole lives, and here were Mother and Elise laughing as if they enjoyed it. They were just alike.

Then he would glance at his father, sitting back, relaxed, smiling in his invalid chair, not allowed to lift his finger, and looking very peaceful. What did Dad have that kept him so serene? He was satisfied that Dad was deeply hurt that all these things had to be, cut to the heart that his wife and daughter must work so hard, that his son could not go to college, yet the lines of care were not nearly so deep on his forehead as they had been some weeks before the bank closed its doors. Was it just that he was relieved to be doing his best toward paying the depositors? No, it must be something more than that. And in spite of himself, he felt a respect for his father's faith. It might have no foundation, but whether it did or not, it was beautiful to see such faith. He found a hungry feeling in his own heart to have something like that to stay his furious young heart upon. Yet he told himself he never could believe in a God who would do such things to trusting people, and he readily hardened his heart when he heard his father pray, always beginning his petition with thanksgiving. He simply could not understand it. Elise was only a child, of course. She enjoyed every new thing that came along, even moving into a little seven-by-nine dinky house on a back street, like a child playing dollhouse. His mother was merely glad that his father was up and around again. Neither Mother nor Elise had any sense of what it was going to mean, this terrible change in the family fortunes. But his father understood, and yet he bore up. It was inexplicable.

Yet somehow, in spite of all predictions, when the paint and paper were in place and the few old sticks of furniture disposed about, that had been saved from the wholesale carnage, even the old golden oak sideboard and dining room table and chairs from the servant's dining room took on an air of comfort. Chris couldn't explain it.

There were draperies, too, that Chris remembered in the nursery when he was a kid, cheery linens with tie backs, long since packed in an old chest in the attic and only pulled out for home charades when they needed costumes. But now they seemed to make, out of the little shanty on Sullivan Street, a cozy nest where comfort might be found in the midst of a desolated world.

It was that first night that they had supper in the new home.

Elise and her mother, in plain cotton dresses, were in the speck of a kitchen getting supper, and a savory smell was already beginning to pervade the house. The rooms were too near neighbors to have any secrets from the parlor of what was going on in the kitchen. Chris knew there was one of those savory stews he always liked so much, and he was hungry for it already. Anna, the departing maid, had cooked it that morning in the old house before the last load of things they were allowing themselves to call their own from the attic came over. Chris knew that Anna had also made doughnuts and a couple of mince pies on the sly between other duties. He had brought over the stone jar containing the doughnuts and the basket with the mince pies early that morning that Anna's surprise for his mother might be complete. Oh, there would be a good supper.

Elise was setting the table, humming a cheerful little tune that never gave hint of the tears that were so near the surface. His father was sitting beside the old attic table in the faded old Morris chair with his feet on the extension, reading the evening paper and resting as happily as if he had been in his gorgeous leather chair in his own library, with the carved desk beside him and an alabaster lamp of old world design to light him. Didn't his father know the difference? Didn't he care at all?

And now came a call for Chris to go after a loaf of bread.

"It's only a couple of blocks or so up the avenue, Chris," said Elise cheerfully, as she saw a frown gather on her brother's brow. "I'd go but Mother needs me. Dinner'll be quite ready when you come back. It's one of those grocery stores, the second block on the right. I bought a cake of soap there yesterday. You can't miss it."

"Why? Will I see the rest of the box of soap out watching for me?" asked the brother ill-naturedly as he rose and slung his cap on the back of his head. "I thought you got an *A* in English. Why would the fact that you bought a cake of soap there yesterday keep me from missing the store?"

"Quit your kidding and hurry, please. I'm making popovers and they need to be eaten at once when they're done."

Chris sauntered out into the chilly evening air, perversely refusing to wear his overcoat and feeling as if he had been exiled into an evil world again. The cheeriness of the little house that had half angered him only made the outside world seem the more unfriendly. How dark Sullivan Street was. The city ought to put in more lights. He hurried along angrily. It seemed to him as if he had scarcely been anything but angry since the bank had closed.

He found the grocery store, bright and full of brisk business. Everybody was there inspecting trays of vegetables, buying great creamy slices of cheese, prunes, crackers, coffee, flour, and potatoes. One woman had a long list and a pile of groceries on the counter before her, and now she turned toward the meat side of the store and began to select pork chops.

Chris looked around curiously. It was almost the first time since he was a little boy that he had been in such a store. There hadn't been any need. Those things were always well ordered by a capable maid over the telephone. Not even his mother had had to mingle with the common herd this way. The store was bright and cheery.

Everything looked clean and appetizing. There were delightful smells of oranges, celery, and coffee in the air. But no one was paying the slightest attention to him. They gave him a curious sensation. He was used to deference everywhere. Well, of course, no one knew him in this section of the city, and there was relief in that. How interested these people were, as if they were selecting a new car or a Christmas present. What did they care which bunch of carrots they bought? Cranberries! How pretty they were in bulk.

But he must get waited on quickly. He didn't want to stay here all night. He approached a salesman with a lady who was accumulating a great pile of things on the counter. She had come to a pause and was trying to think up something else, gazing up at the top shelves of cereals. He would just cut in on her and get his bread and get out.

But the salesman looked up with a courteous smile.

"Sorry, I'm busy just now. You'll have ta wait your turn. Somebody'll be free in a minute, I guess."

Chris stepped back haughtily and felt as if he had been slapped in the face. So, there were rules to this grocery store game. Everyone was just as good as everyone else. The dark color flung up in his face, and he was about to leave, when he suddenly remembered his recent lowly estate and retreated into the background.

Pinned in a corner by a bunch of brooms and a stack of bargain cans of peaches, watching sullenly for a free salesman, he suddenly heard low-spoken words behind him, not meant for his ear for sure.

"That's him," said an uncultured voice. "He's the old man's son. Some baby! Yep, right behind ya. Nope, he dunno me. I was in grammar when he was in high. He wouldn't know me from a bag a beans. And anyhow, he wouldn't. He always was an awful snob! My goodness, no. I wouldn't speak to him. I wouldn't wantta be snubbed. I hate snobs!"

Cold, angry prickles went down Chris's back, and he felt the very back of his neck grow red. He could hardly come out of his fury when his courteous salesman wheeled upon him at last with a free and easy, "Now, sir, what can I get for you?"

His voice sounded unnatural as he asked for the bread. He didn't remember ever to have bought a loaf of bread before. He wondered if there was a certain way of asking for it. He glowered after the two whispering flappers who had been behind him. They were over at the meat counter now, giggling and chewing gum. The one with the red hair and freckles was vaguely familiar as a kid who once tried to run through a football game in the schoolyard and made all the fellows furious. She wasn't any account, of course, but was that the way all of the school had regarded him, as a snob?

Then his humiliation would be the greater. They would gloat over his loss of caste. He had never regarded himself anything but a self-respecting son of his father. A snob was one who looked down on most other people. Well, perhaps he had, but he had always supposed they didn't know it. He had rather regarded it as a breach of etiquette to let others know that they were despised. He must have failed sadly.

He had his loaf of bread at last and went with the check and his money to the cash window, hastily, to get out before he might meet those two disrespectable flappers and have to recognize them as fellow buyers.

He handed in his check at the little glass window and was suddenly aware of a pair of friendly eyes looking up at him and a shyly hesitant smile.

Chapter 7

Natalie Halsey! Here? Her pale little friendly face seemed like a pleasant oasis in this strange, unfriendly environment.

"Hello!" he said, almost eagerly, his face lighting up with a strange relief. "Is this where you hang out? I didn't know it was in this neighborhood."

"Yes." She smiled again. "This is where you picked me up in your new car the other day and took me home. I'll always be grateful to you for getting me home so soon. Mother had had a bad spell just before I left, and she was getting very nervous about my being gone so long. She might have had a relapse if I had been much longer."

"You don't say!" he said, startled, half pleased to be commended for something he had done after the unpleasant whisper he had just heard behind his back.

"You are home from college for the Thanksgiving holiday, aren't you? Or—that would be over wouldn't it? It must be a weekend," she commented in a momentary lull from her store activities.

"No such luck!" he said, a dark cloud of remembrance passing over his face. "I didn't get to go to college."

"Oh," said Natalie sympathetically. "Someone said you were at home, but I wasn't sure. You—are working somewhere? But you'll enjoy that, too. It's nice to be doing something real."

He looked down at the sweet, childish face, a little weary, a little blue under the eyes, and felt a sudden tenderness for her, and anger at himself. She was doing something real. She had found it for herself, and he, Chris Walton, couldn't get *anything*. Not *anything*!

"I wish I were," he said wistfully. "I've walked all over this little old town and nobody wants me."

There was a strange humility about his words. Natalie looked up in wonder.

"You don't know of a good job, do you?" he added wistfully.

"Oh"—breathed Natalie, her eyes thoughtfully watching him. "Yes, I do. But—you wouldn't want such a job. I'm sure you wouldn't."

"Try me and see," said Chris, with sudden determination as he thought of the little cozy room shut in by the curtains and his beautiful mother in that tiny kitchen getting supper. He must somehow make good. He was desperate.

"But," said Natalie, growing a bit red and confused, "it's only—a—it's not in keeping with your—position," she ended bravely.

"My position, lady," said Chris, with a grim humility upon his face that made his chin look rugged and firm, "is away down at the foot of the ladder. I'm groveling at present, if you know what that means. If you have any such jobs as that, please lead me to them."

A woman snapped in between them with a five dollar bill to be changed, and two others followed with their checks to be paid, and Chris had to step back for a moment.

He noted Natalie's pale fingers as they flew among the dirty bills, checking off dimes and nickels, and wondered that he had never noticed before how delicate and fragile she was. Then the three women moved on and there was another moment's cessation.

"It's only right here, in this store." She eyed him anxiously. "You wouldn't want to work here, would you, in a plain, common place like this?"

"I don't know why not," said Chris gamely, swallowing hard at a surprised lump in his throat. "Is there a chance here, do you think? I must get a job."

"We're losing a man today," said Natalie. "He got a telegram that his father had died, and he must go back to Wisconsin and stay with his mother and get a job there. Our manager is very cross about it. He needs someone right away, but he is very particular. I don't know whether he has found anyone yet or not, and he must have someone Monday. If you could come back at a quarter to nine—we keep open till nine on Saturday nights, you know—I could speak to him about it. There might be a chance. But it's only an under position, you know."

Some women were approaching, loud-voiced among themselves, sticking out checks and money, all talking at once.

"I'll be back," said Chris, with sudden determination, and walked away out into the night and the evening smells of the common district where he had come to live. Pork and cabbage, and a fish frying in old grease. *Pah!* What a neighborhood! And he was going to be a common grocer's clerk and sell cheese and rat traps and pickled pig's feet to those gossipy women! Instead of halfback on the college football team, president of his fraternity, and son of a banker!

He saw himself going around in that crowded store, weighing sugar and cutting cheese and bringing up great cases of cereal and canned stuff. Girls like those two who had pointed him out would think they could say fresh things and kid with him. How his mother would hate it! How he would hate it!

Yet, there was a kind of elation about him to think that, perhaps, there was a job in sight. Besides, hadn't he heard that there was a promotion in these stores? Of course, he would not stay a common clerk long. If he had inherited any of his father's business ability, he could build up and get ahead. And when he got a little money saved up, if he didn't like the grocery line, he could get into another line. But, after all, why weren't stores where they sold eatables the best thing to tie to? People had to eat, no matter how hard the times were, nor what happened. That was an idea, too.

But he wouldn't say anything about it at home until he knew more about it. And then, he hadn't got the job yet, either. Natalie had only promised to speak to the manager. There might be another man by this time, or the manager might think him a snob, too. There was no telling in this strange, new, sad world into which he had come to live, it seemed.

He was almost home before he remembered that he had not thanked Natalie. Little pale-faced, eager, wistful Natalie, with her soft halo of hair and her tired, trusting eyes. It was kind of Natalie. He had never done anything for her, except to take her home that once with her bundles. Well, he would go back and see, anyway. He wouldn't have to remember that he had turned any job down, no matter how unsatisfactory.

He came swinging into the house, whistling under his breath, forgetting his troubles for the moment. He was thinking that perhaps he was going to get some kind of a break after all. Only a grocery, but something better might turn up later. At least, if he could get it, he wouldn't be exactly a slacker while he was looking around for something better. Of course, the salary wouldn't be large at first, while he was learning.

They sat down to dinner as if it were a picnic. Somehow it didn't seem so mournful, after all, as he had expected. Chris thought he would always remember his father's first blessing at the little golden oak table, with mother's coarsest tablecloth upon it and the old dishes that had been used mostly in the kitchen at the other house. It was, "Father, we remember that Your Son had not where to lay His head, at times, when He was upon the earth. We thank You for this comfortable, quiet home that You have given us and for this evening meal. Make us to show Your glory by the strength of it. Amen."

Chris was very quiet and thoughtful during the meal, jumping up to get a pitcher of water and replenish the popovers from the pan in the warming oven, to save his mother and sister.

"We have much to be thankful for," said the father, looking around on his family. "Mary, what wonderful children we have. I haven't heard a murmur out of either one of them."

"Why, Daddy, we're having the times of our lives," said Elise cheerfully.

"Same here!" Chris tried to say, guiltily choking over his glass of water and having to retire behind his napkin. He felt in his heart that it was not quite honest for him to say that. But he couldn't bear not to be a good sport when his father and mother were so wonderful. Well, he was going to get that job in the grocery, if it were a possible thing.

He helped Elise clear the table and put away the dishes in order, and about half past eight, he took his hat and went out.

"Oh, I thought we'd all go to bed early," said his mother, looking at him in a troubled way as he opened the door.

"I won't be long, Mother." He tried to reassure her. "I want to see a man about a job I heard of. I can't get him at any other time. It might turn out to be something."

"Well, come home as soon as you can. You know this is a strange neighborhood, and we aren't sure yet what kind of people live around here. I shall worry—"

"No, you don't worry, Mother," said Chris quickly. "You've been a good sport, and you're not going to worry anymore."

She looked after him wistfully as he went out, although she summoned a faint smile. But he knew that she was exceedingly weary, and in spite of all her brave smiles and cheery demeanor, this day must have been very hard for her. He felt condemned that he had thought so much about his own part of the disappointment.

As he neared the grocery store, his soul rebelled. How could he go in there and ask for a job recommended by a girl? A poor girl, who really knew him very little, too? Oughtn't he to go back and get his father to write a letter, or get in touch with the head of all these stores, or do something that would place him on a regular footing and give him a worthwhile salary?

Then suddenly the words of those two obnoxious girls came to him, that he was a snob, and somehow he felt that he would rather stand on his own feet and work his way into any possible favor, than to try to hang on to the old life with its power and influence. So, he held his head up and walked in.

There were still a few last customers keeping the tired salesmen busy, and Natalie, in her little glass house, was busy, too, counting change and getting her cash register ready for the night. But she smiled at him distantly and briefly, as he stood by the door and waited until she seemed to have a moment of leisure. Then he went over and spoke to her in a low voice, as if he were just another customer.

"Wouldn't you rather I came in Monday morning and went to the manager myself? I don't want to keep you or bother you. And all these men look so doggone tired, I hate to butt in on them now."

"No," said Natalie quickly, "he expects you. I found a chance to tell him you were coming. I didn't say much; I thought you'd rather do your own talking. I just said I knew a man who wanted work and I had told him to come around. He seemed relieved. He's been worried all day about it, but he had no time to go out and look up anybody. And the district manager went to New York yesterday, so he can't call on him for an extra man. There he is now, over by those crates, opening them. Now is as good a time as any to talk to him. There aren't many customers left. His name is Foster."

Chris summoned his nerve and walked over to the young fellow in the white linen coat and apron. Why, he didn't look much older than himself!

"Is this Mr. Foster?" he asked, trying to remember that he was asking a favor, not granting one, by being willing to work in that store. "I heard you needed a man. Would I do?"

Foster looked him up and eyed Chris keenly, then grinned at him.

"Take hold and help me put these cans on the shelves, and let's see how you can work," he said. "After that, we'll talk."

Chris flung his cap on a barrel top and set to work stacking the cans in orderly rows on the shelves, saying nothing, but taking great armfuls from the crates and stalking back and forth as if his life depended on it. Foster did not appear to be watching him, did not even seem to be aware of him, except now and then for a necessary direction. And they worked away as if they had always done this. Chris found that it was actually interesting to put those cans in their ranks quickly and get back for another load in record time.

When the crates were empty, Foster gave him another grin.

"That's all. You seem to have pep enough. Just take those empty crates down to the cellar, door over to your right, smash them up with the ax you'll see at the foot of the stairs, and pile them with the other wood against the wall. When you come back, we'll talk business."

When Chris came upstairs, the customers were gone and the front door closed. Natalie was putting on her hat and coat in her little glass den.

Foster had a pencil and notebook, and began asking him questions. His name, age, experience. Was he a stranger? Was he willing to obey orders?

Chris answered briefly and studied his new boss. A quick, keen, alert young man without conceit. He liked him.

"All right," said Foster, "you report Monday morning at eight o'clock. You understand I haven't authority to hire you permanently. But I'll try you out for a week and report to my boss when he gets back next week. If you make good, I'll be glad to have you.

You worked well tonight. Good night. See you Monday." And the interview was over.

Chris went out just behind Natalie, and they walked down the street together, she a little shy and beaming.

"He liked you. I could see," she said.

"I guess you've been saying something pretty nice about me," said Chris gratefully. "That was awfully nice of you. I appreciate it. If I get the job, I guess I'll owe it to you."

"Oh, I just told him you were all right, steady and dependable, you know. He used to know my grandmother and my father, and he knows I wouldn't say that if it were not so." Natalie walked gravely beside him, putting aside her part in the matter as if it were very slight. "I told him we had been in the same school and you always had good marks."

"Well, I won't forget it," he said with a friendly smile. "Say, let me carry that bundle. Sorry I haven't any car, anymore, to take you home."

"Oh, I'm used to bundles." She laughed. "You mustn't go out of your way for me. We're just fellow laborers. You mustn't feel that way about it. A working girl has to carry her own bundles."

"Not if there is a gentleman about," said Chris, masterfully possessing himself of the heavy carton she was carrying.

"You'll have your own bundles to carry presently," she said. "You know employees get a low price on things, and sometimes there are perishable things Saturday nights that they let us have for almost nothing. I save a lot that way, carrying things home."

"I suppose you do," said Chris thoughtfully. "I hadn't even thought about saving on things like that. I guess I'll have to take lessons from you. Though my mother used to tell us stories about how they lived on very little when she was a girl."

"She'll know then," assured the girl. "It doesn't take long to learn to save. But, really, you mustn't go out of your way for me. Please let me take it now. This is my corner."

"It's not out of my way," said Chris gravely. "You didn't know I lived on the street next to yours, did you?"

"Oh!" said Natalie, startled. Then "Oh!" in a sorrowful little voice. "I'm sorry you had to leave that lovely home. I always enjoyed looking at it. I saw your mother coming out the door one day. She's beautiful. I thought she fitted there so well. I liked to think of her living in such lovely surroundings. My mother had a nice home, too, when she was young."

Chris looked down on her with interested eyes, his heart warming toward her because she admired his mother, and because she was sorry about his lost home. There seemed, somehow, a bond between them.

"I guess it's hard for a girl"—he hesitated shyly, fumbling around in his mind for the right words—"to grow up, not having everything she wants."

"Oh, I don't know," said Natalie, with her cheerful little laugh again. "We've had some wonderful good times. When Father was alive, we used to enjoy what we did have, much more than some people seem to who have everything. But, it was always nice to hear Mother tell about the hardwood floors and oriental rugs and lovely things they had in her home when she was a girl. Of course, when we didn't have things, we usually made them, somehow, if it was possible."

"It's rotten for a girl like you to have to do that," he said impulsively.

She looked up at him, surprised.

"Why no! I don't think so," she said gravely.

"You don't think so?" It was his turn to be surprised.

"Not at all." Her tone almost held reproof. "Nothing that God allows to come to His children is a rotten deal. He loves us and knows what we need most. He wouldn't let it come to us if it wasn't for our best."

"You believe He sends such things then?"

"He lets them come," she said seriously. "Nothing can come to us unless it first passes through His hands." There was a sweet trustfulness about her tone that filled him with sudden reverence toward her. "Of course, some of the hard things are testings for us, but He permits them, and what He permits must be best for us."

"What possible good could come out of having to be poor and work for your living and carrying bundles too heavy for you?"

"Well," said Natalie with sudden whimsical laughter. "It might be to keep me from being a snob. I'm afraid I would have been an awful snob if I had a lovely home and all the nice things some girls have."

"You?" said Chris wonderingly, and then he laughed, too. "Do you know, I just heard myself called a snob, this afternoon, back there in the store by two little snub-nosed, lipsticked flappers that used to be in the grammar school when we were in high."

"I know who you mean. But they only thought so because you weren't fresh with them, the way some of the other boys were. You never were a snob. You were always kind and pleasant to everybody. Look how you picked me up and took me home, with all my bundles, in your beautiful new car."

"But why shouldn't I?"

"That's it," said Natalie, decidedly. "You're a gentleman. You never were a snob. Now, Bob Tyson wouldn't have done that. He wouldn't even have seen me as he whizzed by."

"Well," said Chris, "it's comforting that you didn't think I was a snob. But I'm not so sure I wasn't in a fair way to become one, come to think of it. You see, your instance of my courtesy wasn't a fair one, for I recognized the lady in you. I'm not so sure I'd have picked up those two flappers, even if they had a whole truckload to carry. So, you think the raw deal that has been handed out to me is to teach me something, do you? You think I ought to be thankful for it? Losing my home and my college diploma and my car and everything that makes life worthwhile?"

"You haven't lost your home," said Natalie quickly, "nor your father and mother and sister. You still have a place to live, and I'm pretty sure it's a real home, even if it isn't as big and elegant as it used to be. And maybe there are bigger and better things than college diplomas in life."

Chris stared. "Say, you talk like the fellow that preached in our church the last Sunday before the crash. He said we ought to be thankful for everything that's handed out. But I didn't know anybody ever really took it to heart."

"Yes," said Natalie simply, "he's wonderful. He has charge of the mission in Water Street. Did you ever go down there? It's very interesting."

"No," said Chris shortly, "but I guess if he had a little of the hardness he's talking about handed out to him, he'd sing a different tune. I don't see singing praise when the earth is reeling under you. He doesn't know what he's talking about."

"Yes, he knows," said Natalie sadly. "He lost his wife and two children of smallpox over in China. He was a missionary there. He's only been back on a year's furlough, on account of a very severe operation he had to have. He's going back in a couple of months now, going to take charge of a leper hospital, and doesn't expect ever to return to this country. But he's a great man, and he knows what it is to praise God under heavy trial. He calls it 'singing in the rain.'"

"Good night!" said Chris earnestly. "I guess I'd better shut up. I'm not even in the same class with a man like that. He must be some kind of superman."

"No," said Natalie quickly, "he's only an ordinary man with a great God. God can do great things with people who are willing to let Him."

They had reached Natalie's door now, and Chris handed her the bundles.

"Well, you sure have given me something to think about," he said gravely. "Good night, and thank you, more than I can tell, for what you have done for me."

Chapter 8

Natalie's mother looked at her anxiously as she came in, noticed the bright color in her cheeks, the light in her eyes, and sighed.

"Did someone come home with you, dear?" she asked guardedly.

Natalie turned a disarming smile on her mother and put down her armful of bundles.

"Why yes, Mother," she said happily. "I don't know how I should have managed all these bundles if he hadn't. My arm has been aching like the dickens all day where I twisted it, wrestling with that window with the broken cord last night. Just look at what I've got, Mother, a whole lot of celery. Isn't that great! It has just been frosted on the outside and turned brown and doesn't sell very well in consequence, but the heart of it is as sweet as can be. I tasted some and it's wonderful. We can make apple salad, and meat salad, and celery soup, and a lot of things besides eating the best of it just plain."

"It wasn't one of the store men, was it Natalie?" asked her mother as she wiped her hands on the roller towel and came over to look at the celery. "I wouldn't encourage them to continue to get intimate, if I were you. It isn't wise. If you let one of them come home with you, another might, and you don't know what they are all like. Even if we have to go without some things, I wouldn't bring so much you can't carry it yourself. Or—of course, sometimes Janice might come up and meet you about closing time."

"Oh, Mother dear!" laughed Natalie, stooping to kiss her little mother. "Don't you worry. Every one of those boys in the store is nice and pleasant and courteous. They don't hire any other kind there. And they all have their girls. You don't need to worry about me. They don't want to go with me. They tell me about their girls every chance they get, at noon time or in the morning. They say where they went the night before and ask my advice about what to get them for Christmas. I'm a regular old-maid auntie in the store, so I'm perfectly safe. Nobody thinks of me there as a girl, you know; I'm just the cashier. But this wasn't one of them. At least he isn't yet, though he's going to be Monday morning. They've just hired him. Mother, it was Chris Walton!"

"Chris Walton! Again!" said the mother with a strange alarm in her voice. "Oh, Natalie, I'm just afraid you will get interested in him! Why does he keep coming around you?"

Janice appeared in the front room doorway then.

"What do you mean, Natty, Chris Walton working in the store? Your store? How did he come to do that? Goodness! You'd think his father could get him a different job, in some bank or lawyer's office or something, wouldn't you? Mother, did you hear what Natalie said? Chris Walton is going to work in the grocery store."

"Oh," said the mother in perplexity. "Not *really*? Is that what you said, Natalie? How strange!"

"Isn't it?" said Natalie. "I couldn't believe he would. He's always seemed so exclusive and somehow remote. But he came into the store this afternoon to buy bread, and—"

"Natalie, has he been coming there to meet you?" asked her mother, quick to apprehend any possible danger to her offspring.

"Why no, of course not," said Natalie shortly, her brow quite vexed looking. "How silly! Why, he didn't even know I was there till he came to pay his check, and then he stopped a minute and said he was looking for a job. He hasn't gone back to college, Mother, though it's his senior year. He said he had walked all over the city and couldn't find anything to do *anywhere*, and he laughingly asked me if I knew of a job. Of course, then I had to tell him we had an opening right there in the store, just came that day. It was Tom Bonar's job. He's the one with the red hair, you know. He got a telegram that his father died, and he had to go back to Wisconsin right away and stay with his mother. And our manager had been terribly upset about it all day because he didn't know where to turn for the right man. I didn't suppose Chris would look at it or think about it, but he seemed so terribly in earnest that I had to let him know about it. But Mother, he just jumped at the chance. He was real humble about it. Said he was right down at the foot of the ladder, ready to do anything. He had a good spirit, Mother. And so he came back at closing time, and they hired him."

"Oh, dear Natalie, child, I'm afraid you are going to get interested in him. He'll be right there in the store all day, and you'll see him a lot."

"Why shouldn't she get interested in him, Mother?" broke in

Janice. "He's a *prince*. I should think you'd be glad she could have such a friend."

"But he'll not stay there," said the anxious mother. "He'll get something pretty soon and sail off into his own social standing again, and Natalie will be left lonely and heartbroken."

"Oh, Mother dear!" said Natalie. "Please, please don't think of me always in terms of matrimony. I have no desire to fall in love or get married or break my heart or any of those tempestuous things. Forget it, and trust God. Chris is just a nice boy I knew in school. And there's nothing wrong about his carrying my bundles home once in a while, although I'll manage it, of course, not to have it necessary. I guess you've brought me up decently, Mother, and I hope you can trust me. Besides, I don't wear my heart on the outside where every passing thing can knock against it and break it. He was only grateful to me for telling him about the job tonight. He probably won't have time to even look at me again. We're busy in that store, Mother. We haven't time for nonsense. But, here's something, I had a chance to witness for Christ tonight." And she told of her conversation with Chris.

When she had finished, her mother came and kissed her gently on the forehead.

"Forgive me, dear, for being overanxious. You and Jan are all I have, and I keep fluttering about you like an old hen over her chickens, I suppose. I guess I can trust my girl to be careful and discreet, and I am glad you were brave enough to talk to him that way. I've always heard his mother and father were good Christians. His father is an elder in our church, you know. But, of course, I've never known them personally. And you can't tell these days what a son is just by what his father was."

"Well," said Natalie, "I told him about our mission and the Bible study. Maybe he'll go sometime. He seemed interested. Now I suppose you'll go and worry about that. But if Jan fixes her lessons so she can go Monday nights with me, we'd be together, and it isn't the least likely he'd walk home with us anymore. Mother, he's just an old schoolmate being polite. For pity's sake, don't make me so self-conscious about him, or I'll have to get another job."

"No, no, I won't dear," said her mother quickly. "I shouldn't have spoken at all, I suppose, only I'm so afraid for you and so sorry about you that you don't have the right companionship."

"I should worry about companions!" said Natalie cheerfully. "I've got Jan, haven't I? What's better than a perfectly good sister? Is that cocoa on the stove? Look, it's boiling over! My, I'm hungry. These late Saturday hours and the rush at dinnertime make me like a little starved street child! Isn't that great? Can't you all sit down and eat something, too?"

"Yes," said Janice. "We saved our oranges from this morning, and yours, too. You didn't eat yours at breakfast, you know, so we are going to eat together."

Then the three sat down to a simple little meal in the neat white kitchen and had as good a time as if they had been three girls, chatting and planning.

"Natalie, I'm sorry I said what I did. I don't want you to think I don't trust you, and I'm glad of the way you are using your influence with that young man. We'll all pray for him, shall we, that he may find the Lord and get to know Him?"

"Oh yes, Mother, that will be wonderful. We'll claim that promise 'Where two of you shall agree,' won't we? Mother, he would be a power, if he were really saved. You know, of course, he's a member of the church like most of the rest of the young folks that go to our church. But the way he talked, I don't think he ever prays or reads his Bible, and it seemed as if he didn't really believe anything much. He spoke as if it were just all a big lot of guesswork and it might as well be any other religion as Christianity. It isn't likely I'll have another chance to speak about it to him. He'll probably go his own way after tonight. But we can pray, and that will reach him without his knowing we have anything to do with it."

"Dear child!" said the mother, with a loving look at her eldest daughter.

Meantime, Chris had walked thoughtfully, briskly, down the street. As he neared his own door, he remembered that he had a job, and he began to whistle cheerfully. His mother heard him as she was hanging up the cleansed dishtowels on a little string above the range, and smiled. It was the first time she had heard her boy whistle since the crash came.

"Well," announced Chris as he came in, "I guess I've landed a job at last. It isn't manager of the Standard Oil Company, nor president of the Rockefeller Foundation, but I guess it'll at least salt enough for our means."

His father looked up from the evening paper, a light of pleasure in his eyes. His mother came in and beamed at him, and Elise appeared in the doorway behind her, eagerly.

"What is it?" asked his sister.

He took a deep breath as if he were about to plunge into a cold ocean and said, "Errand boy in the grocery store!" And then watched them keenly to get their first reaction.

"A grocery?" said his sister, aghast.

"Fine!" said his father quickly.

"That's a clean business," said his mother interestedly.

Then Elise, with bright, fond eyes, smiling at him—"I'm proud of you, Chrissy!"

Chris drew another deep breath, this time of relief, and grinned.

"Well, don't get too set up," he said sheepishly, "they're only going to try me out Monday. They may not keep me. I may prove too good for 'em, see?"

They had family worship, Father giving thanks for them in the funny little crowded rooms, where even a bed and a small old-fashioned bureau made too many things in the room. Boy! But he had a game family! Look how they took his grocery job! Even Elise, who, being in school might get kidded about it! They amused themselves calling back and forth to one another through the thin partitions and trying to make a joke of the strangeness, but after all there was a hominess about it that had a pleasant side. Even Chris had a throb of thanksgiving as he realized how sane and well and altogether normal his father was. In fact, now that he thought about it, his father was more cheerful than he had been for the past year or so. Probably the bank's affairs had been growing more and more complicated and worried him, and now it was good to be down to rock bottom and try to climb up bravely again.

On the whole Chris felt happier than he had since the trouble came. He got into bed with a pleasant thump of his pillow and a cheerful good-night to them all. But he did not sleep at once. He began to think of Natalie and what she had said. What an unusual girl she was. Not at all the shy mouse of a thing she had seemed in school. He wished he had known her before, when he was in a position to show her some nice times. It would have been fun to give her rides and take her to class entertainments and parties. Now that he thought of it, he couldn't remember ever having seen her at one. Probably the girls had snubbed her, too. Well, she had a lot more to her than any of them. If he ever got the chance, he'd let them all know it, too.

Strange things she had said about God and being thankful for the hard things in her life. He didn't know another girl who would talk like that. He wondered how she got that way and fell asleep thinking how well she had answered everything he had said. Well, perhaps there was something in it after all. Dad seemed to have something to lean upon. He couldn't understand what it was. He vaguely wished he could.

Then he gave a bitter thought or two to his old high school friends off in college. Not a line to him about their frats or how the last football game had gone. Never a cheering word or regret that he was not with them. Oh, at first, of course, that time they came after him, but when they found they couldn't carry him off in triumph to be their hero in college as he had been, that was the end.

True, he hadn't written to them, but that was different. He hadn't anything to write about.

Suddenly, he knew as plainly as if a voice had spoken it that their ways had parted definitely. Life had swept them into separate worlds. Would it ever bring them into touch again?

Chapter 9

W hen Natalie started for the store on Monday morning, she noticed a man standing at the corner of the street with his hat drawn over his eyes and a watch in his hand.

A look of annoyance passed over her face. The same man had been there three times before, watching her come out of the house, almost as if he were waiting for her, timing her. He always gave her an ugly, familiar look as she passed, though she never seemed to notice him. She shrank from encountering it again. He was a big, tough-looking man, and she felt almost afraid of him, although it seemed absurd in broad daylight on a street where many people passed.

Impulsively, she turned the other way and walked around the whole block to escape him. But when she reached the avenue, there he was again at the next corner, standing in just the same position, watching her, but this time with an ugly, amused leer on his face, as if he wanted to let her know that he knew she had gone out of her way to escape.

She turned her face the other way and tried to act as if she had not seen him. It was getting on her nerves to have him do this way. The expression on his face somehow made her shudder. Perhaps he had no idea of watching her at all. Perhaps it was all her imagination.

And then, as if to answer her thought, the man spoke.

"Hello, girlie! Can't get away from me, can ya?" he said, and her heart beat wildly. For an instant she wanted to run, but her feet felt like lead, and it occurred to her that she must control herself and walk steadily. She must not let him know she was frightened. She had made a mistake, of course, going out of her way. He must have seen her hesitate at her own door and then turn the other way to avoid him. She would not do that again. She would just hold her head and walk by him, as if he were not there. Perhaps she ought to warn Janice. It would be terrible if he got to bothering Jan on her way to school.

She forced herself to walk steadily down the avenue, but she was trembling so, she could scarcely stand up.

She made a distinct effort to put the man out of her thoughts. She would not look back to see if he were following her. He was probably just a common fellow without very high standards. There was nothing to be really afraid of and, of course, there were police- men whom she'd call upon if he attempted to follow her. She might report it to the one that often came into the store. It was just as well to have a man like that cleared of the neighborhood. It really wasn't safe for a fifteen-year-old girl like Janice to have to pass such a man. Of course, Janice would have to learn to take care of herself, too. But somehow she felt ages older than her sister and as if she must protect her. Above all, she must not let her mother find out that that man had spoken to her. It would frighten her so that she would be anxious all the time either of them were away from the house.

She tried to concentrate her thoughts on the dress she was planning for Janice, on the other dress she meant to make possible for Janice's commencement next spring. She wondered how much she dared put away each week from her meager salary to save for that time? She herself hadn't minded so much staying out of the activities of her school at commencement time, but she hated to have Jan miss everything. Jan did love good times so much, and she had so few of them. Jan had been so sweet and good about staying out of school while Mother was sick, and now that Mother was well enough to be left alone all day, she did hope that Jan could have a little more freedom. Work would come soon enough. Also, now that Mother didn't have to have extra food and medicine and a doctor all the time, there would be more chance of saving a little for a spring wardrobe for Janice. It was so hard for Janice to always wear makeovers because she was the smallest in the family. For once she should have a dress, perhaps two, which she might go to the store and pick out for herself and try on.

Suddenly, the thought of the man burst into her thoughts again. What if he should hang around and frighten Mother? It was silly, of course, to think that, and what could she do about it but pray? "Oh, God, take care of Mother dear, and Janice, please," she prayed again and again as she walked down the street, her heart gradually growing quieter and more trustful, her nerves steadying.

As she neared the store, she remembered Chris. Would he

really come there to work that day, or would he back out of it after thinking it over? Somehow, she couldn't make it seem real that Chris Walton, the banker's son, the most popular boy in high school—popular, too, she had heard, in his college—should be coming to work that morning in the store just as she was—to measure sugar and potatoes and bring up kegs of mackerel from the cellar. Probably, when his people found it out, they would put a stop to it. Probably, his lady mother would do something about it. She would want him in a profession. But anyway, Natalie herself was glad that Chris himself had been willing to do any good, honest work. It fitted so perfectly with the ideal she had formed of his character as she had watched him from afar through four years of high school. Natalie liked to keep her ideals of people she admired. Her standards were high, and not many came up to them. So far, this young man had. She would likely never have much to do with him. Her life and his were far apart as the poles, of course. Even if he came into the store for a time, there would presently be found something else for him, something more in the line of profession, and this little spurt of work in a store would only be used as a step to something fitter. But if he came, while he stayed she hoped he would make good. He would never be anything to her, of course, but she liked to think there were such fine, noble people in the world, a few such young men. It made the world more worthwhile to live in.

Of course, he had been kind to her, and just now he happened to be grateful to her for having him put on to the position, but she mustn't presume upon that. She must keep her quiet, aloof way. Her act of introducing him to the manager had been the merest trifling kindness. Anyone would do that. She mustn't let him think that she was expecting him to pay her any attention whatever. Indeed, she must manage to get away before he did, so that it would not look that way. He must not think he had to carry her bundles home for her.

However, if he came, and if he stayed, he would probably soon be so busy he wouldn't think anything about it. The routine of the day would take care of that. He would be so tired by evening that he would want to get home quickly and wouldn't have time for the little cashier. She needn't worry about that. She only hoped he would make good—if he came.

But he was there before her, waiting outside the store, and they stood together talking a minute or two. It was very pleasant to have him so friendly, the boy whom all the girls admired. And she couldn't blame them. She had admired him herself, always. Had liked to listen to him recite in school, because he always did it as if he enjoyed it and knew what he was talking about. She had seldom had the pleasure of going to a school game because she had always had to hurry home to help her mother right after school. But she had often stood at the schoolroom window with a book spread on the windowsill before her, and watched the boys practicing in the yard below. And always she had singled out Chris as the most finished player, and exulted in the way he led them all and they deferred to him. Well, now she was enjoying a pleasant little contact with one whom she could enjoy as a friend, if their circumstances in life had been different. But she must not let her head get turned by it. He was Chris Walton, and she was Natalie Halsey, born into different worlds and stations. Of course, her family had been good, too, but the world had forgotten that, though all the families of the earth were one, after all! But then, she knew what people thought of a poor girl allowing a friendship with a boy who was in a higher social class, and she didn't intend to put herself in such a position. So, as soon as the store opened, she retired to her little glass den and began to work with her cash register and her books. And Chris stood back by a counter and watched the day in the store open before him.

It interested him that he was to be a part of this busy new world.

Almost at once people began to swarm in, for coffee and butter and yeast cakes; for a loaf of bread and a box of Aunt Jemima's prepared buckwheat; for cereals, dried beef, and glasses of jelly for lunches.

There came a lull in half an hour, and the manager started him to work, giving him a linen coat and an apron, setting him to picking over a barrel of potatoes and putting them up in paper sacks, so many pounds to a sack. There was to be a bargain sale of potatoes that day. And when the potatoes were all measured, he had a barrel to go over and pick out the perfect heads. Strange, bitter thoughts came to him now and then as he remembered the other boys in his class, all in college now, going about with college caps, whistling on the campus as they went from one class to another, wearing their fraternity pins and planning their pleasant careers for the future, while he sorted decaying vegetables.

But for the most part, Chris was rather interested than otherwise in what he had to do, conscientious to do it thoroughly, and ambitious to see how quickly he could get it done. He was too busy to contemplate the fate that had thrown him into a chain grocery instead of a college.

Now and then he cast a glance over at the little glass den where

Natalie worked, busy every minute, making change, smiling pleasantly at the customers, a crowd always around her little window. How patient and sweet she looked. Her delicate face shone out, too fine for such surroundings. Of course, the store was nice and clean, and the people were all decent, respectable people, and there was nothing really unpleasant about her work. But somehow she looked a lady, made to be waited upon. There was a quiet refinement about her. What was that nursery rhyme Elise used to sing, "Sit on a cushion and sew a fine seam, and feed upon strawberries, sugar, and cream." Somehow Natalie's face made one feel like putting her at ease and caring for her.

So Chris's thoughts moved, in and out all day, between the cabbages he brought up from the cellar and the empty crates and cans that he carried down to the cellar. He was literally an errand boy as he had said, taking orders moment by moment, never through with one activity before another was handed to him. By noon, he was hungry as a bear and ready to devour eagerly the hot coffee and sandwiches the manager had sent in for his helpers from the pie shop nearby, because he couldn't spare any of them to go out and get it for themselves.

They inhaled the food, standing in the back room where the stores were kept, leaning back against the big refrigerator, or sitting on the cellar stairs or an empty crate, swallowed it down hastily, one at a time in turn, and hastened back to work again. Chris wondered that they had so much business all the time. He had never supposed that a grocery store would be such an active place. There seemed always to be somebody wanting something. By night, he was dog weary and sore in every muscle. Some muscles he hadn't known he possessed. And he had thought that every muscle he had was in perfect training. He wondered why it seemed so much more strenuous than playing football. Perhaps because it was utterly new, and he was a little excited about it, anxious to please.

He heard that first day that the district manager would be around in the middle of the week, and his fate would probably be decided then. The district manager would possibly have a new man to put in the place, and Chris, being only a substitute, would have to step out.

That made it a sort of game, and Chris worked harder than ever. He might not have picked out the grocery business for a life work, and he might not want to remain in it forever, but he didn't want to be put out of anything he had undertaken. He wanted to be so good that they would beg him to stay, even if he was leaving of his own free will for a better position. So he pitched into his work with all his might.

He discovered that his fellow workmen were most friendly among themselves, but they regarded him with suspicion. He had not yet won their confidence. He had to do that. They regarded him as an entire outsider. Perhaps some inkling of his former estate had already penetrated to their knowledge.

They answered him shortly, gave him no more information regarding his work than was absolutely necessary, and left him to find out for himself in every case possible. They let him search for an article in the cellar, instead of telling him how close it was to his hand, and were generally just as unpleasant as they could be without actually descending to open fight.

Chris was rather amazed at first, and then indignant. He longed to take them out and thrash them one by one. He found his heart in a continual fume over some rudeness or unnecessary taunt.

It did not help his cause that on the third day of his presence in the store there came an influx of young women, three of them. They were dressed up, apparently, for an afternoon tea. They breezed in, holding their dainty chiffons and handsome fur coats back from the barrels and boxes. Somewhat pompously, they demanded to see Christopher Walton.

Chapter 10

Chris was cleaning the cellar. He had been at it all day. There was to be a new arrangement of boxes and stores that were kept down there, and everything in the whole cellar had to be moved and thoroughly cleaned. He had never done anything quite like it before, except the washing of those windows in the Sullivan Street house, but he was working away like mad trying to get done before night. He was wearing a pair of borrowed overalls, which did not fit him, and his hair was sticking every way. He was just awkwardly wringing out a wet mop when the man from the meat counter yelled down the cellar stairs.

"Hey, there, Walton! Some dames up here wantta see ya! Make it snappy!"

Chris dropped his mop in dismay and stared up the stairs.

"I can't come!" he shouted at the disappearing heels of his informant, but the only answer that came back was another "Make it snappy! The boss hates a mess of ladies around in the way. This ain't no social tea!"

Angrily Chris started up the stairs, wiping his wet hands on his overalls on each side, and dashing them wildly through his disordered hair. What he meant to do was to get a glimpse from the back of the store and see whether this was some practical joke or not. If the boss had sent for him he would go, of course, but otherwise he would retreat again to the cellar and pretend not to have heard. Surely neither his mother nor Elise would come to bother him.

But Irene Claskey, Ethel Harrower, and Anna Peters had not stayed where they were. They had followed down the length of the store and stood just outside the doorway of the storeroom into which the cellar stairs led. So he came upon them before he realized, and they all clamored at once.

"Hello, Chris! Congratulations!" they screeched.

"So, it's really true! You've got a job! How long will it last?"

"Oh, Chris, but you're a scream. Whose overalls are those? Did you borrow them from your butler?"

And then they let out wild, hilarious laughter that arrested the attention of everyone in the crowded store.

White with fury, Chris stood glaring at them, his chin lifted haughtily. Every eye was upon him now. Even the boss coming down that way with a grin on his pleasant face. The boss had been fine. He must do something about this.

"Did you want something?" he asked in a clear, stern voice. Even Natalie heard him away up at the front of the store in her little glass den. His voice was so impersonal that you would have thought he was merely addressing a customer.

365

"Sure we want something!" clanged out Irene, rather enjoying her large audience than otherwise, and openly exulting in Chris's discomfort. "We're going to have a high school reunion next Saturday night, and we want you to help us out. We're having a spree up at the Rabbit Inn on Horndale Pike, and we want you to take a bunch up there."

"I haven't got any car!" said Chris shortly.

"Oh, we know that," went on Irene. "We can get a car if you'll drive it. Dad said you were a good driver and he'd trust our car with you. We have to start at five o'clock, and we're meeting at my house—"

But Chris stopped her voluble details with a clear ringing word.

"Nothing doing!" he said firmly. "Sorry to seem unaccommodating, but I have to work. Good afternoon!" And he turned on his heel and vanished down the cellar stairs, shutting the door behind him.

The customers turned back to their bargains with smiles and knowing looks toward the discomfited girls who stared for a moment, and then with many giggles and contemptuous remarks picked their way hilariously out of the store.

Chris stayed down in the cellar the rest of the afternoon and worked like a fiend. He had no mind to go upstairs and be kidded by the entire store force. He made that cellar look like a parlor. The floor was scrubbed clean enough to eat from. Every box and crate was set to mathematical exactness, arranged in logical order. Each row was labeled with a number on the beam overhead and the same number chalked on each counter. The cellar was so systemized that anything could be found in a jiffy. But Chris had been working with only half of his well-trained mind. The other half had been raging, rending him, lashing itself in fury over his humiliation. Those girls! *Fools!* he called them, and took out his revenge on the cellar floor, using up to the handle the bristles of the old scrubbing brush. Never was the cellar floor so clean before.

When all the others had gone home, the boss came down and looked around, well pleased and full of commendation. Chris listened in silence to his comments of praise for the way he had arranged things, and then he burst out.

"I'm all kinds of sorry, Mr. Foster, that those fool girls came around and made a scene. They're not any special friends of mine and they just wanted to play some kind of joke on me, I guess. I certainly was angry."

"Oh, that's all right, Chris," said the boss, a warm light coming into his eyes. "I understand. Some girls are just naturally made that way. Don't you worry. You've done good work this afternoon. Forget the other. You did 'em up all righty, and I was glad to see it. They hustled away after you left them like a row of little dogs with their tails tucked in. They certainly didn't get a rise out of you."

Chris looked up with his heart warming toward this young man who was his superior and grinned. It was the first time he had called him Chris, and somehow he did not resent it. It seemed rather pleasant.

"Thank you," he said heartily. "It's great of you to take it that way. One thing's certain. I didn't want anything more to do with those girls, never did have much, only we were in the same class at school."

"Well, they're no ladies," said Foster. "Now take our Miss Halsey, she's a lady. She may not wear such highfalutin' clothes, nor run around to parties, and she may have to work for her living, but when it comes to acting like a lady, boy, she can put it all over those three. She's a fine girl."

"She certainly is," said Chris heartily, and felt a strange little thrill of pleasure at hearing Natalie commended.

"Well," said Foster, "guess it's time for us to quit tonight. You've made this cellar look like a palace and no mistake. You're going to make a go of it here, I can see that already. Well, good night!"

Chris went home that night walking on air. His boss had commended him and had actually hinted that his job was practically a sure thing. He was surprised at himself that he cared so much to keep it.

He had almost forgotten about the unpleasant incident of the girls that afternoon, till suddenly it occurred to him that he had not seen Natalie all day except at a distance. She hadn't waited on him. Perhaps she had heavy bundles to carry and had to carry them herself with her slender arms. In the only glimpse he had caught of her she looked pale and tired. He wondered if her mother had perhaps been worse and she had been up all night with her. He found a distinct cause for worry in the thought.

Then he began to wonder if Natalie had seen those girls. Of course she must have. She could not have missed them. No one could. That fiendish Irene had taken care of that. Did Natalie think that was the kind of girls he liked? Did she perhaps hear the invitation and think he was going to accept it and take those girls to a class spree at that infamous road house, Rabbit Inn on Horndale Pike? Somehow he did not want Natalie to think he was intimate with those girls.

Of course he had known Irene Claskey and Anna Peters since kindergarten days, but Ethel Harrower was a comparatively new arrival in town with a rather unclassed social standing. None of the girls but Irene and Ethel had taken her up. She used too much rouge and lipstick and smoked a good deal in public. People like Mrs. Walton didn't consider her nice. Somehow it gave him an unpleasant feeling to think that Natalie had supposed her his friend. Was that the reason Natalie had hurried home? He wished he knew. He would try and get out early the next morning and get a chance to speak to her in the store before people began to come. Though it had been his policy, and hers too, apparently, to keep their distance. Well, perhaps he could catch up to her on the way and get a word with her. He wasn't just clear what he could say. He was too well bred to just sail in and blast those other girls. Yet he certainly did not want Natalie to think he belonged to that crowd. Well, it wouldn't be long till tomorrow now and, anyhow, he was glad at what the boss had said. He would tell Natalie that. She would be pleased, too.

So he whistled cheerily as he went up the walk to the little old house that looked so desolate on the outside and was so cheery and shabby inside.

His father looked up at the sound and said to his mother, "Our boy is coming through in good shape after all, Mary."

And she smiled, mother-wise, and said, "I knew he would, didn't you?"

They had a cheery supper that night in spite of simple fare. The mother was resurrecting all her old recipes, plain, wholesome food, cheaply bought, and deriving its savory taste and smell from the old deftness in seasoning, the trick of long cooking and careful preparation. Perhaps because of its very difference from what they had been eating for years, its simplicity rather charmed the family. Bean soup was made with tomatoes, potatoes, and celery tops, a "mess of pot-tage" the mother called it. Brown bread, baked apples and cream, even bread pudding with a dash of chocolate to make it tasty. Hash! Yes, they loved it, Mother's hash. That was different. Mother could make hash taste like stuffed turkey. It all seemed so good, and they were so hungry from their work. For Elise had found a job looking after two small children afternoons after school, and she came in from riding them up and down the streets in their toy wagon, tired and hungry and happy over the fifty cents she had earned. Elise was standing up well under the family calamity.

When they had finished the bean-tomato soup and the baked apples were served, Chris told them in an offhand sort of way about what the manager had said to him.

Chris couldn't quite comprehend the look of utter joy in his father's face. He didn't see why he should be so moved when he tried to speak.

"Chris, Son, that is great. You've won a bigger battle this week than ever you won in school or on the football field. You've got into the game of life now, and you've begun to conquer yourself. You've made good in a game you didn't like and didn't want to play, and under circumstances that were most trying. Don't think I haven't understood."

"But Dad," interrupted Chris, "I—you—"

"It's no use trying to deceive me, boy," said the father, laying his hand tenderly on his son's arm. "Your mother and I knew how hard it was for you to give up college and go to work. That kind of hard, uninteresting work, too, and to which you were so unaccustomed. We dreaded it for you more than you possibly could for yourself. We had great ambitions for you, Chris. You know that. You are our only son, and there was no height too high for us to dream of your scaling. But I've come to see, through my own humiliations, that one cannot grow strong without being humble. One cannot do great things while self-interest rules. You, my son, have gained one great victory this week over self. I hope it may go on. There are still greater heights to scale. You will have setbacks. You'll find that self is a hard thing to conquer. It will come alive. But if you have really found that you can set self aside and do the thing well that is hardest for you, you have reached a great place in life. There is but one thing higher than that, and that is to let the Lord Christ come in and take self's place. If you can learn those two things, I'll know why God let all this reversal come to us. I have known all along that there must be some reason why we should thank Him for what has come, and now I begin to see a possible reason."

Chris looked at his father in amazement, a deep embarrassment upon him, a sudden feeling that he had always been a failure as a son in his father's eyes.

"Why, Dad," he said huskily, deeply moved, "I didn't know—I never thought—that you felt that way."

"Well, I do, Son, and your mother feels that way, too. Go on and win the game of life. Let Christ come into your life as the ruling power, and we will be too proud to contain ourselves."

Chris thought about it when he went up to bed, thought how his father had spoken in much the same way Natalie had talked. In fact, there were three of them, for there was that minister who had said we must thank God for hard things. The minister, and Father, and Natalie! All saying the same thing. Was it possible that God had been sending these things into his life for a special purpose? Possible that God, a great God—if there really was one—had thought enough of his little individual life, among all the lives of the earth, to turn the affairs of a great bank upside down, and bring changes into other people's lives, with any thought of its affecting him in his relationship to himself, to life, and to God Himself? And yet, most of the professors and students at college felt that if there was a God at all, He was only a sort of impersonal force. Well, it was worth thinking about. Somehow, the idea did not make him angry either, as it had done a week ago.

He went to sleep thinking about what Natalie had told him of that missionary's life and bitter disappointments, thinking of Natalie's face when she had said, "What He permits must be best for us." And what was that other phrase she used in speaking about the missionary? "He's only an ordinary man with a great God."

The last thing he remembered, as he dropped away into slumber, was the earnestness in Natalie's eyes as she had said it and the way her soft hair fell about her forehead. And he decided that the first thing in the morning, he would tell her what the boss said to him last night. She had got the job for him; she had a right to know that he was making good with the manager.

He hurried through his breakfast, and away, that he might catch her and walk with her to the store, but when he passed her corner, he saw only an ugly-looking young boy standing there, with his hat down over his eyes, peering out and up the street. A quick look ahead told Chris that Natalie had already got the start of him and was far on her way.

The boss was just unlocking the door as he reached the store, and although it was early, Natalie slipped into her glass den at once, with only a little distant smile for Chris, and went to work as if she were very busy.

Chris felt a distant drooping of his spirits. Now, why did Natalie have to act like that? Was it just because those other girls had come in and asked for him? Was she perhaps ashamed of him because he had had such visitors? She didn't want to be known as having anything to do with him? Well, if she felt that way, he wouldn't bother her. He held his head high and went to the boss for his orders, unhappiness in his heart and eyes.

They put him to measuring out sugar in small quantities in paper bags. All day long he measured out sugar and rice and put them up in small packages. He worked with set lips and said nothing to anybody. The other men in the store tried to kid him about the "dames," as they called them, who had come to visit him, but he maintained an unsmiling silence. If they wanted to be ugly to him, let them. He could keep to himself.

He tried to stay his unhappy mind on the words his father had said to him the night before, and on his mother's satisfied smile, but he had mixed them up so hopelessly in his thoughts with Natalie and her words to him, that he got little help from them. He was hurt deeply by Natalie's attitude. All day long he kept utterly out of her sight, thereby deepening her feeling that she ought to keep out of his.

For, indeed, the visit of those other girls had affected Natalie more than she realized. It made her feel that she had been entirely right in her decision to have nothing to do with Chris, at least of her own accord. These other girls were, of course, in the same social rank where he belonged. While she never had admired their loud, arrogant ways, she knew that most of the town counted them as standing high in the social scale and would regard her as an outsider. Chris Walton should never have to say it of her that she chased after him after getting him a job in the same store where she worked. As far as she was concerned, she would go her own way quietly, just as she had gone to school. He probably would soon forget she existed, just as he had apparently done while they were in school together.

The free and easy way in which those flashy girls yesterday had marched into the store, as if they owned the earth, and demanded to see him, talking to him in that loud, familiar way, had made her see how utterly out of his world she was. He probably liked these girls. They had been among his crowd in school and knew him so much better than she did. She had just idealized somebody again, as she was always doing, and getting a hard knock when she came to earth and found them human. If she could only keep herself from liking people so much and making them out to be so much better than they were, it would save her many a hard time.

So, Natalie kept to her glass den, meekly ate her little sandwich at noon, without going for a walk, and sat late at her work in the evening until she was sure Chris was gone. No, nobody, either in the store or out, should ever be able to say that she had chased an aristocrat!

Chris had slipped away out the back door, after hovering in the shadows of the back room, his hat in his hand, watching to see if Natalie would go. She did not even look up. She wanted to avoid him. Very well, then he would not trouble her. So he went out into the dark street with bitterness in his heart again. All the joy of the night before had left him, and he was downright cross and tired and hungry and disappointed. He didn't care whether he had pleased the boss or not. Self was in the ascendency, and he felt he was being ill-treated by fate or God or somebody. Perhaps it was Natalie.

As he passed the end of Natalie's street, there he saw that same tough-looking man standing at the corner, watching down the street. Was it possible that he was a friend of Natalie's? Perhaps Natalie was going out with him? Yet, he knew in his heart, it was not so. And when he had passed on to Sullivan Street, he turned back and saw him still there, looking down the street. And even as he watched, the man started down the street toward the store.

Then a sudden frenzy possessed Chris. That man meant no good. He knew a hard-boiled, tough man when he saw one. Chris hesitated only a second, and then bounded swiftly across the avenue, darted on down Sullivan Street a block, and rounded the corner of the street that ended back of the grocery store. With the swiftness of a trained athlete, he sped till he came to the back of the store and slid through the alley just beyond.

Chapter 11

Chris reconnoitered a moment, peering around the corner of the building. He was satisfied that he had reached there, a full block ahead of the other man, who had loitered as he walked, apparently on purpose. Yes, far up at the next corner, he could see a figure lounging under a street light, looking, just now, back toward Sullivan Street. He was not too late. He peered into the store. Natalie was coming out, fastening her coat. The boss was back in the store arranging cans on the counter for tomorrow. Two other men had been detained to help him. He drew a deep breath. Now, should he walk boldly up and speak to her, or should he let her go and follow at a distance to protect her, if she needed protection, or at least to watch and discover whether she met this fellow as if he were an acquaintance? She had a right, of course, to choose her own friends.

Yet as he considered this, his feet seemed to carry him of their own volition up to the door of the store as Natalie came out, her arms full of bundles.

As naturally as if he had always done it, he stepped up to her and took her bundles.

"Well, you've come at last!" he said, trying to laugh naturally, as if she had not kept away from him all day. "I thought maybe you had brought your dinner and overnight bag and meant to stay till tomorrow and save walking home."

"Oh," she said, in relieved delight. "Oh, but I thought you had gone home long ago. I was waiting—That is, I thought—"

"All right. Say it! Say you were waiting till I got away so you wouldn't have to walk home with me. It's best to be entirely frank among friends. I wouldn't want to intrude. If you want to know the truth, I did start home. Got away up to the corner of Sullivan Street. I'm not entirely blind. It was plain as the nose on your face that you didn't want anything more to do with me after what happened yesterday afternoon. And I didn't intend to bother you anymore, of course, if you felt that way. But when I got up to the corner of your street, I saw a bum standing on the corner right where you had to pass, as if he were waiting. And I couldn't see having you go there alone, so I sprinted around down the alley and came after you. But, if I've made a mistake and he's a friend of yours, why just say the word and I'll let you go on your way."

"Oh," said Natalie, with a little frightened cry, catching hold of his sleeve impulsively. "Why, I don't feel that way. I'm so glad you came! He tried to speak to me last night, and I was so frightened I could hardly get into the house. And I didn't dare tell Mother. She wouldn't have let me come to the store today. He's been there for three mornings now, and he called me 'girlie.'"

She caught her breath, and he could see there were tears in her eyes. His heart came right up in his throat, and he felt a great righteous anger stirring in him, but his voice grew calm and manly sounding.

"Well, if that's the case, let's cut through the alley and go around the far block and avoid him. I'm here to look out for you. If that dirty sucker shows his face around you, I sure will let him know where to get off. You needn't worry now."

He slid a protecting arm within her own, putting her on his right side, away from the watching lounger up the street, and guided her swiftly through the dark alley and up another block where they could not be seen.

"Now," said he, "if that's the case, why haven't you spoken to me all day?"

"Why, I did speak to you. I said 'good morning'!" Natalie gurgled between a sob and a happy little giggle.

"Like an icicle, you did!" said Chris grimly. "What had I done to you, I'd like to know? Did you suppose I staged that scene in the store yesterday, with me dressed in overalls for the part? Did you suppose I made a date with those foolish girls to get the limelight on me before the boss and spoil my chance of keeping the job? Didn't you know those girls just did that to get me in wrong? I never did like that Peters girl, anyway. She's crazy, and Irene is always playing to the gallery. The whole thing was, Irene wanted to get back on me for refusing to take her to a roadhouse one night. She wanted to rub it in that I don't have any car, now, to take nobody anywhere in. Wanted me to be their chauffeur. Did you hear what she said?"

"I certainly did," said Natalie indignantly, "and—I didn't think any of those things about you—I didn't indeed. I just thought that I—that you—"

"You just thought you didn't want to appear to have anything more to do with me after all that publicity," said Chris bitterly. "I understand, and I don't blame you, but you needn't look quite so much like an icicle. I won't bother you if you don't want to be friends."

"Oh," said Natalie, and now he saw she was crying in earnest. "I didn't think any such thing. I just thought—after I saw those girls all dressed up—and I knew they belonged to the crowd you used to go with—and I knew they wouldn't recognize me if they saw me, and wouldn't speak to me if they did—it just kind of made me see that I wasn't in your, well, social class. And I mustn't make you think I was chasing you and wanting you to walk home with me and carry my bundles all the time. I hate girls to do things like that. I wasn't brought up to do so!"

They had come now to a comparatively quiet block of houses, with no one else about, and their steps slowed down.

"Good night! Natalie, I didn't mean to make you feel that way! Don't cry!" Chris suddenly fumbled in his pocket and brought out a comparatively clean handkerchief. "Here"—he shifted his bundles, and reaching across them, wiped her eyes awkwardly—"as if anybody could ever think *you* were like that! Why, Natalie—you're wonderful! I think you're just *wonderful*!"

There was a strange new tenderness in his voice. He had a sudden longing to kiss her on her trembling lips and on her sweet, wet eyes. But he wasn't a boy who went around kissing girls. His mother had brought him up with fine, old-fashioned ideas of reverence for girls, and he felt a deep reverence now for this girl. So he drew her arm closer within his own, caught her hand in a good strong grip, and struggled for new words to make plain what he was feeling.

And Natalie struggled to get her composure.

"Thank you," she said softly. "I thank you. It's nice to feel you are friendly and haven't misunderstood me or thought me forward!"

"As if I could!" he said. "I—why—I think you're *wonderful*!" he repeated, failing to find better words to express his admiration. "I think you are the kind of girl I want for a real friend. I've been thinking a lot about what you said, about God passing on everything before it gets to us. Why, how could I misjudge you after that? You've done a lot for me. Not just introducing me to the store, though I'm grateful for that, of course. But you—why, you gave me back a decent assurance and faith in somebody, something. God, I suppose. I almost lost it when things began to happen. And then I saw that you, who have lost so many more things than I have, were standing by and believing in Him, and it kind of made me think, and I've been lots happier since. I don't know that I understand things any better, but I somehow *feel* better. You know, at college almost nobody believed anything much. Besides, you made me see myself."

"How do you mean, see yourself?" asked Natalie wonderingly.

"Well, you made me see that I had been kind of snobbish. I may as well call it by its right name. You made me see that I had really been a conceited snob. And God, if there is a God who cares about such things, probably had to hand me out all this to show me before I got too hard-boiled."

"Well," said Natalie, with a little bit of a laugh in her voice, "I can see you're just what I've always thought you were, and—I'm glad. I hate to be disappointed in people. It's been just beautiful to have you speak out and be so frank with me, and I can't tell you how nice it is to have you so friendly. I've been awfully lonesome ever since I came to town to live. And I'm so glad you haven't thought me forward or anything."

"Well, I'm awfully glad I've found you, and I hope we are going to be wonderful friends. What are you doing tonight? Could I see you somewhere? I'd like to talk to you more about this. I've been all tangled up, and you seem to understand me."

"Why"—Natalie hesitated—"this is my night to go to the Bible school—if Mother is well enough for me to leave."

"Couldn't I go with you? Couldn't I take care of you? I don't like to have you going around the streets, in the dark, with a fellow like that tagging after you. May I come for you? What time?"

"Oh, would you go there? You'd like it, I'm sure. The man I told you about speaks tonight. It's to be at eight o'clock. But I hate to have you feel you must take your time looking after me. Maybe your people will not like it."

"Why not?" asked Chris, looking down at her sweet eyes.

"I'm not your social class, you know," she said gravely.

"Neither am I, anymore," said Chris quickly and laughed, suddenly realizing that the fact did not hurt him as it had. Somehow, there seemed a bond in the fact that they could both laugh over this.

They had come to her door now, and she reached out to take her bundles. Quite a staggering load she had dared that night, because she had been sure that he had gone home and he would not feel he had to carry them. But he did not surrender them.

"These are too many for you to lift. May I come in and put them away for you? That's potatoes, that sack. I know the feel of them after filling nine million bags of them, more or less, today. You shouldn't attempt to carry loads like that. A girl isn't strong enough. That's a man's job."

"Oh, I'm quite strong," laughed Natalie, and tried once more to take them.

"No, please. I'm taking them in, if you don't mind," insisted Chris.

Natalie had a quick vision of her mother, in a big apron, getting supper; Janice setting the table, horrified expressions perhaps on their faces; and her cheeks flamed scarlet in the dark to think that now her mother would worry again. But there was something in Chris's cultured, pleasant voice that made it necessary for her to surrender. And with a quick prayer that all might be well within, she threw open the door into the tiny hall.

Mrs. Halsey was just taking a lovely bread pudding out of the oven, crisp and brown on the top, and the spicy odor of cinnamon reached out into the hall fragrantly to the hungry boy.

"My, that smells good!" he said as he strode through the hall into the tiny kitchen at the end where the door stood wide open. He walked straight over to the clean kitchen table and deposited his bundles, then turned toward the astonished mother, sweeping off his cap.

"Good evening!" he said with a courteous grin. "You don't know me. I'm just the delivery boy from the grocery store. I hope you don't mind my lack of ceremony. I had to lay these down before I take off my hat."

"Mother, this is Chris Walton," said Natalie, appearing behind him with shining eyes, very red cheeks, and a belated introduction.

Mrs. Halsey arose to the occasion beautifully, almost cordially.

"You've been very kind," she said, studying the engaging face of the young man searchingly. "I've told Natalie she shouldn't bring so much at once, and she ought not to impose on your good nature."

"Oh, that's nothing," said Chris with a disarming smile. "I live near here, you know, and I'm glad to be of use. How cozy you look here. Is that the pudding that smells so good? It certainly smells good enough to eat."

"Won't you stay and help us eat it?" asked the mother, smiling cordially.

"Oh, I wish I could, but you see I've got the butter for supper in my pocket, and I expect Mother is flattening her nose against the windowpane this very minute, watching for me. Sorry. That looks like a real pudding, and I'd like to sample it. Perhaps you'll ask me again sometime?"

"Why of course," said Mrs. Halsey. "If you really care to come."

"That's settled then," said Chris, turning to Natalie. "There, Natalie, don't you forget to fix that soon. If you do, I'll have to remind you. Now, I must hurry or I'll get a good scolding for not bringing the butter sooner. I'll be back to go to that school with you, Natalie—at seven thirty, did you say? Or is that time enough?"

"Why, it really isn't necessary to start before quarter of eight. It's only a short distance, you know," said Natalie, not daring to look at her mother.

"I suppose you've forgotten me entirely," said Janice, suddenly appearing in the front room doorway, algebra and pencil in her hand and her curly hair tossed up in a very little-girl way.

Chris whirled and looked at her, bewildered.

"You're not by chance the little girl with the red tam that I used to draw to school on her sled my last year in high school, are you? Those look like her eyes."

"The very same," said Janice, dimpling. "It's several years since I've had a ride on a sled, or anything else for that matter."

"Sorry, I haven't a bus to take you out in, but I don't even own a wheelbarrow anymore. But say, you've grown up fast! I suppose you're in high school now. My, doesn't that make us seem ancient, Natalie? And it only seems yesterday that I took you on your sled to school. Well I must run along or this butter will melt. See you later."

And Chris hurried away. But as he rounded the corner into the avenue, he noticed a slow-moving figure in the shadow on the opposite side of the road, pausing now and then to look furtively up and down the street either way. He was glad he had decided to take Natalie to Bible school.

It was Janice that brought the question to debate as the door closed behind him.

"How did that happen, Natalie? I thought you had eschewed the society of gentlemen forevermore and were going to hold Mother's hand."

"Oh, Janice, you make me tired!" said Natalie nervously. "It wasn't my fault. I waited late so he would be gone because I wanted to bring home those lovely potatoes before they were all sold tomorrow. And when I came out the door, there he was, outside. He hadn't gone at all. I tried to make him understand I could carry my own packages, but it wasn't any use. He even was almost offended at me, said he wouldn't bother me if I was annoyed by him, so there was nothing else to do but let him come. And I can't help it that he is going to Bible school, can I? It was entirely his own idea."

Mrs. Halsey looked at her usually placid daughter in surprise.

"Why, Natalie, dear, I never meant to have you feel that way about it," she said anxiously. "I'm sorry. Please forget it, daughter. It was just that I couldn't bear to have you looked down upon by a rich man's son, or get interested in someone who might be beneath you, morally or spiritually, or who might show you attention that would make you care too much, when he meant nothing but trifling. But dear, I see I should have trusted you. He seems a very nice boy, and most humble, not a bit spoiled by his wealth."

"But he isn't wealthy anymore, Mother," said Natalie earnestly. "They're living over on Sullivan Street near the railroad, next to the woman who used to wash for them. They have given up everything they had and are as poor as we, I guess, from what I hear."

"Well, dear. I was wrong to judge anyone by money or position. I liked him very much in that brief minute or two, and if you want to ask him here to our plain little home, do just as you think best. He'll be welcome with me. Only guard your heart, my precious girl, and don't let it go dreaming. You're my wonderful girl, you know, and I can't bear to think that anything should hurt you."

Natalie turned away and pressed her hand against her hot cheeks, as she suddenly remembered the genuine tone in which Chris had said, "I think you are wonderful, you know."

Then Janice, eyeing her sharply, began to chant in a comical tone:

"You may go and nibble, nibble, nibble,
At the cheese, cheese, cheese,
Little mouse you may nibble
If you please, please, please,
But be careful little mouse,
Of the cunning little house,
For you may someday find
That it's a trap, trap, trap!"

Janice had a sweet, clear voice, with a mocking resonance in it, and the words rang out comically through the kitchen. Natalie, almost on the verge of tears, suddenly sat down in a chair and began to laugh hysterically as Janice's soprano rose in an improvised chorus:

"Oh, my cunning little mouse,
Oh, my darling little mouse,
Oh, you wonderful, wonderful, wonderful little mouse!"

Then Natalie suddenly straightened up and looked soberly at her mother and sister.

"Look here, you two dears. You've got to stop this now, once and for all. I just won't be teased this way. I haven't any idea of throwing my heart out in the street for every young man to trample over. And I guess when a girl trusts her life to the Lord for leading, He isn't going to let her go the wrong way and give her thoughts to the wrong one, is He? Chris is a nice boy and, of course, I like him to be polite and kind to me. But I haven't any funny notions, and you needn't think I have. If the Lord has someone for me to fall in love with someday, He'll likely show me without a question when the time comes. But at present, I'm just a girl, and when anybody is friendly and seems to have right ideas about things, I don't know why I shouldn't be friendly with them to a certain extent without having to pass an inquisition. Now, if you don't both think I'm right about that, I'll go upstairs and stay there, and give him any excuse you like for my not going with him. But I won't stand for all the anxieties and fears any longer. It takes the joy out of life. If you don't want me to speak to him, I won't, but I don't want to hear any more about it."

"The worm has turned!" said Janice solemnly into the silence that followed Natalie's outbreak, and then suddenly they all broke down and laughed together.

Finally, the mother came and put her arms around Natalie, and kissed her softly.

"There dearie," she said, "you're perfectly right. I had no idea we were persecuting you so. Forgive it, precious. And I'll tell you this. He's a fine, nice boy. I can see that at the start. And if you can help him to know the Lord Jesus, it will be a great thing. I'm with you. And I know I can trust you every step of the way. It's a great thing when a mother can say that of her child. Now, quiet down, precious, and let's have supper. It's getting late."

"And so I am with you," proclaimed Janice. "I'm so much with you that I'm going to study my algebra this evening and not go to Bible school till next week. There! How's that for sacrifice?"

Natalie stopped short in the middle of the kitchen with her hat. "I'll help you with your algebra after we come home. But I'm determined you shall start in this class right at the beginning of the first lesson. We're going to take up the book of Hebrews, and it's important to hear the introduction or you won't get the same interest. If you stay at home, I shall stay, too."

"All right, Captain! I'll go then," said Janice cheerfully. "I want to sacrifice myself in any way possible to keep peace in this household."

Then Natalie turned upon her, laughing, and the two girls chased each other round and round the kitchen to the living room, to the hall and back to the kitchen again in a gale of laughter, till they suddenly realized that their mother was doing all the work and dropped their nonsense to help put the dinner on the table.

There was a pleasant excitement on them all as they ate. It was a new thing for the girls to be going out with a young man. Even Janice, scarcely more than a little girl, felt greatly elated, and the mother seemed as pleased as any of them.

"You'd better put on your other dress, Natalie," said her mother as they began to gather up the dishes. "You run up and dress and I can do these few dishes just as well as not."

"No," said Natalie determinedly. "I'm not dolling up just because a boy I used to go to school with is going along. If he doesn't like me the way I am, he needn't go. It's a plain school, and people don't dress up to go there. I'm going to do these dishes. You got dinner, and I can see you're tired."

In the end they all did dishes, the mother sitting down and wiping the silver, and they were done in a trice. And then Natalie did change her blouse and wear her Sunday hat, but neither of them said anything about it. Indeed there wasn't time, for they could hear Chris's quick, crisp step on the walk and his clear whistle, and then came the sound of his knock on the door.

"Seems like being regular people, doesn't it?" said Janice softly under her breath as she started for the door. "The Halsey family is out among 'em!"

And as they started off happily with their escort, Mrs. Halsey sighed half sadly, to think that a simple little pleasure like going out to a religious meeting could bring such delight. They were dear girls. How little real youthful pleasure they had in their lives. If their father had only lived—

Then she slipped up to her room and knelt a long time by her bed, asking for wisdom to guide and guard her children aright, wisdom that should show her distinctly, step-by-step, what the Lord would have her do, and help her not to get her own will in the way of the Lord's way.

Chapter 12

Chris went to the Bible school that night and heard a wonderful talk from a man who spoke as if he were personally acquainted with Jesus Christ, had talked to Him, face-to-face, and received his instructions from a Bible that seemed to be vivid and real, not just mystical sayings mysteriously handed down from dim, uncertain ages almost forgotten. Chris was deeply stirred.

Under this teacher, words, phrases, even verses and chapters with which he had had verbal acquaintance since childhood suddenly sprang into new, wonderful meaning. It seemed like magic. He looked around on the earnest company who were listening, Bibles and notebooks open on their laps, their eyes fixed on the speaker. There wasn't one among them who had the look of a doubter. Their faces seemed almost illumined with inner light. And when he glanced at Natalie, she had had the same rapt look. Even young Janice seemed deeply engrossed.

How did this man find out all these wonderful things? Were they merely interpretations? But no, he did not seem to be twisting the words, for he read them as they were printed. Natalie had found the place and handed him a Bible. He could follow along, and lo, the story with which he was familiar was there, and yet meant as clearly as print just what the teacher said it meant. That was entirely obvious. And all just because the teacher had explained the meaning of a Greek word and made them turn to several other references.

The teacher said more than once that scripture must be interpreted by itself, comparing scripture with scripture, and it certainly was wonderful how it worked out and made things clear. Why, some of the passages that were read he had learned by heart when he was a child in the primary class, but nobody ever took the trouble to make them plain to him, and they had never meant a thing in his mind except a lot of words.

He caught a slight vision of the symbolism all through the Bible, of the significance of numbers and the meaning of every proper name in the Bible. He heard references to dispensational truth that made clear as day sentences that he had always considered vague.

When the lesson finally closed with a prayer that left its imprint on his heart, he found that he was distinctly sorry it was over. It seemed as if the talk had been only about ten minutes duration. He would be glad if there were to be another lesson immediately following. He would have enjoyed asking a lot of questions, but he would sooner have cut off a small piece of his tongue than own to it.

The teacher stood at the door as they went out, took Chris's hand in a warm, quick grip and called him brother, with a sweet, bright look that seemed, when he thought of it afterward, like lightning coming from a strong place with both joy and sorrow.

When they were out in the night again, a silence fell upon the three. At last Janice spoke.

"I think he's wonderful, don't you, Natalie?"

"It's a wonderful book we're studying," said Natalie thoughtfully. "And he knows it well."

"There's one thing I'd like to know," said Chris, more as if he were thinking aloud than really expecting to be answered. "He kept talking about 'saved ones.' What did he mean? *Who* did he mean? How could anybody tell whether they were saved or not?"

"Oh," breathed Natalie earnestly. "You can, of course! Don't you know whether you're saved?"

"Why no," said Chris. "Of course not. Nobody knows about it till after they're dead, do they? And anyhow, what does it mean, saved from what?"

"Why, saved from the consequences of sin, which is death."

"I've never felt that I was such a great sinner," said Chris, just the least bit loftily.

Natalie was silent a moment, then she lifted her head bravely. "We're all great sinners," she stated quietly.

"I don't see that," said Chris stubbornly. "What have you done that's so awful? What have I? Of course, little things. But I've always tried to live a pretty decent life."

"Of course, the great sin, the only sin, after all, that is terrible, is not believing in Him. Rejecting Him when He did so much for us. The Bible says that in God's sight 'all have sinned and come short of the glory of God.'"

"Of course, I've heard that line all my life, but down in my heart I never did see why so much emphasis was put on sin. Most respectable people are pretty good livers. I never had any real desire to be bad. I can't really feel that I'm a great sinner, and I don't see why I should try."

Natalie was praying silently that she might be given the right answer, and now she said half shyly, "People never do feel they are sinners till they've had a vision of Jesus, do they? When you see what He is then you begin to know how far short you fall."

"Oh!" said Chris blankly. Then after a moment—"How could you do that? He isn't here. You can't see a person that isn't here."

"Yes, you can. You can find Him in His Word. And you can find Him in prayer. The Holy Spirit has promised to reveal Him to us if we ask Him. But you've got to come believing. Belief is the key that unlocks the Word and makes us see things that we could not understand without it."

Chris looked at her wonderingly.

"How could one believe something they *didn't* believe? Something they were not convinced was true?"

"Belief is an act of the will," said Natalie, "not an intellectual conviction. It is something you deliberately will to do. It is taking God at His Word and letting Him prove to you what He promises is true. That is the way it was put in Bible school the other night, and I've proved it is true."

"*You* have?" he eyed her curiously in the soft darkness of the street.

"Oh yes! Ever since I was saved."

"There it is again," said Chris perplexedly. "You say it just the way he did tonight, as if it were some sort of charm. What does it mean? How do you get that way? What do you have to do?"

"Oh, you don't have to *do* anything. Just accept it. Salvation is a free gift, and you've only to take it. The moment you accept it, you are saved, and nothing, not anything, can take you out of His hand. For you are His, and from that time forward you are under His care. And He says He is able to present you *faultless* before the presence of His glory, without spot or wrinkle or any such thing. That's not because you are without fault. That's because He is faultless, and because He has given us a right to wear His *righteousness*. It is only through His righteousness that we could be faultless." Natalie was talking earnestly now, herself filled with wonder that she had been given opportunity to say these things.

"But I don't understand," said Chris. "How does that make you know you're saved, just to accept a thing? Just to believe?"

"Why," said Natalie thoughtfully, praying that she might be led to the right words that would bring light to the questioner, "if you were a prisoner, condemned to die, and you were told that someone else had taken the death penalty for you and you might go free, all that would be left for you to do would be to accept his death for yours, to believe what you were told. He has said that the minute you accept His grace and believe His word, you are born again, and are one of His saved ones. He also says, 'He that believeth *hath* everlasting life, and *shall not* come into condemnation, but is *passed* from death unto life.'"

"But I don't just see how believing a thing could make any difference in the way you feel."

"Well, you couldn't see, because belief is the thing that makes it possible for you to see. It is the key that unlocks the mystery, and you can't find out until you try it yourself. Nobody can make you see it. You have to take that key of belief and unlock it for yourself.

You do it in other things. Why not trust God, as well as men? Suppose you are very much in need of something at the store, and you ask the manager about it, and he says he'll get it right away. And then you don't worry about it anymore. You just trust it to him. Yet you don't really *know* he will do it. You haven't *proved* him, perhaps, but you take it for granted he will keep his word. You will to believe him till he has disproved himself. Why not take God at His word?"

Chris was silent, pondering. At last he said, "But I'm a church member, you know. Doesn't that make it all right?"

"No," said Natalie sadly. "He didn't say, 'If you join the church you are saved—passed from death unto life.' He said, 'He that believeth.'"

They had reached the house now and were pausing at the door.

"Won't you come in?" asked Natalie shyly, wondering if her mother would approve of her asking him.

"No," said Chris, "it's getting late, and you and I have to be up early. But—I'd like to know more about this. We'll talk about it another time. Perhaps I'll join that class. I like that bird. He's sincere; you can see that. Well, good night!" And he left them abruptly.

"Strange," he said to himself as he walked home. "I never knew she was a girl like that! How different she is from the other girls I used to know in school. Fancy any of them telling about how to be saved, or caring about it!"

He kept asking himself why he hadn't known this lovely girl before. Why hadn't he sought her out and taken her places, instead of some of the fool girls he used to go with?

Oh, those other girls weren't all silly girls, of course. Janie

Anderson and Marguerite Manning and Roxana White were sensible, bright, fine girls. He had sometimes taken them here and there. But no girl had ever stirred him as this sweet spirit who had sat by him tonight, listening to that most unusual message. He realized that much of the pleasure of the evening had come from watching her lovely, earnest face as she listened.

As he swung up to his own door, he told himself that a strong tie had been welded between that girl and himself that evening. Of course, they were both young, and it was not time yet to think of more serious things, but his heart felt that the friendship with Natalie Halsey had come into his life to stay. Here was a character with something more to it than froth. Something more even than a good education, pleasant manners, and a desire to please. Life had early sifted her and tested her. Her face bore the marks of experience that had not hardened her, but brought a lovely peace upon her brow and a charming light in her eyes. He felt a wistful longing to understand and have the same secret that she possessed.

Chapter 13

The days that followed were full of hard work, but it was somehow very pleasant work to Chris. The fellows in the store were still a little belligerent, jealous of any word the manager spoke to him, ready to criticize and sneer behind his back. But there was always the boss now, liking him and saying nice things occasionally about his work, for he was selling now the rest and understood the stock as well as anyone. And there was always Natalie to watch when a moment of leisure came. Natalie, in her little glass cage, making change with her pale fingers, smiling to the women customers, gravely courteous to the men, sending the ghost of a little bright flash from her eyes to him across the store, now and then, when no one would be watching.

They were very careful not to let their friendship be known. It seemed too indefinite, almost too sacred to be dragged through the store and joked about as it inevitably would have been if it had become known. None of their fellow employees knew that Natalie had recommended Chris, he discovered. She went her quiet way among them, smiling shyly to each one, but holding aloof. Even the manager spoke most respectfully to her, and they all called her Miss Halsey, not Natalie.

Every night Chris lingered in some place agreed upon and they walked home together, he carrying whatever bundles she had. But they managed their meetings around the corner, or after the others had left. The tramp man who had troubled their first acquaintance seemed to have disappeared. He stood no longer at the corner of the street in the mornings when Natalie started out, and she was greatly relieved.

The weeks went swiftly by.

"Mother, I think Chris has a girl," said Elise one evening when they were waiting for Chris to come to dinner. Sometimes he was unaccountably later than need be.

"Oh!" said his mother, looking up a little anxiously. "Do you think so? I—suppose—he—would—sometime, but—he seems so young."

"He's no younger than I was when I fell in love with you, Mother," said her elderly lover, looking unexpectedly from his paper.

"Well, that was different," said Mother, smiling. "You were—I was—that is—"

"Exactly so," said Father with a twinkle. "I was just thinking that myself."

"What makes you think he has a girl, Elise?" asked her mother.

"Well, I've seen him twice walking with her, very slowly, when I went down for Daddy's paper. It's just after the store closes."

"Oh, I hope it's not Anna Peters," said the mother, with quick apprehension in her voice.

"No, it's not Anna," said the sister triumphantly. "Chris can't bear her. He says she's bold."

"She is!" agreed the mother.

"It's a girl around here," announced Elise discreetly.

"Around *here!*" There was consternation in the mother's voice.

"Yes, I think she lives over on Cromar Street. I thought I heard his voice the other night as I was crossing at the corner. If it's the house where he was standing, her sister is in my class in school. And she used to be in Chris's class in high school."

"Who is she?"

"She is one of the Halsey girls. I think her name is Natalie. Her sister is Janice Halsey. Janice seems nice, only we don't any of us know her very well. She always has to hurry home. Her mother's been sick. Janice wears made-over dresses."

"That's nothing against her," said the mother sharply. Her own daughter would probably come to that very soon.

"Well, she's pretty, but the girls don't invite her much."

"Better get acquainted, daughter, and bring her around," suggested Father. "It would be nice to know what the family are like. Of course, there may be nothing serious in carrying bundles. Chris is a gentleman, and it would be natural to walk with one who lived near here. But Mother, if Chris is getting acquainted with someone, you'd better find out who she is and invite her here. That will make a friendship safe and sane, you know. Chris is young, and of course the girls have already liked him. It's natural he'll want friends."

"I will," said Mother with a sigh. And just then Chris came

whistling up the porch, his face the picture of happiness.

The next afternoon, as she was coming down the high school steps, Elise caught sight of Janice Halsey just turning out of the school pavement into the street, and called to her.

"Janice! Janice Halsey! Oh, I say, Janice, wait for me a minute!" she called, hurrying down the steps and after her, swift as a swallow.

Janice paused in surprise. She was accustomed to hurrying away as soon as school closed and not lingering to talk with the girls. Her mother had needed her for so long that it had become second nature with her, even when the need for haste was not quite so urgent. And the girls had fallen into the habit of not counting her in things when they planned for parties and festivities.

"Oh, she wouldn't come!" someone would say if ever her name was mentioned by some newcomer in school. "She has to work or something. She's always in a hurry!" And they let it go at that. So Janice, who used to play with them down in the primary grades, and knew them all, was no more one of them than her sister had been when she was in high school.

So now she stood and waited, gravely surprised, her eyes speculative. What could Elise Walton want of her? Only some message from the teacher probably, maybe about the essay she was to write for the Friday class. Or perhaps it was to tell her of the class banquet. They always went through the gesture of inviting her to it, though they knew she never accepted because she hadn't the two dollars a plate that it cost.

She stood poised, half impatient, and waited until Elise caught up with her, breathless and friendly, with a real smile. She had always admired Elise from afar, especially had she admired her clothes. They were always so lovely, so exquisite, so perfect in every detail, with so many little touches of distinction about them. And Janice delighted to get a closer view of them that she might sometimes copy a little feature in her own made-over garments.

"I wondered," panted Elise as she fell into step with Janice, just as if they had always been close friends, "if you wouldn't take pity on me and explain that algebra problem that you did on the board this morning. You did it so beautifully, and so quickly, but the period was over almost as you finished, and I didn't have time to see what you did. Where did you get that quotient? I simply can't figure it out. I've been working for the last ten minutes over it. You see, there's another almost like it in our lesson for tomorrow."

"Why, of course I'll show you," said Janice in surprise. "But you are always quicker at algebra than I am. You wouldn't have any trouble getting it if you took a little time."

"But I haven't the time," said Elise, rather breathlessly. "You see"—she laughed half ashamedly—"I'm in a hurry today because Mother and I are going to try papering a room. We've never done one before, and I don't know how it will come out. But I'm so excited about it, and I don't know what to do. You see, it's my brother's room, and we want to surprise him with it. Did you ever do any paper hanging?"

"I certainly have." Janice smiled in a superior way. "We always do ours. My sister is a clipper at it. She can put it on as smooth as the skin on your face. Only she's busy all day. She works in the grocery store up on the avenue."

"Oh!" said Elise, with a bit of a gasp at the thought. "Which sister is that?"

"I haven't but one sister," said Janice. "There are only three of us, Mother and Natalie and myself, since Father died."

"Oh, I didn't know your father died," said Elise sympathetically. "How hard that must have been. My father almost died a few weeks ago. We didn't know for days and days whether he was going to get well or not."

"Yes, I know," said Janice sympathetically. "Mother read about it in the papers. You know, he's the president of our bank, and we were interested—" Then she stopped suddenly and realized that was something she should not have spoken about.

"Oh," said Elise, with sudden trouble in her eyes. "Were you among the people who lost all their money through us? Oh, I'm so sorry—"

"Don't worry," said Janice, trying to laugh it off cheerfully. "We didn't have much there to lose. Mother had just had to draw almost all of it out to make the last payment on our house."

"How fortunate!" said the other girl. "But Father says he hopes everybody is going to get back all they lost in a little while. As soon as he gets stronger, he's going to try and do something about it; I don't know what. But oh, I hope you'll get yours soon."

"Oh, I don't think there was enough there to matter," laughed Janice again, wishing she hadn't said anything about it. "What's this about the problem? Do you mean the one about the pumps? Why, you divide the quotient by nine, don't you see?" And Janice opened her book, and the two girls walked slowly along with their heads together over the algebra.

"Oh yes, of course, how stupid of me!" said Elise at last. "My, I'm glad I asked you. Now it won't take me ten minutes to get my work finished for morning, and I can go papering right away before dark. The man who sold us the paper told us a little about putting it on, but I'm scared to death about the ceiling. He told us to get a new dust brush and smooth it ahead, down the middle of a strip of paper, but he warned me it was hard to keep it on, and hard to go straight. I'm afraid I'll make a mess."

Janice laughed.

"It is hard till you get used to it. The first time I ever put any paper on a ceiling, it came down behind my shoulders just as fast as I put it on. And when I got to the end of the strip, I was all wound up in it. Oh, I was a mess."

The two girls laughed over this and Elise made a wry face.

"I expect I'll make a mess of the whole thing," she said, "but I've got to try. For my mother was going to do it herself, and I can't have her getting up on chairs and stepladders and breaking her hip or something. My mother put on some wallpaper once, when she was a young married woman."

"Well, mine didn't, because she didn't have to then; they were well off. But she had to later when we lost all our money, and Natalie and I have been brought up to do everything that we could. If we didn't make things, we didn't have them. But it's kind of fun to make things and do things like papering, don't you think?"

"Sometimes," laughed Elise. "I'll tell you better when I get this paper on the wall. I wish you could come in and sort of coach me."

"But I've got to hurry right home. Mother has been doing some fine sewing for a woman and she wants it before five o'clock, so I must take it. But if there's anything else I can do to help later, I'd love to."

"Thank you," said Elise. "I may call on you yet. By the way, why don't you come over and see me? We're rather near neighbors, aren't we?"

"Yes, we are," said Janice consciously, as if she had considered the matter before but hadn't expected it to be recognized. "I'd love to sometime, if I can get the time. You see—well, we're pretty busy, all of us, most of the time. Since my sister got the position in the grocery store, I have to take her place getting dinner and doing a good deal of the housework, because Mother has been sick, and she really isn't able to do the housework and her sewing, too. And we really need the money from her sewing."

"Well, we're busy at our home, too," said Elise frankly. "I've got a job taking care of kids three times a week, so now I am proud to say I rank in the laboring class, too. I guess I've been pretty useless most of my life, but I'm trying to make up for it now as well as I can. You know, you don't realize when you don't have to what a difference it makes. But honestly, I think it's kind of fun."

Janice looked grave.

"Well," she said sadly, "it's fun sometimes, of course, to put up with things and try and make ends meet. But when someone you love is very sick and there isn't enough money to get the fruit and things all get snarled up, it isn't so much fun."

Elise looked at her speculatively.

"I like you," she said suddenly. "I wish we could be friends. I don't know why we haven't been before."

"I've always liked you," said Janice, grinning, "but I never had time for being friends with anybody. It's nice to know you want to be friends though, and I'd love it."

"Well, let's go to school tomorrow together," proposed Elise. "What time do you start? I'll wait in the house till I see you pass our corner."

"All right!" said Janice, with dancing eyes, "I'd love that. I've never had anybody to walk to school with since Natalie finished high school."

"Well, you have now," said Elise, reaching out impulsively and squeezing Janice's hand. "It's going to be nice. I'm glad."

The two girls parted happily, and Janice hurried home eagerly.

"Mother, what do you think?" she cried as she burst into the house. "Elise Walton ran after me and asked me to help her with her algebra, and she wants to be friends. Do you suppose her brother made her do that? She was really pleasant and lovely about it, as if she meant it."

"Then I wouldn't question it, dear," said her mother, looking up wearily from her sewing. "Did you like her?"

"Oh, she was lovely," said Janice. "And Mother, she isn't the least bit snobbish. She and her mother are going to paper a room this afternoon. She says her mother used to do it when she was first married. I was telling her about putting on ceilings, how careful you had to be."

Mrs. Halsey looked surprised.

"Are they really as hard pressed as that, I wonder?" she said. "I've heard Mr. Walton has been most honorable about giving up his property, but I did not suppose it would really bring them down to doing such things for themselves. It must be very hard for them."

Then after a moment of thought—"I wonder if they have a roller to make the seams smooth? Suppose you take ours with you and go around that way when you take Mrs. Graves's night dresses home. It certainly would be easier for them to have one, and if they own one, it can't do any harm to offer a little neighborliness."

So Janice hunted up the roller they used in their paperhanging and started joyously on her errand.

Elise found her mother up in the room they were to paper, wearing an old dress, with her sleeves rolled up and a pretty good imitation of scaffolding rigged up with the ironing board, the kitchen table, and two chairs. She had just finished cutting the last length of ceiling paper as Elise burst into the room.

"Mother! Where are you? You haven't broken your promise and begun, have you? Oh, Mother! You carried up that kitchen table all by yourself!" she cried.

"No, I didn't. Chris ran home a little while ago to get his overcoat instead of his sweater. The store is sending him in town on an errand, and he was afraid he would be cold. He brought the table up for me. And go look in my room and see what a nice pasting table I've got fixed up, with the two cutting tables and some boards I found in the cellar. No, I didn't carry them up either. I got that little Jimmy next door to bring them for me when he came home at noon, and I gave him ten cents and a big red apple to pay for doing it. Hurry up and let's get at this. The paste is all ready."

While Elise changed into an old dress, she talked.

"Well, Mother dear, I scraped up a friendship with the sister of Chris's girl," she announced as she slipped out of her pretty school dress.

"Oh, my dear! I don't know that I would call anyone Chris's girl on so slight a foundation. Surely if she meant anything special to Chris, he would say something about it to your father and me."

"I wonder!" said Elise, meditatively.

"I'm quite sure he would," said the mother, as if she wished to convince herself.

"Well, anyhow, I liked her a lot, the sister I mean," said Elise. "I guess she's been lonely. She didn't say so, but she seemed very glad that I wanted to be friends."

"Is she—refined, dear? I don't mean, of course, that we should despise her if she isn't—but—well, you know what I mean. I wouldn't like Chris to be interested in bold, forward girls—or coarse ones."

"She's not any of those things, Mother. Really, she's nice. I'm sure you would call her refined. She has a low, sweet voice and a way of looking straight at you, quietly, and waiting for you to speak, instead of rushing in as if she knew it all."

"Well, that sounds good. But you don't know about the other sister, do you? This one is the youngest. The other may be different."

"Yes, I found out about the other one. I don't suppose you'll like it, but—well—she works in the grocery store!"

The mother turned around and faced her daughter, an anxious, thoughtful look upon her face. "You don't say!" she said, perplexed. "Of course that might explain the bundles. Chris may be only showing kindness to a fellow workman. But—it is so easy for people thrown together that way to get interested in each other when they're not truly congenial. I should hate to have Chris spoil his life by getting attached to a common girl. But still, it does seem as if Chris would have sense about it. I am sure he has fine ideals."

"Of course, Mother. He has. I wouldn't worry. And—it may not be anything but a little kindness as you say. I don't see, Motherie, why you can't just trust things like that to God. You trust a lot of other things just as big."

Mrs. Walton looked at her daughter with a startled glance. Elise was not one to speak much of God. She wondered if she had been giving a poor witness.

"I suppose I should," she said, with a smile. "One forgets at times when a new peril looms that life is not all in our own hands to plan for. Elise, dear, wasn't that a knock at the door? Can you run down, or shall I?"

But Elise was already on her way.

She opened the door, and there stood Janice with the little roller.

"Mother thought you might not have a roller and would like to use ours," she said, half shy again before this girl whom she had held in awe so many years.

"Oh, how wonderful! It was darling of you to think of it. No, of course we never even knew there was such a tool. How do you use it? Won't you come in just a minute and show me? Come upstairs and meet my mother. She'd love it. No, I won't keep you but a second, but I do want you to know my mother, and then you can show us how to use this cute thing."

So, much against her will, Janice consented to go upstairs.

"It's Janice Halsey, Mother," called Elise as they mounted the high, narrow stairs. "She's brought us the darlingest little roller to use on the seams of the paper. Wasn't that lovely? Her mother sent it over."

"Oh, a roller!" said Mrs. Walton, coming cordially to the head of the stairs. "How nice! I used to have one, long years ago. I don't know what became of it. Janice Halsey, I'm glad to meet you, and it was very kind of you to be so thoughtful for us. Won't you thank your mother for me?"

Janice didn't stay but a minute or two, and when she was gone, Elise came back and got to work in earnest.

"Didn't you like her, Mother?" she asked as she watched her mother looking out the window after the departing Janice.

"Yes," said the mother, returning with satisfaction from the window, "very much. Of course, one can't judge a person in a minute or two, but she seems well bred. I was watching her walk. She moves with a natural grace. Now, that Anna Peters swags. She can't take a step without swaggering, and when she stands with her slinky coats wrapped around her hips, she looks like a half a hoop. One wonders why her legs don't break off somewhere around the knees, with the balance of her body utterly destroyed as it is. And she goes around smoking on the street and in her car. I've seen her. She's a bold hussy!"

Elise laughed cheerfully.

"Oh, Motherie, you're so funny when you don't like someone. Anna Peters does that on purpose. It's the fashion, Mums, to stand that way, all slunk back."

"Well, don't you ever let me catch you standing that way!" said her mother firmly. "Now, this little Janice is a lady. She must have had a well-bred mother."

"Janice says her mother never used to have to work," said Elise, thoughtfully. "Isn't it strange how people and circumstances just change when they get ready, and you can't do anything about it? You just have to do the best you can?"

"I suppose, dear, that God plans it all," said her mother with a sweet trustfulness.

"Well, if you believe that, why do you ever worry, Motherie?"

Mrs. Walton was silent a moment again, and then gave her daughter a sweet smile.

"I oughtn't ever to, ought I?" she said. "Well, I don't mean to, but sometimes I just forget what a great God we have. Now, dear, shall we get back to work? I'm quite pleased to have you know that sweet child, and someday, perhaps, we'll go and see the mother. I just hope the older sister is as possible."

It was only a few days later that a tall, rough-looking man came into the store and bought a pound of cheese and a box of crackers.

Chris waited on him and noticed a long jagged scar across one cheek. He noticed, also, that he walked about the store, stared at the cash window a good deal, and waited until Natalie was at liberty. Then he pushed his check and the money in. Chris saw his lips move in a remark and twist in an ugly, familiar laugh. Chris felt his anger rise, but he had to turn to his next customer, a fussy old lady who wanted to inspect every orange he put in the bag for her. When he looked up, the man was just sauntering out the door, with a leer and a grin back at Natalie, who had looked away from the door with deep annoyance in her eyes. Chris wondered what was familiar about the sag of his shoulders as he went away, and it was not until later in the day that it occurred to him, and he thought about the bum on the street corner and mentally compared the two. Had that fellow turned up again and hunted out Natalie to annoy her? He felt an undercurrent of worry all the afternoon.

It was a busy day, and Chris had no time to think much. The manager let most of the men go early that night.

Chris was down in the cellar, piling up a lot of boxes that had been thrown downstairs in a hurry that afternoon. He did not like his orderly basement to get in a mess for the next morning.

The boss came down the stairs and spoke to him.

"Walton, they're all gone but Miss Halsey, and I think she's almost through. She has three cents too much in her balance sheet and is trying to find her mistake, but I think it won't take her long. Would you two mind closing up the store tonight? I promised my wife I'd meet her and take her out tonight! Do you mind?"

Chris promised with a smile, proud that he was trusted to close up. The boss usually wouldn't let anybody but himself do it.

He heard the manager say good night to Natalie and go out the door. He put the last box in place, shoved back some tins of canned goods that had been disarranged, picked up some scattered wood shavings, snapped out the light, and came upstairs.

He was wearing old shoes with soft pliable soles, and his footsteps made no sound as he came. He enjoyed the thought of getting a glimpse of Natalie before she saw him. Her sweet face always filled him with exultation that there could be a girl so lovely and unspoiled.

Then he stepped into the store and came within sight of the little glass cage where Natalie sat, and his blood froze with horror. For there, straight within range, standing in front of Natalie was a tall man wearing a small black mask on the upper part of his face and pointing a revolver straight at her!

Chapter 14

For an instant Chris stood paralyzed with horror. Without stopping to think it out, he knew instinctively that Natalie would not be the one to give up easily, throw up her hands, and hand over the cash register. She would not think of herself, and she would fight to the last hope.

And there wasn't any hope. He could see that this man was a hard one who didn't care what he did. It seemed incredible that this could happen, only half past six in the evening, on a street that an hour earlier would have been crowded with passersby, in a store that five short minutes before would have been well protected by a large force of men. Every one of them gone, and he the only one left! Doubtless the bandit knew that—or bandits, for there were probably at least two of them. They must have thought that he was gone, too. He had been down in the cellar for some little time, and the store would seem empty to an onlooker from the street. He must not let them know of his presence till he could first do something to protect Natalie, to protect the cash in the register and safe. He happened to know there was a larger amount of money than usual in the safe, brought in that afternoon after the bank had closed.

And now Natalie would be required to open that safe and quickly, too. Would she do it? He felt afraid that she might stand out against it. Indeed, she seemed to be doing so now.

She was sitting up straight and pale in her little glass room, her eyes big and frightened, looking into that ugly, menacing gun. But she had not put her hands up as she had been told to do.

"Put 'em up, girlie, and dontcha touch that telephone," came the ugly command. "Up with 'em an' you march out here. You gotta open that safe in the back room and do it good and quick, see? Up with 'em, I say! I ain't got time to waste. I'll count three, see? An' ef they ain't up when I gets to three I shoots, see? And when I shoots, I *shoots*. I ain't no softie. I don't mind layin' out a little pretty one like you. I shoots ta kill! One—"

The store was awfully still and Chris felt as if his heart had stopped. It was up to him to do something before it was too late. Could he get out and call for help? He had no weapon. He could not hope to handle a man with a gun, single-handed.

"Two!" The word fell like a bullet deep into his heart. Natalie had not stirred. She had not lifted her hands. Her sweet mouth was set firmly, and she was white as death. Oh there must be something he could do. He glanced around and saw close at his side a big basket of hard green apples. Could he do it? All those years of his boyhood when he had practiced pitching baseball came to his mind, but quicker than any thought came an earlier practice to his lips, a practice learned at his mother's knee in babyhood. *Oh, God, help me save her!*

Silently, he seized an apple, crouched in the old position, and swung his arm. Could he hit that gun out of the man's hand? And if he did, would it perhaps go off and kill Natalie? *Oh, God! Oh, God!* And suddenly he knew that he believed there was a God.

The hard green missile whizzed through the air like a bullet. There was a crash and an explosion, but Chris could not stop to see what had happened. Another apple went whizzing and struck the enemy on the temple. He had started for the door but it dazed him, and as he looked back, Chris gave him another apple, full in the nose, with another in the eyes.

Oh God! Oh, God! Help me! Prayed Chris in his heart, and aimed another apple, when suddenly to his surprise he saw the man crumple to the floor. Could just apples knock a man out? He plunged across the room and was upon him with a wrestling hold he had learned in high school days. The man struggled and kicked out at him, then smashed a blinding blow across Chris's eyes, so that the room was full of stars, bright, hard stars, and his head was swimming, but still he kept his grip on the man's throat. And where was Natalie? She had disappeared from sight. What voice was that he heard? And how did all these people get into the store?

He opened one swollen eye and saw brass buttons. Of course, the police headquarters was almost next door, but how did they know to come? They have heard the report of the gun. Oh, was Natalie killed?

They loosened his hold upon the throat of the bandit, set him upon his feet, wiped the blood from his nose, and patted him on his shoulder.

"Good work, boy!" they said, and he could hear the clink of handcuffs on the arms of the man on the floor, who was struggling for his breath.

"Where is she?" Chris cried out wildly, his heart bursting with fear.

"Where's who? What? You mean the one that telephoned us? Why, who was she anyway? The cashier?"

They jerked the door of the little glass cage open, and there was Natalie, lying on the floor in a heap, with the telephone in her limp hand and her mouth to the instrument, but she did not stir. She was quite unconscious.

Chris was down on his knees at once, lifting her out as if she had been a baby, staggering up with her in his arms.

"He must have got her after all!" he groaned.

"No such thing!" said a man in the crowd, coming closer. "She's just fainted. I seen that gun fall. It went off in the corner, quite harmless. I was just coming by the store on my way, an' I seen that first apple come flyin' an' hit that guy just as pretty! Man, that was some pitchin'! I couldn't rightly make out what was doing. I thought ta myself the men here were kiddin' each other in the absence of a manager. I thought they was wastin' good apples an' oughtta be reported, till I heard that there gun go off in the corner down by the door, almost next ta me. An' then right away I heard the p'lice whistle, and they come flyin' from headquarters, an' I knowed somethin' was doin', but how'd you get onta it? Some buddy come an' tell ya?"

"Call came over the wire, 'Grocery store! Hold up!' that was all," said the chief of police shortly. "It was a woman's voice. Guess she done it." And he nodded toward Natalie. "Boys, get some water," he ordered sharply. "She's gotta be brought to. She's some brave little girl, she is."

Chris laid her gently upon the floor and put water to her lips, took a clean handkerchief from his pocket and bathed her face, and presently she opened her eyes and stared around in amazement at the crowd.

"Oh, are you all right, Chris?" she murmured.

"Sure thing!" grinned Chris in relief. "Don't talk now. Wait. I'm heating you some coffee. There was some left over from what the men had at noon. No, don't get up till I bring it."

More people were gathering now. A woman who occupied the apartment over the drug store across the way said she was sitting at the window, watching for her husband's train to come in and had seen the whole thing. She said the store was light enough for her to see the apples come flying across the room, and it seemed as if there were a bushel of them.

A small boy, who scarcely ever was known to miss a great thrill like that, testified that he heard the gun go off and got on the spot while the apples were flying. He said he saw the big guy get hit in the nose and go down.

The confusion quieted down after a few minutes. Chris brought Natalie a cup of coffee and made her drink it. And when she was able to sit up, they sent her home in a taxi, though she would look after putting her cash register in the safe first, herself.

Chris took her home but insisted that he was coming right back.

"I was put in charge. I think I'll just come back and stay here till I can get the manager on the telephone. He won't likely be back to his house till late this evening, but I'd feel better just to stay here till I get word from him."

He was holding his handkerchief to his bruised cheek now, but he was happy. Boy! he was happy, he told himself, looking across from Natalie, who had her hat and coat on now.

"I think I ought to stay, too," she protested. "Mr. Foster left me here, too, and told me what to do about the money."

"No, Miss Halsey. You gotta get some rest after that bout. You been some brave lady, but it ain't fer a woman to go through them things like you done and then try ta sit up on a stiff, hard stool all evenin' till yer boss comes. You go home an' get some rest or you won't be on hand tamorra, and you'll be needed then, see?" said the natty young policeman who had ordered the taxi.

"Yes, you two done good work," said another policeman, coming up. "We been watchin' that there guy fer about three weeks. He's been hangin' around o' suspicious like, but we couldn't get nothin' on him, an' now we caught him in the act, with plenty o' witnesses. 'Course I ain't sure, but he looks ta me like one o' them guys that's got his mug in the rogue's gallery. If so, you two done even better than you expected. Don't you worry, lady. We'll stick around an' guard this little old store right careful tanight. You just take yer rest till tamorra."

So Chris put Natalie carefully into the taxi, as if she had been a glass vase of priceless value, and climbed joyously in after her.

Chapter 15

For an instant they looked at one another in the darkness, then his hand sought hers and clasped it close.

"Oh, you were *wonderful!*" said Natalie softly, letting her hand lie happily in his. "I stayed conscious long enough to see the first two apples go straight to the mark, and then I felt myself going down and had just sense enough to grab the telephone and take it with me."

"Thank the great God you are safe!" said Chris. "Safe! Oh, I'll never doubt Him again! I prayed, Natalie! All the time I was firing apples at that sucker, I prayed to God to help me!"

"Oh, Chris!" said Natalie, bringing her other hand around and putting it over their clasped ones with a caressing motion, and never realizing at all what she did, "that's the dearest thing of all. I've prayed so much that you might believe."

"You prayed for me, Natalie?" he asked wonderingly.

"Oh, yes. I've been praying for you ever since the day you talked to me about getting a raw deal. I'm so glad, so glad, that you've found Him. Why, I'd have been willing to go through much more terrible things to have you come to see that. It's been the dearest wish of my heart."

"Natalie, darling—" Chris reached over and drew her close to his heart, folding his arms about her reverently. "Oh, you wonderful, beautiful little girl. I love you. I thank God that He has saved you from that devil's gun. Oh, Natalie, I thought he had killed you!" He buried his face on her shoulder, and when she put her hands up caressingly, she found there were tears on his cheek.

Natalie laid her face against his then and touched his wet eyelids softly with her lips. And then Chris lifted his head and put his own lips on hers, and such joy went over him as he had never thought to know on earth. Was love like this?

Then suddenly he sat upright again, his arms still about her, and spoke, eagerly, earnestly.

"Natalie, dear. . .I suppose I haven't any business to be talking about love—in my position. A mere clerk in a grocery store on a starvation salary, with family responsibilities and a burden of debt to help out with, but oh, my darling! If you'll just say that you think you might sometime in the future care for me, I'll work like a fiend. And I'll get somewhere just as soon as I can, where I can discharge all the responsibility and take care of you, too. Do you think you could ever care?"

He held her off anxiously and searched her face in the semi-darkness as the taxi whirled around the corner into Cromar Street.

"Oh," said Natalie softly, catching her breath, "I care *now*. I care with all my heart! It may sound dreadful, but I think I've cared ever since you were a boy in school, and I used to love listening to you reciting."

Then she hid her confusion against his coat, and they clung together.

It was only the taxi stopping in front of Natalie's home that brought them back to earth again.

Chris helped her out, and they made quite a promenade of the walk from the street to the porch, twelve feet by actual measurement.

"But I've got a family, too, and responsibilities," said Natalie, coming to her senses. "I couldn't—"

"Well, of course we couldn't now," said Chris, slipping his arm around her and holding her close to his side. "But with God's help, we'll get where we can. I'll get where I can take care of my responsibilities and yours, too, and then you won't have to stay in a store and work any longer. A store—*our* store is all right, of course," he added loyally, "but it isn't the place for the woman I love, you know, and I want you taken care of, my darling! And now, you ought to get right in and go to bed. I can feel you are trembling. Should I go in and tell your mother what's happened?"

"No," said Natalie, "not tonight. It isn't necessary for her to know about that man—at all—maybe. She doesn't go out much. She wouldn't be likely to hear it, I hope. Because I'm afraid if she knew, she would be frightened every time I went to the store. And—about—*us*—well, perhaps we'd better wait a little for that. She likes you a lot, but—it might seem sudden to her. We'll wait and talk it over a few days first, shall we?"

"I'd like that," said Chris. "It's like having our own secret a few minutes longer. But I mean everyone will know it the first minute I'm in a position to take care of you. And I think we ought to tell your mother very soon."

Then suddenly he stooped and kissed her softly again.

"I've been a poor girl, you know," she reminded him softly again. "I've been in another class from yours almost all my life."

"Thank God for that!" said Chris fervently. "If you hadn't been, you might not have been willing to love me now. Oh, darling, I'm the happiest person alive I believe.

"And to think God had this in store for me. Why, Natalie, I'm glad, glad of every hard thing that's happened to me, when it brought me this beautiful love out of the darkness. Just think, if I'd gone back to college this last year, I might never have known you at all, except as a quiet girl in my high school class And I was angry as could be that I had to give up my college. What's college beside a love like this?"

They might have talked all night, if Janice hadn't come with brisk steps down the little hall inside and flung the door open wide.

"What are you two doing out there in the cold?" she asked keenly. "Nice night for a tête à tête, isn't it, northeaster blowing forty knots an hour, and you two aren't aware of it. There'll be snow before morning, and Natalie took the old ratty fur off the neck of her coat this morning, too. Come on in here, where it's warm. If you two want to talk secrets, Mother and I will stay in the kitchen and you can have the front room."

Chris and Natalie looked up shamefacedly.

"Thank you, I'm just going," said Chris. "I have to get back to the store for a little while. I brought Natalie home. She was—a little tired—at least—she ought to be! She's—worked hard today."

"What was that car I heard stopping out here at the door a few minutes ago?" asked Janice sharply, looking from one to the other of the two curiously.

"Oh why, that was a taxi," explained Chris. "You see, I thought your sister was pretty tired, and there was a taxi—and so—" he finished lamely.

"Is my sister sick?" asked Janice, promptly lowering her voice so that it would not reach the kitchen.

"Not in the least," said Natalie, promptly and briskly. "It was just a notion. I'll tell you about it, Jan, when we get up to bed. It was just—nothing."

"Is she sick?" asked Janice, looking straight through Chris.

"No," said Chris, smiling and facing her clear glaze. "Not a bit, only I think she's had a hard day and she ought to get to bed soon. That's honest, little sister, so run along and don't worry. I must go at once."

Janice grinned at him amicably.

"All right, big brother, I'll see that she gets to bed at once. Any tonic or anything needed?"

"No, just a glass of good milk and something hot to eat, and—I wouldn't worry Mother, if I were you. She'll be all right." He smiled a wonderful radiance at Natalie, and Janice lost none of the radiance as she watched him.

"I still have my senses," said Janice caustically.

Chris took a reluctant leave, and Janice swung the door shut.

"He's getting very chummy! 'Little sister' and 'Mother,' indeed! Sounds almost like one of the family." And she grinned at Natalie. "Come on in, duck-of-a-sister, and eat supper. We thought you were never coming. There's only creamed codfish, but its delickety, if I do say so as-who-made-it. And there are plenty of fluffy boiled potatoes to eat with it, and cranberry sauce for dessert. Mother made that, so you know it's all right. And Mother's interest money has come, and it's five whole dollars more than it was last time, so there! Now, will you be good!"

Janice's manner was gaiety itself, but she gave her sister a keen glance and decided that she must go early to bed.

Chris went back to the store so happy that he scarcely knew what he was about. And found himself quite a hero in the eyes of the whole police force, who hung around the store, kept him company, and talked the attempted burglary over so many times it almost seemed like a great robbery by the time they had got done.

About half past eleven there came a wild ringing of the telephone. The manager had just got home and found the police chief's message that something had happened at the store. He was wild with anxiety at once.

The chief happened still to be in the store and lounged over to answer the call. The story had lost none of its spice in its many times telling, and Foster got a vivid description of the whole attempted robbery with full details and plenty of credit for Chris and Natalie.

Then the manager wanted to speak to Chris and was thankful almost to tears for what Chris had done. He said he knew if anything had really been pulled off when he left the store in charge of someone else, that he would be blamed for it, and his managership probably taken from him. And it would mean losing all he had gained in five years of work in the store, from under-helper up. He declared he was coming right up even though it was late. He wanted to take Chris by the hand. He wanted to be on the spot and hear the whole account over again. No, he wouldn't wait till morning; he was coming right away. Would Chris wait? It wouldn't take him long to get there in his car.

They had quite a session in the store at midnight. All the police force that could be spared for a few minutes, from preventing other incidents that come under the law, were assembled. In fact they had spent most of the evening hovering about and trying to make a hero out of Chris. By the time the manager arrived, Chris was getting bored with it.

"I didn't do anything much," he growled. "There wasn't anything else I could do, was there? It was just a matter of—" he was going to say "luck," but he hesitated and finished—"it was just a little old miracle that I hit that gun and that it didn't go off in Miss Halsey's face instead of on the floor. I was scared still as soon as I'd done it, lest that was what had happened, and I could see the thing I ought to have done was send a big alarm and scare the fellow away. Only—well, somehow, I couldn't see having the bum get away and try it on us again, sometime. He wasn't safe to have around, that guy."

So they praised him and slapped him on the back, and called him "Chris" adoringly and familiarly, and rallied around him till far after midnight.

He had telephoned early in the evening that he was detained at the store. But his mother had not been able to sleep till he came. She called to him softly as he came up the stairs.

"All right, Chris?"

"Sure, Mother!" he said, pushing open her door and stepping in to put a kiss on her lips. Then he slipped out again with never a word about the excitement that had detained him.

When Chris finally got to his own room, he was so excited it seemed to him he would never be able to sleep. He was so happy he did not know himself. After the months of sadness and doubts and darkness, the hard work and bitterness, here was so much joy handed out to him at once that he couldn't take it all in, yet.

But above the kindly words of his manager, the praise of the whole police force, and the glow of pleasure in his heart that he had been able to save the store from loss, rang the sweetness of the thought that Natalie loved him, and the glad thanksgiving to God for letting him save her life.

And she loves me, she loves me! his heart sang as he prepared to turn in. *I know everybody would think I was a fool and all kinds of a cad to tell a girl I loved her when I haven't a cent to offer her, but please, God, I will have, and she understands. We'll just keep our own counsel and talk to God about it, and I'm sure the time won't be far away when I can have the privilege of taking care of my dear girl.*

Then, for the first time in several years, he knelt down and really prayed, thanking God for the way He had led him, and even for all the sorrow He had sent, with which He had brought such glory and joy into his life.

After that he lay down to his rest, but lay awake to think how sweet and shy Natalie had looked when she told him how she had cared for him even when he was a boy in high school. And he thrilled to the memory of the touch of her soft lips on his eyelids. Oh, Natalie was a wonderful girl! And she was going to be his someday! Life had suddenly taken on glory. Even hard work was glorious.

Chapter 16

The family read about it the next morning in the paper as they sat at breakfast, just as Chris had swallowed a bite or two and rushed away, and before Elise went off to school. Chris hadn't stopped to wait for the rest to come down. He said he had to be early at the store.

His fellow workmen met him with marked deference and respect, going out of their way to be nice to him. It made him feel like laughing. A hero he was, all for throwing a few green apples at a man's head instead of aiming a baseball at a mark. He laughed to himself as he went about his work of setting out the fresh vegetables that came in. What a little thing it took to make a hero, after all, and why had he ever cared so much about it?

About ten o'clock the district manager arrived, and then it was all to do over again, the hero-worship business. The district manager had some stately words to say concerning the company's indebtedness to him. It was quite public, for there were even customers going around picking out heads of lettuce and oranges. They paused, all of them, and looked at Chris, and had to hear the story again from the quiet, respectful salesmen who yearned to have been in Chris's boots last night. Albeit, none of them had the reputation as a baseball pitcher that Chris had enjoyed in school, and each knew, in his secret soul, that he wouldn't have made half as good a showing as Chris had done in nabbing and saving the cashier's life.

Then the district manager and the manager called Chris and Natalie into the back room and shut the door. And the district manager told Natalie that the company was greatly pleased with her service in saving the company money and having presence of mind, and they were raising her salary and giving her a little platinum wristwatch, with a suitable engraving to commemorate the event. He then turned to Chris and told him that the company had been watching him with interest during his stay with them and had decided to give him a promotion with a raise of salary in the near future, but that last night's good work had decided them to make the move at once. The assistant manager was moving to the coast, and the company had decided to put Chris in his place. They wanted him to be in position to learn as much as possible from Mr. Foster, with a view to taking a managership himself, someday. And, of course, there would be a substantial raise in his salary also.

Chris was overwhelmed. He tried to thank the manager and the district manager, and he broke down huskily. Then he and Natalie stood, just like two children, with their eyes full of gratitude. Chris's heart was swelling with pride.

That noon he took Natalie over to the tea room for lunch to

celebrate. It was their first real chance to talk it all over alone, for last night they had been too engrossed with each other. But they could only sit and exclaim and beam at one another.

"You were *wonderful!*" said Natalie, her eyes filling with tears in spite of her effort to keep them back. "You saved my life! He was going to shoot me! I could see it in his eyes. He was furious!"

"Oh, my dear!" said Chris, looking at her with something in his eyes that brought the color to her cheeks. "Oh, God was good! Oh, I'm glad, glad, now, that I didn't get to go to college and that I was put here to help save you. I suppose, perhaps, someone else would have saved you, if I hadn't been there, but I'm glad it was I instead of someone else. And come to think of it, Natalie, if the bank hadn't closed and Dad hadn't lost his money, I might never have known you."

They did not do much eating in that half hour of lunchtime, but they went back to their duties radiantly happy.

That night when Chris came in, his family met him with open arms.

"So, Son," said his father, rising to meet him. "You've been making a hero of yourself. Got your picture in the paper and everybody calling up to tell me how fine you are."

"Picture in the paper!" said Chris, disgusted. "How did they do that?"

"Oh, they raked up that old football snapshot, the one with your torn sweater on and mud on your face, the one the girls used to carry around in their schoolbooks," said his sister, with dancing eyes. "Some brother I've got. Look! It's in the evening paper!"

"Good night!" said Chris modestly. "What a fuss about throwing a few apples!"

"Yes," said his father, "and that's not all. Mr. MacLaughlin called up this morning and offered to take you into the Title and Trust Company and train you into a banker. Title and Trust is a good old company, solid as Gibraltar. How about it, Chris? Want to be a banker?"

But Chris shook his head.

"Nothing doing, Dad. They wouldn't have me when I needed it, and now I'm in line for managership of the grocery store, someday. I wouldn't give it up for any old job in a bank, not on a bet. I'd be years getting a pittance, and then some. Then there's another thing—a grocery is a good, solid business. You can't have a run on a grocery. People have to eat. I'm sticking by the grocery store. It's a great institution, and I'll be the head of the whole company."

"But Chris, dear, a banker is always so much respected. Your father—"

"I know, Mother dear, it's a very respectful business, but so is the grocery business, and one banker is enough in the family at a time. Besides, Mother, I didn't notice that respect saved our home when we got in a tight place. Dad was one in a thousand, of course, and everybody understood that and trusted him, but I didn't see that it got him by any better than if he'd been a grocer. And I'm putting my lot in with the grocery store, if you don't object."

"Of course not, Son," said the Father quickly. "Not if you've thought it over carefully and decided that way. I'm proud to have a son like you, and the grocery business is good and honorable, and as much needed as a bank."

"Another thing, Mother," said Chris, getting a little flustered, "I—we—I've decided I want to get ready to do some real kind of Christian work in the world, and that takes money."

They were silent for very wonder, and Chris got red and embarrassed and looked down at his plate.

"You see, we—that is, I–I've come to see things in a different way lately. I used to think what you believed was mostly bunk. Yes, I did. Oh, I know I went to church and all that, but I thought it wasn't quite right, when you and Dad believed so firmly in God, for you to lose all you had. But now I see it differently, and I want to study the Bible and get ready to be of some use in the church and among the people. I don't know how to tell you." He floundered around, searching for words, and was aware of his sister's bright eyes fixed upon him, half mockingly.

"You see, we—that is I, I—You see there's a girl, Mother, I'd like to you to invite to dinner or something!" he blurted out.

"Chris!" said his mother, instantly aghast, "Oh, Chris, you aren't trying to tell me that you want to get married. Not *yet*!"

Chris laughed excitedly.

"What do you think I am, Mother? Crazy? Of course not. But she's just a wonderful girl, and I want you to know her."

"And you haven't been getting engaged either?" she asked anxiously.

"Not exactly engaged, Mother, dearest. What have I got to get engaged on? I've got a family to look out for, and she has, too. We've got to work hard, both of us for awhile yet—but we like each other a lot, Mother, and I want you to know her."

"Is she the girl whose life you saved, Chris?"

Chris looked her straight in the eye, his color rising a bit. "Yes, Mother, if you call it that, though I'm not so sure she didn't save mine instead, calling up the police just in time."

She looked at him a little uncertainly. Then a bright smile

bloomed out. "I'll go and see her tomorrow, Chris."

"Thanks, Mother, a lot. You'll like her, I know."

"I'll try, anyway," said the mother bravely.

"You won't have to try, little Mother," sang Chris, with a lilt in his voice and something bright and beautiful in his eyes. "She's wonderful! I know you'll like her, Mother. She's your kind!"

He stooped and kissed her tenderly.

"Well, I'm sure I hope for your sake that she is," she said with a quivery smile and a mother-sigh.

Chris went back to his chair again and tilted it back against the wall.

"There's another thing, folks," he said, kicking the toes of his shoes gently together to hide his embarrassment. "You might as well hear the whole story at once."

They all looked up, startled, but he did not give them time to worry.

"It's this. I've got to the place where I can say I'm glad from my own standpoint, really glad all this trouble happened to us. I can see that going back to college and all that isn't always the best thing a fellow can have to begin with life, and whatever God hands out is always best. It's Natalie's doings. She's a wonderful Christian, folks, the kind of Christian you are, Mother. And she's made me see it, too. She's had a lot of hard things in her life, and she says she's glad for them—that they've helped her to know God better and not be selfish and all that. And—well—she's got me thinking that, too. And now I feel that I'm really saved. I wasn't before, but now I am, and I want God to have His way in my life. And—we—we're going to study the Bible, evenings, at a class that's been started down at the Water Street Mission. I just thought I'd like you to know the whole thing."

But his father was on his feet now, standing beside him, looking down with shining eyes. And his mother came over and laid her lips tenderly on his hair, where it fell away from his forehead.

Then his father spoke. "Chris, dear son, that's the best thing you ever told me. That's better than health or wealth or anything else in life, to know that you belong to Christ and are learning to be led by His will. I have known all along that God was handing us His best when He sent sorrow and humiliation and scorn and poverty for me and mine, but I didn't see why He did it, and I didn't expect to see why till I got over in the Home Eternal. But He has made me see, now, bless His holy name! I'm glad He gave us trouble when it was to lead to such a great joy as this. And we'll love the little girl, too, for having helped."

"Yes, dear!" said the mother, making it like a promise.

"Well, then, that's all right!" sighed Chris, with joy in his face, getting up cheerfully around the room. "I ought to have known you'd take it like this, but I hated like the dickens to tell you. I wasn't sure I could make you understand."

"You can always make us understand, Son, when you use the language of heaven," said his father with a wonderful smile. "I'd rather have you tell me what you just did than anything else in the world. I'd rather have you know the Lord than be the richest banker that ever lived."

So presently, Chris kissed them all around, pinched his sister's cheek to make her look less solemn, and hurried away to the next street to call on Natalie.

But it was really Natalie's mother that he called on first. He found her sitting in the front room finishing a bit of sewing while the girls washed the supper dishes. He went over and took her work gently out of her hands, and laid it carefully on the table as she looked up wonderingly at him with a half premonition in her eyes.

"Now, Mother Halsey," he said, as tenderly as he would have spoken to his own mother. "I've come to confess to you. I don't know what you will say to me, and I'm sorry if you don't like it, but it's done and you ought to know about it. You see, last night I told Natalie that I loved her. I didn't mean to do it so soon, not till I had an assured position in life and plenty of money to take care of her the way she ought to be taken care of. But—well—I—we—well, I *told* her, and I found out she cares, too, and I thought you ought to know it. I don't want to do anything underhanded. Do you mind, very much, Mother Halsey?"

Natalie's mother looked at the earnest young man who was waiting so eagerly for her answer. Her lip trembled and tears welled into her eyes, but she said, with a real smile and a bit of a quiver in her voice, "You dear boy!" And then she put up her two hands and softly laid them one on each side of his cheeks and drew him toward her and kissed him gently.

Then she whisked out her handkerchief, brushed away the tears, and smiled again.

"I ought to be very glad and proud." She smiled. "I *am*. Of course, it is a little bit sudden, and you are both young, and I was afraid of a rich young man at first. I didn't know how dear you were—"

Her lip quivered again.

"But I'm not rich, Mother Halsey." Chris laughed joyously. "I'm poor as a church mouse. That's what makes it so bad for me to have told Natalie how I feel, when I can't do a thing about it yet. But if you'll trust me, I'll work hard and try to get a place where I can give her the kind of home she ought to have."

"Oh, I meant you were accustomed to riches. I was afraid you were spoiled—you may as well know the truth! But you're not! You're all and more than I could possibly desire in a man for my dear girl. And I'm proud of you, besides. Oh, I've read the papers. You and Natalie thought you had kept last night's happenings from me, and Janice helped, too. But the boy that came to fix the gas stove told me and showed me a paper. He knew who Natalie was, and who you were, and I know all about it, and I'm proud of you both. Of course, I didn't expect this—that is, not so soon, anyway—I guess you had a right—and I can understand."

"You're a peach, little new mother," said Chris, "and I hope I won't disappoint you. The only thing is I wish I could get Natalie out of that store right away, though of course I'd miss the sight of her greatly. But I'd like to relieve her and all of you, at once, of all care and work."

"Well, that's dear of you. But, of course, Natalie must go on working right away, and you mustn't expect to have all you want right away. It won't hurt either of you to work and win your way ahead, and I'm glad that Natalie has real joy in her life. She's never had much of a chance to have a good time—"

"Now, Mother!" protested Natalie from the kitchen doorway, "I've always had a happy life."

"Yes, you've been a good girl and said so." The mother smiled, half ruefully.

"No, but Mother, I have!" insisted Natalie. "I've been happy in my home and family. I've had you and Father and my wonderful sister."

"Yes, she would add that," said Janice, joining them as she wafted a dishtowel over the plates. "She's some sister, I tell you, big brother!"

"You've said it!" added Chris earnestly. "Say, I'm so happy I could swing my hat in the air and shout!"

"But," warned the mother, "you may have a long road ahead full of disappointment and waiting, you know."

"We know," said Natalie, smiling, "and we don't care. We have each other now and those things won't matter so much."

"And it's not going to be so frightfully long either, Mother Halsey, if I can make it short by hard work, see? And I guess it makes some difference, too, that we both belong to God, now, doesn't it?" he added shyly.

"It certainly does," said the mother, with shining eyes. "It makes all the difference in the world to me. I couldn't have given my child to a man that didn't know the Lord, you know, rich or poor. Natalie told me about that last night, and I certainly was glad. For, of course, I couldn't help seeing how things might be going and should have been terribly troubled to have my girl going around with you much longer if you didn't belong to the Royal Family."

He flashed her a bright smile as she slipped out of the room and left him with Natalie.

"Oh, I'm glad I belong!" he said as Natalie came over to sit down beside him on the little old couch. And he took her hand, reverently, and bent over to lay his lips upon it.

But out in the kitchen, Janice was complaining.

"I don't see, Mother, why they need to have the door shut. We are entirely in sympathy with them. Aren't they going to be chummy anymore? If I were you, I wouldn't begin that way."

"Well, Janice," said the mother, "suppose you let them have a little chance to talk things over first. We'll make a bit of fudge and the smell of it'll call them out by and by. There's fresh chocolate that Natalie brought home tonight. Suppose you start it while I finish this seam, and then I'll help stir it."

And so, presently, the enticing smell of cooking chocolate stole silently under the crack of the front room door and brought the two back to earth again from the little earthly heaven they had been planning sometime in the future. And they came out with shining eyes and helped beat the fudge, turn by turn, till Chris claimed the right to finish it all himself.

After Chris was gone home that night, Janice turned back with a satisfied sigh. "Well, I guess it's going to be nice after all, having a brother-in-law. He seems to be able to fit in pretty well anywhere, and anyway my arm always does ache stirring fudge!"

Chapter 17

It was a bright day in the following spring that Chris brought his father down to the bank in an old secondhand Ford he had bought for a song. For the Fidelity Bank and Trust Company had opened its doors again to the public and was rewarded by a long line of depositors waiting to put back into the bank what they had recently received from it.

The bank had been able to pay back every cent of its indebtedness and to get on its feet again for business with a clean record.

It had been nothing short of a miracle that had made this all possible, and the one who had been used to work this miracle was Christopher Walton Senior, the honored president. For he had been unanimously elected president again, even against his own protest. The bank felt that it could not do without his influence and good judgment. They recognized that it had been largely through his wisdom and efforts that the marvelous reconstruction of the bank's affairs had been brought about.

Two things had conspired to make possible this miracle of the business world. Three men, warm friends of Mr. Walton's who had been in Europe at the time of the closing of the bank's doors, had returned and come to the aid of the bank with a large sum of money. This, added to the fact that Mr. Walton had been able to turn over a good figure, a huge block of real estate in which much of the bank's assets had been tied up, had restored the people's confidence, and the bank was in a fair way to be stronger than ever.

Mr. Walton's personal fortune was, of course, gone, but he had friends and his business, and the confidence of his neighbors once more.

"And someday," said Chris Junior as they talked it over one night, "you might even be able to buy back our home, that is, when I get to be owner of the grocery stores, of course." And he grinned. "I love that place and so does Natalie, and I'd like to have it back and see you and Mother in it again. I heard the other day that the chump that bought it is getting restless again and seeking fairer pastures. He says the people in this town are all a set of snobs, and he thinks he'll go to Europe and buy an old palace somewhere in Italy. When he does, I mean to see what can be done toward buying it back. That is, of course, if God is willing," he added softly, half under his breath. "What He wants goes with me from now on."

Mr. Foster had been transferred to the managership of the district, and Chris was now manager of the store. He was as pleased as if he had been made president of the United States. Perhaps even more pleased, for he had developed a genuine love for his store and the goods he handled. His efficiency had been noticed and commended more than once from headquarters.

"Meantime, Dad," went on Chris after a minute, "I've been thinking. I find this house next to us here is on the market at a ridiculously low price, and I'm talking with the agent about financing it. He thinks it can be done at a price that I could carry, perhaps. What would you think about it? It's a double house, you know, and it has possibilities. We could do a lot of little things ourselves to it. And I just thought, if Natalie and I found it possible pretty soon to get married, we could take this side and let Natalie's mother and Jan have the other side, and then we families would all be together. At least that would be for the present till we could manage to get back the old home."

"I think it would be lovely!" said Mrs. Walton quickly, her eyes sparkling. "That won't be like losing you. Oh, Chris, you're a darling boy!"

"Well, Mother dear, that was Natalie's suggestion. She loves you, she really does, and her mother does, too."

"And I love them both, and Janice, too," the mother added, "and so does your father and Elise. I think we are going to be very happy, whether we get the old house back or not. I'm not sure but I'd be just as well satisfied to stay right here. It's cozy, and we're all happy together."

That was the beginning of the talk, but things moved rapidly on, and it wasn't long before the house next door was getting a new coat of paint and paper, outside and in. Natalie was shopping for some very cheap, pretty, bargain curtains, and evenings were exciting times when everybody had come over to see the new house and see the latest thing that had been done to it.

It was Betty Zane's young sister that asked Elise one day, "Say, Elise, is it true that your brother is going to marry that Halsey girl?"

"Yes," said Elise coldly, "it is." Her tone did not invite further comment, but her smile showed that she was entirely satisfied with his choice.

"Mercy," said the other girl disagreeably, "did she work in a store? I should think you'd feel terribly about it."

"Yes, she worked in a store," said Elise proudly, "and so does my brother, but we are just delighted about it. We love her very dearly and are very glad that he is going to marry her. She's choice. Good-bye, I'm going this way today." And Elise swept around the corner, a trifle haughtily.

But it was some weeks later that Betty Zane and Anna Peters were walking down the street together.

"Did you know," began Betty, "that Chris Walton and that quiet little mouse of a Natalie Halsey are being married this evening? The wedding is in the church, and only a few intimate friends are invited. But they say the owner of the grocery stores is coming and that he gave Natalie a whole silver service. Aren't things strange? Chris Walton working in a grocery store and then getting to be manager. But I can't understand his marrying that poor little Halsey girl."

"I heard she came from a fine old family," said Anna.

"Well, what's that when you haven't a rag to wear on your back? I wonder what on earth she'll wear to be married in? Something old or made over, I'll bet."

"Well, it's old, and it'll be made over a little, perhaps," laughed Anna disagreeably. "Our dressmaker is doing it. But she says it's gorgeous. It's her mother's wedding dress, ivory satin, and a thread lace veil that must have cost a fabulous price. Natalie's almost her mother's size. The dress hardly has to be changed at all, just taken in a little on the shoulders. I think she might have invited us, don't you? Her old schoolmates! They say she has some gorgeous presents from the people in the stores. I'd like to see them. I think it was real mean of her not to ask us."

"Well," soliloquized Betty, "I don't quite see why she should. We never acted as if we knew she existed when she was in school. But I suppose, now that Mr. Walton is back in the bank and everything going prosperously, we'll have to take her up."

"I don't see why," said Anna. "They're going to live down on that little old Sullivan Street. Isn't it odd, when they don't have to anymore? I don't see why they should expect us to call on them."

"Well, if you ask me," said Betty's younger sister, "I don't believe they know or care what you do. They live in a world of their own, and they like it. I've been talking with Janice Halsey a lot lately, and she says they all go down to that Water Street mission and study the Bible. I think they're all strange."

"Yes," said Anna, sighing half wistfully, "I guess that's it. They're just peculiar people. They don't seem to mind in the least that they lost all their money and had to go and live down there in the unfashionable district. Fancy staying there when they don't have to? And I guess they are happy, for I met Chris the other day and he was whistling away. And he smiled at me like a beam of sunshine, though I know he can't bear me. I just can't understand it. They are happier than they were when they were rich. And those Halseys seem happy, too."

"I know," said Betty. "I don't understand it. They're happy without things, and I've got a lot, and sometimes I'm awfully bored with life. Wouldn't you think they'd just be desperate to think they had all that money and that lovely home and had to give it up?

And yet, they go around looking as if they'd just inherited a fortune and belonged to a royal family."

Five blocks away from where those girls were talking, Chris was fingering a delicate wedding ring on Natalie's finger, saying, "Natalie, I've been thinking how wonderful God has been to us, to just take me out of the life I was living that I thought was so wonderful and put me where I might know you. Oh, you darling!"

GRACE LIVINGSTON HILL (1865–1947) is known as the pioneer of Christian romance. Grace wrote more than one hundred faith-inspired books during her lifetime. When her first husband died, leaving her with two daughters to raise, writing became a way to make a living, but she always recognized storytelling as a way to share her faith in God. She has touched countless lives through the years and continues to touch lives today. Her books feature moving stories, delightful characters, and love in its purest form.

Grace Livingston Hill began writing stories in 1877 at the tender age of twelve and didn't stop until her death in 1947. But what may be more amazing is that she has sold more than 84 million copies and is still loved by young and old alike.